The Collector's Edition of Victorian Erotica

GW00673303

First Magic Carpet Inc. edition September 2004

Published in 2004

Manufactured in the United States of America
Published by Magic Carpet Books

Magic Carpet Books
PO Box 473
New Milford, CT 06776

Library of Congress Cataloging in Publication Date

The Collector's Edition Of Victorian Erotica

ISBN 0-9755331-0-X

Book Design: P. Ruggieri

THE COLLECTOR'S EDITION OF
VICTORIAN EROTICA

Introduction

I t has been our task, dear reader, to compile for you an extensive collection of 19th century England's best literature of erotica. By erotica we understand not only fictions and poetries but also dramas, sex guides and books of perversion. It is this vast and varied field as written and read in the years of Queen Victoria that this anthology attempts to represent.

'Attempts' I say with deliberation, for after these several years of almost uninterrupted work, I have come to realize that nothing could be more ludicrous than to claim this an exhaustive collection. 19th century erotica comprises not merely fiction, poetry and drama, but also scientific treatises, Para-medical work, faction (a strange combination of fact and fiction embodied in frequently satirical Croniques Scandaleuses, for instance) and satire.

It is for this reason that our selection begins with The Philosophy of Modern Flagellation, which set down the law, and its many possible transgressions, before arriving at passages derived from Victorian erotic fiction. All texts are anonymous in the typical Victorian underground tradition.

No lone soul can possibly read the thousands of erotic books, pamphlets and broadsides the English reading public were offered in the 19th century. It can only be hoped that this Anthology may stimulate the reader into further adventures in erotica and its manifest reading pleasure.

In this anthology, 'erotica' is a comprehensive term for bawdy, obscene, salacious, pornographic and ribald works including, indeed featuring, humour and satire that employ sexual elements. Flagellation and sadomasochism are recurring themes. They are activities whose effect can be shocking, but whose occurrence pervades our selections, most often in the context of love and affection.

The stumbling stone, indeed, is how we might understand pornography. Entire books have been written dealing with the question, 'What is pornography?' and a few points have been clarified. Susan Sontag has shown that to separate literature and pornography is to mislead, and that sexual stimulation can be a legitimate form of literature as well. Morse Pekham has gone as far as to claim that art can be expressed in pornography.

While most critics seem familiar with the etymology of 'pornography' (it means the writing of, on, about – or even for – whores) none seems to have considered the first appearance of the term in the English language. The Oxford English Dictionary lists no reference to the word 'pornographic' or 'pornography' before 1857. The OED, which relates the origin of the word to the Victorian period, rather vaguely defines the term as: The expression or suggestion of obscene or unchaste subjects in literature or art.

Anthony Burgess has ridiculed such a definition by carrying it to its extreme: If anything that encourages sexual fantasy is pornography, he wrote, then pornography lies all about us – in underwear advertisements, even the provocative photographs in the non-class Sunday papers.

Initially, pornography served an entertaining as well as a didactic purpose, gradually becoming a vehicle of protest against establishment and middleclass morality. The rise of erotic fiction is a concomitant development that also has a few links with the straight, bourgeois mentality. Erotica must be looked at as rich subsoil from which the so-called canon of 'high literature' has been informed.

This erotic subculture – the Victorian 'otherness' – is something that was of specific interest to the Victorians themselves, and that remains of interest to us today as we try to understand the past and how we are descended from its surprise and wonder. Thus, dear reader, we offer the term 'erotopia' for the selections we have drawn here for you; erotic/pornographic fantasies that most resemble utopian fantasies.

Take, if you will Man with a Maid in which Jack, the Victorian gentleman jilted by the desirable Alice, vows 'to make her voluptuous person recompense him for his disappointment'. He sets up a cloistered residence – a soundproof room replete with iron rings set into the walls and rope pulleys hanging from the beams – to which he lures Alice and her maid, Fanny. In this 'snuggery' they are gradually introduced to the joys of sexuality.

Then follow Jack into the utopian setting of a country manor in the sequel, A Weekend Visit, in which a charming young widow, her beautiful mother, and their delicious virgin companion delight in a series of theatrical events and intimate games, with a degree of inventiveness particular to characters in the most notorious of Victorian erotica.

Imagine further what would happen to the innocent Mary O'Connor, raised in a parsonage by her ecclesiastic uncle, who takes a job at an 'agency' she soon discovers is but a wild orgiastic bordello. The action in Misfortunes of Mary mostly takes place in that 'chamber on the second floor' where diverse games are played by healthy and diverse Englishmen.

The very existence of the various genres of erotica we have gathered in this anthology explain such recurring themes in the canon of 'high literature' as chastity, virginity, seduction, adultery, fetishism and prostitution, to name a few. According to Freud, the advancement of civilization demands the inhibition of the sex instinct. Freud saw in erotica a larger biological interest and an aggrandizement of sexuality. In his view, the biological drive eventually becomes a cultural drive with Eros as the cultural building power. This process seems to have come to a head in the 19th century, when a revived notion of Eros challenged bourgeois patterns of thought, behaviour and morality. Significantly, the classical Ars Amoris had been confined to an aristocracy or a propertied oligarchy and the first readers and revivers of classical erotica in the early modern period were, again, aristocrats for whom sexual pleasure in fact and print was not immoral but amoral in the classical sense. During the Victorian period, the Ars Amoris gained a dimension it had never before possessed and new readers defined the limits of Eros' realm.

Thus, dear reader, we leave to you the task of defining the limits (or the possible limitlessness) of Eros, by entering our Anthology. It is both poet and reader together who are the lovemakers: Ut Coitus Lectio. Pascal wrote: A force de lire d'amour, on devient amoureux (By dint of reading of love, you fall in love) and we know that to read and speak of love is indeed to make love.

Dr. Major LaCaritilie
East Hampton, N.Y.

Table Of Contents

The Philosophy Of Modern Flagellation

Nature makes her own laws, peculiar and particular, without stopping to bother about the idiosyncrasies of civilization or the virtues of society. We are simply animals with a je ne sais quoi added that is inexplicable. We can only realize it in a weak, helpless, fumbling sort of way. Therefore, when we meet fellow-creatures with queer ideas of lubricity or sexual inversions, do not let us get excited, either with lust or indignation. Instead, try to look the thing squarely in the face and think the matter out, wrestling with the monster, all sentiment thrown aside, and trampling on conventional cant.

We have all been taught that the marriage state, with sober copulation in the intention of perpetuating the human race, is the real ideal of sexual intercourse in this world, and that all other systems of voluptuous indulgence are illicit and criminal, leading besides to eternal damnation.

This theory is (like the basis of all religion) charming, consoling and too sweet to be true. It means goodwill on earth, virtue, and denial in both sexes.

All sensible people know that our passions prevent this utopian state ever being attained, and are obliged to confess that simple coition with a legal mate (sparing of forbidden caresses, and mysteriously carried out in darkness) is rarely satisfactory even to the most pure and ethereal couples.

Whether married or unmarried, the love of creation generally accompanies the act with a peculiar set of antics, which vary according to taste, age, and climate. Very often these preliminaries and hors d'oeuvres are preferred by both parties. In love's drama, the prologue is sometimes more enjoyable than the dénouement.

To try to catalogue these aids to pleasure would necessitate a lifetime, and, although no doubt a universal dictionary of lascivious manias is wanting in every erotic library, the genius who could compile such a desirable work has yet to be born. Our task is merely to glance at a single branch of the prolific tree bearing the fruit of good and evil, and to say a few words about 'flagellation' as a help to enjoyment when man links his robust body with woman's sculptural frame.

Plunging boldly into the midst of our subject, we begin by stating the well-known fact that cruelty is inherent to the human race. Also, education stops our natural instincts. We show those instincts as boys by our ill-treatment of dogs, cats and insects, until it is thrashed out of us and we are taught to know better. Enough of this feeling remains in some to create intense sensual excitement when holding under physical or moral domination a creature of the opposite sex.

'…*Tu auras fait le mal à un être humain et tu seras aimé du même être: c'est le bonheur le plus grand que l'on puisse concevoir.*'

It is of course possible to classify and catalogue the degrees of violence that cruelty applied to voluptuous passion contains, but they evidently range from downright horror and murder, as exemplified in Suetonius, to the comedy of two lovers whipping each other in turns for fun. There is no doubt also that the voluptuary – who gives large sums to a procuress to ravish virgins – possesses also this mania, and the pain he inflicts upon his mistress of the moment lends additional zest to his enjoyment.

Some flagellants will only whip young girls and the Mysteries of Verbena House will please all those who wish to know how boarding-school discipline is carried out.

The flogging desire is generally supposed to flourish with extraordinary vitality in England and to be the pet vice of the Anglo-Saxon. Without seeking to exonerate this robust race, whose strong shoulders can well bear the burden, if true, we seriously think that all over the world the same pleasure of whipping and being whipped is to be equally found. There is not a brothel in any city where rods and whips are not kept in reserve, to use on the posteriors of the customers, or the delicate charms of the venal nymphs, according to wishes expressed and paid for.

References both serious and in jest will be found in all erotic libraries, and the Kama-Sutra gives chapters on various modes of striking, biting, and scratching women; in all erotic books in every language there can be found episodes concerning all kinds of whippings.

There are women who like to be ill-treated, ranging from the prostitute who takes a black eye from her bully as proof of love, to the patrician dame who begs her perfumed swains to pinch her plump arms and prick her soft skin with her own, golden, be-jewelled bonnet-pins.

Cruelty exists among Lesbians too, either when jealousy is aroused or as a spur to mutual enjoyment. Some men experience pleasure in beating or being beaten and humiliated by their own sex, as shown by Krafft-Ebing. Passive sodomites, too, often delight in being roughly handled by their partners.

But the commonest form of flagellation and mild cruelty is the voluntary submission of men to women. They love to be treated as if they were veritable slaves, and generally pay dearly to be thus ill-used. Indeed, they themselves draw up a program of the penances they wish to have inflicted. Severe flogging is often asked for, with binding or strapping down stipulated. Sometimes they are satisfied with being insulted and forced to perform repugnant tasks and obscene acts. One such is mentioned in La Corruption Fin-de-Siecle, where an individual of this type is delighted to lick the seat of a water-closet in a Paris house of ill-fame.

The philosopher must not be astonished at any vulgarity however lewd, horrible and repulsive or simply grotesque, when venereal passion forms the motive.

We hope these few foregoing words have proved what we wished to show, namely that there exist all over the world, a large number of men and women who delight to practice flagellation and cruelty in all its forms. They serve as an accompaniment or as an inducement to love's paroxysm. In our own enlightened times, obeying the fatal necessity of classification, we place Jack the Ripper at the top of the class. At the bottom we place the anonymous voluptuaries who answer advertisements of this kind in the newspapers of London and Paris:

'Electric Baths et Massage – Nurse and six lady assistants receive patients, eleven to nine, Sundays included. Rheumatism cured. Discipline treatment.'

Sporting Times, London, May 8, 1897
'Jeune femmes, tres jolie, magnifique chevelure blonde, Venitienne,

elegante et fine cravache, habituee aux hommageset agissant en maitresse absolue, desire union avec monsieur aise, de preference age, soumis et sans volonte. Ecrire, Altesse,' etc.

'Jeune femme, 25 ans, brune, joli type oriental, connaissant a fond l'education anglaise, cherche union aisee avec personne serieuse, douce et soumise. Ecrire a,' etc.

Le Journal, Paris, May 22, 1897

The following is a copy of a reply sent by one of the above fascinating Parisian lady flagellants to a would-be client:

> *Paris*
> *Dimanche,*
> *'Nous verrons ce que valent vos belles protestations d'obeissance et de soumission lorsque vous viendrez demain, lundi, au rendez-vous que je daigne vous accorder. J'eprouverai un apre plaisir a vous humilier, a vous tenir subjugue, aneanti, sous mon fouet, dans le collier de chien qui vous attend; a satisfaire enfin sur tout votre etre devenu 'ma chose', les fantaisies les plus tyranniques de mon imagination. A genoux, des votre entree, vous me remercierez de l'honneur que je vous fais de vous recevoir comme esclave, et preparez-vous a subir, sans le moindre geste ou mot de revolte, toutes les epreuves ou sombrera, sous ma volonte, votre fameuse dignite d'homme. Donc, à demain, lundi, 4 h 30 m. precises, apres-midi. Je vous crois deja assez obeissant pour etre exact.*
>
> *Votre maitresse absolue.*
> *Alice de Villefranche*

We have left to the last a few remarks upon the medical side of the question, as flagellation is always to be found quoted as an aphrodisiac in treatises on impotency and sluggish venereal action. Meibomius, in his well-known, pleasantly-written little pamphlet A Treatise on the Use of Flogging in Venereal Affairs, of which there are many editions in all languages, sums up as follows: Stripes upon the back and loins, as parts appropriated for the generating of seed, and carrying it to the genitals, warm and inflame those parts, and contribute very much to the irritation of lechery. In Aphrodisiaque Externe, ou Traite du Fouet, the same idea is stated.

We timidly put forth the following theory, as a personal opinion given for what it is worth and without pig-headed prejudice. If warmth and irritation applied to the back posteriors and loins are conducive to copulation, would not more simple means answer the purpose? Friction with horsehair gloves and alcohol in mild cases, mustard plasters and blistering in others, should have the same effect.

In La Generation Humaine by G. J. Witkowski, we find: *Le Dr. Roubaud preconise la flagellation contre l'antonie des organes genitaux. Il a fait construire, a cet usage, un balai metallique forme d'une centaine de fils flexibles, qui par la diversite de leur composition (cuivre, laiton, fer, platine, etc.) degageraient une certaine quantite d'electricite et dont l'action stimulante s'ajouterait a celle de la flagellation.*

Until proof of the contrary, we think this metallic broom would be most effective in the hands of a pretty woman. We have never yet heard of a used-up husband being secretly treated by a disciple of Dr. Rouband, and then, fresh from the stimulating electric effect of the flogging, rushing, a new man, into the conjugal alcove, where his devoted wife is peacefully sleeping, ignorant of the learned preparation and the surprise in store for her. Such, we take it, should scientific flagellation be, if such exists at all.

So, we venture to think that Meibomius and others following in his wake, wishing to air their views on this very fascinating and tabooed subject, were careful to stress the medical, to avoid the rigors of police censorship and reassure the casual reader.

Flagellation, we think, is useless without the adjuncts of lascivious exposure of the body and salacious subjugation. Pain, shame, and humiliation are exciting to the highest point the nervous system of the givers and takers in either sex.

Jean Jacques Rousseau, who is always quoted on this point, says in his Confessions: *...j'avais trouvé dans la douleur, dans la honte même, un melange de sensualite qui m'avait laisse plus de desirs que de crainte.* (The italics are ours.)

The same transparent and excusable mockery is often met with in works bearing upon the vice of sodomy. The authors all begin by abusing the unfortunate creatures who are afflicted with the penchant for sodomy, so as to be able to present their work without being branded as propagators of immorality. A little cynical frankness might be advantageous in such instances, enabling us for once to trip up an old proverb and touch pitch without being defiled.

But from recent signs, we are pleased to see that these misleading attacks of false indignation are fast growing out of fashion, and nowadays we are beginning to write of vice because vice exists. Is any other excuse necessary? It ought not to be, but as we pen these lines we are perfectly aware of the fact that we run the danger of being called 'bloodthirsty floggers,' simply because we gossip about the whipping mania.

We have endeavoured to obtain the views and opinions of medical men on the subject of castigation, but some of our friends were too occupied with their interest in the question, and begged to be excused because of their inability to write for the press. This fear of putting the frank, honest thought to paper for lack of literary practice troubles precisely those people whose judgment is most worthy of appeal.

The following 'notes' were sent us by a doctor practicing in the 'modern Athens' of the North. We think they will prove of some interest to our readers. At first our friend, like others, declined.

A FEW NOTES AND OBSERVATIONS ON THE SUBJECT OF FLOGGING AS A STIMULANT TO THE SEXUAL PASSIONS

This is a subject that has engaged the attention of mankind from the earliest times. It was largely practiced in ancient Greece and Rome. Indeed, it may have reached its greatest perfection during the orgies of Imperial Rome. It has gone on more or less in all countries to the present day, but notably perhaps in the 17th and 18th centuries, when, in France especially, it was largely indulged in. Women in all ranks of society took special delight in flogging the posteriors of their male admirers.

It is a well-known fact that flogging the bottom of a man or a youth excites the most lascivious desires, so much so that many men like to be well whipped before they attempt connubial intercourse. It is seen in the animal world as well, for when a stallion cannot be got to cover a mare a few sharp strokes with a ship across his loins will make him do his duty at once.

Of course, most young lads, just entering puberty, are bursting with lust and desire, and have no difficulty, when opportunity offers, of proving themselves men. But there are some youths, eager for the fray, and yet all too shy, timid, or modest to make the first attempt. For them a good sound birching on their bare bottoms will soon bring them to reason.

I remember being told a rather whimsical story many years ago by a physician long since dead. One day, sitting in his consulting room, a young gentleman was shown in. He was a very good-looking and well-dressed young fellow, but seemed very shy. After a good deal of hesitation he said that he had been married just a week, and that he and his wife were staying in a neighbouring hotel on their wedding tour. He explained that, much to his mortification, he had never yet been able to have his wife properly, that he much wanted to, and that he knew what he ought to do, but that he could not get an erection.

The medical man listened to him intently and then said that, if he would put himself entirely in his hands and submit to a drastic remedy, he thought he could cure him. The young gentleman promised implicit obedience to his directions, whereupon the physician said, 'I shall call upon you tonight just before you and your wife go to bed. When you are in bed I shall come into your bedroom and then give you the necessary medicine.' All this happened, and when the young couple were quietly in bed, the doctor appeared with a ladies' small riding-whip in his hand. He rapidly pulled the covers down, and before the young man knew what was going to be done, he found himself quietly turned over on his face. His nightshirt was pulled up, and a quick succession of stinging cuts rained down on his backside.

This went on for some time until the doctor, putting his hand underneath him, found his patient's cock stiff and hard, when he said, 'Mount your wife at once, Sir, and do your duty like a man.'

To his intense delight, the patient found that he could do so, the doctor continuing the flogging all the time of copulation until the final act came. He then retired, saying to the bride, 'My dear lady, whenever you find your husband cannot do his duty, repeat this medicine. It will never fail. In fact, I should advise you always to take a whip to bed with you.'

Some few years afterwards, the doctor received a letter from his patient, thanking him for the treatment and saying that he was the father of three children!

Women have been known to take great delight in whipping the bottoms of both girls and boys, because it causes such lewd and lascivious feelings. What is perhaps more extraordinary, and it is a well-known fact, is that many boys of all ages, young men and men grown-up, take delight in having their bottoms well whipped, especially by a woman. When a woman whips them, it excites a randy feeling to a most marked degree.

I was told once by a gentleman who kept a large establishment of servants, grooms, and footmen, that he used to go into their bedrooms of a morning and call them. He did so in the most effectual of all ways, by giving them a good flogging. He invariably found that if their cocks were not 'standing' at the moment he began, but a few stinging cuts with a whip soon made them as stiff and hard as possible, very often leading to the final discharge.

Just a few words about the portion of the body so erroneously called 'the private parts'. Up to sixteen or seventeen, all boys' bottoms are very much the same – white, soft, round, firm, and plump. But after about seventeen they very often change, and seem to take on an individuality of their own. Some always remain white, soft, and plump although, of course, they get bigger. Others get red and beefy, others get hard and almost horny, and some, I have seen, almost covered with hair. But, all feel the influence of being touched up with one or the other of the different implements in use – the birch, tawse, cane or whip, and of these four the last two are certainly the best.

It is curious and at the same time very interesting to see their cocks gradually stiffen and get hard under the influence of a whipping, and there is no doubt that many boys and youths, far from disliking it, really get fond of the discipline. They would ask for it for the sake of the pleasurable sensations it causes.

A lad's virile powers do not always depend upon his being strong, hearty, and lusty. Some of the most lascivious youths I have seen have been frail effeminate-looking creatures. One would scarcely have supposed were capable of anything, but I think that they are the worst. When you see a lad with a big, large bottom you may feel pretty certain that he is strong after women, even if, as is generally the case, he has got a small cock. It is a curious thing that you will find a large bottom generally associated with a small cock and vice versa. As a rule it is the large-bottomed lad who soonest gets a woman in the family way.

One of the biggest bottoms I ever saw belonged to a young fellow (now a soldier) who had a tiny cock, and yet he could never touch a woman without getting her with child. I suppose it was the powerful muscles behind that did it.

THE PHYSIOGNOMY OF THE HUMAN BACKSIDE

Our doctor's observations on the contour and formation of that most noble and necessary part of the human frame, the arse, is hardly original even if exceedingly interesting. We quote the following from Pisanus Fraxi:

'Mr. Hotten cut out of the Preliminary Address two passages in which prints are mentioned, and suppressed in total a curious and facetious letter (covering, in the original, four pages). The correspondent, Philopodex, communicates to the editor his opinions and advice respecting illustrations for a very superb work to be forthcoming very soon entitled An Exhibition of Female Flagellants.

'In the first place then (he observes) I hope (a hope the title seems to encourage me in) it will consist of a display of female backsides, for though I consider a Lady's bum uncovered to be an agreeable and diverting object, I would not give a farthing to see a man's arse. This I believe is only agreeable to persons of a certain description, too bad to be countenanced.

'But to see the representation of an agreeable young lady having her petticoats pulled up, and her pretty pouting backside laid bare, and seeming to feel the tingling stripes of a rod, is amusing enough. Such is that excellent print of yours, the Countess Du Barry's whim, which is nearly perfect in its kind, I would, therefore, have your book contain such subjects and such descriptions.

'Now, a word or two to the engraver, let him portray the lady's backside, which no doubt will be the principal figure in the piece, round, plump and large – rather over than under the size which the usual proportion of painters and statuaries would allow. Let him in general present it full and completely bared to the eye, though in some plates, for variety, he may give it to us sidelong. If a little bit of the lady's under petticoat or shift shades some part of it, that would be satisfactory as well.

'Let it be remembered that – if he has complete knowledge of his subject as I imagine he has, and he is a man of genius – a large field is open before him to display it in. He may show us several different sorts of backside, all of them natural and proper, all elegant and handsome (for there is almost as much difference in tails as in heads) but not all alike. He certainly will not give the little round firm backside of fifteen to a matron of thirty-five, for instance, nor the full mellow bum of the middle-aged Lady to the boarding-school Miss.

'Philopodex proceeds to give directions as to the implement to be used, not a great wisp of something, which they suppose will do to represent a rod, but a stinging tickle-tail, the dread of naughty Miss. Or a tingling rod, which the admirers of this diversion might know to be made of their darling birch. Further he hints: It is probable that in some of these prints there will be other figures besides the principal, the bare-assed lady. Now, although we cannot have the satisfaction of seeing the pretty bums of them all, an ingenious delineator might so contrive it, to heighten the lusciousness of the whole piece, that one by some careless posture might show her legs, another her breasts, and the dress of others might be so managed, as to give us the idea of a very large and full backside, concealed under the swelling drapery. Thus would each plate present us with a very beautiful and entertaining tout ensemble, and these little circumstances and adjuncts would prove a seasonable relief to the eye. We may be fatigued and overpowered by the blaze of beauty, from the naked arse of the lady enjoying the sweets of the birch, darting full upon us without the least bit of petticoat or smock interposing. But by way of cloud, we can ease our scorched senses.

'Philopodex concludes in a PS: I thought it unnecessary to advise you that all the figures should be dressed. Every lady should have her shift on, at least. Nakedness must always in these matters be partial, to give the highest degree of satisfaction.

'The second part of the Exhibition of Female Flagellants is similar to the first – a collection of anecdotes about birchings administered by female hands. The use of flowers in re venerea is dilated upon: After she had finished (whipping her) she took Miss N. to the garden, and picked for her a beautiful nosegay, so monstrously large that she was almost ashamed to wear it. However, as her friend wore one of an equal size, she pinned it to her bosom. 'I see, my dear,' said she, 'you are not acquainted with the secret influence of flowers. Know, my dear girl, that their sweet perfume has an uncommon effect on many men and women. But to have that effect on men they most adorn a lovely bosom, like yours. According to the correct fashion, the bouquet should be very large, and worn on the left side of the left breast.'

THE EVILS OF EXCESSIVE WHIPPING

It should not be forgotten that the fustigation may be carried to lengths that reason and nature alike reprove. For grown-up girls troubled with hysteria, or disobedient wives afflicted with flippancy, there is and can be nothing as necessary as a sound and vigorous smacking on the buttocks. But children should be treated with more care and leniency. The following remarks by a French doctor illustrate our meaning.

SMACKS ON THE BUTTOCKS

If flagellation, fustigation, palletation (smacking the face or the hands with a leathern pallet) and other punishments of the same kind are no longer inflicted in our schools, there is an infantile correction still employed, not by school-masters, but by fathers and mothers themselves. We allude to smacks administered with the flat of the hand on the buttocks, the lumbar region, and the back part of the thighs of juvenile delinquents.

We must admit that this manner of operating is as injurious as were fustigation and palletation. Whether administered by the naked hand, or by the hand armed with a pallet, a cane, birches or rods, blows on the buttocks or on their neighbourhood have the same effect: They inflame the genital organs, determining in them heat; they excite and erect them and thus prematurely develop the idea of pleasure in beings who endeavour to profit by the discovery. In children everything may lead to evil, and parents ought to know it if they do not wish to become the involuntary accomplices of the acts of their offspring.

BEATING IN BROTHELS

The following adventure of Ned Ward is curious, and affords us at the same time a picture of the brothels in his day being one night with his friend, at the Widows Coffee-House, in conversation with the 'Airy Ladies' of the establishment:

'Who should grovel up stairs but, seemingly, a sober citizen about the age of sixty. Upon which the old mother of the maids call'd hastily to Priss, then whispering ask'd her if there were any rods in the house? I sitting just by overheard the question.

'The wench answer'd, "Yes, yes, you know, I fetch'd six penny worth but yesterday".'

'Upon the entrance of this grave fornicator, our ladies withdrew themselves from our company, and retir'd like modest virgins to their secret workroom of iniquity.

'Then left the old sinner, in the winter of his lechery, to warm his grey hairs with a dram of invigorating cordial, whilst we pay'd our reckoning.

'We were lighted down stairs, and left the lustful satyr a Prey to the two strumpets I believe, he found himself in a much worse condition than a breech between two stools or lot in Sodom, between the merry cracks of his buxom daughters.

'I ask'd him what was the meaning, when the old lecher came into the coffee room, that Mother Beelzebub ask'd the Wench whether they had any rods in the house. He smil'd at my question, and told me he believ'd he should teach a new vice to me, one which I scarce had heard of.

'That sober-seeming saint, says he, is one of that classes in the black school of sodomy who are call'd by learned students in the science of debauchery, flogging cullies. This unnatural beast gives money to those strumpets you see, and they pull down his breeches and scourge his privities till they have laid his lechery.

'He all the time begs their mercy, like an offender at a whipping post, and beseeches their forbearance. But the more importunate he seems for their favourable usage, the severer vapulation they are to exercise upon him, till they find by his beastly ecstasy, when to withhold their weapons.'

A LADIES PRIVATE WHIPPING CLUB

These female federates are chiefly matrons grown weary of wedlock in its accustomed form, and possibly impatient of the cold neglect and indifference that after a certain term, became attendant upon them. They are determined to excite, by adventitious applications, those ecstasies that in the earlier period of marriage they had experienced...

The respectable society or club of which we now treat, are never less than twelve in number. There are always six down, or stooping down, and six up. They cast lots for the choice of station, after a lecture, which is every evening read or spoken extempore. The lecture is upon the effects of flagellation, as experienced from the earliest days to the present moment, in monasteries, nunneries, bagnios, and private houses.

The six patients take their respective situations, and the six agents place bare those parts that are not only less visible, but less susceptible of material injury. They may also be the most exquisite in point of sensation. Thus begin the courses of practice.

The chairwoman for the meeting accommodates each participant with a stout engine of duty, and being herself the fugalwoman in the evolutions. She takes the right hand of line, and pursues the manual exercise in whatever manner, and with whatever variety she pleases. The rest of rank keep a watchful eye upon her performance, not daring to slip under a penalty of a double dose of the same nostrum, which is sometimes more than the offenders can endure, either at or after the ceremony.

Agreeably to the fancy of the chairwoman, sometimes the operation is begun a little above the garter, and ascends to the pearly inverted cone, then is carried by degrees to the dimpled promontories, which are vulgarly called buttocks, until the whole, from a milky white, as Shakespeare says, 'Becomes one red!!'

Sometimes the wanton, vagrant fibres are directed to the more secret sources of painful bliss! Sometimes the curious, curling tendrils bask in the Paphian groove! And sometimes, as the passions of the fair directress rise, they penetrate even the sacred cave of Cupid!

There it is that the submissive patients generally, with one voice, cry out, 'It is too much!' and rising from their stations, they express in the most feeling language their several sensations.

The fair president now resigns her rod, the emblem and engine of her office, to whom she thinks the most adroit and capable, and together with the remaining five, take the several stations of their predecessors.

The course is recommenced with whatever additions and improvements the new performer pleases. Sometimes the process is reversed, and beginning at the grove and cave already mentioned, with gentle applications proceeds to the swelling mountains, where the strokes grow more fierce and frequent. Then the second file of patients cry out in their turn for mercy!

WOMAN'S PASSION FOR WHIPPING

The passion for whipping in women is very great, it has often been remarked. The following lines depict it with some vigour:

> *To look at her majestic figure,*
> *Would make you caper with more vigour!*
> *The lightning flashing from each eye*
> *Would lift your soul to ecstasy!*
> *Her milk-white fleshy hand and arm,*
> *That ev'n an Anchorite would charm,*
> *Now tucking in your shirt-tail high,*
> *Now smacking hard each plunging thigh,*
> *And those twin orbs that near 'em lie!*
> *They to behold her diamond rings,*
> *Ev'n them you'd find delightful things!*
> *But above all, you'd love that other*

That told you she was your stepmother!
Then handing you the rod to kiss,
She'd make you thank her for the bliss:
No female Busby then you'd find
E'er whipped you half so well behind!
Her lovely face, where beauty smiled,
Now frowning, and now seeming wild!
Her bubbies o'er their bound'ry broke,
Quick palpitating at each stroke!
With vigour o'er the bouncing bum
She'd tell ungovern'd boys who rul'd at home!

BRANTOME ON THE GREAT LADIES

I have heard it said of a great lady in the world, very great, who was not satisfied with her natural lasciviousness, for she was versed in harlotry. Having been married and become a widow, she was wont to undress her dames and maids. Delighting much to see them thus, she would then with the flat of her hand beat their bottoms with many hearty smacks and vigorous bangs.

'When the girls had done anything wrong, she had them well birched, and her satisfaction was then to see them jump, moving and twisting their bodies and buttocks, which according to the strokes they received were very strange and diverting.

'At times, without stripping them, she would make them lift their garments. As they wore no drawers, she would smack or whip them on the bottoms according to their offence, or to make them laugh, or else cry. These visions and contemplations would so sharpen her appetite that she would then, often with good intent, go and satisfy it with some gallant fellow both strong and robust.'

SCHOOLBOYS AND THE MISTRESS

The following experience is extracted from a letter, dated March 13th, 1859, written by a gentleman whose name I am not at liberty to divulge, but whose veracity may be relied upon:

'In my boyish days, it was customary in preparatory schools to have boys and girls together under a woman, and where the rod was used on all occasions with the utmost severity. We used to be birched in the presence of each other, the girls across the knee, or held under the arm, the boys on the back of a maid-servant.

'This latter used often to come to our rooms, and play the school-mistress, as did most of the girls. I have a vivid recollection of some extraordinary scenes in this line which have given me the perfect conviction of numerous women possessing the taste in question.

'In the school mentioned above, the female who always assisted the mistress was evidently most fond of seeing the operation, though she liked us all, and was herself a great favourite with the boys. But it was always with a giggle and a joke that she told several boys almost every morning that they were not to get up until Missus had 'paid them a visit,' or after seeing them in bed, telling them they were to keep awake until Missus should have had 'a little conversation with them.' Moreover she said that she might be expected every moment with a couple of tremendous rods.

'This girl put us up to a great deal, and I fear developed our puberty far too precociously. She had a very large breast, and she arranged her dress so that, while being horsed, our hands completely slipped into it, feeling her bubbies. The rocking and plunging used repeatedly to bring on emission. Many of the boys used to try to get whipped merely to experience this sensation. Although forty years have elapsed since all this, yet the remembrance is as vivid as if it had occurred only yesterday.'

THE WIDOW AND HER MAN-SERVANT

The following passage, writes Pisanus Fraxi, which I extract from the memoirs of John Bell, a domestic servant, London 1797, is still more to the point:

'The next service in which I found myself was that of a widow lady of fortune, whose family consisted of two nieces in their early twenties and a younger nephew. She had been a handsome woman, and had still a fine person. When she engaged me, she said she should expect me to assist her in anything that she required, which I at once promised to do.

"What this 'anything' was soon appeared, for when I brought in breakfast the next morning, she asked me whether I had ever been servant in a school, and helped to whip the children? I answered I had not, but had often whipped my brother, whom I had taught to read.

'Some half-hour after, her nephew ran against me when I had a plate in my hand. It fell to the ground and was broken.

'"Now, John," said she, "hold that boy fast, while I get a good rod for his impudent bottom." She speedily produced it from a press, and handed to me, adding, "Sit down, and give it him, as you did your brother." •

'I lost no time in stripping the fellow and administering to him a proper correction, my mistress looking on with evident satisfaction.

'"Very well,' she said, 'you see what that boy wants, and you can give it him whenever he deserves it, but only in my presence. Mind that."

'I now perceived she had a violent passion for whipping, but my astonishment was excessive when, the same evening after tea, she ordered me to perform the same ceremony on the two nieces. It was indeed something novel for the young ladies of a house to be flogged by the footman, and to have their white thighs brought into contact with his red plush breeches.

'When my mistress perceived that I hesitated, she looked sternly at me and cried, "Instantly, on that sofa or you leave this place." Pulling up the elder girl's petticoats, and pinning her shift high up, she pushed her towards me. I laid her gently across my knees, and though pretending to use force, tickled her so lightly that she was soon up again, more frightened than hurt.

'Not so the other sister, who was short and stout, with a cross, ugly face, but magnificent posteriors, which I am ashamed to say I lashed vigorously with far different feelings from those I experienced in chastising her slim and handsome sibling. A slight second whipping for the boy closed the day's entertainment. I need not detail the various modes in which I executed my new and unexpected duties. In the morning she generally liked them whipped, while she sat at her work, counting the cuts and her stitches. In the evening she usually took it over her tea, sipping it out of her saucer, saying quietly, "Please, John, a little more on that right buttock. That will do!"

'This occupation, however, took up so much of my time that I required the assistance of a page to get through my work. My mistress at first refused, but acquiesced when I remarked that he would probably require a great deal of correction. So I chose a lad from the workhouse, sturdy and chubby, who, the master said, "took a deal of hiding."

'I made him sleep in my room, so I could keep him always clean, and his backside fit to be exhibited to a lady. As he was hard to hold, four staples were, at my suggestion driven into the Drawing Room wall, to which he was attached like a spread eagle. These were concealed from notice, the two upper by pictures, the two lower by a footstool.

'You may imagine that a stout urchin, inured to punishment, afforded my mistress more occasions for her favourite diversion than the three genteel young people put together.

'But these scenes, as far as I was concerned, drew rapidly to a close. Notwithstanding this lewd taste, my mistress was practically a dragon of virtue, and on discovering that a tender relation existed between her pretty waiting-maid and myself, she turned us both out of the house at a moment's warning, and at great discomfort to herself.

'How she got on afterwards I don't know, as another service took me into a distant part of the country. I heard, however, that my two pupils, having considerable fortunes, made good marriages. I have frequently seen them in their carriages in London streets, and thought how little their husbands knew of the part I had taken in their education.'

The Mournings
Of A Courtesan

I t was July, and frightfully hot. The heat excited me. At ten o'clock in the morning, I found myself at little Coralie's just as she was coming out of the bath.

She was stretched on a settee (why not call it a fouteuse?) enveloped in a woollen wrapper and attended by her two chambermaids, Rosine and Nana, both in their shifts.

By the warmth of the kisses I gave her on my entrance, Coralie comprehended that I was in a gallant humour.

'So,' she said, laughingly, 'you come to ask charity?'

'Oh, Madame,' said Nana, who came to assure herself that her mistress spoke the truth. 'Madame, it is rigid!'

'It is standing!' repeated Rosine.

I took two sovereigns from my pocket, and holding out one in each hand, I asked these two amiable girls to throw off their mistress's wrapper and to strip off their own shifts, requests they did not refuse.

They were both brunettes; Coralie, on the contrary, was a blonde, small enough, a little dumpy even, with breasts that resembled balls of ivory, well-developed flanks, full thighs, and corpulent leg. But her ankles tapered off to perfect feet, such as one never meets but in Paris or Spain. As for her pretty, rosy backside, all the beau monde, masculine and even feminine, had pinched it, bitten it, slapped it. What a charming, smutty look Coralie had! Fie! The impudent pretty little face! What eyes for the damnation of all our souls! And what a mouth, made equally to love and to laugh in the face of the human race, whilst devouring its money!

'Hold,' she said to me, throwing her foot up to my face. 'Kiss the instrument of thy pleasure; I am going to do thee between these two little feet!'

Well enough! But the bell sounded at the outer door.

Nana, in the costume of Mother Eve, ran to see who was the visitor, and returned aghast.

'Madame, it is the Duke. I have shown him into the boudoir.'

'My sweet friend,' said Coralie to me, raising herself, 'allow me to go and earn fifty pounds.'

Drelin, drelin, drelin! It was Rosine's turn to receive the comer.

'It is another fifty pounds, sure enough,' cried Coralie, clapping her hands.

Drelin, drelin, drelin! This time the two girls ran to the door together.

'Madame, it is little Lousteau!'

'He is good for a one-hundred pounds,' said Coralie, 'but by a bill payable when he comes of age. One must coin money in the best way one can when one deals with children. Ah, well! Let all three of them wait! My girls, give me the lovely member of my friend!'

Rosine and Nana pulled down my trousers obediently. Coralie took, and commenced to roll between her two feet, what she rightly called my lovely member.

Are you not aware that the women of Corinth were renowned for their exquisite knowledge of the art of provoking with their feet the venereal orgasm of their Athenian or Boeotian lovers? Coralie's feet are as prettily shaped as they are agile. They seized my member between their satiny soles.

She ordered her maids of honour to arrange themselves on either side of her, one on the right, the other on the left, and commenced tickling one with each hand. Her two pretty little hands disappeared in the black pussies of the two girls. Her two feet glided, flew; turning themselves round my enflamed prickle. Anon they scratched sweetly with their nails on the balls which contained the divine liquor. Soon they adventured from the tip of my member even unto the passage of Sodomy.

All at once she stopped.

'Suppose I dismiss my three lovers,' she said.

'Madame,' said Nana, 'shall I go and ask them separately to return in two hours?'

'What a fool you are!' cried Coralie. 'If you want them to come back, rather tell them to go to the devil!'

This was done. As Nana re-entered the room, after having fulfilled this delicate mission, she was able to see a white jet shooting into the air. My semen was spouting.

'Madame!' cried this charming girl, with an air of consternation, 'isn't this a good thing lost?'

'Yes,' said Rosine sententiously, 'one ought not to waste the gifts of the good God, Madame.'

Coralie screamed with laughter.

'My children,' she cried, 'will you restore our good friend to the state that pleasures you?'

Dear girls! Already they brought their charms into play, and extended their hands.

'Don't touch it!' cried Coralie. 'It is by the eyes that we must reanimate our friend. Come, then, my girls! Come, then.'

At the same time she stretched herself along the sofa, her thighs open and slightly raised.

'Who loves me, kisses me!' she said.

Rosine and Nana darted forward together. Nana reached the goal first, and Coralie's bush disappeared under her libertine mouth. Rosine consoled herself as best she could by embracing her mistress, and sucking her titties. As for me, I clitorised and postillioned Nana's croup, which was close in front of my face. Cries, sighs, and impious imprecations announced that Coralie was ejaculating.

'Nana,' she cried, 'see if it be standing yet!'

Nana assured herself of this by pushing a little backwards her croup, which encountered my member in a state like brass.

'Yes, Madame,' she sighed.

In the position in which she was, it was to Coralie's coynte she spoke. The frivolous thing heard to a marvel. Coralie made me sit in the middle of the sofa, and perched herself upon me. In this posture the pleasure is slow in coming, and the sugarplum-gulf does not close itself so tightly.

Following the orders of her mistress, Rosine came and knelt in front of us. The dear creature commenced to lick us both at the same time. A blow of the tongue to Coralie's clitoris, another blow at the root of my member. I drew it out, and she swallowed it up entirely. It re-entered Coralie's coynte, and I recommenced this charming game. Nana, on her knees behind Rosine, held her comrade's crupper tightly between her thighs and clitorised her.

The bell rang once, twice, three times. It was the three amorists who had been sent to the devil, and who were returning in search of Paradise.

'Yes, yes,' said Coralie, quite swooning, 'after pleasure, business. I go to earn my two-hundred pounds!'

What a glorious life is that of a courtesan! She kisses, she enjoys, and she enriches herself. She has every joy at once.

Mounted In Silver or The Leucadian Leap

Blanche de Beauvoir to the Marquise de la Galissière: 'Madame, I saw you yesterday at the Italian Opera. I love you.'

The Marquise de la Galissière to Mademoiselle Blanche de Beauvoir: 'Mademoiselle, I received a strange letter from you yesterday. It is certainly a mystery. Explain yourself.'

Blanche to the Marquise: 'If you ask me to explain myself, it is because you have understood me with half a word. Ah well, yes! I love you, I desire you. My eyes eagerly devoured you the day before yesterday. Are you above the prejudice that rejects the sweetest and most solid of pleasures, the sweetest because it is forbidden fruit, the most solid because it is the only one durable? Is it true that you have slept with the Princess Edwige? I am as apt as she.'

The Marquise to Blanche: 'Are you silent as the grave?'

Blanche to the Marquise: 'Silent as the grave, burning as the flame.'

The Marquise to Blanche: 'When I used to visit the Princess Edwige, I found her with a handsome cavalier. He too put the finish to our interview when we were tired of chatting together.

With three, the time slips along more sweetly.'

Blanche to the Marquise: 'I will do what is necessary to extinguish the fire I have kindled. I will procure this handsome cavalier, Marquise of my heart. Till tomorrow.'

The Marquise to Blanche: 'But he must not show himself until we call him.'

Excuse me, fair reader, the handsome cavalier which this madcap Blanche was going to offer to the Marquise was your humble servant.

I found Blanche at her toilette and I can tell you that it was one of great nicety, in which I aided her to the best of my ability. It was I who covered her with essences, and with poudre à la maréchale. She is a fine girl, white, fair, and rounded in form.

The two of us were together, I making some drops of eau de Portugal roll down her golden-haired mount, she receiving this libation with a feverish impatience. I wanted to take some liberties. She stopped me.

'Let us both preserve our strength,' she said.

The waiting-maid entered, carrying a sealed parcel addressed to Blanche. We eagerly opened it. The packet contained a superb dildo in a silver case bearing Royal arms, with this inscription engraved: 'Edwige to her angel.'

Whilst we were admiring this curious article, a carriage stopped in front of the house. Blanche bustled me into a room adjoining her boudoir.

'I will introduce thee when it is time,' she cried.

'Eh, morbleu! Why not at once?' I started shaking the door, but she had firmly bolted it. I tried to peep through the keyhole. I could see nothing; but I heard.

I heard whisperings, kisses, the clucking of amorous hens, a froufrou of dresses slipping to the ground, light boots thrown to a distance, then a silence.

'Stark naked, stark naked!' cried Blanche. 'Ah! I hold thee, Marquise!'

'Call me Whore!' said the great lady.

'Oh, the pretty bibi! The lovely coynte!'

The sofa groaned. Then there were sighs, furious yells. Suddenly there was an interruption caused by Blanche, who coughed, spat, and choked.

'Dear angel,' said the Marquise, 'what is it then, one of my hairs in thy throat?'

'One has never seen such long ones! Ah, here it is!'

And the sighs began again.

'My love,' cried the Marquise. 'The man, is he here?'

The door opened. What a spectacle!

Blanche, naked as a savage queen, led me forward. I saw her accomplice stretched on the sofa, in the same costume of nature, her body marked all over with kisses and bites, her thighs widely opened, her flanks agitated with convulsive thrillings, her head thrown back on the cushions, and her face covered with a handkerchief.

'Blanche,' she murmured, 'I can do no more. Let him come.'

Parbleu! I came. These abundant thighs and the black bush half-opened, it all transported me with a sacred fury. I sprang on the sofa, I encoynted the fair one. At the first stroke, which she returned me, the handkerchief fell.

'My cousin la Galissiere!'

'My cousin de le Brulaye! Ah, so much the worse! I – I am feeling it!'

'I dis – I discharge!'

The spasm had seized us both like a flash of lightning, and spared us the embarrassment of so strange a meeting.

'Then you have kissed me, my cousin.'

'Then I did futtere you, my cousin.'

Blanche fairly writhed with laughter.

'They are relations!' she cried. 'They are relations!'

However, the Marquise, in a languishing voice, asked Blanche where the Princess's dildo was. Blanche brought forward the monster in triumph, and at a sign from her accomplice, fastened it round her loins. Then she wanted to put it into the Marquise.

But she was not amused with games so simple! She made Blanche lie on the sofa, and straddled across her resolutely. The enormous dildo did not enter without making her groan; but it did enter at last. The Marquise, then addressing herself to me, said, 'My cousin, take what remains for you.'

That which remained, of course, was her backside.

I accommodated myself to it, as you may well imagine. The entrails I was to penetrate were those of my own family! As I presented myself a little brusquely, my cousin stopped me by a well-applied blow of her satin crupper.

'Do you only know how to commit sodomy?' she said to me. 'Ah, Richard, the skill is not to push to the very end. There is at the entrance a muscle, a ring which closes…'

'Yes, the sphincter,' I replied.

'And it the pressure of this that will give you pleasure! It is this that will make you feel delicious contractions. Do not thrust right in, don't thrust right in!'

'Ah!' cried Blanche. 'What a woman! How she knows everything!'

Who would have told me that I should receive lessons in Socratic's from my cousin la Galissiere! I obeyed her instructions – I placed myself just within the sphincter. She caused me to feel these divine contractions!

'Do you see? This is the kiss of the backside!' she said to me.

The Convents
À La Mode

I t was the Regency, then. No, it was the Empire only, the Low
Empire, small epoch of little cynics to lying senses and a
trembling heart. Strange epoch in which strange modes were
introduced! One took one's daughter to church and one's mistress to the brothel.

This is what Therese de Charnac, whose slave and plaything
I was at that time, said to me. She related to me that her dearest friend had been conducted last night to Saint-Vigor. She
added, 'It is the mode!'

She was tall, a brunette, moderately thin, this Therese,
admirably made for wearing men's clothes. I gave her a suit of
mine, and put on her trousers myself. 'En route for the Convent
of Saint Vigor, and whip up, coachy!'

'Good,' murmured the nuns, on seeing her enter, 'another
tribade!'

'You hear them?' I said to Therese.

'They deceive themselves,' she said. 'Tribade? Not yet!'

There reigned in this room, brilliantly lit up, a strong odour
of iris mingled with perspiration, of musk and semen. Otherwise

the place was furnished and hung with red velvet. Nothing could have been colder or more banal. Not even an erotic image on the walls. One would have said it was the boudoir of a notary.

The servant cried, 'All ladies to the saloon!'

The ladies came in from all sides. One saw them enter by every door, in yellow dresses, red dresses, blue dresses. Corsages open even to the waist, allowing the throat to be exposed and protrude itself, petticoats fastened by a single thread, ready to fall at any moment. Venus, obscene Venus, emerged quite naked from this wave of velvets, laces, and silks. Naked, quite naked, absolutely stark naked.

Therese seated herself, trembling and confused in spite of her natural hardihood, at the end of a sofa. The cynical troop came wheeling round her.

'Good day, pretty lad.'

'Make your choice, my fine man.'

'See! I know who you are; I will lick thee, I will suck thee. Oh, we are accustomed to amuse the ladies of the Court!'

'Make your choice!' cried the servant.

'Come, my man,' said a stout girl who loved a joke, 'you are just what I want. How much do I ask? A sovereign and ten inches! This gallant ought to be mounted as a horse!'

But a tall and strong ribald whore, who wore, why one knows not, a Swiss costume, with floating tresses, and who was called Gretchen, came and sat on Therese's knees, and passing her hand over the pantaloons of the fair one with a comical gravity, cried out, 'It stands!' Then there were cries, shouts, laughter, and stamping of feet throughout the room.

'Gretchen, let him do thee in front of us!'

'In the greyhound style, in the greyhound style!'

'It stands! It stands!'

And the servant repeated, 'Make your choice!' in a voice of thunder.

At a sign, which I gave them, Gretchen, the Swiss, and one of her companions, who was called Ida, carried Mlle. de Charnac away. I followed them. Therese murmured I know not what unintelligible protestations. I said to her, 'It is the mode!'

In the room we entered there was a great bed, entirely surrounded by looking-glasses. Gretchen set herself to the task of stripping off the trousers of her fair visitor, whose teeth chattered as if she had been led to the place of execution, notwithstanding that the fingers of the adroit Swiss were already tickling her.

Ida said to me, 'Give us your little present.'

I placed four sovereigns on the mantelpiece. And as this girl was pressing round me, I showed her Therese entirely stripped of trousers and drawers.

'Everything for her!' I cried.

Speedily, I beheld all three of them naked. The mirrors that surrounded the bed reflected these three interlaced bodies. The two prostitutes of the people held embraced between them the prostitute of the fashionable world. They placed her at the edge of the bed. Ida, kneeling behind of her and holding her two legs on her shoulders, conveyed the fire of her kisses to her anus. Her tongue wriggled in the path of sodomy.

Gretchen the Swiss was lying across the bed, and sucking Therese's breasts. Her mouth glided along and descended, lapping the brown skin. She opened with two fingers the gate, not of sodomy but of nature, and seized her clitoris between her lips. Therese cried out, writhed, and called to me.

'Enjoy, you little whore,' I said to her. 'Enjoy till you burst, till you give up the ghost. Be licked! It is the mode!'

It was the fashion at court at that time. They said the Queen had a sacred troop of maids of honour whose most intimate and profound charms had no secrets for her. They said that, armed with a dildo, she had had the first fruits of them all. What remained was for the dignitaries of the Empire.

All this Mlle. de Charnac knew well.

'Haven't you a dildo here?' she sighed in a dying voice.

Gretchen sprang to a wardrobe, in which she opened a drawer. Dildos – there were ten, there were twenty! The Swiss assured me that they were only used for the ladies of the Court. This made me say, 'Have they the pox?'

But already the Swiss was armed with a magnificent article, which she had fastened to her waist, and darting on to the bed, she threw down Mlle. de Charnac, panting under her.

These women of high rank have, as the saying goes, eyes bigger than their bellies. They must, then, have very big eyes? Doubtless. But it is also true that the artificial member of Gretchen the Swiss was enormous!

It entered nevertheless. Ida directed it with art. Gretchen thrust with measured movements.

'My friends, you are ripping me open. You are assassinating me! Ah, I am – I am quite full!'

We heard something like a cracking. Then she uttered a terrible cry.

'Do not complain,' I said to her, 'it is the mode.'

Long after, very long after, until an advanced hour of the night were these games à la mode prolonged. The last stroke of the concluding part was the most piquant. In truth, they gave me the honour of taking part in it, in this manner.

Represent to yourself your servant stretched horizontally along the bed. Mlle. de Charnac, or the prostitute of the fashionable world, was at the side, threaded by Gretchen after the fashion of beasts. Ida, squatted under her, licked her sweetly, and the great lady herself, throwing herself on me, sucked me with fury. Then raising herself, her eyes troubled, reeling and giddy, Mlle said to me, 'Dress me again, and let us go home.'

When we were once more in the carriage, I began to contemplate her with admiration, as a person worthy of her rank by her luxury.

'Are you contented?' I asked her.

She raised her shoulders slightly, 'Bah!' she said. 'It is the mode!'

The Pearl-Grey Stocking
And The Red Star

The fair Lamperiere was a widow with clear eyes, very rich, and with a form as opulent as her purse. Perhaps she was not in every point as perfect as the Venus of Arles, to whom her flatterers compared her. One could even find something a little heavy, a clumsiness in the chiselling of her figure, and her shoulders exposed a skin tolerably thick and too close. As a set off, nature had given her a leg! And at the end of this leg, an alert foot. She was ordinarily shod in hose of pearl-grey silk with rose-coloured slippers. Is there a voluptuary who does not know that a pearl-grey stocking is the utmost expression of pleasure?

At the moment I present her to you, the fair Lamperiere is very much engaged, for I am seated in an armchair, in front of and quite close to her. I hold her in my embrace, even passing a hand under her petticoat!

Although one belongs to the best society, one is not the less sensitive. The tickling, from which she could not defend herself, greatly incommoded the fair Lamperiere.

'Am I dreaming?' she said to me. 'What... this is the second time you have seen me alone! You have no esteem for me!'

'I should like to esteem you three times running without drawing breath,' I replied, not knowing what I was saying. 'Besides, it is the fault of your pearl-grey stocking.' My hand did not quit its post, and the following dialogue took place between the fair Lamperiere and myself:

She: This pearl-grey stocking is not a reason.

I: It gives you a celestial leg. God is my witness that I whished at first only to touch your ankle. But, on my faith –

She: Ah! You are crushing my knee!

I: No, it is not your knee. It is higher where I am caressing. What a skin! Of rose-coloured satin, like your slippers.

She: Yes, yes! I am well enough content with my skin. If you continue, I shall call out.

I: Ah, the dainty little navel!

She: I shall call my maid.

I: I have paid her!

She: You have paid my maid! Monster! Will you let me be!

I: Good! You can't guard every place at once! If you defend the front, I shall attack the behind!

She: You are a man without delicacy. Who do you take me for, Sir?

I: For myself!

She: I am an honest woman, and since the death of M. de Lamperiere no man has ever...It is an abomination, a rape, a murder!

I: I beg of you, open your dress a little, instead of calling me all these things without reason. Give me this lovely breast. Truly, one could say that it is too firm!

She: Ah, well, yes! But you must leave the rest alone. Hold, here it is. I have even the complaisance to draw it from its prison for you!

I: The nipple is the colour of chocolate. I am going to eat it!

She: No, no. Brrrr – that gives me a shiver.

I: Now, offer me your mouth.

She: My mouth! Ah, well. Ah! you are making me swoon! No, I don't wish – no, I will not unclose my thighs. Your hand shall not pass. Your are doing wrong. What nails! But you are stripping me quite naked! At least will it please you to lower my dress?

I: Certainly, certainly! Why shouldn't I close the curtains as well! I love much better to look at what I am holding. Gods! These pearl-grey stockings! You have a finely nurtured form, my dear. I am going to bite you to pieces. Do you see this black muff?

She: Three fingers are too much. Two only! Ah, rub more gently! What a man! Great God! I – I!

I: You have ejaculated, you're content. What shall we do now? Do you wish to have my tongue in the mouth of this pretty pussy?

She: As for that, today, no! No, no, no, no! You have left me no time to make my toilette.

I: This need not trouble you! I love the taste of the fruit. But why do you draw away thus, my sweet?

She: Nothing – a pain which –

I: At the bottom of your stomach! A little colic. You draw back again, you wish me to do so!

She: Yes, I wish you. Above all, I am opposed to what you proposed to me.

I: Minette? Oh, oh! You don't pardon me for not having made a declaration to you in regular form!

She: My regulars! Who has told you? My regulars! No, no, not yet. If my calculations are right, they will not be until tomorrow.

I: The devil, if I thought of that. But what are you looking at, then, in the fold of your chemise?

She: It is nothing! It is nothing! I was sure of it!

I: We will say, then, that your regulars do not commence until tomorrow, even although you are having them now, my dear!

She: You say that. At the bottom you are like all men. Women are more amorous in these vile moments, but you do not profit by it. It disgusts you!

I: Wait a bit! Let me look! Just here, in the crease of your thigh, is a little red trace!

She: Horrible! Loose me! Go! Come back in three days. Leave me!

I: Bah! Struggle as much as you like, I hold you. Rather take off your dress. Take it off, will you? Quite naked with your grey stockings, on which the little red drops will fall. That will be charming!

She: Ah, Richard! If I believed you were sincere, I would do what you wish.

I: Regard, the proof of my sincerity. Is it not stiff enough? I am all on fire!

She: Would you put it like that, in the blood?

I: I can tell you that I am not going to leave you wearing even your chemise.

She: But...What are you doing? I have nothing on but my stockings! Truly, I am ashamed.

I: Where shall we go to do our pretty little game?

She: In the next room there is a bed.

I: There is a couch of red silk, and red goes well with you. There, come in front of the mirror. You will see this great thing, which is so stiff, enter your pussy and come out again.

She: What an idea! I like it well.

I: Hold, place yourself on your knees. I come in from behind. See, the mirror reflects your stomach, your breasts, and this brown hair! Your buttocks are like marble.

She: Leave me the pleasure of putting you in! It enters. Today, I am big. The blood is coming, and it makes the passage humid; but ordinarily –

I: Do you see, it goes, it comes – I slip out, I re-enter quite sweetly – I go to the bottom. Hurrah for the blood! Hurrah for the blood! A red star on the grey hose! I am going to tickle you.

She: Richard, Richard! Not such shocking words. Tickle strongly!

I: The blood! Flic, Flac! How I am dabbling!

She: I want to embrace you. I cannot. Hold, I will embrace you in the mirror. Ah! I enjoy thou also! You are flooding me!

I: Sacre dieu!

She: Withdraw yourself, my darling.

I: I have the appearance of having steeped my member in the blood of all the enemies of France!

She: What are you looking for?

I: A napkin.

She: The blood is ugly to look at now that your passion is glutted. You no longer have anything but disgust!

I: Parbleu! I will prove that well enough to you immediately, when I am in a state. You shall replace me with your hand as soon as I have wiped myself. My dear, you kiss to distraction.

She: Ah! Richard! Richard! How I love thee! Come and seat yourself on this sofa. The napkin which you are looking for this napkin ce sera ma bouche.

Venus
School Mistress

The school-mistress was the widow of an officer. She was rather pretty, but corpulent. Though nicely formed, possessing a dignity that captivates while it awes, she was confoundedly fond of whipping her scholars. In short, it was her ruling passion. When she flogged a bigger scholar who was pretty, she (as the Sister Grise mentioned in Manon's Memoirs) would thrust into her victim's body a monstrous dildo. Then she would whip the culprit with a large birchen rod as hard as she could, squeezing her between her own thighs all the time, till a copious spending cooled her burning lust.

The number of boarders was confined to twenty-five, but we had several day-scholars, among whom were many boys; notwithstanding this, the mistress never kept but one English teacher, always very young, besides an old woman who acted in the capacity of housekeeper. I had scarcely been a week in the house, when I had occasion to complain to the mistress of one of the girls who was learning, but was extremely idle and inattentive. The mistress told me with a tone of authority to flog her myself. And for the future, said she, 'I desire you will not complain to me anymore, but punish them yourself. I expect my teachers to help me in correcting the children, as well as in teaching them, and you are big enough, Miss, and strong enough for the purpose.

She could not have given me a job I loved better, for like Manon, I had a particular itch for flogging. I learned from one of the servants, that my predecessor, who was a young girl of about twenty, exercised her flogging talents in such a manner as to give great satisfaction to the widow. To gain her approbation in this respect, it was necessary to do it till you were out of breath and the culprit's arse a gore of blood.

But to return to the mistress's direction, I went immediately to her closet, where she kept her rods, and chose one of a tolerable good size, and stripping the girl, and tying her hands before her, as the widow always did, I flogged away for ten minutes at the least, with all my force. The governess watched me all the time, as if her eyes would start out of her head. When I had finished, she said 'That's the way I would have you flog. You will make an excellent schoolmistress in time. Indeed she was tolerably right, for though it was my first attempt, I left the girl's backside in a sad condition. I was not a little proud of the liberty she gave me of whipping, for scarcely a day passed that I did not exercise the rod upon some delinquent or other.

There was a man she employed every Monday to bring a regular supply of fresh-cut birch brooms for the use of the school. Sometimes she whipped the bigger scholars, particularly the boys for we had several great boys, behind a large folding screen. It was at the bottom of the schoolroom, and concealed the closet door where she usually deposited her store of birch and from which a back staircase led to another part of the house. Sometimes she flogged in her bedroom, but more frequently in the school. I once saw her flogging a great girl who had taken some money privately from one of her school-fellows' pockets. The mistress gave it to her for near half an hour, and wore out two large birchen rods, well steeped in vinegar, over the girls' thighs and buttocks. She had that day more the appearance of a fury than a rational being. Passion and lust, by turns, discovered themselves in her countenance.

She used also a kind of cat-o'-nine tails, or rather, o'-sixty tails, for it had about sixty lashes to it, of the length of the arm. It was made of thin slips of parchment, moistened and closely twisted, with five knots at the end. But she made use of it only when she flogged the bigger boys or girls, and even then, preferring the birch upon most occasions. It was but once during my residence with her that I saw her apply it then to a girl who had been detected in frequent acts of pilfering.

I had nearly forgot to mention one of the bigger scholars, who frequently assisted me in hearing the younger ones in English, and who had permission to use the rod upon their hands, but nowhere else. She was very pretty, a great favourite with the widow, with whom she slept. Sometimes she whipped the youngest girls, but only when she had particular orders from the mistress for that purpose.

The widow received very often from one of the trustees of the school, an old friend and a consummate libertine, a large bouquet of costly flowers. As she was subject to the headache, she would sometimes make her favourite girl or myself wear it, though on certain occasions she would wear it herself. I was, like Manon, passionately fond of having a large nosegay in my bosom to smell at when I exercised the rod, as the fragrance of the flowers always excited in me the most pleasing sensations.

One day she received a most beautiful one, almost as big as a broom, and she insisted on my wearing it. She tied it herself to my bosom, so high that the flowers shaded almost the left side of my face. 'That is the way,' said she, a young girl should wear a nosegay.'

I flogged that day two grown-up girls who richly deserved it. The governess was so well pleased with my work that she gave me many kisses. When the school day was over, she ordered me to flog a beautiful boy who had been kept for that purpose. He was learning English, but of a very idle turn. His mother had desired that he might be forwarded as much as possible, and to that end suggested that the rod should not be spared. I said I was ashamed to whip so big a boy. She told me, with a great deal of nonchalance not to have that kind of mock modesty, and to do my duty. 'You are the English teacher,' she admonished. 'You are obliged to correct your scholars. To tell the truth, I was dying for a fair opportunity of whipping a big boy. I was afraid I was not strong enough. I nevertheless attempted to unbutton his pantaloons, but I could not affect it. I called Julie, the girl I just mentioned, for she frequently helped me in holding such refractory scholars as I could not manage myself. We soon tied his hands, and as the mistress was in the school, he did not dare make any more resistance.

I then stripped him to his heels, fastening his shirt up to his shoulders, and began scourging his backside with an excellent rod, and with a degree of force that only lust could inspire. 'Oh! Mademoiselle Miss,' cried he, for he thought that was my name as everybody in the house called me so. 'Forgive me, pray forgive me. I will learn my tasks better in the future, I will indeed.'

I paid no attention to his entreaties, but kept flogging on, my face buried in my nosegay, till at last the rod dropped out of my hand. I remained for a few minutes in a kind of lascivious stupor, and I confess that I felt that day such sensations as I had never experienced before. Perhaps, too, the luxurious fragrance of my bouquet might have contributed to excite them, for I kept smelling at it all the time I scourged him.

I held him under my arm, resting upon a high table, and kept him closely shut up between my thighs. I am sure I gave him more than a hundred lashes, the widow crying out the whole time, 'Don't let him go yet, whip him,' etc. The birch appeared to pinch him very much, for he plunged and writhed his body in the most wanton manner.

As soon as the boy was gone, the mistress, who had eyed me with a great deal of attention, and guessed very well what was passing within me, came to me. There were only ourselves in the school, as the children were playing, under Julie's inspection, in an adjoining court. Giving me burning kisses, as in the morning, she said, 'I am going into my bed-chamber, where I wish you would follow me in a few minutes, as I have something to say to you.' She then left me, passing through the closet where the birches were kept. I could not possibly guess what she meant, but was still determined to go. Her chamber, I must observe, was on the attic story. I found her very busy tying up a great bundle of birch, and as soon as I entered she locked the door. I began to be alarmed, thinking she meant to give me a flogging. My fears were soon dispelled, however, when she said, sitting on her bed, and pulling me after her, 'My dear girl' I have a favour to ask of you: I am very much afflicted at times with rheumatism in my backside, and suffer a great deal from it. The physician has prescribed to me the use of birch. Will you do me the favour to give me a good whipping with this rod?'

I stood petrified, and really thought the widow out of her wits. She perceived my astonishment, but at last persuaded me to acquiesce. I told her I was ready to do any thing to oblige her, but was afraid I should hurt her.

'On the contrary,' said she, 'you will do me a great deal of good.' Then she began kissing me again, and smelling at my nosegay, or rather my sweet bosom, the scent of which seemed to augment her lust. She passed her hands all over my body, and in fact acted with me as men do with women to excite desire before enjoying them.

After this little preamble, she tendered me the rod. 'Forget who I am,' she said and whip me as you whipped the boy just now.' Then placing herself upon her belly across the bed, and stripping herself as high as she could, she uncovered to me a bum that might vie with the Venus of Medici's.

I really think, if I had been a man, that I should have begun pushing away immediately in it. I took the rod, however, and began flogging her as if she had been a child.

'Harder,' said she, 'harder, faster, faster, and by no means stop till I say the word enough.'

I therefore whipped away lustily, at least as fast and hard as I could. There was a large looking-glass opposite her, so that she could see how I laid it on all the while. I suppose I was at it a full quarter of an hour, and her beautiful arse only displayed red strokes, as the rod was not calculated to fetch blood, being made of very slender twigs of birch, quite green.

She uttered half-broken expressions from time to time, as if sighing or out of breath, saying very often, 'Oh, my dear Miss Birch, forgive me, do, pray, pray,' etc.

At last she said the word 'enough' and I immediately discontinued. Then turning towards me and stripping me, she drew me violently to her, and made me lie upon her with my bum on her private parts. Grasping me between her thighs, she gave a deep sob, and continued in this posture for some minutes. The reader will easily guess that she had taken care to fix into her the Dildo she made use of, particularly when she flogged the bigger boys.

As soon as she recovered herself, she got up, thanked me and said, 'I suppose, Miss, it will be totally needless to advise you to keep this a secret, for you may depend upon it, if I ever hear it transpires, I shall find ways to be revenged.'

I assured her that she need not be alarmed on this, and we immediately separated.

When I was alone, I reflected upon the occurrence, and made no difficulty in concluding in my own mind, that the widow was a most complete libertine. It is not that she hated men. On the contrary, she found in birch discipline the gratification of one of those arbitrary tastes, for which there is no accounting.

As for myself, I acquired from that day a most ungovernable inclination for all sorts of sensual indulgencies, and particularly for flogging.

Among the pupils who were learning English, there was a tall young man, who received lessons from me about three times a week. He was the son of the bookseller who supplied us with school-books. I think he was then about eighteen years old, well made, and rather handsome. He was, also, rather bashful.

I soon found that I had captivated him, and I was not a little fond of him as well. But I had taken care to conceal it from him, for I always took a delight in teasing men.

I frequently detected him, instead of studying his lessons, staring at my springing bosom, for I had a very full one. Upon these occasions, I used to give him two or three gentle boxes on the ear, which pleased him very much.

Whenever I wore a nosegay he was always smelling at it, and I discovered that he was passionately fond of seeing me with a very large one. He would frequently bring me one, and then help me to fasten it to my bosom, taking care to slide his fingers, as if by chance, over my bubbies. I then pretended to be very angry in order to scold him and give him boxes on the ear. But his touches, far from displeasing me, procured me the most delightful sensations.

Before we began our lessons, we sometimes went, with the widow's permission, for a walk on the banks of the Seine. He would make love to me there, and like most lovers, tell me stories that had neither head nor tail. The widow, who had perceived my great partiality for him, desired me to encourage his addresses, as he was, she said, an excellent match for me.

One day he brought me a remarkably fine nosegay of very large size. It was the custom at that time, and I believe even now, for young girls of age to be married to wear enormous ones, always composed of the most odoriferous flowers, and to have their heads adorned with a wreath of the same. As I had a most beautiful one just fixed in my bosom, which the widow had given me, and had just been gathered, he appeared very much annoyed. He requested me repeatedly to wear his.

Lovers, like children, fret themselves for nothing, and their mistresses would be doing them a great service, when they grumble for nothing, if they would give them a good hearty whipping. Since we are the mistresses of men, we should use our authority to some purpose.

But to return to my lover, this was exactly his case. By way of frolic, I offered to untie my bouquet, and to mix the flowers with his to make one out of the two. Mine was stuffed with a quantity of moss-roses, tuberoses, jonquils, myrtle, etc., and his chiefly with carnations and jasmine. This proposition gave him apparent satisfaction.

As soon as I had arranged it, and tied it up tightly, I attempted, or rather both of us tried, to fasten it to my side. But we could not effect it on account of its monstrous size. With the help of two or three pieces of strong ribbon, however, I at last contrived to manage it.

'Here,' said I to him, looking at myself in a large glass. I could not help remarking what a voluptuous and effeminate air a large bouquet gives to a woman. 'Here is a nosegay fit for a duchess. How do you like it? I hope it is big enough now, for it nearly covers the whole of my face. The ladies on the Continent always wear their bouquets very high on the left side, so as to have the flowers play with their cheeks'

'Oh, a pretty girl like you,' says he, 'cannot wear a nosegay too large.'

'So, to please you,' said I, 'a pretty girl must make herself ridiculous.' In truth, however, I had seen many young girls with a nosegay in their bosoms as large as the one I had on, and I did not think it a bit too large.

As it was rather early, I requested the widow's permission to take a little walk with my lover, which she immediately granted, saying to me with a smile, 'You'll be taken for a young bride, with your great bouquet in your bosom. Don't, however, be late, for I sup in town tonight. I hope your scholar is diligent, she added in jest. You know we have plenty of birch in the house for idle ones.'

I was highly pleased to have an opportunity of exhibiting myself with my great nosegay, and my pride privately gratified by the attention of the passing crowd. I frequently heard people behind me say, 'Here's the jolie Anglaise. See, she is as beautiful as an angel.'

After we had taken a few turns, and I'd been stared at through and through, particularly by the men, we set for home. When passing, by chance, close to the home of the woman whose son I had so soundly whipped, she happened to be standing at the door. She invited me in to refresh myself with a glass of wine, it being the trade in which she dealt, thanking me repeatedly for the chastisement I had given the boy.

We accepted her invitation, and my lover and I drank several large glasses of good old Champaign, for we were both very thirsty. However, it tasted to me like small beer, and from not being accustomed to its strength, it made me more merry than usual. Then we left her to return to the school.

The children were already in bed, and the mistress had taken Julie with her. My scholar and myself betook ourselves to a kind of study, a room quite on the back part of the house where he and others generally read their lessons to me. We rested a little while on a sort of settee, where the governess sometimes fastened the bigger boys or girls in order to flog them more easily.

As he wished to kiss me and take other liberties with me, I got up, and we sat down to a table to read. He performed so indifferently that I began to scold him. But he could not take his eyes from my bosom.

I had told him to learn the verb 'to love,' and in repeating it, he said in the present tense, 'I love you.' When he came to the future, 'I shall love you forever,' I did not appear to understand him, but said in a kind of joke, 'I have a great mind to follow the governess's direction, and fetch a good rod to make you more attentive.'

'He began laughing, and said, 'I'll wager twenty kisses that you may whip me as long and as hard as you can, before I'll tell you to leave off!'

'Done – let me try,' I replied, for the wine had so far got into my head that I neither knew what I did or said. Besides, I had grown, since I had whipped the widow, very bold and wanton. I rose to fetch a rod, and chose the largest and greenest I could find.

During my absence he had pulled off his breeches, which I did not discover at my re-entrance, as he had on a long great-coat such as young men frequently wear on the Continent in summer. 'Come,' said I, shaking the bundle of birch at him. 'Come, young man, down with your breeches, and let me see what effect this birch will have upon you. I think it will make you more attentive.'

He immediately took off his great-coat. I was not a little astonished at seeing him in his shirt; nevertheless, forgetting myself entirely, I lost no time in tucking it up to his shoulders, and took him under my arm, as if he had been one of our scholars. Leaning him against the table, I began flogging him like one of the children, with my face buried in the flowers of my nosegay, which almost overcame me with its odoriferous exhalations.

Though he did not open his mouth with a complaint, I could see very well the marks of the birch on his backside. But who is the man who would not have liked to be in his situation, whipped by a pretty girl? Oh, ye male readers, I think I see you smile, but it is no less true.

I still kept on, that I might win the wager, but in vain. I had given him I don't know how many lashes, when I began to feel his weapon; it was glued, as it were, to one of my thighs, for I had on only a thin muslin gown. Swelling to a considerable size, and so stiff, it caused me to reflect on my frolic, but too late. Breathless with my exertions, I was obliged to yield. I then attempted to escape, but he had taken the precaution to fasten the door and hide the key.

As he had won his wager, he seized me, and, smothering me with kisses without losing a moment, he threw me on the settee and stripped up my shift. In spite of the resistance I made, which only served to inflame his lust, he got the head of his engine into my belly, grasping me closely all the while in his arms.

He soon became ungovernable, tearing into me without mercy, his thrusts growing increasingly more furious. After causing me a great deal of pain, he thrust at last up to the very hilt, all the while sucking my neck, for I had turned my face and buried it among the flowers, that I might not see him.

I arrived by degrees at an excess of pleasure, through my excess of pain. So keen was the sensation I felt when I received the emission of his seed that I scarcely knew if I had any life in me I soon expired in the arms of the murderer of my virginity in an agony of bliss.

As soon as we recovered ourselves, finding I did not speak, and had the appearance of melancholy, for I was greatly ashamed of what had just taken place, he broke the ice, saying, 'I have made you a woman, but I swear by the love I have for you, that I will marry you as soon as you choose.'

As I was more to blame than he, I freely forgave him the outrage, and after mutually exchanging kisses, we separated like true lovers. In order to give me incessant proof of his affection, he hired at his laundress's, whom he bribed for the purpose, a small garret, and bought a neat bed for it. Thereafter, we frequently met in private to renew our libidinous gambols, which always terminated in luxurious coition.

Julie and I became very intimate. She told me in confidence that she often whipped the widow, with whom she slept, as mentioned before, particularly in the morning before they put their clothes on. She would turn the widow upside down, press her in her arms, and at last die with pleasure under her. At other times, she would fasten with belts round her waist a dildo, the flat hilt of which covered her pretty slit. The mistress had taught her to imitate the motions men make upon women in the act of coition, and by these means allay the burning fire within her.

One day she was gone, and by chance had left the key to the drawer where she kept the appliance. Julie showed it to me, and I could not help admiring its contrivance. It was made of whalebone covered with velvet. The head had a bladder over it, and in the middle of it was a small pipe. The construction was such that in pressing the imitative balls that hung from it, she received a bedewing, a shower of the warm milk contained in it.

So when she flogged (particularly the bigger boys) she entwined their legs and thighs between her own, and the smart of the birch would make them struggle and writhe in such a manner as to cause at the last critical moment her own 'ejaculation'. I have brought a few of them from France. I have often used them, and still do, whenever I whip the bigger girls or boys. Even men, when I like them, sometimes get themselves flogged.

One afternoon the widow and I had been flogging a tall, awkward girl more than usual. She was remarkably idle, and I had flogged her that day most severely. I believe I had given her more that a hundred lashes, though four or five dozen strokes, properly applied, were the common punishment of the school. We always fastened to the side of the bigger girls a large bundle of birch, in lieu of a nosegay, to make them more ashamed, and as she could not bear this additional punishment, she got away from me just as I was going to tie to her bosom the birchen bouquet.

I went after her, but she had taken refuge on the far side of a long table near the folding screen. I got upon it in order to take hold of her, but was surprised to see, by the elevation at which I stood, the trustee. He was peeping through a crevice in the screen, observing what was going forward in the school. I did not, however, pretend to have seen him. Instead, I brought back the young slut and fastened, in spite of her struggles, her birchen nosegay.

I was some time after this an observer of a far more lascivious scene than what I have just described. I had been out to make a purchase, and at my return, as I did not see Julie in the play-ground with the children, I naturally concluded that she was in the school. I was going to open the door, but was prevented by finding it fast, which rather surprised me.

At the same time, I distinctly heard the birch applied with the utmost severity to a boy who was bawling as loud as possible. In another part of the school I plainly distinguished the voice of a girl who was undergoing the same chastisement.

I had not the least doubt that the school-mistress and Julie were both at work at the birchen business, and with a view of satisfying my curiosity, I went to the private staircase that led to the closet where the birch was kept. Its door also happened to be fastened, but as there was a small window over it that looked upon the room, and admitted some light into it. I got upon an old table that happened to be there. I then saw again, not without astonishment, the trustee flat upon his belly, with a young girl under him, whose neck he was devouring with kisses. She was also almost at full-length upon a table, which appeared to have been put there for the express purpose. She was stripped to her shoulders, and his weapon was engulfed in her backside, his stones resting on her plump buttocks. At the same time, he was peeping every minute through the hole in the screen, watching the beautiful Julie flog a girl with all her strength. He could also see the widow who had just whipped a boy. The lad, reading before her with his pantaloons down, was kept between her thighs. Pressing with one of her hands, which was round his body, his naked arse upon her private parts, she held his most tremendous rod in the other.

This curious scene lasted, I suppose, half an hour. Observing the trustee retire his flagging instrument from its hiding-place, I hastily withdrew. As soon as I saw Julie, I told her what I had seen, but we could never discover who the girl was. She appeared to be very young, handsome, and with a most beautiful skin.

This scene had in a great measure confused my ideas, for at that time I was not acquainted with the different propensities of men, and I thought that this way of being conducted was perhaps as natural as the other. I had even an intention to try it with my lover.

I had observed that the widow sometimes retired into her bedroom with the trustee, as well as with a cousin of hers, who was captain of a merchant ship. I did not suppose that it was merely to enfiler des perles (as the French say), as she passed with them sometimes several hours. I ransacked my brains to find some way or other to see their sports, but to no purpose. There was a passage that led to the widow's bedchamber, but it was always fastened up on these occasions. It was impossible either to see or hear what was going on in her room.

One day I was in my room, which was on the same floor with hers, musing on some method to gratify my curiosity. I perceived I could pass along the gutters from my room to hers, for there was a parapet that made it not only practicable but safe. I had also observed that, when she expected a visit from any of these gentlemen, she would wear the nosegay, or rather the sweet-broom the trustee sent her almost every day. That evening I saw her go into her bed-chamber, with her bouquet up to her ear, by the private staircase, the trustee following her on his tiptoe. I went directly into my room, and getting out the window, I placed myself a little on the side of the widow's. She could not form the least idea that she was overlooked.

The trustee was already before her in a supplicating attitude, and almost naked. The school-mistress, armed with nearly half of a birch broom, was fastening his shirt up to his shoulders. She ordered him to lie across the bed, before the mirror glass, that he might contemplate her during the birchen operation. Then she began to whip him like a Russian school-mistress.

When he had received about two hundred strokes, he got up, kissed her beautiful bosom, folded her in his arms, and placed her at last on the bed. After he stripped her, I thought he was going to serve her in the same manner as he had the girl behind the folding screen, but however I was deceived, for he got into the right channel, and began to work away like a Monk.

Another time I discovered by the same means her cousin, the captain, a portly gentleman of about thirty. She gave him also a severe whipping, but after she had worn out a famous bundle of birch upon his bottom, she took the cat-o'-sixty tails and began flogging him with it, sometimes on the buttocks, sometimes on his back, for he was quite naked.

She would now and then stop for a few minutes, and rub his nose with his shirt, saying, 'You dirty scoundrel, will you piss your breeches again? Will you, will you,' etc., flogging him again as violently as she could.

After this tender preliminary, he placed her upon her belly, with her shirt stripped up to her shoulders. I saw him then thrust his Maypole into the widow's backside up to the very hilt. He continued in that posture for at least twenty minutes, working his arse up and down with all his force, pressing his balls upon her beautiful buttocks.

All these pretty scenes caused the fire of lust to burn violently in my veins. Fortunately my lover, a vigorous young man, appeased in some degree the heat or I don't know what I should have done. We met each other almost every evening before supper. He had begged me several times to give him another whipping, for the one I gave him on the day of my faux pas had made such an impression upon him that he was longing for another.

With a view to gratifying him, I armed myself one evening with a very large rod, composed of fresh and tender twigs of birch, which I knew would twitch him very much but not do the least injury. He had sent me that evening, for it was my fête a bouquet similar to the one I wore the day he got my maidenhead. I had on besides a beautiful white muslin gown, almost as light and transparent as gauze. Instead of a wreath of flowers round my head, as I generally wore, I had on a cap à la paysanne, which was then very much in fashion, and which made me look still more lascivious.

I went rather early to our room, and lay on the bed, waiting for him. The emanations of the flowers of my beautiful nosegay, for I counted more than five dozen moss-roses, and as many carnations and pinks and other flowers, intermixed with a quantity of jasmine and myrtle, invaded voluptuously my senses. I was surrounded by an atmosphere of perfumes – I felt self-languor diffusing itself through my body, my heart as it were, expanding. While I was yielding to the most delightful sensations, ideas of the most delightful sensations, ideas of the most pleasing kind pervaded and filled my soul.

Oh, ye lovely maids, who think a large nosegay spoils your sweet bosoms, when on the contrary it adorns them with an irresistible charm, try the experiment when you are performing any of the rites of Venus. You will soon find that the sweet perfume exhaling from your bouquet will not only excite your desires, but aggravate very much a venereal enjoyment, if you take care to wear it large and high enough to be able to snuff up its lascivious scent during the performance.

I was in that voluptuous state, when I heard my lover walking up. As soon as he saw me he smothered me with kisses, and without losing a moment extended me on the bed. Lying himself upon me, in a few minutes he made me swoon with pleasure under him.

He had brought with him a bottle of Champaign, which we immediately emptied, the effects of which made me soon ready for another engagement. Before, however, we began our sport, by way of a treat, I took up my bundle of birch, which I had concealed under a table, and began playing the school-mistress with him with a vengeance. I whipped him as hard as I could for a full quarter of an hour, which wound him up to such a pitch of lechery that he was eager for another touch at me. Throwing me on the bed, he pushed his dart into me, as if he would have split me up, all the time devouring my bubbies.

I kept the rod with me, and tried to continue flogging, with my face, as usual, buried in my lascivious bouquet, but I was obliged to stop for want of strength. Suddenly I felt such ravishing pleasure, diffusing itself into the innermost recesses of my body, accompanied with dear delirium, intimating the delicious moment of dissolution in which enjoyment itself is drowned, that I thought my existence was upon the point of being dissolved in bliss.

I had passed nearly two years in a continual succession of delight, when my lover's mother came one morning, overwhelmed with grief, to tell us that her son had drowned the evening before. He often went to bathe, and it was supposed the cramp had suddenly seized him, and being alone, without the power of receiving any assistance, he was drowned.

I fainted at the intelligence; and when I came to myself, I felt all the weight of my situation, for I was nearly three months gone with child by him. I remained for a considerable time swallowed up in grief and despair, but time and youth, by degrees, moderated the violence of my sufferings.

Some time had elapsed since I had received any letter from my mother, when one evening I saw her enter with a young lady of uncommon beauty. It was Manon, or rather Mrs. Duverger, who was going to embark at Le Havre with her husband for Philadelphia. My mother had got acquainted with her on the journey. As the ship was not quite ready to sail, she stopped for very near a month here at Rouen. It would have been one of the most agreeable months of my life if it had not been for the recent death of my lover.

As Mrs. Duverger's time of departure was now arrived, we parted with regret, for she entertained for me a particular friendship. To say the truth, some little gambols had passed between us, which I shall leave to the reader to guess.

She made me several presents, among them nine ostrich feathers of a most enormous size, and a monstrous winter bouquet of artificial flowers. Those were so exquisitely perfumed that they retained their respective scents in a high degree, and when I wore them everyone took them for real flowers. She gave me also her enormous brown bear muff, as well as a copy of her Memoirs, to amuse me, she said, when I should have leisure to read them.

As soon as she was gone, my mother made me a partial confidence of what had happened to her since our separation, adding that the person with whom she had lived had lost large sums by gaming, and had left her in great distress. She intended to return immediately to England, to continue her school with Miss Smart, giving me the choice either of remaining at Rouen or accompanying her to London.

As Rouen, since my lover's death, had become disagreeable to me, I preferred returning. We took our leaves of the widow, who paid me something more than our agreement, and of the beautiful Julie, whom I loved like a sister. Perhaps fortunately for her, Julie was possessed of a very cold constitution, for I often whipped her for pleasure, and even frigged her, but to no purpose. Scarcely anything affected her.

She had, for example, a lover in the son of a writing-master, who attended our school. She liked him a little, she would say, but the proud little wench would scarcely let him kiss her pretty hand. One day the sweet fellow, for he was very handsome and not much more than eighteen, attempted to kiss her sweet bubbies. I am sure, if it had not been for shame, she would have whipped him. She was very near doing it, for she took a rod and flogged his hands and legs as hard as she could, for daring, she said, to take such a shocking liberty with her.

As soon as we arrived in London, my mother went, after resting a day or two, to Chelsea, where she was informed that Miss Smart had parted with the school. She was gone to Ireland with a gentleman, as governess to his nephews and nieces, but also to himself. She informed me afterwards that she flogged him almost as often as her pupils.

About that time I brought to the birthing bed a daughter, the very image of her father. Never shall I forget the great care and maternal affection my mother showed me at that critical period. I have and shall always give her proof of my gratitude.

We passed a year together, without following any particular business. Our pecuniary stock beginning gradually to decrease, my mother took employment at a small haberdashery shop at Islington, and I, for the sake of the country air, went as a teacher to a girls' school in Wales. There I indulged almost every day my propensity for administering the birch discipline, and even carried it to an excess, leaving my little girl under my mother's care.

After spending some time in that school, I returned to London, and took lodgings in Westminster, with an intention to open a day-school, as my mother wished to continue in her little shop, and have still the care of my little daughter. I believe she would at that time have sooner parted with her life than with the little darling.

I took it into my head one day to go to Ranelagh, to see if I could meet with some friends. I dressed myself as elegantly as I could. I went in the evening to a nursery, where I bought a quantity of many kinds of odoriferous flowers, in order to make what is called on the Continent an enormous bouquet de luxure. For the first time, I wore on my head the nine beautiful white feathers Madame Duverger had presented me at Rouen.

I had not been long in Ranelagh, when I was accosted by a gentleman, the same as mentioned in Manon's Memoirs, who was passionately fond of being whipped with green birch by young women elegantly dressed, and with a most enormous nosegay in their bosoms. At times he would make me dress as a lady of the Court, with a hoop of the largest size, and a beautiful muslin gown and train spangled with silver, and drawn up with festoons of natural flowers. He had by him several gowns of the kind, which, with the enormous bouquet and high plume of white feathers. He usually gave me a most lascivious look. I would then whip him for half an hour, impersonating a lady of the first order of beauty and haughty deportment; this pastime always finished, on his part, in an agony of pleasure. I have known several gentlemen who had a similar penchant.

I went out one evening with the monstrous muff Madame Duverger had also given me, for it was rather cold, with an intention to scold my shoemaker, who had neglected to send me a pair of shoes I had ordered. I had got partly upstairs, as the cobbler lodged at the top of the house, when I heard a young woman crying out, 'Oh, pray, pray forgive me, Aunt. Do forgive me, and I will bind them directly.'

Discovering a large trunk in a corner near the door, I got gently upon it, and saw through a small window over the door Madam Crispin, a tall, carroty termagant, about thirty, rather pretty, with a monstrous bosom, tying up the best part of a birch broom, quite green. A big girl was upon her knees, supplicating in vain for pardon. As soon as Madam had tied the rod, she stripped the young thing, and took her under her arm. Raising her a little from the ground, with her buttocks fully exposed, she flogged her till the blood ran down to her heels. She then locked her up in a closet, saying, 'Now go, you lazy hussy, and bind the shoes as I ordered you.'

Her husband, a tall brawny fellow, about forty, who had been watching her all the time, with eyes full of lechery, suddenly left his work, and throwing her without ceremony on the bed soon engulfed his terrible weapon into her. I never saw one of such a monstrous size. He worked her in such a manner that she seemed nearly suffocated with lust and gorged with pleasure.

Not wishing to interrupt them, I returned softly downstairs, without saying anything about my shoes.

I hardly got into the street, when I met a gentleman rather advanced in years, who observing my great muff, for it was enormously large, begged permission to see me home. As soon as we got into my bed room, he undressed himself entirely and asked me to tickle him with my muff all over his body, particularly about his private parts. Leaning upon a table, he placed his tool upon the hollow of my backside, and moving and pressing his stones upon my buttocks, he soon discharged, squeezing me with all his force between his thighs. I was standing all the while opposite a large looking-glass, with my neck exposed and my hands in my muff.

Among the capriccioso who wanted 'to rouse the Venus lurking in their veins' was a young lad, not above sixteen, from Westminster College. I used to whip him with the utmost severity, with a very large bundle of fresh birch, for nearly half an hour. He would be quite naked, with his hands tied up, and I would lean on a table, stripped up to my navel, always with an enormous bouquet in my bosom. When I felt his young staff threatening me, I would leave off, and untie his hands; he would then lay me on the bed, and make me feel unspeakable emotions.

I used also to whip another in the character and dress of a nun, with a cat-o'sixty-nine tails, till the blood ran down to his heels. A third took delight in putting his finger into my fundament while I was handling his private parts. I should fill a volume, were I to enumerate and enter into particulars relating to the various and strange propensities of some men.

My friend of Brompton had enabled me to purchase a boarding and day school, full of large girls and boys, in order to indulge with me in a number of birchen sports. He was particularly fond of enjoying me whilst I was scourging as hard as I could a big girl, selecting always for that purpose some grown-up, wicked, lazy wench with a fat arse – someone I knew to be too stupid to take notice of what was going forward, or rather backward.

One day, as I was reading the Morning Advertiser, a paper I peruse every day, I saw an advertisement to this effect: If Miss R.B. (with a star after the letters) will write a line to J., mentioning where she can be heard of, etc. I immediately recollected I had given Julie that direction, in case she should come to England, and could not find me; I answered it, and I had the pleasure of meeting again the beautiful Julie, who acquainted me that she had married the son of the writing-master I mentioned, but that he killed himself in less than two years by his incessant connections with her. She also informed me that the widow had espoused the trustee, and some other little particulars. We now live together and whip like two little devils both young folks and old ones.

Adieu readers of all descriptions. To amuse you with my juvenile gambols has been my object. You are the best judges if I have succeeded. If I find that you approve of this little bagatelle, I shall perhaps, at a future period, bring forth another birchen production. I have a great deal more to say upon that subject.

Man With A Maid

All the ropes and straps were fitted with swivel snap-hooks. To attach them to Alice's limbs, I used an endless band of the longest and softest silk rope that I could get made. It was an easy matter to slip the band (doubled) round her wrist or ankle, pass one end through the other and draw tight, then snap the free end into the swivel hook. No amount of plunging or snuggling would loosen this attachment, and the softness of the silk prevented Alice's delicate flesh from being rubbed or even marked.

During the ten minutes grace that I mentally allowed Alice in which to recover from the violence of her struggles, I quietly studied her as she stood helpless, almost supporting herself by resting her weight on her wrist. She was to me an exhilarating spectacle, her bosom fluttering, rising and falling as she caught her breath, her cheeks still flushing, her large hat somewhat disarranged, while her dainty well-fitting dress displayed her figure to its fullest advantage.

She regained command of herself wonderfully quickly, and then it was evident that she was stealthily watching me in horrible apprehension. I did not leave her long in suspense, but after going slowly round her and inspecting her, I placed a chair right in front of her, so close to her its edge almost touched her knees, then slipped myself into it, keeping my legs apart, so that she stood between them, the front of her dress pressing against the fly of my trousers. Her head was now above mine, so that I could peer directly into her downcast face.

As I took up this position, Alice trembled nervously and tried to draw herself away from me, but found herself compelled to stand as I had placed her. Noticing the action, I drew my legs closer to each other so as to loosely hold her between them, smiling cruelly at the uncontrollable shudder that passed through her, when she felt the pressure of my knees against hers! Then I extended my arms, clasped her gently round the waist, and drew her against me, at the same time tightening the clutch of my legs, till soon she was fairly in my embrace, my face pressing against her throbbing bosom. For a moment she struggled wildly, and then resigned herself to the unavoidable as she recognized her helplessness.

Except when dancing with her, I had never held Alice in my arms, and the embrace permitted by the waltz was nothing to the comprehensive clasping between arms and legs in which she now found herself. She trembled fearfully, her tremors giving me exquisite pleasure as I felt them shoot through her, then she murmured: 'Please don't, Jack!'

I looked up into her flushed face, as I amorously pressed my cheek against the swell of her bosom: 'Don't you like it, Alice?' I said maliciously, as I squeezed her still more closely against me. 'I think you're just delicious, dear, and I am trying to imagine what it will feel like, when your clothes have been taken off!'

'No! No! Jack!' she moaned, agonizingly, twisting herself in her distress. 'Let me go, Jack; don't... don't!' and her voice failed her.

For an answer, I held her against me with my left arm around her waist, and then with my right hand I began to stroke and press her hips and bottom.

'Oh... don't, Jack, don't!' Alice shrieked, squirming in distress and futilely endeavouring to avoid my marauding hand. I paid no attention to her pleading and cries, but continued my stroking and caressing over her full posteriors and thighs down to her knees, then back to her buttocks and haunches, she, all the while, quivering in a delicious way. Then I freed my left hand, and holding her tightly imprisoned between my legs, I proceeded with both hands to study over her clothes the configuration of her backside and hips and thighs, handling her buttocks with a freedom that seemed to stagger her, as she pressed herself against me, in an effort to escape from the liberties that my hands were taking with her charms.

After toying delightfully with her in this way for some time, I ceased and withdrew my hands from her hips, but only to pass them up and down over her bosom which I began lovingly to stroke and caress to her dismay. Her colour rose as she swayed uneasily on her legs. But her stays prevented any direct attack on her bosom, so I decided to open her clothes sufficiently to obtain a peep at her virgin breasts, and set to work unbuttoning her blouse.

'Jack, no! No!!' shrieked Alice, struggling vainly to get loose. But I only smiled and continued to undo her blouse till I got it completely open and threw it back onto her shoulders only to be baulked as a fairly high bodice covered her bosom. I set to work to open this, my fingers revelling in the touch of Alice's dainty linen. Soon it also was open and thrown back, and then, right before my eager eyes, lay the snowy expanse of Alice's bosom, her breasts being visible nearly as far as their nipples.

'Oh! Oh!' she moaned in her distress, flushing painfully at this cruel exposure. But I was too excited to take any notice; my eyes were riveted on the lovely swell of her breasts, exhibiting the valley between the twin-globes, now heaving and fluttering under her agitated emotions. Unable to restrain myself, I threw my arms round Alice's waist, drew her closely to me, and pressed my lips on her palpitating flesh which I kissed furiously.

'Don't, Jack!' cried Alice as she tugged frantically at her fastenings in her wild endeavours to escape from my passionate lips, but instead of stopping me, my mouth wandered all over her heaving delicious breasts, punctuating its progress with hot kisses which seemed to drive her mad to such a pitch that I thought it best to desist.

'Oh, my God!' she moaned as I relaxed my clasp and leaned back in my chair to enjoy the sight of her shame and distress. There was not the least doubt that she felt most keenly my indecent assault, and so I determined to worry her with lascivious liberties a little longer.

When she had become calmer, I passed my arms around her waist and again began to play with her posteriors, then, stooping down I got my hands under her clothes and commenced to pull them up. Flushing violently, Alice shrieked to me to desist, but in vain! In a trice, I turned her petticoats up, held them thus with my left hand and with my right I proceeded to attack her bottom now protected only by her dainty thin drawers!

The sensation was delirious! My hand delightedly roved over the fat plump cheeks of her arse, stroking, caressing, and pinching them, revelling in the firmness and elasticity of her flesh under its thin covering, Alice all the time wriggling and squirming in horrible shame, imploring me almost incoherently to desist and finally getting so semi-hysterical, that I was compelled to suspend my exquisite game. So I dropped her skirts, to her relief, pushed my chair back and rose.

I had in the room a large plate glass mirror nearly eight feet high which reflected one at full length. While Alice was recovering from her last ordeal, I pushed this mirror close in front of her, placing it so that she could see herself in its centre. She started uneasily as she caught sight of herself, for I had left her bosom uncovered, and the reflection of herself in such shameful dishabille in conjunction with her large hat (which she still retained) seemed vividly to impress on her the horror of her position!

Having arranged the mirror to my satisfaction, I picked up the chair and placed it just behind Alice, sat down in it, and worked myself forward on it till Alice again stood between my legs, but this time with her back to me. The mirror faithfully reflected my movements, and her feminine intuition warned her that the front of her person was now about to become the object of my indecent assault.

But I did not give her time to think. Quickly I encircled her waist again with my arms, drew her to me till her bottom pressed against my chest, then, while my left arm held her firmly, my right hand began to wander over the junction of her stomach and legs, pressing inquisitively her groin and thighs, and intently watching her in the mirror.

Her colour rose, her breath came unevenly, she quivered and trembled, as she pressed her thighs closely together. She was horribly perturbed, but I do not think she anticipated what then happened.

Quietly dropping my hands, I slipped them under her

clothes, caught hold of her ankles, then proceeded to climb up her legs over her stockings.

'No! No! For God's sake, don't, Jack!' Alice yelled, now scarlet with shame and wild with alarm at this invasion of her most secret parts. Frantically she dragged at her fastenings, her hands clenched, her head thrown back, her eyes dilated with horror. Throwing the whole of her weight on her wrists, she strove to free her legs from my attacking hands by kicking out desperately, but to no avail. The sight in the mirror of her struggles only stimulated me into a refinement of cruelty, for with one hand I raised her clothes waist high, exposing her in her dainty drawers and black silk stockings, while with the other I vigorously attacked her thighs over her drawers, forcing a way between them and finally working up so close to her cunt that Alice practically collapsed in an agony of apprehension and would have fallen had it not been for the sustaining ropes which alone supported her, as she hung in a semi-hysterical faint.

Quickly rising and dropping her clothes, I placed an armchair behind her, and loosened the pulleys, till she rested comfortably in it, then left her to recover herself feeling pretty confident that she was now not far from surrendering herself to me, rather than continue a resistance which she could not but see was utterly useless. This was what I wanted to effect. I did not propose to let her off any single one of the indignities I had in store for her, but I wanted to make her suffering the more keen through the feeling that she was, to some extent, a consenting party to actions that inexpressibly shocked and revolted her. The first of these I intended to be the removal of her clothes, and, as soon as Alice became more mistress of herself, I set the pulleys working and soon had her standing erect with her arms stretched above her head.

She glanced fearfully at me as if trying to learn what was now going to happen to her. I deemed it as well to tell her, and to afford her an opportunity of yielding herself to me, if she should be willing to do so. I also wanted to save her clothes from being damaged, as she was really beautifully dressed, and I was not at all confident that I could get her garments off her without using scissors on some of them.

'I see you want to know what is going to happen to you, Alice,' I said. 'I'll tell you. You are to be stripped naked, utterly and absolutely naked; not a stitch of any sort is to be left on you!'

A flood of crimson swept over her face, invading both neck and bosom (which remained bare); her head fell forward as she moaned: 'No! No! Oh, Jack... Jack... how can you?' and she swayed uneasily on her feet.

'That is to be the next item in the programme, my dear!' I said, enjoying her distress. 'There is only one detail that remains to be settled first and that is, will you undress yourself quietly if I set you loose, or must I drag your clothes off you? I don't wish to influence your decision, and I know what queer ideals girls have about taking off their clothes in the presence of a man; I will leave the decision to you, only saying that I do not see what you have to gain by further resistance, and some of your garments may be ruined – which would be a pity. Now, which is it to be?'

She looked at me imploringly for a moment, trembling in every limb, then averting her eyes, but remaining silent, evidently torn by conflicting emotions.

'Come, Alice,' I said presently, 'I must have your decision or I shall proceed to take your clothes off you as best as I can.'

Alice was now in a terrible state of distress! Her eyes wandered all over the room without seeming to see anything, incoherent murmurs escaped from her lips, as if she was trying to speak but could not, her breath went and came, her bosom rose and fell agitatedly. She was endeavouring to form some decision evidently, but unable to do so.

I remained still for a brief space as if awaiting her answer; then, as she did not speak, I quietly went to a drawer, took out a pair of scissors and went back to her. At the sight of the scissors, she shivered, then with an effort, said, in a voice broken with emotion:

'Don't… undress me, Jack! If you must… have me, let it be as I am… I will… submit quietly… Oh, my God!!' she wailed.

'That won't do, dear,' I replied, not unkindly, but still firmly, 'you must be naked, Alice; now, will you or will you not undress yourself?'

Alice shuddered and cast another imploring glance at me, but seeing no answering gleam of pity in my eyes, but stern determination instead, she stammered out: 'Oh! Jack! I can't! Have some pity on me, Jack, and have me as I am! I promise I'll be quiet…'

I shook my head. I saw there was only one thing for me to do, namely, to undress her without any further delay, and I set to work to do so, Alice crying piteously: 'Don't, Jack; don't! Don't!'

I had left behind her the armchair in which I had allowed her to rest, and her blouse and bodice were still hanging open and thrown back on her shoulders. So I got on the chair and worked them along her arms and over her clenched hands onto the ropes; then gripping her wrists in turn one at a time, I released the noose, slipped the garments down and off it and refastened the noose. And as I had been quick to notice that Alice's chemise and vest had shoulder-strap fastenings and had merely to be unhooked, the anticipated difficulty of undressing her forcibly was now at an end! The rest of her garments would drop off her, as each became released, and therefore it was in my power to reduce her to absolute nudity! My heart thrilled with fierce exultation, and without further pause, I went on with the delicious work of undressing her.

Alice quickly divined her helplessness and in an agony of apprehension and shame cried to me for mercy! But I was deaf to her pitiful pleadings! I was wild to see her naked!

Quickly I unhooked her dress and petticoats and pulled them down to her feet thus exhibiting her in stays, drawers, and stockings, a bewitching sight! Her cheeks were suffused with shame-faced blushes, she huddled herself together as much as she could, seemingly supported entirely by her arms; her eyes were downcast and she seemed dazed both by the rapidity of my motions and their horrible success!

Alice now had on only a dainty Parisian corset which allowed the laces of her chemise to be visible, just hiding the nipples of her maiden breasts, and a pair of exquisitely provoking drawers, cut wide especially at her knees and trimmed with a sea of frilly lace, from below which emerged her shapely legs encased in black silk stockings and terminated in neat little shoes. She was the daintiest sight a man could well imagine, and, to me, the daintiness was enhanced by her shame-faced consciousness, for she could see herself reflected in the mirror in all her dreadful dishabille!

After a minute of gloating admiration, I proceeded to untie the tapes of her drawers so as to take them off her. At this she seemed to wake to the full sense of the humiliation in store for her; wild at the idea of being deprived of this most intimate of garments to a girl, she screamed in her distress, tugging frantically at her fastenings in her desperation! But the knot gave way, and her drawers, being now unsupported, slipped down to below her knees where they hung for a brief moment, maintained only by the despairing pressure of her legs against each other. A tug or two from me, and they lay in snowy loads round her ankles and rested on her shoes!

Oh, that I had the pen of a ready writer with which to describe Alice at this stage of the terrible ordeal of being forcibly undressed, her mental and physical anguish, her frantic cries and impassioned pleadings, her frenzied struggles, the agony in her face, as garment after garment was removed from her and she was being hurried nearer and nearer to the appalling goal of absolute nudity! The accidental but unavoidable contact of my hands with her person, as I undressed her, seemed to upset her so terribly that I wondered how she would endure my handling and playing with the most secret and sensitive parts of herself when she was naked! But acute as was her distress while being deprived of her upper garment, it was nothing to her shame and anguish when she felt her drawers forced down her legs and the last defence to her cunt thus removed. Straining wildly at the ropes with cheeks aflame, eyes dilated with terror, and convulsively heaving bosom, she uttered inarticulate cries, half-choked by her emotions and panting under her exertions.

I gloated over her sufferings and I would have liked to have watched them – but I was now mad with desire for her naked charms and also feared that a prolongation of her agony might result in a faint, when I would lose the anticipated pleasure of witnessing Alice's misery when her last garment was removed and she was forced to stand naked in front of me. So, unheeding her imploring cries, I undid her corset and took it off her, dragged off her shoes and stockings and with them her fallen drawers (during which process I intently watched her struggles in the hope of getting a glimpse of her Holy of Holies, but vainly), then slipped behind her; unbuttoning the shoulder-fastenings of her chemise and vest, I held these up for a moment, then watching Alice closely in the mirror, I let go! Down they slid with a rush, right to her feet! I saw Alice flash one rapid stolen half-reluctant glance at the mirror, as she felt the cold air on her now naked skin. I saw her reflection stark naked, a lovely gleaming pearly vision; then instinctively she squeezed her legs together, as closely as she could, huddled herself cowering as much as the ropes permitted – her head fell back in the first intensity of her shame, then fell forward suffused with blushes that extended right down to her breasts, her eyes closed as she moaned in heartbroken accents: 'Oh! Oh! Oh!' She was naked!!

Half delirious with excitement and the joy of conquest, I watched Alice's naked reflection in the mirror. Rapidly and tumultuously, my eager eyes roved over her shrinking trembling form, gleaming white, save for her blushing face and the dark triangular mossy-looking patch at the junction of her belly and thighs. But I felt that, in this moment of triumph, I was not sufficient master of myself to fully enjoy the spectacle of her naked maiden charms now so fully exposed; besides which, her chemise and vest still lay on her feet. So I knelt down behind these garments, noting, as I did so, the glorious curves of her bottom and hips. Throwing these garments onto the rest of her clothes, I pushed the armchair in front of her, and then settled myself down to a systematic and critical inspection of Alice's naked self!

As I did so, Alice coloured deeply over face and bosom and moved herself uneasily. The bitterness of death (so to speak) was past, her clothes had been forced off her and she was naked; but she was evidently conscious that much indignity and humiliation was yet in store for her, and she was horribly aware that my eyes were now taking in every detail of her naked self! Forced to stand erect by the tension of the ropes on her arms, she could do nothing to conceal any part of herself, and, in agony of shame, she endured the awful ordeal of having her naked person closely inspected and examined!

I had always greatly admired her trim little figure, and in the happy days before our rupture, I used to note with proud satisfaction how Alice held her own, whether at garden parties, at afternoon teas or in the theatre or ball room And after she had jilted me and I was sore in spirit, the sight of her invariably added fuel to the flames of my desire, and I often caught myself wondering how she looked in her bath! One evening, she wore at dinner a low-cut evening dress and she nearly upset my self-control by leaning forward over the card table by which I was standing, and unconsciously revealing to me the greater portion of her breasts! But my imagination never pictured anything as glorious as the reality now being so reluctantly exhibited to me!

Alice was simply a beautiful girl and her lines deliciously voluptuous. No statue, no model, but glorious flesh and blood allied to superb femininity! Her well-shaped head was set on a beautifully modelled neck and bosom from which sprang a pair of exquisitely lovely breasts (if anything too full), firm, upstanding, saucy and inviting. She had fine rounded arms with small well-shaped hands, a dainty but not too small waist, swelling grandly downwards and outwards and melting into magnificent curves over her hips and haunches. Her thighs were plump and round, and tapered to the neatest of calves and ankles and tiny feet, her legs being the least trifle too short for her, but adding by this very defect to the indescribable fascination of her figure. She had a graciously swelling belly with a deep navel, and, framed by the lines of her groin, was her Mount Venus – full, fat, fleshy, prominent – covered by a wealth of fine silky dark curly hairs through which I could just make out the lips of her cunt. Such was Alice as she stood naked before me, horribly conscious of my devouring eyes, quivering and trembling with suppressed emotion, tingling with shame, flushing red and white, knowing full well her own loveliness and what its effect on me must be; and in dumb silence I gazed and gazed again at her glorious naked self till my lust began to run riot and insist on the gratification of senses other than that of sight!

I did not, however, consider that Alice was ready to properly appreciate the mortification of being felt. She seemed to be still absorbed in the horrible consciousness of one all-pervading fact, viz., that she was utterly naked, that her chaste body was the prey of my lascivious eyes, that she could do nothing to hide or even screen any part of herself, even her cunt, from me! Every now and then, her downcast eyes would glance at the reflection of herself in the faithful mirror only to be hastily withdrawn with an excess of colour to her already shame-suffused cheeks at these fresh reminders of the spectacle she was offering to me!

Therefore with a strong effort, I succeeded in overcoming the temptation to feel and handle Alice's luscious body there and then, and being desirous of first studying her naked self from all points of view, I rose and took her in strict profile, noting with delight the arch of her bosom, the proudly projecting breasts, the glorious curve of her belly, the conspicuous way in which the hairs on the Mount of Venus stood out, indicating that her cunt would be found both fat and fleshy, the magnificent swell of her bottom! Then I went behind her, and for a minute or two, revelled in silent admiration of the swelling lines of her hips and haunches, her quivering buttocks, her well-shaped legs!

Without moving, I could command the most perfect exhibition of her naked loveliness, for I had her back view in full sight while her front was reflected in the mirror!

Presently, I completed my circuit, then standing close to her, I had a good look at her palpitating breasts, noting their delicious fullness and ripeness, their ivory skin, and the tiny virgin nipples pointing outward so prettily, Alice colouring and flushing and swaying herself uneasily under my close inspection. Then I peered into the round cleft of her navel while she became more uneasy than ever, seeing the downward trend of my inspection. Then I dropped on my knees in front of her and from this vantage point I commenced to investigate with eager eyes the mysterious region of her cunt so deliciously covered with a wealth of close curling hairs, clustering so thickly round and over the coral lips as almost to render them invisible! As I did so, Alice desperately squeezed her thighs together as closely as she could, at the same time drawing in her stomach in the vain hope of defeating my purpose and of preventing me from inspecting the citadel wherein reposed her virginity!

As a matter of fact, she did to a certain extent thwart me, but as I intended before long to put her on her back and tie her down so, with her legs wide apart, I did not grudge her partial success, but brought my face close to her belly. 'Don't! Oh, don't!' she cried, as if she could feel my eyes as they searched this most secret part of herself; but disregarding her pleadings I closely scanned the seat of my approaching pleasure, noting delightedly that her Mount Venus was exquisitely plump and fleshy and would afford my itching fingers the most delicious pleasure when I allowed them to wander over its delicate contours and hide themselves in the forest of hairs that so sweetly covered it!

At last I rose. Without a word, I slipped behind the mirror and quickly divested myself of my clothes, retaining only my shoes and socks. Then, suddenly, I emerged and stood right in front of Alice. 'Oh!' she exclaimed, horribly shocked by the unexpected apparition of my naked self, turning rosy red and hastily averting her eyes – but not before they had caught sight of my prick in glorious erection! I watched her closely. The sight seemed to fascinate her in spite of her alarmed modesty, she flashed rapid glances at me through half-closed eyes, her colour coming and going. She seemed forced, in spite of herself, to regard the instrument of her approaching violation as if to assess its size and her capacity!

'Won't you have a good look at me, Alice?' I presently remarked maliciously. 'I believe I can claim to possess a good specimen of what is so dear to the heart of a girl!' (She quivered painfully.) After a moment, I continued, 'Must I then assume by your apparent indifference that you have in your time seen so many naked men that the sight no longer appeals to you?' She coloured deeply, but kept her eyes averted. 'Are you not even curious to estimate whether my prick will fit in your cunt?' I added, determined, if I possibly could, to break down the barrier of silence she was endeavouring to protect herself with.

I succeeded! Alice tugged frantically at the ropes which kept her upright, then broke into a piteous cry: 'No, no... my God, no!' she supplicated, throwing her head back but still keeping her eyes shut as if to exclude the sight she dreaded. 'Oh! You don't really mean to... to...' She broke down, utterly unable to clothe in words the overwhelming fear that she was now to be violated!

I stepped up to her, passed my left arm round her waist and drew her trembling figure to me, thrilling at the exquisite sensation caused by the touch of our naked bodies against each other. We were now both facing the mirror, both reflected in it.

'Don't! Oh, don't touch me!' she shrieked as she felt my arm encircle her, but holding her closely against me with my left arm, I gently placed my right forefinger on her navel, to force her to open her eyes and watch my movements in the mirror, which meant that she would also have to look at my naked self, and gently I tickled her. She screamed in terror, opening her eyes, squirming deliciously: 'Don't! Oh, don't!' she cried agitatedly.

'Then use your chaste eyes properly and have a good look at the reflection of the pair of us in the mirror,' I said somewhat sternly. 'Look me over slowly and thoroughly from head to foot, then answer the questions I shall presently put to you. May I call your attention to that whip hanging on that wall and to the inviting defencelessness of your bottom? Understand that I shall not hesitate to apply one to the other if you don't do as you are told! Now have a good look at me!'

Alice shuddered, then reluctantly raised her eyes and shamefacedly regarded my reflection in the mirror, her colour coming and going. I watched her intently (she being also reflected, my arm was still round her waist holding her against me) and I noted with cruel satisfaction how she trembled with shame and fright when her eyes dwelt on my prick, now stiff and erect!

'We make a fine pair, Alice, eh?' I whispered maliciously. She coloured furiously, but remained silent. 'Now answer my questions: I want to know something about you before going further. How old are you?'

'Twenty-five,' she whispered.

'In your prime, then. Good. Now, are you a virgin?'

Alice flushed hotly and painfully, then whispered again, 'Yes!'

Oh, my exultation! I was not too late! The prize of her maid-enhead was to be mine! My prick showed my joy! I continued my catechism. 'Absolutely virgin?' I asked. 'A pure virgin? Has no hand wandered over those lovely charms, has no eye but mine seen them?'

Alice shook her head, blushing rosy red at the idea suggested by my words.

I looked rather doubtingly at her. 'I include female eyes and hands as well as male in my query, Alice,' I continued. 'You know that you have a most attractive lot of girl and woman friends and that you are constantly with them. Am I to under-stand that you and they have never compared your charms, have never, when occupying the same bed...'

She broke in with a cry of distress, 'No, no! Not I! Not I! Oh, how can you talk to me like this, Jack?'

'My dear, I only wanted to find out how much you already knew so that I might know what to teach you now! Well, shall we begin your lessons?' And I drew her against me, more close-ly than ever, and again began to tickle her navel.

'Jack, don't!' she screamed. 'Oh, don't touch me! I can't stand it! Really, I can't!'

'Let me see if that is really so,' I replied as I removed my arm from her waist and slipped behind her, taking up a position from which I could command the reflection of our naked figures in the mirror, and thus watch her carefully and note the effect on her of my tender mercy.

I commenced to feel Alice by placing my hands one on each side of her waist, noting with cruel satisfaction the shiver that ran through her at their contact with her naked skin. After a few caresses, I passed them gently but inquisitively over her full hips which I stroked, pressed, and patted lovingly, then bringing my hands downward behind her, I roved over her plump bottom, the fleshy cheeks of which I gripped and squeezed to my heart's content. Alice the while arching herself outwards in a vain attempt to escape my hands. Then I descended to the underneath portion of her soft round thighs and finally worked my way back to her waist running my hands up and down over loins and finally arriving at her armpits.

Here I paused, and to try the effect on Alice, I gently tickled these sensitive spots of herself. 'Don't!' she exclaimed, wriggling and twisting herself uneasily. 'Don't, I am dreadfully ticklish, I can't stand it at all!' At once I ceased but my blood went on fire, as through my brain flashed the idea of the licentiously lovely spectacle Alice would afford if she was tied down with her legs fastened widely apart, and a pointed feather-tip cleverly applied to the most sensitive part of her – her cunt – sufficient slack being allowed in her fastenings to permit her to wriggle and writhe freely while being thus tickled, and I promised to give myself presently this treat together with the pleasure of trying on her this interesting experiment!

After a short pause, I again placed my hands on her waist played for a moment over her swelling hips, then slipped onto her stomach, my right hand taking the region below her waist while my left devoted itself to her bosom, but carefully avoiding, for the moment, her breasts.

Oh, what pleasure I tasted in thus touching her pure sweet flesh, so smooth, so warm, so essentially female! My delighted hands wandered all over her body, while the poor girl stood quivering and trembling, unable to guess whether her breast or cunt was next to be attacked.

I did not keep her long in suspense. After circling a few times over her rounded belly, my right hand paused on her navel again, and while my forefinger gently tickled her, my left hand slid quietly onto her right breast which it then gently seized.

She gave a great cry of dismay and meanwhile my right hand had in turn slipped up to her left breast, and another involuntary shriek from Alice announced that both of her virgin bubbies had become the prey of my cruel hands! Oh, how she begged me to release them, the while tossing herself from side to side in almost uncontrollable agitation as my fingers played with her delicious breasts, now squeezing, now stroking, now pressing them against each other, now rolling them upwards and downwards, now gently irritating and exciting their tiny nipples! Such delicious morsels of flesh I had never handled – so firm and yet so springing, so ripe and yet so maidenly, palpitating under the hitherto unknown sensations communicated by the touch of masculine hands on their virgin surfaces. Meanwhile Alice's tell-tale face, reflected in the mirror, clearly indicated to me the mental shame and anguish she was feeling at this terrible outrage; her flushed cheeks, dilated nostrils, half-closed eyes, her panting, heaving bosom all revealing her agony under this desecration of her maiden self. In rapture, I continued toying with her virgin globes, all the while gloating on Alice's image in the mirror, twisting and contorting herself in the most lasciviously ravishing way under her varying emotions!

At last I tore my hands away from Alice's breasts. I slipped my left arm round her waist, drew her tightly against me, then while I held her stomach and slowly approached her cunt, Alice instantly guessed my intention! She threw her weight on one leg, then quickly placed the other across her groin to foil my attack, crying: 'No, no, Jack! Not there! Not there!' At the same time endeavouring frantically to turn herself away from my hand. But the close grip of my left arm defeated her, and disregarding her cries, my hand crept on and on till it reached her hairs! These I gently pulled, twining them round my fingers as I revelled in their curling silkiness. Then amorously, I began to feel and press her gloriously swelling Mount Venus, a finger on each side of its slit! Alice now simply shrieked in her shame and distress, jerking herself convulsively backwards and twisting herself frenziedly! As she was forced to stand on both legs in order to maintain her balance, her cunt was absolutely defence-less, and my eager fingers roved all over it, touching, pressing, tickling, pulling her hairs at their sweet will. Then I began to attack her virgin orifice and tickle her slit, passing my forefinger lightly up and down it, all the time watching her intently in the mirror! Alice quivered violently, her head fell backwards in her agony as she shrieked: 'Jack don't! For God's sake, don't! Stop! Stop!' But I could feel her cunt opening under my lascivious tit-illation and so could she! Her distress became almost uncon-trollable. 'Oh, my God!' she screamed in her desperation, and as my finger found its way to her clitoris and lovingly titillated it, she spasmodically squeezed her thighs together in her vain attempts to defend herself. Unheeding of her agonized plead-ing, I continued to tickle her clitoris for a few delicious moments, then I gently passed my finger along her cunt and between its now half-opened lips till I arrived at her maiden ori-fice up which it tenderly forced its way, burying itself in Alice's cunt till it could penetrate no further into her! Alice's agitation now became uncontrollable; she struggled so violently that I could hardly hold her still, especially when she felt the interior of her cunt invaded and my finger investigate the mysteries of its virgin recesses!

Oh, my voluptuous sensations at that moment! Alice's naked quivering body clutched tightly against mine! My finger, half-buried in her maiden cunt, enveloped in her soft warm throbbing flesh and gently exploring its luscious interior!! In my excitement I must have pushed my inquisitiveness too far, for Alice suddenly screamed: 'Oh… Oh! You're hurting me! Stop! Stop!' her head falling forward on her bosom as she did so. Delighted at this unexpected proof of her virginity and fearful of exciting her sexual passions beyond her powers of control, I gently withdrew my finger and soothed her by passing it lovingly and caressingly over her cunt; then releasing her from my encircling arm, I left her to recover herself. But, though visibly relieved at being at last left alone, Alice trembled so violently that I hastily pushed her favourite armchair (the treacherous one) behind her, hastily released the pulley-ropes and let her drop into the chair to rest and recover herself, for I knew that her distress was only temporary and would soon pass away and leave her in a fit condition to be again fastened and subjected to some other torture, for so it undoubtedly was to her.

I produced a large bottle of champagne, and pretending that the opener was in my alcove I went there – but my real object was to satisfy in Fanny the raging concupiscence which my torturing of Alice and then Connie had so fiercely aroused in me.

I found her shivering with unsatisfied hot lust. I threw myself into a chair, placed my bottom on the edge and pointed to my prick in glorious erection. Instantly she straddled across me, brought her excited cunt to bear on my tool and impaled herself on it with deliciously voluptuous movements, sinking down on it till she rested on my thighs, her arms 'round my neck, mine 'round her warm body, our lips against each others. Then, working herself divinely up and down on my prick, she soon brought on the blessed relief we both were both thirsting for –

and in exquisite rapture we spent madly.

'Oh, sir, wasn't it lovely?' she whispered as soon as she could speak.

'Which, Fanny?' I asked mischievously. 'This or that!' pointing to the room.

She blushed prettily, then whispered saucily: 'Both, sir!' as she passionately kissed me.

I begged her to sponge me while I opened the champagne, which she did sweetly, kissing my flaccid prick lovingly, as soon as she had removed all traces of our bout of fucking from it. I poured out four large glasses, made her drink one (which she did with great enjoyment) then took the other three out with me to the girls.

I found them still in each others arms and coiled together in the large armchair, Alice half sitting on Connie's thighs and half resting on Connie's breasts, a lovely sight. I touched her and she started up, while Connie slowly opened her eyes.

'Drink, it will pull you together!' I said, handing each a tumbler. They did so, and the generous wine seemed to have an immediate good effect and to put new life into them. I eyed them with satisfaction, then raising my glass said, 'To your go health, dears, and a delicious consummation of Connie's charming and most sporting suggestion!' Then I gravely emptied my tumbler. Both girls turned scarlet, Connie almost angrily. They glanced tentatively at each other but neither spoke.

To terminate their embarrassment, I pointed to a settee close by, and soon we arranged ourselves on it, I in the centre, Alice on my right and Connie on my left, their heads resting on my shoulders, their faces turned towards each other and within easy kissing distance my arms clasping them to me, my hands being just able to command the outer breast of each! Both girls seemed ill at ease; I think Connie was really so, as she was evidently dreading having to be fucked by me, but with Alice it was only pretence.

'A penny for your thoughts, dear,' I said to her, curious to know what she would say.

'I was thinking how lovely Connie is when naked,' she murmured softly, blushing prettily. I felt a quiver run through Connie.

'Before today, how much of each other have you seen?' I asked interestedly.

Silently both girls pointed to just above their breasts.

'Then stand up, Connie dear, and let us have a good look at you,' I said, 'and Alice shall afterwards return the compliment by showing you herself. Stand naturally, with your hands behind you.'

With evident unwillingness she complied, and with pretty bashfulness she faced us, a naked blue-eyed daughter of the gods, tall, slender, golden-haired, exquisite, blushing as she noted in our eyes the pleasure, the contemplation of her naked charms was giving us.

'Now in profile, dear.'

Obediently, she turned. We delightedly noted her exquisite outline from chin to thigh, her proud little breasts, her gently curving belly, its wealth of golden-brown hair, standing out like a bush at its junction with her thigh – the sweep of her haunches and bottom, and her shapely legs!

'Thanks, darling,' I said appreciatively. 'Now, Alice!' And drawing Connie on to my knees, I kissed her lovingly.

Blushingly, Alice complied, and with hands clasped behind her back she faced us, a piquant, provoking, demure, brown-eyed, dark-haired little English lassie, plump, juicy, appetizing.

She smiled mischievously at me as she watched Connie's eyes wander approvingly over her delicious little figure!

'Now in profile, please.'

She turned half around, and now we realized the subtle voluptuousness of Alice's naked figure, how her exquisitely full and luscious breasts were matched by her somewhat prominent round belly, both in turn being balanced by her glorious fleshy bottom and her fat thighs. The comparative shortness of her legs only added piquancy to the whole, while her unusually conspicuous Mount Venus, with its tousle of dark clustering silky hairs, proudly proclaimed itself as the delightful centre of her attractions.

'Thanks, darling!' we both exclaimed admiringly as we drew her to us and lovingly kissed her, to her evident delight and gratification.

'Now, Connie darling,' I said, 'I want you to lie down on that couch!' I removed my arm from her waist to allow her to rise.

'No, Jack!' she begged piteously and imploringly, her lovely eyes not far from tears, 'please, Jack, don't insist!'

'You must do it, darling,' I said kindly but firmly as I raised her to her feet and led her to the couch and made her lie down. 'I must put the straps on you, Connie dear,' I said, 'not that I doubt your promise, but because I am sure you won't be able to lie still. Don't be frightened, dear!' I added as I saw a look of terror come over her face. 'You are not going to be tortured or tickled or hurt, but will be treated most sweetly.'

Reluctantly, Connie yielded.

Quickly, Alice attached the straps to her wrists, while I secured the other pair to her ankles; we set the machinery to work and soon she was lying flat on her back, her hands and feet secured to the four corners – the dark brown upholstery throwing into high relief her lovely figure and dazzling fair hair and skin! I then blindfolded her very carefully in such a way that she could not get rid of the bandage by rubbing her head against the couch. Now that Connie was at our mercy, I signalled to Fanny, who gleefully rushed to us noiselessly and hugged her mistress with silent delight.

'Now, Alice dear,' I said, 'make love to Connie!'

'Oh!' cried Connie in shocked surprise, blushing so hotly that even her bosom was suffused with colour. But Alice was already on her knees by Connie's side and was passionately kissing her protesting mouth in the exuberance of her delight at the arrival at last of the much desired opportunity to satisfy on Connie's lovely person, cunt against cunt, her lascivious desires and concupiscence.

I slipped into a chair and took Fanny on my knees, and in sweet companionship, we settled ourselves down comfortably to watch Alice make love to Connie. My left arm was around Fanny's waist, the hand toying with the breasts, which it could just command, while my right hand played lovingly with her cunt.

After Alice had relieved her excited feelings by showering kisses on Connie's lips with whispered fond endearments, she raised her head and contemplated, with an expression of intense delight, the naked figure of her friend, which I had placed at her disposal! Then she proceeded to pass her hands lightly over Connie's flesh. Substituting the feminine pronoun for the masculine one he uses, Shakespeare sings: To win her heart she touched her here and there, Touches so soft that conquer chastity.

This is what Alice was doing. With lightly poised hands, she touched Connie on the most susceptible parts of herself – her armpits, navel, belly, and especially the soft tender insides of her thighs – evidently reserving for special attention her breasts and cunt. Soon the effect on Connie became apparent – her bosom began to palpitate in sweet agitation, while significant tremors ran through her limbs. 'Is it so nice then, darling?' cooed Alice, her eyes dancing with delight as she watched the effect on her operations on Connie's now quivering person. Then she rested her lips on Connie's and gently took hold of her breasts.

'Oh, Alice!' cried Connie, but Alice closed her lips with her own, half-choking her friend with her passionate kisses. Then raising her head again, she eagerly and delightedly inspected the delicious morsels of Connie's flesh that were imprisoned in her hands. 'Oh you darlings!' she exclaimed as she squeezed them, 'you sweet things!' as she kissed them rapturously. 'Oh, what dear little nipples!' she cried, taking them in turn into her mouth, her hands all the while squeezing and caressing Connie's lovely breasts till she faintly murmured, 'Oh stop, darling!'

'My love, was I hurting you, darling?' cried Alice with gleaming eyes, as with a smile full of mischief towards us she reluctantly released Connie's breasts. For a moment she hesitated as if uncertain what next to do – then her eyes rested on Connie's cunt, so sweetly defenceless, and then an idea seemed to seize her. With a look of delicious anticipation, she slipped her left arm under Connie's shoulders so as to embrace her, placed her lips on Connie's mouth, extended her right arm, and without giving Connie the least hint as to her intentions, she placed her hand on Connie's cunt, her slender forefinger resting on the orifice itself!

'Oh, Alice!' cried Connie, taken completely by surprise and wriggling voluptuously.

'Oh, Connie!' rapturously murmured Alice, between the hot

kisses she was now raining on Connie's mouth, her forefinger beginning to agitate itself inquisitively but lovingly.

'Oh, darling, your cunny is sweet!' she murmured as her hand wandered all over Connie's private parts, now stroking and pressing her delicate Mount of Venus, now twisting and pulling her hairs, now gently compressing the soft springy flesh between her thumb and forefinger, now passing along the delicate shell-pink lips, and finally gently inserting her finger between them and into the pouting orifice!. 'I must... I must look at it!' Quickly she withdrew her arm from under Connie's shoulders, gave her a long clinging kiss, and then shifted her position by Connie's side, till her head commanded Connie's private parts. Then she squared her arms, rested herself on Connie's belly, and with both hands proceeded to examine and study Connie's cunt, her eyes sparkling with delight.

Again she submitted Connie's delicious organ of sex to a most searching and merciless examination, one hand on each side of the now slightly gaping slit, stroking, squeezing, pressing, touching! Then with fingers poised gently but firmly on each side of the slit, Alice gently drew the lips apart and peered curiously into the shell-pink cavity of Connie's cunt. After a prolonged inspection, she shifted her finger rather higher, again parted the lips and with rapt attention she gazed at Connie's clitoris which was now beginning to show signs of sexual excitement, Connie all this time quivering and wriggling under the touches of Alice's fingers.

Her curiosity apparently satisfied for a time, Alice raised her head and looked strangely and interrogatively at me. Comprehending her mute enquiry, I smiled and nodded. She smiled back, then dropping her head she looked intently at Connie's cunt, and imprinted a long clinging kiss in its very centre.

Connie squirmed violently. 'Oh!' she moaned in a half-strangled voice.

With a smile of intense delight, Alice repeated her kiss, then again and again, Connie at each repetition squirming and wriggling in the most delicious way, her vehement plunging telling Alice what flames her hot kisses had aroused in Connie. Again she opened Connie's cunt, and keeping its tender lips wide apart she deposited between them and right inside the orifice itself a long lingering kiss which seemed to set Connie's blood on fire, for she began to plunge wildly with furious upward jerks and jogs of her hips and bottom nearly dislodging Alice. She glanced merrily at us, her eyes brimming with mischief and delight. Then she straddled across Connie and arranged herself on her, so that her mouth commanded Connie's cunt, while her stomach rested on Connie's breasts and her cunt lay poised over Connie's mouth, but not touching it. Her legs now lay parallel to Connie's arms and outside them.

Utterly taken aback by Alice's tactics, and in her innocence, not recognizing the significance of the position Alice had assumed on her, she cried, 'Oh, Alice, what are you doing?'

Alice grinned delightedly at us, then lowered her head and ran her tongue lightly half a dozen times along the lips of Connie's cunt and then set to work to gama-huche her!

'Oh! Oh!' shrieked Connie, her voice almost strangled by the violence of the wave of lust that swept over her at the first touch of Alice's tongue. 'Oh! Oh! Oh!' she moaned in utter bewilderment and confusion, as she abandoned herself to strangely intoxicating and thrilling sensations hitherto unknown to her, jerking herself madly upwards as it to meet Alice's tongue, her face in her frenzied movements coming against Alice's cunt, before it dawned on her confused senses what the warm moist quivering hairy object could be! In wild excitement, Alice thoroughly searched Connie's cunt with her active tongue, darting it deeply in, playing delicately on the quivering lips, sucking and tickling her clitoris and sending Connie into such a state of lust that I thought it wise to intervene.

'Stop dear!' I called out to Alice, who at once desisted, looking interrogatively at me. 'You're trying her too much! Get off her now, dear, and let her recover herself a little or you'll finish her, which we don't want yet.'

Quickly comprehending the danger, Alice rolled off Connie, turned around, contemplated for a moment Connie's naked wriggling figure, then got on to her again, only this time lips to lips, bubbies to bubbies, and cunt against cunt. She clasped Connie closely to her as she arranged herself, murmuring passionately: 'Oh Connie, at last, at last!' Then she commenced to rub her cunt sweetly on Connie's.

'Oh, Alice!' breathed Connie rapturously as she responded to Alice's efforts by heaving and jogging herself upwards. 'Oh, darling!' she panted brokenly, evidently feeling her ecstasy approaching by the voluptuous wriggles and agitated movements, as Alice now was rubbing herself vigorously against her cunt with riotous down-strokes of her luscious bottom. Quicker and quicker, faster and faster, wilder and wilder became the movements of both girls, Connie now plunging madly upwards, while Alice rammed herself down on her with fiercer and fiercer thrusts of her raging hips and buttocks, till the delicious crisis arrived! 'Connie! Connie!' gasped Alice, as the indescribable spasm of spending thrilled voluptuously through her. 'Ah... ah... ah!' shrieked Connie rapturously, as she spent madly in exquisite convulsions! Connie was dead to everything but the delirious rapture that was thrilling through her as she lay tightly clasped in Alice's clinging arms!

The sight was too much for Fannie! With the most intense interest, she had watched the whole of this exciting scene, parting her legs the better to accommodate my hand, which now was actually grasping her cunt, my forefinger buried in her up to the knuckle, while my thumb rested on her clitoris, and she had already spent once deliciously. But the spectacle of the lascivious transports of her mistress on Connie set her blood on fire again. She recollected her similar experience in Alice's arms, the sensation that Alice's cunt communicated to hers, the delirious ecstasy of her discharge, and as the two girls neared their bliss, she began to agitate herself voluptuously on my knees, on my now active finger, keeping pace with them, till with an inarticulate murmur of, 'Oh… oh, sir!' she inundated my hand with her love-juice, spending simultaneously with her mistress and her mistress' friend.

As soon as she emerged from her ecstatic trance, I whispered to her inaudibly, 'Bring the sponge and towel, dear.'

Noiselessly she darted off, sponged herself, then returned with a bowl of water, a sponge and a towel just as Alice slowly raised herself off Connie, with eyes still humid with lust and her cunt bedewed with love-juice. I took her fondly in my arms and kissed her tenderly, while Fanny quickly removed all traces of her discharge from her hairs, then proceeded to pay the same delicate attention to Connie, whose cunt she now touched for the first time.

A Weekend Visit

The day passed uneventfully, and at half-past ten we all met in Helen's room, three ladies in visible but suppressed excitement. 'We won't waste time,' I said briskly, 'so everyone naked please!' and in a trice I again had the pleasure of viewing their charms. Then I produced the wristlets and straps, the sight of which produced much laughter. Under my direction, Helen and Alice quickly fastened them on Maud's wrists and ankles.

I made her lie face-upwards on her mother's bed, and secured her wrists to the opposite bedposts by the straps. Then, to her surprise and consternation, and to Alice's undisguised delight, I directed Helen and Alice to pull Maud's legs widely apart and strap her ankles to the corner posts, so she lay spread-eagled, exposing all her charms to us and rendering her utterly unable to prevent us from doing what we wished to her! In silence we gloated over the provocative spectacle. Turning to Helen and Alice, I said, 'My dears, Maud is at your absolute disposal for fifteen minutes after which I shall want her for myself! Now, go ahead!'

With a cry of joy, Alice threw herself on Maud's prostrate and helpless self and excitedly showered kisses on her lips and cheeks and eyes. Then turning herself slightly, she seized Maud's breasts.

After kissing the pretty coral nipples, she took them between her lips and sucked each in turn, all the while squeezing and handling the breast – Maud lying helpless in shamefaced confusion. The colour on her cheeks came and went, and a nervous smile passed over her face when her eyes met ours.

I glanced at her mother, Helen. Helen's eyes, glittering with a peculiar light, were riveted on her daughter's naked body. As I stealthily watched her I noticed that she was shivering! It certainly was not from cold, and recollecting how she was fascinated and excited on the first evening when her daughter stood before her naked for the first time and how she from that moment seemed never tired of looking at Maud's naked beauties, I guessed that unknown to herself a lusting desire after her daughter had sprung up in her.

Seeing that Alice and Maud were absorbed with each other, Alice in the hitherto untasted pleasure of playing with another girl's naked body, Maud with the also hitherto untasted sensations of having her most private parts invaded and handled by feminine fingers, I drew Helen out of earshot and whispered to her, 'You look as if you want to have Maud, eh dear?' She coloured vividly and nodded vehemently with a conscious smile, too embarrassed to speak. 'Why don't you then?' I continued. Helen stared at me in surprise. 'Get on Maud, grip her tightly, and rub your cunt against hers sweetly.'

'Oh, Jack, really?' Helen stammered in growing excitement, her bosom heaving with her agitation.

I nodded with a reassuring smile, adding, 'Try it, dear! Lots of women solace themselves in this way when they cannot get what they really want!' She looked incredulously at me. I smiled encouragingly; then her eyes wandered to Maud, who was lying motionless save for an occasional quiver. Alice had deserted her sweet breasts and was now busily engaged with her cunt, which she was kissing and stroking and examining, the procedure evidently giving Maud the most exquisite pleasure judging from her half-closed eyes and her beatific expression – a most voluptuous sight, which apparently swept away Helen's hesitation.

She turned to me and murmured almost inaudibly, 'I long to do it, Jack, but she wouldn't like it!'

I took her trembling hands that betrayed her lust, and whispered coaxingly, 'Maud has got to put up with anything that any of us wishes to do to her during her twenty-minute turn, dear. When she guesses what you contemplate, she probably will protest, but as soon as she feels your cunt on hers she will love you more than ever! Try her, dear!'

Helen hesitated, looked hungrily and longingly at Maud and then at me, then back at Maud. At that juncture Alice exclaimed, 'I'm only keeping on till you come, Auntie!'

Helen shivered again, her eyes now glittering wildly with lust and desire, then with an effort she muttered huskily, 'Jack! I must… I must have her!' and moved toward the bed.

'Come along, Auntie! I've got Maud nicely excited, and you can now finish her off in any way you like!' exclaimed Alice merrily. After imprinting a farewell kiss on Maud's cunt, she rose as if to make way for Helen, while Maud languidly opened her eyes and dreamily smiled a welcome to her Mother. But when she saw Helen scramble onto the bed and place herself between her widely parted legs in an attitude that could only indicate one intention and noted the lust that was glittering in Helen's eyes, she became alarmed, and cried, 'No, no, Mother, no, no!' as she desperately tried to break loose.

Alice flushed as red as a peony, her colour surging right down to her own breasts as she intently watched Helen with eyes widely open in startled surprise. Helen paused a moment, as if gloating over the naked beauties of her daughter, then she let herself down gently on Maud who again cried, 'No, no, mother, no!' as she felt her mother's arms close firmly round her. Helen arranged herself on Maud – first breast against breast, then cunt on cunt. Then having her daughter at her mercy, she began to move herself on her lasciviously, as if she was lying impaled on a man!

Hardly had she commenced to agitate herself on Maud than the latter exclaimed in an indescribable tone of astonished delight, 'Oh!…oh!…oh!…Mummy…dar…ling!' which sent Alice's blushes surging again all over her bosom as she glanced shamefacedly at me. I crossed over to her and slipped my arms round her, noting as she nestled against me how she was quivering with erotic excitement!

Helen had evidently set her daughter's lust on fire, for Maud now was wildly agitating and tossing herself about beneath her mother and heaving herself furiously up as if to press her cunt more closely against her mother's as she passionately kissed Helen.

Suddenly she wriggled violently, then spent in delicious thrills and quiverings. Alice's gentle but subtle toying had so inflamed her that little was needed to finish her! Recognizing what had happened, Helen suspended her movements and rested lovingly on Maud. She set to work to kiss her ardently, evidently enjoying the thrills and spasms that convulsed her daughter as she spent.

Soon Maud began to respond to her mother's provocations and agitated herself under Helen in the most abandoned and lascivious way, which set Helen off in a fresh frenzy of uncontrollable lust. With wildly heaving buttocks and tempestuous wriggling of her hips and bottom, Helen pressed her cunt more closely than ever against her daughter's, rubbing her clitoris against Maud's till Maud again spent rapturously.

Suddenly, Helen's body stiffened and grew rigid. An indescribable convulsion swept violently through her, and with incoherent ejaculations and gasps she spent madly on Maud's cunt, then collapsed and lay inert on her daughter, motionless save for the voluptuous thrills that quivered through her with each spasm of spending!

And so Mother and daughter lay in a delirium of ecstasy, their cunts pressed against each other, utterly absorbed in the sensations of the moment and the divine pleasure that for the first time in their lives they had mutually given to each other!

In delighted silence, Alice and I watched this voluptuous episode, and when the delirious climax had passed she turned to me and huskily whispered 'Jack! oh Jack!' and looked pleadingly into my eyes. I saw what she wanted. I drew her closer against me and slipped my hand down to her throbbing and excited cunt. She was so madly worked up that it only required one or two quick but gentle movements of my finger to make her spend ecstatically.

Her thrills of rapture as she stood upright supported by me nearly set me off! With a strong effort I controlled myself, for in a minute or two I had to fuck Maud. So I bade Alice away to freshen herself, and to bring the feathers with her when she returned. Being curious to see how Helen and Maud would regard each other when they came to themselves, now that their fit of lust had been satiated, I watched them closely.

Very soon, with a long drawn breath of intense satisfaction Maud dreamily opened her eyes. She seemed hardly conscious, but when she found herself unable to move hand or foot and recognised that her Mother was lying on her, the happenings of the evening instantly flashed through her brain and sent the hot colour surging over her cheeks and bosom at the consciousness that she had just been ravished by her Mother. When her eyes caught mine, she coloured more furiously than ever, but smiled gratefully as I noiselessly clapped my hands together with a congratulatory smile.

Then she turned her face towards her mother and a look of intense love came over her as she regarded her still-unconscious

Mother. She brought her lips to bear on Helen's cheek and kissed her lovingly, whispering, 'Mummy! Mummy! Mummy, darling!'

Then, with a deep sigh, Helen came to herself. She quickly realized her position and flushed scarlet as she half-timidly sought Maud's still humid eyes. When she read in them her daughter's happy satisfaction, she kissed Maud passionately and murmured in evident relief 'Oh, my darling, I couldn't help it, you looked so sweet, and you were so luscious!' After another long clinging kiss she slipped off Maud.

Alice had just rejoined me, and, as Helen rose to her feet, our eyes inquisitively sought her cunt and that of Maud. They were a curious sight; both mother and daughter must have spent profusely as their hair was sticky and plastered down by their joint spending. Noticing the direction of our looks Helen glanced at Maud's cunt and then at her own, and, horrified at what she saw, she exclaimed in charming confusion, 'Oh Alice, do see to Maud!' and rushed off to her bathroom followed by our hearty laughter. Maud merrily joined in with pretty blushes when told the cause.

Helen soon returned and joined me. 'Well?' I asked mischievously. She blushed and replied softly, 'Jack, it was just lovely, just wonderful! I couldn't have believed it! Maud was simply luscious!' I laughed. 'Make Alice do me presently, Jack! I'd love to feel her on me!'

I nodded laughingly, then glancing at the clock I exclaimed, 'Only seven minutes more for Maud! She must now be really tortured for four minutes, and then she is to be brutally outraged in your presence! Now set to work and give her a severe tickling!' and I handed a feather to each.

'No, no, Jack!' cried Maud, flushing painfully and tugging at her fastenings. 'No, no, don't tickle me! I can't stand it!' But Helen and Alice joyously arranged themselves one on each side of her and with a smile of anticipated enjoyment they began to touch her lightly with their feathers – first in her armpits, then under her chin, then all round and over her lovely breasts. Helen took one and Alice the other, Maud all the time struggling and squirming in the most provocative way as she begged them to desist.

From her breasts they passed to her navel, then on to the lines of her groin, and finally along the soft and sensitive insides of her thighs, Maud now plunging wildly and evidently suffering real torture from the subtle titillation she was being made to undergo. Then after a short pause and a significant glance at each other they applied their feathers to Maud's cunt!

'Ha! Ha! Don't! For mercy's sake, stop!' Maud almost shrieked, writhing frantically and straining at her fastenings. Half alarmed at the effect of their action, Helen and Alice stopped and looked at me as if for instruction. I glanced at the clock, there was rather more than one minute left. I felt positive that Maud could endure the sweet agony for that time and that it would make the ensuing fuck all the more delicious to her. So I determined that she should go on being tortured.

I signalled to them to re-commence. To prevent the house from being alarmed I held my handkerchief firmly over Maud's mouth so as to stifle her cries. Promptly Helen and Alice complied, their eyes gleaming with lustful enjoyment at the sight of Maud's naked body quivering in agony, applying their feathers again to her cunt they tickled her delicately but cunningly all along its sensitive lips. When they poutingly opened involuntarily under the stress of the titillation and disclosed the coral flesh of her interior, Alice delightedly plunged her feather into the tempting gap while Helen amused herself by tickling Maud's clitoris, now distinctly visible in angry excitement!

Maud by now was nearly frantic – twisting, wriggling, squirming and screwing herself madly in vain attempts to escape the torturing feathers. In spite of my handkerchief, her shrieks and cries were distinctly audible. It was evident that the limit of her endurance was being reached and that she was on the point of hysteria, so I signalled to Helen and Alice to stop; just as I did so she cried frenziedly, 'Fuck me, Jack! oh fuck me!'

In a moment I was on her, with two strokes I buried my prick in her raging volcano of a cunt and began to fuck her. Hardly had I started when she spent deliriously! I suspended my movements, for a few moments during which I kissed her ardently, then with renewed lust and unsatisfied desire I again began to fuck her. The sensation of holding her naked struggling, body in my arms plus the knowledge that she was tied, helpless, and at my mercy, imparted a most extraordinary piquancy to the operation!

Furiously I rammed into her. Deliriously she responded to my fierce down-thrusts by jerking herself madly upwards! Then the heavenly climax overtook us simultaneously, and – just as she for the second time spent rapturously – I shot my boiling tribute frantically into her. She received it with the most exquisite quiverings and thrills.

As soon as Helen saw that the ecstatic crisis had come and gone, she and Alice unstrapped Maud; and as soon as I slipped off her they carried her off, while I retired to my room for the necessary ablutions. But to my surprise Helen came in before I had commenced.

'Alice is looking after Maud, so I have come to attend to you, Dear,' she said archly. Sweetly she sponged and freshened my exhausted prick, finally kissing it lovingly.

I asked her if she thought Alice would be equal to twenty minutes torturing such as we had administered to Maud, also whether Alice's cunt was fit to receive me again. (I had broken her maidenhead the previous evening.) To the latter enquiry she gave a decided affirmative adding that Alice was eagerly looking forward to being fucked. She agreed with me that we had better reduce the term of Alice's torture to fifteen minutes.

I asked with a smile if either she or Maud proposed to fuck Alice, so that I might arrange accordingly. She replied that she would not, as she might reserve herself for her own approaching turn. She would not be surprised if Maud was tempted, she told me, only Maud was very exhausted by her struggles while being tickled. With a conscious smile and blush, she added, 'I am almost sure she intends to have me when my turn comes!'

So we settled that Alice should be thoroughly well felt by her and Maud, then I was to suck her, then we should tickle her cunt, and finally I should fuck her.

When we returned to Helen's room we found Maud busy attaching the straps to Alice's slender wrists and ankles, and soon she and Helen had Alice securely fastened to the four bedposts. I noted with amusement that they pulled Alice's legs much wider apart than I would have done, so widely in fact that the lips of her cunt were slightly open.

She looked perfectly delicious in her helpless nudity, her pretty cunt exhibited to perfection. As Helen and Maud gazed silently at her, I could see that their erotic desires were being rekindled. Suddenly they threw themselves on Alice and showered kisses on her. They proceeded to feel her all over, their hands visiting caressingly her most private parts, after which they squeezed her dainty breasts and kissed her cunt, laughing delightedly as she wriggled and flinched under their provocative touches.

'Come Mummie, let us see the result of Jack's work last night,' cried Maud merrily. With gentle fingers they opened Alice's cunt and eagerly inspected its interior, noting with amusing animation the changes caused by her violation. Presently, Helen gently inserted her finger into the newly opened passage, watching Alice carefully as she did so, laughing as Alice winced when the sore spot was touched. But she confirmed her opinion that Alice was fit to be fucked, thereby receiving from Alice a smile of satisfaction. Then they glanced at me, as if awaiting instructions.

'Now Alice, you're going to be sucked,' I said with a meaningful smile, to which she responded, evidently not objecting to this sweet form of torture. Turning to Helen and Maud, I directed them to play with and suck Alice's breasts while I attended to her cunt. With charming eagerness they addressed themselves to the exquisite morsels of Alice's flesh allotted to them, preluding their operations with ardent and salacious kisses, then proceeding to feel and stroke Alice's dainty bubbies, first holding them up by their little pink nipples, then imprisoning them between both hands and gently squeezing them. Alice betrayed her rising excitement by her quick flushes and nervous laugh.

Presently, Maud pressed between her hands the breast she was torturing so sweetly so as to make the delicate nipple stand up. Then she lovingly took it between her lips.

'Oh, Maud!' ejaculated Alice, squirming voluptuously. Helen promptly followed suit, her action eliciting another irrepressible cry from Alice, now rosy red at the sight of her breasts in the mouths of Helen and Maud and the tickling sensations imparted to her by the play of their warm tongues on her sensitive nipples. I considered it about time I joined in the play, so lowering my head and placed my lips on Alice's cunt, I fondly imprinted lascivious kisses all along her tender slit.

'Ah, Jack!' she cried as she commenced to wriggle divinely. When I ran the tip of my tongue gently along her cunt's lips and delicately licked and tickled them, she began to agitate herself voluptuously, twisting as much as her fastenings would permit and wildly thrusting her cunt upwards to meet my tongue.

Presently I noticed that its lips began to open involuntarily. As they did so, I forced my tongue between them, thrusting, darting, and stabbing downwards as deeply as I could into the almost virginal interior. I created in her an almost ungovernable erotic fury, under the influence of which she writhed and tossed about in the most lascivious fashion. It was clear that she was quickly approaching the blissful crisis. So withdrawing my tongue from her sweet orifice, I seized her clitoris between my lips and sucked it fiercely while my tongue cunningly tickled it.

This finished Alice off. With an indescribable wriggle, she spent in delirious bliss and collapsed in rapturous delight, punctuating the spasms of her ecstasy with the most voluptuous quivers and thrills. Then she lay inert and exhausted, with turned-up and half-closed eyes. But very soon she opened them again, and murmured faintly, 'Oh, please kiss me!'

Helen and Maud instantly threw themselves on her and showered loving kisses on her helpless cheeks till they restored her to life again. Then they tenderly sponged and washed her cunt and gently got her ready for her next torture, while I removed from my lips and moustache the traces and remains of her spend.

When I returned I found Alice was herself again and keenly curious to know what now was going to be done to her. In response to the enquiry in her eyes, I leant down and told her we now proposed to tickle her cunt. Did she thing she could stand it? She trembled nervously then said, 'I'll try, only stop me from screaming!'

'Then we'll gag you, dear,' I said, and carefully I twisted a large handkerchief over her mouth. I signalled to Helen and Maud to commence torturing Alice.

It was just as well that I gagged her, for at the first touch of the feathers on her sensitive cunt, the muscles of her stomach and legs violently contracted as she involuntarily tried to escape from the tickling tips. When this natural movement was frustrated by the straps, she shrieked as the feathers continued to play on and between the lips of her cunt. Oh how frantically she struggled and wriggled.

A delighted smile now appeared on the faces of Helen and Maud at the sight of the delightful agony that Alice was suffering. Joyously they continued their delicious occupation, tickling her cunt! Alice now was an exquisite spectacle. In her desperate efforts she twisted and contorted her lovely naked body into the most enticing attitudes, while the sound of her stifled hysterical screams was like music to us!

Although it was only a few minutes since I had fucked Maud, my prick became rampant and stiff, as if eager to renew acquaintance with Alice's cunt. It was evident that the subtle titillation was trying Alice severely, but so delightful was the sight of her struggles and wriggles that I allowed Helen and Maud to continue the sweet torture, till Alice hysterically begged me to stop. I then reluctantly did.

As I removed the gag from her mouth she gasped, 'Oh Jack, it was awful!'

'But you liked it, dear!' I said with a smile.

'Well, yes,' she admitted with a constrained laugh, 'but it is too exciting for me. Please don't torture me any more,' she begged prettily.

'Very well, dear,' I replied, 'but then you must end my torture,' and I pointed to my rampant prick. Alice blushed, smiled, and then nodded lovingly to me, and promptly I slipped between her legs. Bringing my prick to bear on her excited cunt, I gently forced it in – using every precaution not to hurt her – till it was completely buried in her warm, throbbing and fleshy sheath.

'Ah,' she murmured rapturously, as she felt herself possessed again by me, but this time without pain! I clasped her closely to me till her breasts were flattened against my chest. Then I set to make Alice taste the pleasure of being fucked!

She was terribly excited both by the tickling her cunt received and by her eagerness to again experience the exquisite raptures she had enjoyed in my arms the previous night – in spite of the pain of her violation. As I commenced to move myself on her slowly, sweetly, I could feel her straining at the fastenings to accommodate the sensations of the moment.

As I proceeded to fuck her, she murmured ecstatically, 'Oh… oh… oh, my darling, how heavenly!' She closed her eyes in rapture and wriggled and quivered under me voluptuously as she felt my prick working up and down in her cunt. Soon the blissful ecstasy began to overwhelm us both. Alice agitated under me in a perfectly wonderful way as I rammed furiously into her. Then her body suddenly stiffened, an indescribable thrill quivered through her as she rapturously spent. At the same moment, I shot into her frantically my boiling tribute of love. Then we both collapsed in delicious transports, oblivious to everything but our voluptuous sensations – Alice enraptured by the exquisite pleasure she was now fully able to taste, and I overjoyed at again having fucked her deliciously dainty self.

We soon came to ourselves. Meanwhile, Helen and Maud had set Alice at liberty. After a long passionate kiss, I slipped out of her and retired to my room accompanied by Maud, Helen taking charge of Alice. Sweetly Maud attended to me, and then somewhat eagerly asked what I proposed to do to her mother, confessing with a blush that she was longing to enjoy her!

'Certainly do, dear,' I replied, delighted at the prospect of again seeing the Mother and daughter relieving their lust by means of each other, naked. Joyfully Maud kissed me, and we hurried back. Helen and Alice had returned and were awaiting us.

Alice evidently was full of elation at her newly acquired sexual freedom. Eager to enjoy her privileges, she caught hold of Helen and drew her to the bed, at the same time calling to Maud to help her fasten Helen to the four corner posts. With great glee Maud complied, and very soon Helen lay extended on her back with her limbs strapped to the posts and a hard pillow under her bottom. She was at our absolute mercy.

'Now Maud, you may have your mother to yourself for the next five minutes,' I said. A vivid blush surged over Helen as she heard her fate and glanced shamefaced at her daughter. Maud smiled lasciviously at her with the assured air of a conqueror. Alice arranged herself alongside of me, slipped her arm round me, and with her unoccupied hand gently played with my balls.

Maud bent down and kissed her mother first on her lips, then salaciously on each breast, and finally on her cunt. Seating herself alongside Helen, she gently ran her delicate forefinger along the lips of her mother's cunt. 'Oh, Maud, don't,' cried Helen, shifting herself uneasily and squirming deliciously under the licentiously free touches of her daughter's finger. But Maud continued deliberately to irritate her mother's cunt till she had worked Helen into an almost uncontrollable degree of erotic excitement, making her plunge and wriggle and twist in the most voluptuous manner.

It was a charming sight to watch the daughter's delicately slender forefinger at work on her mother's sexual organ, half hidden in the luxuriant growth of hair that crowned Helen's cunt, driving her slowly to the very verge of spending, but forbidding her the blessed relief, and making her tug wildly at her fastenings in her semi-delirium. No longer able to endure the maddening desire to spend, Helen cried in agony, 'Oh Maud, do finish me!'

With a gratified smile, Maud leisurely placed herself between

Helen's widely parted legs, and with eyes glistening lustfully, she mounted her mother so that their breasts and cunts rested on each other. Fiercely seizing Helen's helpless body, she set to work to rub her cunt against her mother's. 'Ah! darling!' exclaimed Helen in ecstatic delight, as with half-closed eyes she surrendered herself to be fucked by her daughter, jogging herself spasmodically upwards so as to press her cunt more closely against Maud's.

Soon their movements became furiously tempestuous, especially Maud's she plunged and rammed and curvetted herself on her mother's fastened-down body in her efforts to bring on the madly desired crisis.

Suddenly she cried, 'I'm coming!' and with a hurricane of down-thrustings she spent deliciously on her mother's cunt just as Helen, with an irrepressible ejaculation of, 'Ah!' yielded to nature and collapsed, spending ecstatically in her daughter's arms.

As soon as her paroxysms of pleasure had died away, Maud kissed her mother lovingly, rose off her, and rushed to the bathroom, shielding with her hands her cunt from our inquisitive eye. But Helen, being tied down, had to remain as she was, her cunt fully exposed, all glistening and sticky from her daughter's spend. With charming confusion and shamefaced blushes, she endured our amused scrutiny. Catching Alice's eyes, she murmured, 'Please, dear,' whereupon Alice prettily proceeded to remove all traces of the double spend. By the time Maud returned, Helen was ready to be submitted to Alice's caprices.

'What now, Jack?' she asked hesitatingly.

I pointed to Alice. 'You've to satisfy her lust now, dear. Go ahead, Alice.' Installing myself comfortably in an armchair, I drew Maud on my knees, so together we might watch Helen under Alice's hands.

For a moment Alice stood undecided, her eyes wandering over Helen's helpless and naked self. Then she set to play with Helen's beautiful breasts, which she stroked and squeezed and caressed, finally sucking each in turn. Her eyes were fixed on Helen's tell-tale face as if to assess the result of her toying. What she concluded evidently encouraged her, for, with a wicked smile, she armed herself with a finely pointed feather and placed herself by Helen's side in a position from which she could command Helen's cunt.

'No, no, Alice, don't tickle me!' cried Helen hastily as she nervously tugged at her fastenings, laughing nevertheless at her predicament. Alice, however, only smiled mockingly at her and proceeded to apply the feather to Helen's cunt, passing the tip lightly but searchingly along its sensitive lips that were still excited from the friction induced by Maud's cunt. 'Don't, Alice!' again cried Helen, squirming charmingly, but seeing that she was doomed to undergo the sweetly subtle torture, she nerved herself to endure it, clenching her teeth and firmly closing her lips so as not to cry out.

Then followed a lovely spectacle! Having had her own cunt severely tickled, Alice had learnt where the most sensitive and susceptible spots were, as well as the most telling way in which to apply the feather to them. Availing herself of this knowledge, she so skilfully tickled Helen's cunt that in a very short space of time she had Helen struggling and writhing in the most frantic contortions, straining at her fastenings so frenziedly that the bedposts began to creak.

Helen's closed eyes and clenched lips, her heaving breasts, her palpitating bosom, heightened the provocative effect of her naked, tossing, agitated self. But although she heroically refrained from screaming, it was evident that she was fast reaching the limit of her powers of endurance. Meanwhile, the gaping of her cunt dumbly indicated the excitement erotically raging there. I succeeded in catching Alice's eye and signalled to her to stop, which she instantly did. Not unwillingly. Her flushed face and glittering eyes betrayed the lustful concupiscence that now possessed her, and that she was longing to satisfy by means of Helen's naked helpless body. She dropped the feather and impulsively threw herself on Helen, and was proceeding to work herself on her as she had seen Maud do, when Helen gasped, brokenly, 'Wait... a moment... darling!'

Although she now was absolutely trembling with unsatisfied lust, Alice sweetly and sympathetically suspended her movements. She clasped Helen tightly to her, her breasts resting on Helen's, and showered ardent and salacious kisses on Helen's flushed cheeks and quivering lips till Helen had sufficiently collected her disordered faculties. Then Helen opened her eyes and, smiling amorously at Alice, murmured, 'Now, darling!'

Alice needed no encouraging! Gripping Helen tightly, she furiously rubbed her cunt against hers, her deliciously youthful figure and her frenzied and uncontrollable but exquisitely graceful movements forming a wonderful contrast to Helen's mature but voluptuous body, so rigidly strapped into virtual passivity.

So new was Alice to the art of fucking that, in place of prolonging the exquisite pleasure and slowly bringing on the sweet climax, she concentrated all her energies to procuring the satisfaction of her erotic lust. Wildly she rubbed her cunt against Helen's till the ecstatic crisis overwhelmed them both. Then simultaneously they spent, Alice with a rapturous cry of 'Auntie! Oh, Auntie!' accompanied by the most voluptuous thrills of carnal delight, while Helen ejaculated deliriously 'Oh... oh... Alice, darling!' as she lasciviously quivered in her amorous transports!

In silence and spell-bound, Maud and I had watched Helen

and Alice, but the sight was too much for Maud. When Alice set to work fucking Helen, Maud whispered hoarsely to me, 'Jack! Jack!' and agitated herself on my knees in such a way that her desire was unmistakeable. Instantly my hand sought her cunt, there being no time for any sweet preliminaries, my finger went straight to her throbbing clitoris and so adroitly did I frig her that just as Helen and Alice were surrendering themselves to their lust and beginning to spend, Maud also distilled her sweet love-juice with an ecstatic discharge all over my hand!

I let the three women rest undisturbed till the throes of their spending had ceased. Then, when Alice slipped off Helen after passionately kissing her, Maud seized her and dragged her to me, exclaiming 'Show us your cunt, dear.' Bashfully, Alice stood still as we delightedly inspected her sexual organ, all smeared with the love-juice that had proceeded from herself as well as from Helen.

I showed her my hand. 'This is Maud's,' I said with a wicked smile. Wiping it gently on her hairs, I added, 'Now your cunt carries the sweet essence of all three of you, darling.' Maud terminated Alice's blushing confusion, by dragging her off to the bathroom.

Helen was still in her semi-swoon looking most fetching in her exhausted nudity. Quietly I armed myself with sponge and towel and gently set to work cleaning her cunt. This roused her from her torpor, and he slowly opened her eyes, but when she recognized me and what I was doing to her, she started into full life and, hotly blushing, exclaimed, 'Jack! Oh, darling, that is not for you to do.' Suspending my work for the moment, I replied, smiling significantly, 'My darling Helen, as I am about to be the next occupant of this sweet abode of love, may I not put it in order for myself?'

She smiled tenderly at me and raised her face as if inviting a kiss. As I bent downwards, she whispered softly, 'Darling, may I suggest my next torturing?' I nodded with an encouraging smile. Helen blushed deeply, then murmured bashfully, 'Do you mind… sucking me? I have never had it done to me yet, and I would like to try it!'

'Certainly, dear,' I replied, delighted at her request. 'And after that?'

She blushed again, then replied softly, 'Fuck me, darling!'

Enraptured, I kissed her passionately in token of compliance. Then I set to work again, and thoroughly sponged and purified her sweet cunt inside as well as out. By the time Maud and Alice reappeared, Helen was herself again, and eagerly anticipating the new experience she was about to taste.

When the two girls returned I placed them on the other side of Helen. They guessed from my position what I was going to do to her, and with expectant smiles they quickly took their places. Then lowering my head I brought my lips to bear on Helen's eager cunt and kissed it sweetly, first in the very centre of her clitoris – each kiss making her shiver with pleasure. Next I began to pass my tongue backwards and forwards along her slit, licking it delicately but provokingly.

'Oh, Jack, oh… oh!' Helen exclaimed, agitating her bottom and hips voluptuously while a smile of beatitude crept over her face! Seeing that she was now revelling in the erotic sensations aroused by my tongue, I continued to lick and tongue-tickle her till her cunt began to gape and pout amorously. Then I darted my tongue into her orifice as deeply as I could, and tickled the deliciously warm, soft interior.

This set Helen raging with erotic lust. 'Oh, oh, Jack! My darling!' she gasped as she violently wriggled in lascivious transports while I first tickled this sensitive part of herself with my tongue and then took it gently but firmly between my lips and passionately sucked it!

This finished Helen! Her struggling body suddenly stiffened, a violent convulsion swept through her, and with an incoherent, half-strangled cry she spent rapturously with the most lascivious quivers and thrills!

As I reluctantly raised my head from Helen's cunt, the two girls noiselessly clapped their hands gleefully, evidently delighted by what they had witnessed. With Helen still absorbed in her ecstatic oblivion, they accompanied me to my room, watching with much amusement the removal from my lips and moustache the traces of Helen's spend.

'What next, Jack?' they eagerly asked.

'The usual finale, dears,' I replied smiling. 'Only I am going to pull the straps so tight that Helen won't be able to move at all, and so will lie like a log while she is being fucked! When I give you the signal, just tighten the straps as much as ever you can, even if she cries out!'

Helen had come to herself when we rejoined her, and she welcomed us with her usual kind smile. The girls at once kissed her warmly, and eagerly enquired how she liked being sucked. Helen blushingly confessed that she had found it just heavenly! 'As good as what you are about to receive, mother dear?' asked Maud teasingly.

Helen laughed. 'Do not forget, dear, that I have tried it only once, while the other, well, I know and love,' she replied evasively.

'Well, Helen,' I intervened, 'I was going to fuck you, but would you prefer to be sucked again?'

She blushed, hesitated, then said gently, 'The old way, Jack, please. I like to be in your arms, dear, and to feel myself possessed by you, and to… to spend in response to you!'

'Then fucked you shall be, darling,' I replied as I kissed her tenderly. 'Shall I do it now?'

'Give me a minute or two, please Jack,' she pleaded, then turning to the girls she said softly, 'Dears, will you try to work me up?'

'I know a better way for both of us,' I said. Straddling across Helen, I seated myself on her chest, placed my prick between her breasts, and with my hands I pressed them together, around and over it, at the same time lasciviously squeezing them. I gently logged my prick backwards and forwards between them, revelling in the delicious contact of Helen's full, soft breasts against my now-excited organ. Its stiffness together with the provoking friction seemed to communicate to Helen some of its ardour, for in spite of her shamefaced confusion at the sight of her breasts being put to such a use, her bosom soon began to heave and palpitate, and her colour to come and go.

I nodded to the excited girls, and they immediately set to pulling the straps as tight as ever they could, laughing merrily at Helen's dismay and protests when she found herself practically unable to move at all! 'Now, darling,' I said.

Working myself backwards over her stomach, I slipped into position between her legs, threw myself on her helpless and rigidly extended body, and with one powerful stroke I drove my prick up to its roots in Helen's longing cunt. I took her in my arms and began slowly to fuck her.

'Ah, Jack!' she breathed blissfully. My sensations were extraordinarily piquant! Although Helen lay motionless under me, I could feel that she was involuntarily struggling desperately against her fastenings by her muscular contractions and broken breathing and the agitated movements of her only free part, her head. She rolled and tossed so restlessly and unceasingly that I had the greatest difficulty in catching her lips to kiss them. Her up-turned eyes, clenched teeth, and half-closed lips indicated that her inability to indulge herself in the relief afforded by even slight wriggles was concentrating the whole of her erotic lust and lascivious cravings in the battlefield itself, her terribly excited cunt!

The tension was evidently getting too much for Helen, so I set to fucking her hard, plunging and ramming myself into her quicker and quicker, more and more wildly, till the blissful climax arrived. Madly, I deluged the recesses of her thirsting cunt with a torrent of boiling love-juice, which Helen received with incoherent ejaculations of rapture as she herself spent ecstatically in transports of lascivious delight!

Leaving Helen to lie in happy oblivion I slipped off her, and, with the aid of the girls, I freed her from her fastenings. Just as this was achieved she came to, and dreamily rolled off her bed. Maud at once took charge of her, while Alice accompanied me into my room and again sweetly bathed and dried my exhausted prick. Then she suddenly stooped down and kissed it lovingly, blushing hotly as she did so.

It was the first time she had let herself go, and I augured so favourably of her action that I ventured to whisper as I kissed her, 'Before long, dear, you must let me teach you to suck it as well as kiss it,' in response to which she looked lovingly at me and nodded her head with a tender smile of promise.

We re-entered Helen's room simultaneously with herself and Maud. Helen threw herself into my arms and kissed me lovingly, seemingly overjoyed by her experiences. We chatted together for a little, and then after affectionate goodnights we all sought our respective rooms, well pleased with ourselves and each other.

Misfortunes Of Mary

James Barrington wore a terrifying smile, or rather a sneer. Had Mary looked at him at that moment, she would have realized the terrible danger that threatened her.

He had sat down again in the same armchair and continued smoking a cigar with an absent-minded air. He gestured her to approach, indicating with a finger a spot on the carpet directly in front of his feet.

'You want to prove that you are grateful to me, Mary? Well, that's the easiest thing in the world. All you have to do is simply to obey all my demands.'

'Oh, yes Sir, willingly. I promise to be the most devoted, obedient, and attentive of secretaries.'

'Hum, very good, very good. Kneel down here, in front of me.'

'Kneel down? But why?'

'Don't argue, Mary. You've promised to be obedient. I have to begin by completing your education, which is very wanting in spots.'

A little confused but filled with the desire to please in all ways her generous protector, Mary fulfilled his request. Like any meticulous young girl, she discreetly raised her skirt as she lowered her knees to the carpet in order not to wrinkle it.

He stared at her for a long time, admiring her pretty face, her candid and confident eyes, and her sensual mouth. She finally lowered her eyes, and his stare fixed itself on her shoulders and then her chest, both completely hidden by her loose-fitting blouse. Then, taking a long drag on his cigar, he blew the smoke violently in her face. She drew back abashed, coughing, and looking at him reproachfully as her eyes filled with tears. He laughed.

'You're not accustomed to smoke, Mary. I must insist that you become so.' He remained silent for a moment, and then suddenly said, 'Mary, undo your blouse and let me see your breasts. I insist that my secretary have a good chest.'

Had lightning struck at her feet, she could not have been more surprised. Her heart caught in her throat. She could not move, and thought that she had misunderstood.

'I repeat, Mary, and I don't like to repeat myself. Show me your breasts. I want to see them.'

Stupefied, she cried, 'Sir, oh, Sir, you're not aware of what you're saying! What do you mean? There's no rhyme or reason... I don't understand...'

'Don't search for the reason. You have just signed a contract in which you agreed to serve with loyalty and devotion, isn't that right? You have given me the authority to complete your education by whatever means I should deem necessary. Is that right or isn't it? And that's what I am doing. As of now I am undertaking your sex education, a subject that in your case has been completely ignored till now. A good secretary must be perfectly documented in this matter. Show me your breasts of your own free will. Undo your blouse with your own hands. Obey quickly, or else I have the means to make you...hmm... hmm...'

Mary was dismayed. She was completely baffled. She was gripped by a terrible anxiety. She looked around her and saw the footrest, the leather-covered bench, the large praying stool, and the crucifix on the wall. Then she noticed the large couch covered with cushions.

The Colonel took her by the arm and gripped it tightly.

'You're hurting me,' she trembled.

'Do what I ask of you with good will, Mary, or else you'll be sorry.'

'Sir, let me go. Oh, leave me alone. I'd rather go and give it all up. I'll never do what you ask; it's awful. Let me go…ouch, you're hurting me, I tell you.'

'Once more, are you going to uncover your breasts? Yes or no?'

'Never! You can't be conscious of what you ask. It's shameful.'

'That's not all you'll be asked, you little idiot. You're going to be asked to show calves, thighs, your back, and your ass too, even your stomach and finally your whole body. Nude, all nude, from head to foot. A good secretary, you know… I'm going to make a perfect secretary of you. A secretary for the day, yes, but especially one for the night. Ah…' His own words rendered him giddy and whipped up his passion. He held his prey firmly by her biceps and kept her from getting up or making any movement. She twisted and turned in his grasp, trying with all her might to get loose. He stood up, spreading his legs apart, and then bent her savagely forward underneath him. Then, closing his knees, he gripped her torso between them. He brought her wrists back across the small of her back and taking a rubber thong from his pocket, tied them together. Bending over, he took her skirt and folded it back, up and onto her back, doing the same with her slip, which left her dressed simply in her panties. He got excited.

'Ah, so you don't want to obey, well, I'm going to train you, my little pigeon. Those ladies at school never whipped you when you were bad? Well, I'm going to give you a good spanking, something that has been missing in your education. Let us hope it will render your character more supple. The first time we'll whip you on your bare skin. You hear, on your bare ass! I'll make them blush a little; that'll warm them up a bit.'

Mary begged, protested, and began to make promises of obedience. She was terrified at the idea that a man, and worse yet a stranger, would perhaps force her to show this most intimate part of her anatomy. It was terrible for her, all the more so since she didn't understand what it was all about. She was being punished for having refused to obey a most shameful demand, to uncover her breasts before a man, a stranger she had known for barely an hour. Her mind was in a turmoil. The world was upside down. All her principles of honesty, all her education of a nice girl brought up in a religious environment, were being trampled and overthrown. 'Aie! Oh... aie!' she cried as she felt the first blows.

Barrington leaned forward over the moon embedded in the tiny panties, stretched to bursting by the position he had forced Mary to take, and he began laying into her. She twisted about, rolled her ass in all directions, and cried, implored, and tried in vain to undo the thong which held her. Methodically and unhurriedly, he struck with his large hand first to the right and then to the left. Thus he covered all of the accessible terrain with some twenty blows.

Mary involuntarily shook and quivered her rear end in a most lascivious manner and cried: 'It's vile to treat me in this way, Sir. Let me go. You have no right. I have done nothing wrong. Oh... oh, you're making me suffer...'

'Have you decided to show me your tits?'

'Oh... never, as long as I live...'

'Then I'll go on, but this time on bare skin.'

'No... not that. Oh, gangster!' This heartfelt cry escaped her despite all the respect she felt she owed a man who was old enough to be her father. She felt the searching hands of her tormentor unfasten her panties and then pull them down over her thighs. The panties, despite her efforts to keep them from sliding down her tightly pressed legs, were soon down to her knees, leaving uncovered the entirety of her beautiful moon of white flesh.

Barrington's eyes glittered at this sight. The two hemispheres were magnificent and in full bloom, covered by a milk-white skin that was beginning to turn rosy from the spanking it had just received. He revelled in contemplation of the double crescent of her cheeks greeting each other across that dark crevice.

Mary was desperately trying to free herself from the bindings that were choking her. But all efforts were in vain. The Colonel held her firmly and the contortions of the young girl's attempts to free herself were imparted to her ass which only added to the delectation of the lascivious voyeur.

Vigorously and without sparing her, excited by the beautiful flesh which rebounded under his fingers, he began his torture.

'Oh, Sir, have pity on me. I'm so ashamed. Stop… stop, I beg you. Let me cover myself. Oh my God… oh… oh, not there, not so low, not there, higher! You're torturing me. You'll wound me. Oh…'

In effect, Barrington had ceased to strike her on the peripheries and had begun to attack the lower meridian, as close to the top of her thighs as possible. His upright position, however, prevented him from reaching the more sensitive part underneath. 'Have you had enough, my little recalcitrant lady? Are you going to give in? Have you decided to show me your pretty tits of your own free will?'

'Never… I'd rather die…'

'And do you think, my little imbecile, that a spanking never killed anyone…?'

'Oh, I'm too unfortunate!'

'Yes or no?'

'No... no...'

'Well, you've asked for it...' Reaching for the table, he took up the ruler, a nice square ruler, twelve inches long, and, without a moment's hesitation, let it fly against her right cheek. The cry of a wounded animal sounded in the room and the poor girl's body gave a sudden jerk. One of her legs stretched out with the pain and her panties split. But she immediately drew her leg back, as if by instinct, fearing that she was uncovering too much of her person. He managed to keep her pinned between his legs nevertheless. Then another blow struck her other cheek. More cries, more contortions, more tears, more supplications, and he stopped for an instant. 'Mary, if you don't accept, the third blow will fall between the last two, in the middle. And that really is going to hurt you, and you will have gained nothing. I'm going to hit you right here.' So saying, he reached down his hand and ran his fingers up and down the length of her crack, muttering, 'Here... here...'

At that Mary's resistance was finally overcome. Fearing the worst, she decided to accept the bargain. Quivering and with a voice filled with fear, she said, 'I accept.'

'To show me, by yourself, your chest?'

'Yes,' she said in one lengthy breath.

No sooner had she said it than Barrington let go his hold of her, put the ruler back on the table, and sat down again in the armchair. He was breathing heavily.

Before him the poor girl remained on her knees, trembling and sobbing, her head lowered and covered by her hair which had become undone.

He quickly untied her hands. She rubbed her aching wrists as she continued sitting on her heels, lost in her misfortune.

Barrington gave her a moment to pull herself together. He was in no hurry. He had the whole evening and all of the night.

A few seconds later, full of disarming candour, Mary made a last attempt: 'Are you really going to persist in your demand, Sir?'

'Why, most certainly.'

'But why? Why ask me such a thing? Why have you mal-treated me in this way?' she cried, sobbing.

'I wouldn't have, Mary, if you had obeyed me. You're now a private secretary. It is entirely your fault. As to my desire to see your breasts, it is perfectly legitimate. I have just hired you for three months. During that time we shall be living very close, one to the other, and I want to assure myself that you have a nice body and that it is pleasing to me.'

'But what does my body have to do with the work you wish me to do?'

'Mary O'Connor, it is precisely your body that is of great importance to me. Far more so than you can imagine, and I must tell you that as of tonight I plan to inspect it in detail, my dear child, piece by piece.'

'Oh, my God, have pity, kind Sir. Let me go. Mrs. Coates will surely find you another girl as qualified as I, even prettier than I. I cannot accept the thought of... I'm going!' And getting up on her feet she made a dash for the door before Barrington could move from his chair.

A laugh rang out in the room. Barrington hadn't budged.

Leaning against the closed door which she had not been able to open, Mary, haggard and eyes popping out of her head, repeated the fatal words that she had just uttered: 'Crook... I'll report you to the police...'

Sniggering, Barrington approached his prey slowly. Before he could grab her she dodged to the side like a cat, but his outstretched hand managed to retain a small piece of her blouse.

She reached the window and opened it violently, saying, 'You've asked for it.' Closing her eyes and letting out a terrible scream, she threw herself out into space. Luckily, she didn't fall very far. She fell to the thickly matted floor outside this fake window, and, of course, was completely unhurt. With the terror of a trapped animal, she got back on her feet, and, looking about her, she understood the trick. She also understood that she was a prisoner and at the mercy of her employer.

Barrington stepped over the sill to join her, and Mary, leaning against the wall with her face in her hands, began to cry.

'Come, Mary, let's be reasonable. As you can see, all has been foreseen for subjugating recalcitrant young girls. You cannot escape your fate. Now be good.'

She let herself be led back, her resistance completely broken.

Back in the room, Barrington resumed his place in the chair and made her take up the same position as before. He said not a word.

With the back of her hand, Mary threw her golden hair back over her shoulders, and looking him straight in the eye, she said, 'It's you who are forcing me to sin, but God will forgive me, as you will be punished by Him.'

He smiled without a word and apparently remained altogether indifferent to this distant threat.

Slowly, her fingers trembling, she began undoing her blouse. Once it was undone, she drew back the borders, so uncovering her white neck, and then lowered the blouse to her elbows. But her breasts remained covered by her slip and a jersey held tight by her corset.

'Take off your blouse altogether, Mary.'

She obeyed once more and uncovered to his eyes her beautiful shoulders, her plump arms. Only the narrow shoulder straps of her slip and jersey remained to hide her exquisite flesh.

'Continue,' he ordered.

She became white as a sheet. With a trembling hand she slid the tissue over her elbows and then, with a rigid movement, she folded back the jersey and the nylon over her corset.

Barrington's eyes sparkled at the sight of the two magnificent tits. They couldn't have been whiter had they been washed in snow. Oh, the two rosy-red nipples, and the whole was bigger and juicier than he had imagined it. Was the little one in an unconscious state of heat? This thought made his 'Mr. John Thomas' jump in his cage.

Mary didn't move. Her head was lowered, red with shame.

Barrington stretched out his hands. Sacrilegious contact, so delicious for him and so filled with horror for her, took place. He first touched her two round shoulders. She shuddered and drew back instinctively with a sob, but his fingers sank into her smooth flesh, holding her and drawing her toward him. He kneaded the fleshy shoulders and caressed her arms, and then with all of his ten fingers he enveloped the round mounds.

Mary whimpered in despair, 'This is horrible.' Her shame was complete. She no longer made a motion. She reasoned that if she were obedient, the sooner this newer torture would end. But she could no longer hide from herself a strange feeling being awakened in her – that of finding herself naked for the first time before a man. Feeling the flesh of her breasts caressed, squeezed, caused in her a strange confusion of emotions. She would have liked to run away, yet a dumb force kept her glued in place. It wasn't altogether unpleasant to have one's tits caressed and… oh… now he was gently pinching, twisting, and fondling her nipples with his fingers. And now her ass-cheeks, her breasts, were burning with a deep twanging, and till then unknown, heat. What was the meaning of all this?

It was so plain to Barrington that Mary was getting hot that he said in a vulgar manner, 'So you enjoy having your tits squeezed, my lovely?'

She blushed and kept her silence.

'Oh,' continued Barrington between his teeth, as if talking to himself, 'I'll have to see for myself if all this is having an effect on her.' He got up, but he had such a hard-on that he had to put his hand in his pocket to shift his dick up against his stomach. Then he said, 'Come here, Mary. Kneel before this crucifix and ask God for forgiveness for the sins you are going to commit.' Without giving her time to arrange her clothes, leaving her arms bare, her tits flapping, her blouse hanging about her waist, he dragged her to the praying stool and forced her to kneel on it.

Innocently, she placed her hands on the back of the stool, full of shame at being nude before Christ, who appeared to have a look of reproach mixed with pain on the features that bore down on her. It must be said that this particular icon had something of the peculiar about him. His expression was rather one of intense ecstasy than one of suffering, in addition to which he was fixed to a St Andrew's cross in the shape of a large X, his legs and arms spread wide.

Barrington bustled about. Again taking out the rubber thongs, he tied Mary's wrists to the top of the stool's back, one on either extremity. Then sliding back two bolts, he swung the stool backrest frontward till it lay horizontal to the floor. The poor girl was now leaning on her elbows with her knees propped higher up on the seat of the stool. Her head therefore was now lower than her buttocks. Her tits still hung bare, but her skirt had fallen down again, covering her calves.

'Mary, you must pray and give penitence. I am putting this crucifix before your eyes so you may beseech it for forgiveness.' So saying, he did just that.

Mary was completely bewildered. She couldn't understand what her tormentor was driving at now, and feared some new punishment. The anxiety she felt, and the confusing state that had overtaken her during the last moments were suddenly doubled when she felt her skirt and slip being raised over her back. Her rump and thighs were again exposed in all their nudity and she shuddered with fear and shame.

Fearing that she might try to interfere with his projected inspection, he fastened her knees with two belts he had fetched from the closet. 'Put your knees onto the stool.'

The unfortunate girl was perfectly aware of the base posture she had been forced to take. She made one more supreme attempt to resist, beseeching, supplicating, imploring, trying to make James understand that it was impossible to steep her in greater shame than she already was experiencing.

'Further discussion is useless,' he replied dryly, and with one of the belts he gave her a stinging blow on the thighs.

'Another fifty like that one if you persist in your refusal. Your white skin will be bloody.'

She jerked violently, let out a piercing scream, and spread wide her knees.

In the twinkling of an eye, he secured her calves and feet to the legs of the stool with another two belts. His mouth drew to a thin line and he became even more vile. 'Mary, you are very beautiful in this position. I can look at your whole body now. I see 'everything' in every detail. The warm valley is entirely exposed to my view. There is nothing now to hide your tiniest treasures from my eyes. And a little while ago you were snivelling because I made you unbutton your blouse and show me your tits. Now I'm feasting my eyes on your juicy buttocks. I'm getting down on all fours right behind you now. I see your little hole encrusted between two thick hills. I see your delicate, oblong little trough, from which flows forth the fountain of your golden piss. I see the soft wild silk that covers your mound of Venus, and the gently round-ed hill of your belly, and… oh, your velvet thighs…' For what seemed like a long time, he remained silent, devouring with his eyes those hot and innocent parts spread out in such a disgraceful manner before him. 'Now let's see if you have any spirit.'

Mary hadn't said a thing, nor made any protestations, for her moral suffering was too great. Yet physically she was gripped by the most disturbing feelings, the source of which she could not deter-mine. These sensations were by no means unpleasant, an inexplica-ble phenomenon for her. She would have liked to scream out her disgust, her resentment, her shame, but she had neither the strength nor the willpower. A strange languor misted her thinking. The heat radiating from her beaten ass caused the most troubling sensations. She hated herself for being so vile but she was unable to react.

Barrington was panting, deriving from this little exhibition the greatest cerebral satisfaction. Kneeling behind the delectable ani-malism of this virgin captive, he stretched out his hands and enveloped gently with his palms the two firm tits on which two nip-ples now stood quivering and erect. He grabbed the nipples between his fingers and began to massage them skilfully. Mary became rigid, breathing heavily. The gentle caress was paying off.

Barrington kept his eyes glued on the little vulva, searching in the folds of this still innocent organ the first signs of the heat he was try-ing to provoke. He did not have to wait long, for soon the lips began to move and palpitate. He pinched and pressed the nipples of her tits. The vulva yawned, opening suddenly and spasmodically by force of her belly's contractions. His hands let go of her bosom and began to knead gently the beautiful flesh of her buttocks, thighs, and belly.

Mary's nylons got in his way and he undid them and rolled them down to her knees. The beautiful young girl was getting agitated, little shivers running along her skin as the result of these sacrilegious caresses. Her ass contracted and distended, oscillating from left to right. Her cunt became gripped by a violent animation.

Just then, Barrington reached for the crucifix stretched out beneath the young girl's eyes, and removed the tiny cloth wrapped around its loins.

Mary was struck with horror. Pointing straight at her was a stiff prick. She had never before seen the sexual organ of a man, and thought she would go out of her mind. Her eyes ran over the tensed body before her. It was not a Christ there before her, but a faun in heat. She was able to distinguish now the tiny horns, which had been hidden at first by the crown of thorns. His feet were goat's hooves, his legs hairy, and his cock was stiffly pointing at her lips... oh, horror... madness...

Barrington, having noticed the involuntary sexual reaction indicating the passionate nature of the young Irish girl, could no longer resist attacking the cute vulva that was going mad. His caressing fingers ran lightly and ardently down the entire length of the cleft. He grazed past the asshole and ran along the side of the adorable cleft, which was by this time quite moist.

Mary quivered with a mixture of shame and pleasure. He brought his face up to her cunt, and with his thumb he folded back the love-enamoured husk. He breathed deeply the pungent perfume distilled by this rosebud. This was followed by a wild contraction of her ass muscles. A dumb gurgle issued from Mary's throat; was it the death-rattle or the purring of a cat in heat? In any case, he was now convinced that he had found Mary's most vulnerable spot. He nibbled at her with passion, sticking his tongue deep into the moist crevice. At the same time, he continued to tease her breasts. Soon he noticed an agitation in the small of her back and the very globes of her ass, sure signs that she was getting close to coming. He was careful not to lick her clitoris, now well in view, for he didn't want her to come yet. For the moment, he just wanted to create such a degree of excitement in her as to make her putty in his hands. He stopped playing with her. Her vulva was red, irritated, moist, and in full eruption. The time had come...

He got up, untied the young girl, and made her sit down in the chair behind the desk. He went over to the chimney and spoke into the speaking-tube of the dumbwaiter, ordering a light meal and some hard liquor. Two minutes later the sound of the rising lift between the thick walls announced that the order had been delivered.

Mary was as if in another world. Almost completely nude, her clothes in a mess, she did not seem to think of fixing herself up. However, her eyes were glowing, even if they did stare, with an unknown fire. From time to time she trembled convulsively.

Barrington brought over the tray laden with two plates of cold chicken, rice pudding sprinkled with paprika, and a basket of fruit. In addition, there were bottles of cognac, gin, vermouth, and a bottle of seltzer in a bucket of ice.

The Colonel began to stuff himself. He found a moment to place one of the plates before Mary, but she took no interest in it. He drank some cognac with a little seltzer, and was soon finished. Mary hadn't touched a thing on her plate.

'Take a piece of fruit, if you're not hungry.'

'No thank you,' she said in an exhausted tone of voice.

'Well, drink this then,' he said, handing her a glass half full of gin in which he had poured a finger of vermouth.

'I'll do my best,' she murmured. She sipped the beverage slowly till she had finished it. It burned her throat and oesophagus, but it did her good.

'Some more?' he asked. 'A good secretary should not be afraid of a little alcohol.'

'Oh, what difference does it make… if you say so,' she said resignedly. She drank another glass and her head began to turn, but she felt better. The alcohol picked her up, warmed her heart, and gave her courage.

He let her alone for some time while he considered how he should pursue the adventure. He took advantage of this moment of calm to visit the neighbouring bathroom where he undressed and put on a large bathrobe and comfortable slippers. He then came back and sat down again in the chair and called to her, 'Mary, come here and kneel down before me as you did before.'

The young girl shuddered and implored, 'Haven't you humiliated and tortured me enough? Have pity. Don't ask me to do any more shameful things. I can't go on. I'm on the edge of despair.'

'Not at all, my little one; on the contrary, all this is very normal. We have to educate you in the matters of love, and I shall succeed in doing so. And with your help…'

'Oh, my God, I'm lost…'

'You won't say that an hour from now; you'll be thanking me for having opened your eyes,' he said. And something else too, he thought to himself.

She came forward slowly, her blouse still undone, her arms bare, although she had covered her breasts with her body linen. She kneeled down before him and with nervous fingers she slid down the shoulder straps of her linen and blouse and removed both entirely, throwing these garments on the table. Once again his eyes feasted on her lovely bosom. He did not tire of looking at these virgin breasts with their proud and stiff little buds pointing at him. For some time he caressed these exposed charms.

'Mary, answer me truthfully. Did you never give yourself

pleasure, all alone, at night, in your bed, during the warm days of spring when the birds sing and the flowers bloom? Did you never have the desire to... rub yourself... here... with your finger?' So saying he stretched his hand toward her belly and touched her gently on her skirt where her pubic bone was.

She drew back her pelvis, frightened.

'Answer me. Tell me the truth. Must I take up the ruler again in order to get an answer out of you?'

'Oh, Sir... this is horrible. No... no... don't hit me again.'

'That depends on you.'

'I... I don't understand what you mean.'

'You know very well now. I'm asking if you have before felt strange sensations of heat, something eating up your whole body, especially in a certain part, as you felt them just a little while ago when I was caressing you on the praying stool.'

'Oh, never, never... I've never felt anything like that before.'

'Is it really true?'

'I swear it on my uncle's head.'

'Well, in that case I'll believe you. And was it agreeable?'

'Oh...'

'It was, wasn't it? And you don't dare admit it. But of course it's pleasurable to be caressed, kissed, and even jerked off. You don't understand? I'll explain it to you. Come closer...' He grabbed her head between his two hands and drew it to him and kissed her gluttonously on her full mouth.

Mary, in her surprise, tried to back away.

He held her with one hand while with the other he began once more to titillate the nipples of her tits. In a flash Mary melted in his arms. He felt her getting excited once more. She resisted no longer, and when he tickled her with his tongue her lips parted, then her teeth. She accepted his lunging tongue, which began reaming the inside of her mouth. She answered his caress. He felt triumphant and was getting caught up in his own excitement. He drew away from her slowly. 'Isn't that good, a loving kiss?' he asked.

Shyly, her eyes half closed, she murmured very low, 'Yes...'

'You are all hot once again, Mary. Your pulse is beating faster, your blood is surging through your arteries, and your little cunt must be quivering. But you know it's the same with me. I too desire to be relieved. Oh... I feel like... yes... Mary, would you, with your mouth...?'

'With my mouth?'

'Give me pleasure?'

A heavy silence followed.

Barrington looked at her with insane eyes. He put a hand on the back of her neck and slowly pulled her toward him, till her face was next to his thighs. With a sudden movement of his other hand he undid the belt of his bathrobe. It fell open, uncovering to Mary's eyes his male member, stiff and menacing. The odour of a wild animal struck her nostrils and she cried out in fear. He murmured, 'With your mouth... with your lips. Have you never seen a man's organ, little one? Well, have a feast. I have the pretension of having a damn handsome cock. You can kiss it the way I did you. You can lick it, as I licked you there. You can suck on it. I want you to suck on it and make me come...' As he said these words, he had brought her lovely face in contact with his cock and was rubbing her nose, cheeks, lips, and neck with it.

'Open your mouth and lick it with your tongue, or I take up the ruler again.'

Mary had one last violent reaction of modesty. For a moment, after the disturbing first kiss she had ever received from a man, she had weakened. But she was incapable of committing the base act he now demanded of her. An infinite disgust took hold of her. She struggled and managed to get out of Barrington's clutches, yelling, 'No, not that… you're a vile creature!'

Barrington jumped to his feet. 'You'll have asked for it, Mary. I'll make you do it. It's just too bad for your hide.' He went for the closet and took out a switch and two riding whips, a thick one and a thin one, and several leather belts. He had the look of a madman, his eyes throwing darts.

Mary, still kneeling, followed his movements with frantic eyes. She heard him mutter terrifying threats.

'I'd rather whip the hide off her ass and tits than give in. A little-mannered bitch like that, she'll find out what sort of stuff I'm made of.' He threw his instruments of torture on the table and yelled, 'Get up, Mary, and take off your clothes. I want you completely naked this time. I've had enough of your airs.'

Terrified, Mary got up.

Menacingly, he was waving one of the whips, demanding, 'Let's hurry it up. Take it all off, my pretty. That'll teach you to stall.' Before she could even raise her arm in defence, he struck her a sharp blow across both breasts with the back of the whip. The blow had been well calculated, but Mary, in her utter surprise, doubled up, let out a blood curdling scream, and brought her hands up to her offended breasts. He took advantage of her position to let her have another blow on her buttocks, which protruded too temptingly. She cried again, but more from surprise than pain, for with all her clothes the blow couldn't have hurt her too much.

'Hurry, Mary, make up your mind. I want you naked. It's terrible, isn't it, having to show oneself before a man? A man one doesn't know and who is neither one's husband nor lover? And one has never undressed before him? Your uncle Ted, did he never see you in the nude? While you were taking a bath, for example, on the pretext that he wanted to be sure you were soaping yourself properly?

No? Never?'

She nodded her head in the negative and hid her face in her hands, crying.

'Are you going to make up your mind, or aren't you? Or do I have to rip your clothes off, piece by piece?'

She knew that there was no hope now, and so this adorable and modest girl began to undo her skirt and her slip, which she let fall to her feet, sobbing all the while.

Barrington had regained his comfortable armchair and was smoking another cigar as he contemplated his victim.

The corset followed and she now stood in her panties. Her blouse, only half off, hung about her waist, as did her jersey. And her stockings were crumpled down in accordion folds about her calves.

He stopped her. She was adorable this way, her torso completely nude, her beautiful round arms, her shoulders gracefully curved, and her pointed tits arrogant and clearly defined. 'Fold up your clothes neatly, Mary, and put them on that chair over there.' He indicated the chair behind the desk, just next to his own. Thus he was able to watch her as she moved. As she bent down to pick up her skirt he noted that her bosom was really firm, for it did not move a fraction of an inch. He continued to watch her as she went past. She was embarrassed, red with shame, yet graceful in all her movements and attitudes despite it all.

When she had neatly put away her things, as he had ordered, he commanded her, 'Take off your shoes and your stockings now. Rest your foot on the chair. The carpet is so thick that one can walk comfortably on it barefoot.'

She turned her back to him, so he was able to look at the small of her back and her ass, still covered by her panties. One after the other, she undid her stockings. It was then that he noticed the perfect shape of her legs, the delicate roundness of her knees, the slimness of her ankles, and the ravishing loveliness of her well-kept little feet.

Well, Mrs. Coates certainly hadn't taken him for a ride this time. He would willingly pay her the fifty guineas he still owed, and even more if she should demand it. What a marvellous creature. So musing, he called her over to him once again. He was still holding the fine riding whip in his hand, snapping it in the air from time to time in such a way that it made a hissing sound.

Mary, her hands folded in front of her, gave him one last suppliant look. 'Must I, really?'

'I never take back an order once given.'

'Oh, but why? Why me? What misery. Dear God, what have I done to deserve such a fate?'

'It's because you're such a ravishing young person with a magnificent figure you want to hoard and keep to yourself when I desire to admire it in all its splendour. All these charms, which till now you have so wrongly and jealously hidden, must now be given up to others. Thus, Mary, in another instant, you shall be entirely nude before a man for the first time in your life. And I hope for your sake that it won't be the last. I may even say that, on that question, I'm certain that it won't be. With your beauty you should be shown in the streets of London, standing on a pedestal drawn by six white oxen as naked as yourself. Well, I'm waiting. Or do I have to use this whip again?'

'You are a base cad. You are taking advantage of your strength in a shameful manner. But you'll pay dearly for this. The police will protect me, and you'll be hanged. Hanged, do you hear, you bastard? Oh, God has forsaken me. Because of you I have known anger, and I blaspheme. I'm going crazy.'

'You have known anger, and soon you will know love. It's much nicer, and it gives you fewer complexes. In a little while you'll be less of an idiot. I'm going to fuck you. I'll make love with you and I'll force you to share my pleasure, and then you'll understand. Do you know what it is to fuck? Have you ever heard speak of it, to make love? I hope that you haven't, for I want you to be virgin both of mind and of body... but you hurt me terribly a little while ago, when you refused to lick me. So now I'm going to punish you and make you do it despite yourself. Naked, all naked... quickly...' And the whip whistled menacingly, cutting through the air with its sharp cry just in front of her.

She drew back a step, terrified. He got up and his robe stuck out like a vertical tent, but she didn't notice it. Trembling, she hastily unbuttoned her panties which were closed at her hips. They slipped to the ground and lay there, encircling her ankles in all their whiteness. Her blouse was still hanging from her waist and she couldn't make up her mind whether to undo it. Everything began whirling. She became terribly dizzy. The idea of showing the middle of her body from the front appalled her.

The whip hissed again, this time lashing her calves. She clutched the linen around her waist in her two fists and pulled it down a few inches, then staggered and suddenly fell to the ground. In the hapless movement of her legs, she did a split and tore the cloth down the greater part of its length. Her blouse came loose and lay next to her thighs. She was naked and half unconscious. The shock had been too brutal for her young nerves.

Barrington got down beside her and removed the linen that had gotten entangled around her feet and admired in ecstasy her marvellous body, whose only movement now was an occasional convulsive shudder. Her eyes were closed and her hair flowed in disorder around her head and shoulders. He put his ear to her heart and he heard it beat violently. This first contact between his cheek and her skin enraptured him. Reassured, he gave the nipple closest to him a big lick and heaved himself up.

He hurriedly got some cognac, and supporting her head with his hand made her drink several mouthfuls. Almost immediately, she opened her eyes and breathed deeply. Her eyes were terribly red from crying, and she appeared to be lost, not understanding where she was or what had happened to her.

'Drink some more. That'll put you back in shape, Mary.'

On hearing his voice, she trembled again and looked at him strangely. Nevertheless she opened her lips and drank another half glass of alcohol. It picked her up immediately, and once more she became lucid. Her first gesture was to place one hand over her pubic bone and the other over her breasts with a movement of adorable modesty.

Barrington said with a sneer, 'You'll see, you little fool. Once I have you tied in the shape of a cross, then you can try and hide your cunt and tits.' He went back to his chair, lit his third cigar, and poured himself a drink of gin while looking at Mary stretched out on the carpet. 'Are you going to remain there forever, Mary? It's an excellent position for a whore.'

Mary was terribly insulted. She understood that word and so she sat up, red as a beet with shame, and hesitated before getting up, so confused was she by her complete nakedness.

'Up we go, you lazybones, let's have a good look at you...' The whip was again being brandished.

Mary was frightened, and with supple movements of her pretty, curvy body she raised herself to her feet and turned her back to him.

He admired her magnificent stature and perfect proportions. Her back, wide at the shoulders, well-fleshed, did not give away her shoulder blades. Her waist was small, but the swell of her belly was full for such a young woman. A handsome ass. Her long legs, well-jointed at the height of her thighs. Her calves, nicely rounded, tapered to a pair of slim ankles. The whole had a line he had not expected to find in a girl of such a modest background. Perhaps she had been the fruit of a maternal extramarital error committed with a young lord of the aristocracy. Her beautiful golden hair, with natural curls crowning her still girlish head, fell down in long graceful waves over her shoulders and back. He couldn't tire of looking at her, admiring her. After a considerable silence, he stretched out his arm and gave her a lash across her close-pressed calves, shouting, 'Turn around, I've seen enough of your back. Let's have a look at the front.'

Mary jumped from surprise and let out a yell as she shifted her weight from one foot to the other. There was a thin red line swelling across her calves. Victim of her fear, especially for her delicate skin, she turned around, flaming red.

'Well, finally,' said the Colonel. He was completely dazzled by this living statue. Without a word he admired this masterpiece of nature, which by the wildest chance, and with the help of underhanded means, had fallen into his clutches. 'Put your hands behind your back and be quick about it.'

Mary turned from red to dead white. Her last bastion of modesty crumbled as she obeyed him in desperation.

Barrington licked his lips like a gourmet enjoying every morsel of a rare dish.

Mary, her head bent, cried bitterly. She had reached the depths of abasement and shame. Even though she had been forced by most vile means to the present moment, this did not obviate the fact that she was the pure niece of a preacher who had raised her in an atmosphere of the purest of Christian virtues. And here she was, this most honest girl, naked and undergoing the vilest of perusals, the most abominable and degrading possible. The shame and embarrassment that now possessed her were of the most atrocious sort. She couldn't but realise that she was being treated as in ancient times when the chiefs of savage tribes used captured women as booty, as a slave. This humiliating examination that she was undergoing; the physical contacts which had already been forced on her, and that she knew would be forced on her again; these contacts that she detested, but which she could not deny had afforded her pleasure – despite her will – that they shouldn't; the frightful whippings that burned her delicate skin and forced her to give in to the most vile demands; the foul caresses that had been imposed on her when she had been tied to the praying stool; the filthy tongue; the unknown words whose meaning she could guess; all these horrors were marking the inexorable stages of her frightful downfall.

Barrington rose and moved toward her. 'Don't move while I look you over close-up.' He put the whip underneath his arm. Once again his detested fingers brushed her mother-of-pearl flesh, slid around her neck, her shoulders and then her breasts, which he caressed gently, massaged, and kneaded. Then he stroked her hips, her rounded belly, and tickled the pretty orifice of her navel. A second later he moved down to her crotch. Trembling, desperate, crying, she no longer dared to protest or make a move to defend herself. He caressed the abundant wild silk of her cunt, curled it around his fingers, and gave it little tugs at which she yelped. 'It's ugly, all this hair… you have too much of it.'

He went to the bathroom, the entrance to which was hidden by a draw-curtain, and came back with a hairbrush and a pair of scissors. 'Your hair is all in a tangle, and I'm going to brush it out for you.' He began with her head. He busied himself with the hair, brushing it briskly back, uncovering the forehead and temples, bringing the whole back over her shoulders. He wrapped a silk scarf around her head so as to draw her hair away from her mother-of-pearl ears. 'Look at yourself in the mirror. How do you like your hairdo?'

Mary gave a timid glance at herself and uttered an 'Oh!' of surprise. The turban gave her a little roguish air that she didn't at all appreciate. In addition, it changed her entirely from her customary self.

'Raise your arms gracefully and cross them above your head, Mary.'

She assumed this graceful pose without realizing at first that in so doing she exposed her armpits and their red-haired furnishing. Her breasts were magnificently raised and almost arrogant.

The Colonel fingered caressingly the moss of her armpits. He then brought his fat face close to the intimate hollow.

Mary made a movement as if to fend him off, and immediately received a lash of the whip for her pains.

'Don't move, and keep your arms up. Hum, that smells pungent under there,' he gurgled as he breathed in deeply the acid odour of her armpit. Then he straightened up and began to brush the short kinky hair.

Mary uttered tiny little cries and begged him to stop.

'Does that tickle?' he asked, laughing. After having played at his game for a few minutes, he turned to her cunt bush. First he brushed from the top down, then from the bottom up.

Mary was maddened. She pressed her legs together, hoping thereby to prevent the brush from going too far under. But soon a delightful tingling sensation ran up her spine and her cunt came aflame again. She lowered her hands and tried to push away the brush that excited it in such an odious manner.

Barrington let her have it with the whip across her fingers. 'Mind your hands,' he cried. At that, he grabbed a handful of her cunt hair and pulled it up. Then, taking the scissors, he began cutting.

Mary was frightened and let out a yell. She tried to pull her belly away. But his hold on her fine bush was firm, which caused her considerable pain. Her wriggling did not prevent him from cutting all her hair the length of her slit.

Showing her the cut curls, he said, 'I wanted to keep a souvenir to remind me of you, namely these little curls of your cunt hair. And now, each time I look at them, I shall be reminded of this marvellous day.' And he continued with little snips of the scissors to completely remove her curtain of modesty. To do so he had kneeled down, and he threatened to cut her skin if she made a move. Soon the whole area was clean, with the exception of a few freckles. By the same token her slit was now outrageously exposed. 'And now on to more serious matters, for I'm beginning to get famished for a little love. My bursting balls are beginning to kill me.'

Naturally, she understood none of these words, but she suffered on hearing them nonetheless.

'Are you ready to give me the relief I expect of you with your mouth, which you refused me a little while ago? Answer me, Mary.'

The unhappy creature was terribly troubled. She remembered the horrible contact between her face and her tormentor's hard, burning flesh. She remembered in particular the frightful odour that had revolted her nostrils. It had so nauseated her that she had been unable to consent to embrace the cylinder, as he had demanded. An uncontrollable disgust had mounted in her throat. 'Don't ask that of me, please, it's too... too horrible.'

'Unfortunately, I'll ask you but one more time, for you're going to do it whether you like it or not, Mary.'

'Oh, my God, save me!'

'Leave the Good God be. He has other cunts to whip without worrying about yours. Ha!'

Mary was dismayed, for she suspected what would follow. Thinking to soften him, she said in a desperate voice, 'Your... your flesh... its odour was too strong, I couldn't... have pity. Let me leave. Haven't you tortured me enough?'

He sneered. 'Ah, so you think I smell bad? Well you better get used to it for I like that particular caress the best, and a good secretary must be able to perform it perfectly for her boss, and at any time, it's indispensable.' He took her by the arm and dragged her over to the bench. 'Stretch out on your belly.'

She shuddered. What was going to happen? He pushed her savagely, and as soon as she was stretched out he fastened her to the bench with a belt, which he pulled over her back and under the bench. Then he tied her wrists to the bench's front legs, but in such a way that her tits overlapped the edge of the bench. Across the opposite extremity of the bench he attached a long piece of wood, which had been hung beneath. He then tied her ankles to this crosspiece in such a way that her legs were completely spread-eagled. All the while, Mary resisted with all her might, screaming continuously, begging her executioner to spare her, to forgive her her faults (which she had not committed) and not to make her suffer.

But Barrington, much too excited by now, paid no heed to this heartrending music. For more than an hour he had manipulated, both physically and morally, this unfortunate young girl, and as a result his senses were so violently excited that he required immediate relief. His whip whistled, bitingly, cruelly, and bit into the flesh spread out helplessly before his eyes. Slowly, he moved the lash up the length of the calves, up her thighs, and just as slowly down the shoulders to the small of her back. She screamed without pause, and finding that she was too rigidly tied, he loosened the belt around her waist and began whipping her chubby ass. He was careful to strike only with the tip of the whip, spreading the stings of the lash evenly over the whole surface of the two cheeks. Her eyes were bulging. Her beautiful, white body, becoming striped like a zebra, bounded convulsively under the stinging bites of the whip. As Mary was fastened by only her wrists and ankles, she had enough leeway to contort her body convulsively, and these movements of flesh in pain ravished the cruel flagellant. The young girl screamed all her suffering, begging him to end her torture and her shame. But her wriggling contortions filled him with far too much pleasure for him to stop so soon.

He accorded her a moment of respite while he went to the bathroom to fetch a mirror. It was mounted on a stand with casters and he rolled it to the foot of the bench, facing her widespread legs. He approached her once more, but this time he took up his place by her head. Thus he was able to see, by means of the mirror, all her hidden treasures as he continued his torture. With each blow he saw the beautiful buttocks quiver, flatten out, and then spurt back out as if propelled by a violent contraction in the young girl's stomach. He struck to the right, then to the left, and ended by a few down the middle, in the slit, on the most sensitive flesh that was already wildly boiling. During this time, Barrington's robes had come undone and so uncovered his cock's hard-on jerking about as he administered the blows.

Mary let out a strange cry, one of mixed pleasure and pain, and Barrington noticed the great confusion that was animating her sexual region. Her loins were jerking about like trip-hammers, knocking her love mound hard up against the bench. The cheeks of her ass contracted and distended wildly, leaving exposed to his view the sexual trough in full excitement. She was no longer screaming, but moaning quietly. Barrington smiled. He kneeled before her on the carpet and dangled in front of her lovely face his rigid, ready-to-burst dick. He slipped his hands underneath her and placed them on her tits, which he caressed gently. Oh, the round beauties filling his hands like… like dingle berries…

Mary shuddered and recoiled, gazing wildly at the cock saluting her at a distance of only a few inches. Just then, Barrington pinched her erect nipples, and Mary's mouth opened as if to cry out, while her neck stretched out full length. He immediately pushed his big tool into her mouth and let out a wild bellow. After no more than two wild jerks, he came, emptying his overflowing balls into her pure throat. His haggard eyes remained fixed on her mad cunt, which he could see clearly in the mirror, and which was spurting juice in which her little fish was jumping.

Barrington let out another hoarse cry, the bellow of an animal in heat, as the wild sensation of coming surged through him again. His sperm shot out in hot spurts into the depths of the unhappy girl's throat. She made vain efforts to free herself from the gag of flesh that was choking her. Several times she almost strangled. She coughed and ejected some of the thick, gooey liquid around the edges of the thick cylinder on which her face was impaled. Nevertheless, she was forced to swallow a considerable amount. Barrington was in full heat now and was no longer recognizable. He was hungry for this body that he had been manipulating for more than an hour. He wanted to come again and again in the flesh of the beautiful virgin.

He straightened up suddenly, and like a crazy man, his eyes bloodshot, he ran his hands wildly over her hot body as it lay at the mercy of his lasciviousness. He pinched her, scratched her, and murmured a stream of incoherent words. 'A virgin… no, two… I'm going to take one and then the other. Mary, you won't interfere. First your little asshole… this one…' and his fingers rutted down her ass slit till they reached her contracted anus. 'And then your little cunt next, your pretty vulva, which I'm going to force open, penetrate, spread out, rape. Ha, Mary, a good secretary, a perfect secretary, as it says in your contract… I'm going to instruct you in the profundities of life, ha…ha…ha…'

He had, while muttering to himself, unloosened Mary's feet and hands. Yet she didn't dare move. She only closed her thighs and breathed deeply, her heart beating like a trip-hammer, and waited in anxiety the forthcoming tortures. He grabbed her around the waist and picked her up like a feather. He carried her with her ravishing posterior and dangling legs just under his nose. He slapped her rear with his wide-open hand, carrying her all the while toward the praying stool. A moment later she was again fastened tight to the stool. Her bosom was even lower this time, for it was her shoulders that he had attached to the horizontal back of the stool rather than her elbows. Thus her loins were considerably higher than her head.

Again he knelt. This time, with the savagery of a dog in heat, he lapped the hot and tender flesh, all the while caressing the rest of her body, her hips, belly, tits, arms and back. Then getting up suddenly, he said: 'I can't take it any more. I just have to bung-hole you, honey.' Standing behind her, he placed the end of his instrument against the brown spot, which he had just licked and lubricated with his saliva. The disproportion between his tool and her orifice made his intention seem like the height of conceited ambition. And yet he went about it in such a skilful manner that in no time he had arrived at shoving the half of his tool into the anal casing, which was now distended to its very limits.

To describe her screams, her contortions, her protestations and her supplications is impossible, but they were all to no avail. Impeccably, Barrington reamed out a passage by the knowing twists and circling motions of his dong, pinching all the while her buttocks and the tender flesh of her belly, rubbing her clitoris and cunt lips from below, teasing her tits and their tender nipples. This all provoked such contortions of her back and loins and hips that, without realizing it, she greatly facilitated his task.

He bent forward over her back so that his thighs were glued to hers, and began to move back and forth. He knew that he mustn't sink his tool in too deep, for in doing so he would risk hurting her or giving her such pain as would obviate the pleasure he desired to make her share with him. He began moving about in a livelier fashion, with more precision. While he continued to concentrate his attention on her breasts and clitoris, he continued to ream out with greater and greater speed the narrow tunnel. He pushed a finger in between the erect lips of her vulva, spreading apart the tender folds of flesh cushioning her hymen. Mary uttered a cry of pain and his loins quivered. He stiffened, then plunged his cock in to the hilt and froze at the instant that his burning juice tore down the canal of his urethra, bringing with it the maddening sensation of ultimate pleasure.

Mary, half unconscious and battered about by the most contradictory feelings, her spirit drowned in fumes of alcohol that was served to her with great generosity, her nerves completely on edge, her senses awakened to the extreme by the extravagant caresses she was undergoing, was sinking little by little into a morbid pleasure. It was purely physical, and she could no longer defend herself against it. At the same time, as Barrington felt the final moment approaching, he shoved his finger with a sudden thrust as deep as it would go. He felt the inner drum of skin give way, and the flood of virginal blood envelop his finger. He redoubled his efforts on Mary's clitoris, and a few seconds later brought on the orgasm he had sworn he would bring in her. At the same moment, he overflowed in his own sexual climax. Mary groaned with pleasure and wallowed in her physical downfall. She was certainly a very hot-blooded girl, full of sexuality and sensuality. Those now dominated her, as her orgasm shook her spasm-racked body.

He slowly got up, looking over the battlefield of his second encounter with bleary eyes. His cock stayed up, and wouldn't stop throbbing. He walked about the room, his pecker pointing straight ahead, still covered in a reddish slime, and with a drop of come still hanging from his gaping pee-hole. He went into the bathroom and took a sponge-bath, washing in cold water his enflamed sexual parts, but nothing had any effect on his cock, which was still hard as a piece of granite. He was too excited for the cold-water treatment to have any effect.

He returned to where Mary lay, still tied to the bench, her ass kissing the air and spread wide. He had a towel soaked in eau de Cologne, and with it he began rubbing down the back, ass, thighs, and loins of his victim in the hope of speeding the healing process on all the bruises he had inflicted with the whip.

Mary gave a terrible jerk, for the alcohol burned her flesh. She screamed and contorted herself within the confines of her bonds, begging him to stop his rough treatment. Then he rubbed the towel between her legs and right into the half-moon slit of her cunt and ass. At this, Mary was unable to keep back a blood-curdling scream.

The towel came away covered with blood. He threw it into a corner and untied his victim. 'Go and wash up a bit in the alcove there, while I stretch out to rest and have me a cigar.'

Staggering, her back, cunt, and asshole burning, Mary went out to the washstand.

Barrington again seated in the comfortable chair, was lighting up his fourth cigar and listening intently to what Mary was doing. He heard water running from the faucets, the toilet being flushed, and the shower. Mary was most likely trying to get some life back into her bruised body.

After a while, no longer hearing anything, and she not making a reappearance he shouted, 'Mary, you've got to come back. I still have to take your real virginity. Let's not cheat. I'm to use you according to my will…'

A pale and undone Mary reappeared in the room with a large towel wrapped around her, her eyes red with large dark circles beneath them. She threw herself at his feet and begged him in a most pathetic way to spare her this ultimate disgrace, now that he had already used her in such an abominable way, but with no result.

He had an answer for her, 'How can you ask me to free you? Look at John, still hard as a rock. He's still hungry, very hungry, and demands his normal due. Till now all he's had is a light hors d'oeuvre, honey…'

'Oh, you're horrible, and don't call me honey. That word in your foul mouth is sacrilegious.'

'Ha, sacrilege,' he laughed. 'For one thing, who gave you permission to wrap that towel around you? Take it off. I want you nude, naked, all naked, you're beautiful that way.' He looked at her in a sarcastic manner as he filled a glass with liquor and offered it to her. 'Here, Mary, drink this cognac. It'll do you good. Cheers, and all that rot.' It was the fifth time he'd given her a drink. He hoped that in so doing he'd soften her resistance; that she would give in more easily to his last demand.

Feverish, nauseous, weak, her head pounding, she swallowed the drink at one gulp. Her eyes fluttered, her head turned, and she had to sit on the floor, supporting herself with one of her hands.

'Take off that towel!' he screamed, grabbing the whip.

Shy and filled with modesty, her eyes lowered, Mary let fall the towel. She was again naked before her tormentor.

Barrington devoured her with his eyes, blowing huge puffs of smoke toward the ceiling. He sat there, sunk deep in the chair with his robe half open. It left to view his stomach and his terribly red cock, pointing to the blue, still filled with desire and ready for battle. 'You see, Mary, for a minute I was trying to think of how I was going to de-virginize you. I was trying to decide whether to do it by attaching you to the bench to take you from the back or to tie you to the chaise lounge on your back with thighs well spread and then do it belly to belly, papa fashion… or perhaps to tie you to the praying stool as before and do it doggie style. Or better yet, I'll have you get on me, have you fuck me… Yes, that'll be fun, to make you do the operating. It'll be interesting and will tire me less. Good idea. That's what I'm going to do. Come to think of it though, I'm most comfortable in my chair. You could go to it here, at your ease. Let's go, Mary, chin up, the time has come. We're going to make a real woman out of you.'

Mary was feeling weaker and weaker, her head spinning, her eyes bloodshot. She couldn't move. She remained glued to the floor.

He got up and grabbed her under the arms and lifted her to her feet, giving her three slaps across the face, which caused her to come back to life a bit. 'Come and sit on my lap. I like caressing your eatable meat.' He dragged her to the chair, sat down, and placed her on his knees. She allowed herself to be directed, as she felt lost and hopeless. His hands took possession of her beautiful flesh, rubbing her stomach and tits. Soon he began to run his fingers up her knees, moving slowly and gently up the smooth skin of her thighs till he reached her crotch. Just then, Mary, reaching for support against the back of the chair, fell against him. Her breast was right next to his face. With one hand he kneaded the left tit while with the other he caressed her thighs. His mouth and tongue teased the breast within reach of his lips.

Mary gently opened up her thighs without knowing it. His agile fingers took immediate advantage of nature's invitation in order to determine at what point of excitation the palpitating vulva had reached. Her cunt was flooded. He sniggered. He raised his head and Mary lowered hers, putting her velvety arms around his neck as their lips met in an embrace. The virgin quivered and trembled nervously as she opened her hot legs even wider. All the while he was going over her with his fingers, his tongue was lost between her set of white choppers, which were now wide open. Mary was lost, and she gave herself up to the ineffable pleasure of love.

James knew how to manipulate the sensitive spots of a girl who was giving in. Without removing his lips from hers, he picked her up and changed her position in such a way as to have her kneeling on the seat of the chair. No word was said, and if he had to stop his caresses of her wild cunt, it was only for an instant while he was moving her. He slid lower down between her thighs which now straddled him in such a way that his tool was in position for the final beachhead. Little by little he replaced his fingers with his cock in the quivering temple of her vulva. She was hardly aware of the substitution. She moaned in a sing-song of pleasure. Holding his stiff prick in his hand, he reamed it around at the entrance of her vagina, which was pooled with unctuous fluid. She began imperceptibly to move her hips rhythmically up and down.

Barrington couldn't hold on any longer. The moment had come. He grabbed Mary by her haunches and lifted her up a little. Then, looking straight in her eye, he said, 'Mary, look at me. Open your eyes. You're going to feel my dick slowly penetrate… slowly spread the lips of your cunt, entering little by little… pressing against your flesh… against your virginal barrier. It's up to you to break the barrier by pressing with the weight of your body. It'll crack... your hymen will split under the pressure. You'll feel the inside of your belly being filled by my flesh... to the very depths... up to your womb. After just one moment of pain you'll see, Mary... it's going to be divine... ah... oh... oh!'

Dazed, she lowered herself, and Barrington broke through the obstacle. A flood of vermilion-coloured blood spurted about his oversized cock and spattered their thighs. Mary had become a slave to desire, hypnotized by his words (the monster) dominated by his dirty soul and by an imperious desire that was uncontrollable. She followed his instructions point by point. A moment after her hesitation, at the climactic moment of pain, she had borne down her belly on the male dagger on which she was impaled for the first time in her life. A terrible pain, intimate, deep – the scream of a wounded animal – and Mary sank onto Barrington's shoulder in a faint. Just then he ejaculated into the pit of her innards a torrent of burning sperm.

Mary was now a woman.

Barrington gasped for breath. He continued romping in and out of her cunt with big lunges. He continued plunging in the depths of the narrow passage. He felt his cock perfectly gloved by her tiny trough, and the contact between his flesh and hers was absolute. In a few minutes he came again, spilling out his balls. And Mary, returning to consciousness, was taken by a frenzied sexual intensity. She in turn began wiggling her hips, in the grip of her passionate nature, and came like a mad woman. She gripped in a tight embrace the neck and shoulders of the man. She covered his face with burning kisses and when his hands pressed her swollen tits she melted in a frenzy of ecstasy, whirling her hips, bearing down with her belly, forcing his cock to enter into the passionate depths till its head beat against the dilated and maddened door of her womb. Then she collapsed, out of breath and worn out. He shoved her away from him brutally and she rolled over his legs and fell exhausted to the carpet. Half unconscious, agitated by spasmodic jerks, her arms and legs forming a cross, she was stretched out on her back like a broken doll.

* * *

From the neighbouring room, by means of a two-way mirror, several persons had been witness to this scene. Mrs. Coates, an astute business woman, knew how to put all circumstances to profit, thus her pocketbook was doubly lined. Of course, Barrington suspected nothing, but Mrs. Coates, who had sold Mary's virginity for one-hundred guineas, had thus earned supplementary receipts.

Her three best clients were present, Lord Selwin, a debauchee who looked older than his forty years; the Reverend Nicolas, a libidinous pastor fat and pot-bellied who normally officiated at St Elizabeth's Church; and the Lord Justice C. W. Strongcock, who protected Mrs. Coates by his official judiciary position and would have come to her assistance in case of trouble with the local police. These three despicable creatures had just wallowed for a fee of fifty guineas in the spectacular downfall of an unfortunate young girl.

Barrington was getting dressed, his eternal cigar between his lecherous lips. He had a last drink, went to the speaking tube at the chimney mantelpiece, and asked to have the door opened. With one last look at Mary still lying stretched out on the floor unconscious, naked and covered with gore, he stepped out of the room feeling very happy and satisfied.

Mrs. Coates greeted him politely and enquired whether he had been satisfied with the services of his secretary.

'Entirely so,' he replied. 'This time I must give you my compliments, you old lecherous witch.'

'Oh, Colonel Barrington,' said the old procuress, giving him her hand despite feeling offended.

'Ah, yes, I nearly forgot... I still owe you fifty guineas.' Haughtily, he descended the stairs with Mildred leading the way to the door. He slipped her a sovereign. With a measured stride, calm and full of tranquillity, he directed his steps toward his club, where he proceeded to dine as if nothing had happened.

The Modern Eveline

I am considered by those who have had the honour of my acquaintance to be a pattern of propriety. I am pointed out by anxious mothers as an excellent example of careful training, combined with the advantages of a Continental finishing course at a select pensionnat de demoiselles in the environs of Paris. I am also the invited of very strict old maids, because I affect to enter into their schemes for the conversion of untold savages, am liberal of purse, and reticent of tongue.

The latter quality runs in my family. Our history demands an extraordinary amount of it. There are at least two families of high and ancient aristocratic pretensions whose loud-tongued, drinking, gambling male descendants openly boast that they have never allowed a maiden of their noble line to pass, as such, out of the family and into the arms of her spouse. Ours is a third, only we are not so simple as to publish the fact.

I am not, by any means, a saint in outward seeming. In my appearance and ordinary habits, I am not so straight-laced as I am represented. I do not set out for particular formality in my daily pursuits. I am only quiet, observant, always affable, amiable, and sometimes a trifle volatile. The men call me dull and say, 'A pretty girl, but you know, dear boy, there is no fun in her. No use to try it on, dear old chappie, you'll only come off second best.' 'Fun' in the mind of the society man of the present day means immorality. They adopt the word because it is a light and gay style of describing the loose conditions which bind together all that they care for in the nature of modern society. At present, society is content to parade itself with a superficial and very flimsy disguise over its naked deformity. In a few years' time, at its present rate of progress, it will work bare-faced in the open light of day.

I am not going to moralize; I do not even wish to be a self-appointed censor of the times in which I live. I do not personally care a pin what becomes of society, so long as I succeed in avoiding the arrows of detraction, scorn, and contempt it launches against any luckless member who has the misfortune to be found out. I hardly think it will do so in my case. At any rate, I take all possible precautions to pursue my silent path of sensual indulgence in obscurity and peace.

My father Sir Edward L – – , Baronet, started life a rich man, rich even in these days of treble millionaires, American heiresses, and other innovations. He entered the army, served with his regiment in India, and returning to that empire after a short furlough, met and married a nobody with whom he was shut up for a month or more on his voyage out. She was good-looking, tall, and coarse. He soon tired of her. After dragging her about for three months with his regiment, he sent her home to England. I rejoice to think that I do not inherit any single trait of my mother's personality. She never cared for me or took any particular notice of me.

I had two older brothers. Of the elder, I may speak later. I knew little of him in my childhood. As to Percy, we were companions until I was sent to school and he to Rugby.

I suppose I was always curious and enquiring as a child. I have been told so. Personally, I only remember a few prominent incidents of my early childhood. It was not a joyous or even a happy one. My brother and I were thrown much together. He was curious also. Together we secretly investigated the remarkable differences in our physiological structure. We came to the natural conclusion that such opposite developments must be designed for some purpose, which at present we did not understand.

The tree of knowledge being denied to us, we set about making our own investigations. The result was that we discovered a certain indefinite gratification, even when on being at each end of a large marble bath, our toes encountered certain exposed portions of each other's persons, which at all other times we were told we must hide and never talk about.

Secretly, also, we mutually inspected these remarkably different developments; it was a new field of investigation and insensibly we enjoyed it. We pursued our studies at such intervals as privacy and opportunities permitted. We slept in the same room, and we would steal furtively into each other's beds to whisper and wonder at the delight the feeling and the caressing of these dissimilarities afforded us.

In short, we masturbated each other, until my brother Percy attained a precocious development of his private parts quite sufficient to destroy all vestige of maidenhood in his sister.

Arrived at this age, we were separated, as I have already related. A couple of years at a Brighton Seminary exclusively for 'the daughters of gentlemen' did not eradicate the lessons in physiology I had already learnt, quite the contrary. I listened while my companions compared notes, and I found most of the girls were equally well informed.

Indeed, one or two of the elder 'daughters of gentlemen' would lecture us in the junior classes, while we listened to the absorbing topic with rapt attention, about what a naked man was like, with curly hair on his belly and a thing dangling between his legs. They described it as twice the size of my brother Percy's. They went further, even, and one averred that she had seen and handled one. That they grow quite stiff and stood upright. In that condition men endeavoured to thrust them into girls.

I listened and said nothing, and for my pains they called me a little fool and an innocent. Even at that early period of my existence, I had imbibed the instinct of reticence, so generally absent in young women.

Two years of study on all the subjects conventional and impractical, to which 'the daughters of gentlemen' are subjugated at my age in such establishments, afforded me ample opportunities of acquiring the rudiments of a society education. How much longer I might have remained at the Brighton Seminary I know not, but an untoward accident put an end to my career there, as also to the 'select establishment' itself.

It happened thus. Among the domestics was a page, who had commenced his duties there as a small boy. As he was a very quiet, well-conducted lad, he remained a long time, and, in fact, grew to puberty in the house. Nobody seemed to notice the change. The lad waited, at table, in gorgeous buttons and claret-coloured cloth, and did other useful duties, quite unrestricted, about the premises. One of the elder girls however, whose inquisitive genius had discovered the interesting fact that he had hair on his belly and a thing that stood upright, essayed in secret to take advantage of this development. She induced him to put it in her on more than one occasion, with the result that she was discovered to be enceinte. The fact could not be concealed. The Brighton press took it up, and the 'select establishment' was closed forever.

My father was at this time on military service in India. A comparatively a young man, he had risen to the command of his regiment. I was not allowed to remain at home. My prayer for a governess was peremptorily refused; my mother could not endure my presence. I was packed off to a pensionnat de demoiselles near Paris. It had been specially recommended by the lady mother of two promising and 'honourable' young members of a noble house.

It was at this place that I was destined to be initiated into the more practical knowledge of mankind, so far as their sexual instincts and aptitudes are concerned. The house was large and stood in its own grounds with a short garden in front leading to the loge du concierge, and great iron gates that closed the establishment to the public road.

The lodge was tenanted by a singular individual, a hunchback, who had held the office of janitor for some years. He was a man of some forty-five years, and stood about four feet and a few inches in his boots. His hump was a sufficient disfigurement, but his ungainly ugliness, his long hair and huge hands and feet, added greatly to his weird appearance.

With all this, however, his face was not repulsive, and his manner the reverse of brutal. He was considered a perfectly harmless unfortunate. He bore an excellent character, and he had the entire confidence of Madame St. C, directress of the pensionnat.

When I became intimate with my fellow pupils, I learned that they were quite as well acquainted with natural phenomena as my old friends at Brighton, indeed more than one of the French girls made no scruple of boasting of her exploits. One in particular spoke openly of her acquaintance with a certain playfellow of the other sex, who had obtained from her such favours as only lovers are permitted.

The concierge was allowed to eke out his small revenue by the harmless privilege of retailing sweets, chocolate, etc., to the pensionnaires. The girls, during the hours of recreation, would return from his little den in the lodge with red cheeks, their mouths full of sugar-plums.

I never had the child's weakness for bonbons. I was not fond of them. The concierge and myself remained strangers for a considerable time after my arrival. I often noticed that the man took extra trouble to salute me in passing. He offered such civilities as were decorous and polite. The girls spoke sometimes of little commissions they had given him to perform for them. I soon found he was considered a safe intermediary between the world at large and the elder girls.

When I crossed from Dover to Calais, en route to Paris in the charge of a governess who collected the English pupils, I chanced to sit next to two gentlemen who conversed together of Voltaire and his works. Possessing a girl's natural curiosity, I listened.

They mentioned his allusions to Charlemagne. One exclaimed how he recognized the biting sarcasm of his style. He quoted the account given of the great king's private vices. The other cited Addison to show how little concern the great Frenchman had for virtue in itself. It was a pretty dispute. The raised their voices. I made notes, and determined to read Voltaire and judge for myself. I did not want bonbons, I wanted Voltaire.

One afternoon, I passed the door of the lodge. It was not closed. The concierge had an inner room. There was a curtain across the door between the two. I had seen one of the girls go in a few minutes before. I entered after her.

All being silent, I peeped through a corner of the heavy curtain. The hunchback was standing sideways to me, inclined a little towards the curtain. She was sitting in his big chair before him. Her clothes were disarranged and her legs and her white belly uncovered. The man's big paw was between her thighs. He was fingering her pretty slit.

What struck me most was that he had in front a huge and naked limb. It was quite twice the size of Percy's. It was very straight and stiff. The girl was sucking the big lead-coloured knob, which was rolling in and out of her mouth. He was wriggling backwards and forwards, so that sometimes almost all of the knob appeared. Then he bore forward, so that nearly the whole of it went in between her red lips. Both her hands were clasped round his long thing. She bent her head forward in little bobs. She met his movements. Both were too much occupied to think of the curtain. They thought themselves alone, safe. His eyes were half shut. He had a satanic expression of enjoyment on his face. His lips were apart. His breath came in loud hissing sobs. On the table was a packet of bonbons.

There are certain trifling things one hears when young that make a long and lasting impression. They remain for quite a lifetime. Such was the Brighton girl's description: 'A man with curly hair on his belly, and a thing twice the size of my brother Percy's that got stiff and stood up straight.' Here was one at last, the very thing of which that Brighton girl had told us.

I remained still and looked on. They were only some ten feet from me. They had no idea of my presence. He breathed hard and fast. The girl seemed to like the tickling of the paw that moved crab-like about her thighs. Presently she stopped. She drew back from the shiny thing that stood smoking in front of her young face.

He said something that I could not catch. The hunchback's limb was quite nine inches long and very thick; it was all she could do to clasp it in her delicate hands. He pushed it towards her lips again and pointed to the packet of sweets. She took the terrible morsel once more into her pretty mouth.

He continued his touches. He put his right hand upon the back of her head and pressed her to him. The whole of the big knob was now covered by her moist lips.

Suddenly, he struck her little hands from their hold and took his limb between his own finger and thumb. He drew forward her head with one hand and held her close. He pushed forward. She tried to extricate herself. In vain she struggled. The man's thing was firmly held in place in her mouth. He began gasping and stamping on the tiled floor. She choked and struggled.

He gradually stopped all movement. He looked ready to drop. Slowly he withdrew his limb, which now drooped like a dying flower. It was dripping with a white froth. She began spitting and coughing. I thought she would have been sick. I turned away, and, stealing out, ran up to the house.

That night I dreamed of a man's belly covered with hair, and a long thick limb which dangled between his legs, and could on occasion stand upright, quite twice as big as Percy's.

The third day after was a fête. Most of the girls went out to the Bois de Boulogne with the governesses. I pleaded a headache and remained within the precincts of the pensionnat. In the afternoon I strolled down to the lodge. The concierge had a window that looked up the avenue towards the house. He saw me coming, and was at the door. He asked me why I had not gone with the others. Then he asked me if I liked bonbons. He said I never came to him.

'I have no taste for sweets, but you can do me a little favour. I want a book to read. Do you think you could get me one?'

A wicked look came over his face. 'One with pictures, Mademoiselle, one of those elegant little books about the amorous fancies of young ladies and gentlemen?'

I laughed. I told him I wanted Voltaire.

He promised to try and find me a copy. He would make enquiry. Would I come in, and he would take down the title? He looked up and down the drive, and then led the way into his lodge. On a table lay his assortment of sweets. 'It is a thousand pities you do not like sweets.'

'Does little de Belvaux like sweets? She offered me some yesterday. She must be a good customer. Is it always for sweets she visits you?' I laughed again.

The little man laughed also. He looked a little uncertain. Then his face cleared. He saw I knew more than I cared to say. No doubt there were confidences among the pensionnaires. Doubtless I possessed knowledge of what went on there. He offered me a chair. He leant over me while I sat and wrote the word Voltaire. His breath came hot on my neck. The situation was novel. A strange excitement possessed me. He took the pen from my hand. As he did so, he seized my wrist and pressed it. 'What will you give me, if I get the book?'

'Whatever you like, if I am not found out.'

'All right, come in here, Mademoiselle. You are the most beautiful girl in the pension. I would do all for you for nothing. Why do you laugh? Eh bien, nearly for nothing. At any rate, for something you would like.' He led the way into the inner room;

the window that looked towards the house was covered with a muslin blind. He carefully closed the curtain behind us. I had already seen him shut the outer door. There was another door at the back of the lodge that led into the shrubbery.

He stood in front of me. He took me round the waist. Encouraged by my submission, he drew me to him. He pressed his stunted body to mine. He quite took my breath away. 'You darling! You beauty! You are not afraid. You shall know all. You shall see all. Look at this!' He quickly unfastened his trousers.

I was horribly afraid we might be interrupted.

'Don't be uneasy. There is no chance that anyone can disturb us. Here, my divine little beauty! Give me your pretty hand.' He seized it. He conveyed it to his person. He placed it upon a monstrous limb half swollen with desire. It lolled in my immodest grasp. My fingers clutched it and closed upon it. It was my initiation to a man's parts. He uncovered his belly and fully exposed all. He was covered with short, curly, dark hair. The limb throbbed and lengthened in my hand. 'Rub it like that... so... that's lovely... Oh, That's exquisite! How nicely you do it, Mademoiselle.' His member swelled and stiffened till it was more than half the length of his stunted thighs. The red and blue knob looked like a shiny ripe plum. 'Do you like that, ma belle?'

'Yes, I like it. Are you quite sure we are safe?'

'Quite safe. Go on, ma petite. I will tickle you presently.'

I continued my gentle friction, looking all the while at the strange thing I held in my hand. There was a large hairy purse below, which wagged about as I worked. I rubbed the limb up and down as he told me. It grew as hard as a piece of wood. I grasped the loose skin that could no longer cover the big plum. I pressed it back at each movement. His pleasure seemed to increase. My strokes grew quicker.

'I shall come soon. Je vais jouir! Oh... Oh... go on... go on... faster! Do not let go. Mon dieu, what pleasure! Hold tight... oh!'

With my right hand, I moved up and down as the girls milk the cows. I looked down at his naked limb. He uttered some inarticulate words. Suddenly, as I looked, a stream of thick hot stuff shot out and fell in a shower all over my hand and arm. I worked away until the thing, covered with froth, slipped out of my hand. 'Now you must promise me that book as soon as you can get it, or I shall not return to visit you.'

'I am going tomorrow to the quays on purpose. No doubt I can get it there.'

'Bonjour, alors. I will stop in for it the day after tomorrow.'

'Ah, my sweet dove, then you shall learn something more, something very nice that all young ladies like very much.'

'But I must have my book.'

'Sans faute, au revoir!'

You, Eveline – the girl they all call so delicately beautiful, so refined that they say your noble and ancient blood stands out in your face and figure – you associate with such a being as this! A hunchback, whose ugly head lies deep between his shoulders, whose dwarfed stature barely exceeds four English feet, whose ungainly legs bow apart like the opposite staves of a barrel!

Yes, Eveline pleads guilty. In art it is the rule that all should be in good proportion. All must unite to form a pleasing similarity. In lust it is the reverse. Lust is fed by disparity, by incongruity and perversity. The tall man loves the little woman. The old man's senile passion is stimulated by the immature girl. The elderly lady takes a boy of twenty to her arms and lavishes presents upon him so that his interest, if not his desire, should be involved. Endless requirements arise out of these anomalies.

Then why should the gentle, the graceful, the elegant and the delicately bred and nurtured Eveline not find a similar stimulus in dalliance with a deformed but interesting hunchback? Eveline is perverse. If you do not believe it, please close these memoirs. They are not for you.

But at the same time the hunchback is a strong man with a large limb. Eveline, even at that early age, had conceived a desire for strong men with large limbs.

Two days later, I found an opportunity during the recreation time to wander down to the porter's lodge – not for sweets.

All was quiet. The concierge was at the little window. It commanded the straight avenue to the main building. He had evidently seen me coming.

'I have come to know about my book, my Voltaire. Have you got it for me?'

'Ah, Mademoiselle, as if I could forget such a sweet and beautiful being as you. Of course I have it. Behold it here!' He held up in both hands several small volumes bound in rusty leather, and waved them triumphantly over his ugly head. He deposited them on the table. I looked at the title, Essai sur les Maeurs et l'Esprit des Nations. I picked up Volume I, Charlemagne. 'You are very good. It is what I want. Tell me the price?'

'You beautiful chérie, you have already paid me for anything I can do for you all my life long. Afterwards we will talk of the price.' He struck his great hollow chest a resounding blow. He actually bowed. Then he struck an attitude.

Had I not felt he was assuming a part, I might have believed in his vehemence. As it was, I knew well enough his vicious designs upon myself. I was on my guard. I put the little volume in my pocket.

'Well, now, my pretty one, you will give me my reward.' He pressed his long arm round my waist. He gave a side-glance up the avenue, then with his left hand he coolly undid his nether garment and shamelessly produced his big yard. 'I am a man of few words, dear Mademoiselle. Feel the weight of that!'

I looked upon his nakedness. He took my hand as he spoke. He laid it upon his member. Even as my fingers closed on his exposed nudity, his request had become impossible. Snake-like, the huge thing straightened and lengthened itself. It rose with strong, muscular jerks. It stood proudly up by itself at a small angle with his hairy belly. I looked at it, and at the man himself, with a strong inclination to laugh.

The little fellow was in no humour for jesting. His face, inflamed with the coarsest lust, was opposed to my own. His bandy legs, his squat body, his long ungainly arms appeared to me irresistibly comic. As he stood in front of me, his left arm resting on his hip, his right close to his side, and his long and vigorous limb stretched disproportionately before him, he seemed to me to resemble nothing so much as an exaggerated teapot with a straight spout.

Then a strange sensation of abandonment came over me. I felt excited beyond all self-restraint with the strangeness of the situation. I put my little hand again upon the huge spout. I felt it throb. The man's lust extended its influence to me. I was quite ready to meet his salacious advances. I seated myself in his armchair. He placed himself in front of me. I examined the big limb. I caressed it with my hand. I shook it and played with it, wondering at its size and elasticity.

'Now it is my turn. I must find where all your pretty charms hide themselves, ma belle.' He suited the action to the word. He thrust his hand up my skirts. He reached my thighs unopposed. I was not in a humour to resist his audacious proceedings. Suddenly, he threw up my clothes. He saw the most private portion of my person fully exposed to his eager view. Instantly, his face approached me. Sinking on his knees, he glued his lips to my orbit. I felt his hot tongue licking me like a dog, as he darted it backwards and forwards. Presently a sensation of voluptuous pleasure overpowered me.

I shivered, and was conscious of having experienced the climax of sensual delight. The hunchback, however, continued his employment with evident relish. Very soon I found the same tingling spasms of pleasure pervading me, and my head fell back against the soft cushion while I lay in a sort of dreamy faint. I was aroused by finding the concierge standing close before me, his long stiff member pressed against my cheek.

'Ma cherie, how you have come! You have had pleasure. Tell me, was it nice? Now you will do for me what I have done for you, ma belle, will you not? Kiss it.' He pressed the knob of his thing against my lips. I kissed it just upon the small opening which showed on the end. I opened my mouth to speak. Instantly he pushed the big member forward. The knob passed in between my moist lips. It tasted nice. I liked it. I let him have his way. I did not care, I wanted to enjoy, and so did he. I clasped the broad shaft with both hands, there was space and to spare for both. I sucked it. I thought it was delicious. He writhed about. He worked up and down. He was plainly enjoying the liveliest sensations of pleasure. I tickled all round the little hole with my tongue. I withdrew my wet lips. I could look down it a little way. The big knob grew more purple and tasted like hot cheese. I held tight to his member. I worked my hands up and down it.

'Oh! Oh! Oh, it's delicious. Go on, ma belle! Oh! Oh!'

I determined to go on. I suspected what he wanted to do. I did not mind. I would let him have his will. I continued sucking.

Sometimes he almost withdrew the red nut from my lips, and sometimes he thrust it as far as it could go into my mouth. His features worked with convulsive enjoyment. I also experienced a distinct, undefined pleasure in the act I was committing.

Presently, some slippery drops came from his limb. I felt half inclined to draw back. Before I could do so, however, he pushed forward. A perfect flood of hot stuff flew from the orifice and filled my mouth. I pumped with both hands, and sucked with my lips. I only desisted when he became calm. He groaned with ecstasy while he was discharging. He seemed a very long time about it. I received it all in my mouth. It ran from my lips in a stream.

I found an opportunity a few days later to visit the concierge. Madame St. C – – was never tired of sounding his praises. He was such a conscientious little man. He strictly observed his religious duties. He so well knew how to drive away the people who tried to gain admittance with begging letters and other means of practicing upon the unwary. In short, he was inestimable.

I only found him useful, and his singular passion excited my precocious lust for knowledge of the male sex. He was an embodiment of very ordinary erotic desire, and as such I made use of him.

He was as usual in his lodge. He welcomed me with a snort of obscene triumph. After seeing that all was secure, he invited me into his sanctum and, pulling open his blouse and trousers, produced his truncheon. I loved to grasp the long thing in my little hand. Before it could swell to its full size and be stiff and self-supporting, I put my lips to it and sucked. I thought it delicious. Evidently he was of my opinion. It quickly – too quickly for my fancy – swelled and stiffened till I could hardly close my lips over the whole of the big knob.

He was plainly enchanted with my willingness. He had no idea how lewd a well-educated, well-bred young girl can be when she is absolved from all fear of the consequences of her indiscretions.

I revelled in my discovery of the male organ in all its strength and virility. We were utterly alone. We both knew it. The fact supplied the confidence necessary for the full development of our lasciviousness. He had never found so free and capable a pupil. I had never discovered a chance so favourable to the gratification of my precocious instincts.

I have given our dialogue in English, but of course, it was carried on in French. I was accounted one of the best of the English girls, as to my fluency, and I was told frequently by my masters that my accent was exceptionally un-English and good.

It was early in the afternoon. There was a long interval from study. We felt ourselves safe. I hardly remember all that passed. The hunchback held himself in reserve. I allowed him to visit my person to greater advantage than before.

He tried to profit by my simplicity to make me a real victim to his lust. I repelled all such attempts, not entirely because I feared either the consequences or the violence of the aggressor. I had my own views. What those were will appear later.

Finding me obdurate, for I would not consent to the admission of his monstrous truncheon between my thighs, he fell again to sucking my parts. He revelled in this exercise. He reduced me to a condition of exhaustion. Then he presented his huge limb to my lips. The previous scene was repeated.

I acquired the remaining volumes of Voltaire. I stole through the shrubbery to the house, my little volumes in my pocket.

Forbidden Fruit

My stepmother took her breakfast in bed so I went to say good-morning and kiss her. She was asleep, and I had a grand view of her magnificent bosom, as being very warm weather, she had on only a low necked chemise. How long I stood to admire the snowy whiteness of the large, full bosoms, as they rose and fell under my gaze at each respiration, I know not. I was going to awaken her by kissing them, when a sudden idea pleased me better. Going to the chest of drawers, I selected a pink silk chemise, and was about to take a pair of black silk panties, only my eyes lighted upon some open-network tights of dark blue silk, a pair of golden garters, lovely blue silk hose, and a pretty pair of Turkish slippers, which looked just made for my small feet. Looking in the wardrobe, I spied a duck of a dressing gown, of almost transparent white muslin, which would show the figure inside and display the most attractive charms.

Running away to the nursery on the next corridor, I soon put off my own things, arrayed myself in the feminine attire and, looking in the mirror, opened the dressing gown and lifted up my chemise to see how I appeared beneath.

Neither my stepmother nor her sister could be called big

women. They were rather what I call the thoroughbred type, about the Venus height, and slim, with splendid bottoms that must have been cultivated by the wearing of corsets from the earliest girlhood. So, being a well grown boy, the things just suited me.

But to return to the looking-glass... it made me in love with myself, the pretty stockings, legs, garters, the slippers. But what almost took my breath away was the sight of the blue open-network tights, which my ample thighs filled up so that they fitted me to perfection, the blue showing up the flesh tint beneath in a most ravishing manner. My cock actually began to stand as I contemplated the sight of myself, and thought of the effect it might have on my mamma. I felt so wicked. As I passed along the corridor, a pretty young chambermaid remarked, as I passed her, 'La, what a pretty girl you make, Master Percy.'

'Do you think so, Patty?' I replied. 'Just look at my chemise and how I am dressed underneath.' I opened my robe to give her a view. I felt so full of devilry that I was half inclined to pull her into the nursery for a game.

'My Goodness,' she exclaimed in surprise, 'tights and all. You don't look quite comfortable, but you'll do.' Her eyes must have caught sight of my state of erection. 'See what your Mamma will think of you,' she added, with a curious look on her face.

'Kiss me then, Patty,' I said, giving her a hug and pressing my lips to hers, which she freely returned.

'Now, go along and don't be rude. Mary must have taught you something.'

'Could you teach me anything, Patty? Will you give me a lesson one day?' I asked, looking full in her eyes. 'I think you can.'

Blushing crimson, the girl got away from me, and ran into one of the rooms. Perhaps she expected to be followed, but I had other games in view. The pretty Patty was relegated to some future opportunity.

Entering Mamma's bedroom as quietly as possible, I again contemplated that divine bust till my prick was rampantly stiff. The compression of the network tights seemed only to increase the lascivious desire that inflamed it more and more every moment. I was hot all over, and my trepidation was so great, my knees knocked together. A shiver passed through my frame. Dare I kiss them? How awful should I be repulsed. Desperation gave me courage.

'My beautiful mamma, do let me kiss your lovely titties,' was all I could say, almost in a whisper as my voice quite failed, so great was my agitation. First laying my burning cheek by the side of her heaving bosom, I took a nipple between my lips. But hardly had I done so when I heard, 'My darling boy, are you kissing your Mother's bosom? I was just dreaming of my Percy. How nice of you to awake me like that.' But then, seeing my get-up, she started in surprise. 'What have you got on? My things? Oh, you funny boy!' Drawing my face to hers, she gave me such kisses as I had never had from her before. They were like flames, making my blood boil in a moment.

'Now, let me see how you have dressed yourself, Percy,' she said, opening the muslin robe. 'Ah, my chemise, too; none of your own things.' Playfully lifting it up, you should have seen her eyes start as she caught sight of my lower parts encased in her own open-net, blue tights. She saw how Mr. John Thomas was excited and seemed fit to break out at that instant. 'They are not big enough, Percy. They irritate you. Let me get them off,' she said, raising herself. As the bed-clothes fell back, I had a sight of her golden-haired mount for a moment, as she quickly pushed her chemise over it. It was perfectly maddening, but I had to act the innocent, the know-nothing. 'Come on the bed, and then I can pull them off, you silly boy. Why did you put them on?'

I mounted the bed by her side, and she removed the tights,

lingering, as I thought, unnecessarily long in doing so. 'Now, I can cuddle my boy. I haven't had you to myself for ever so long, and how this thing of yours has grown! That network chafed you my dear or it would never get like that.' Saying which, she made me lay by her side, clasping me tightly to her bosom, which heaved tumultuously. 'Poor thing, how hard and swollen it is,' she said, putting her hand on my affair. 'Let me soothe it. There... there... it will be all right soon.' But I could feel her heart beating furiously, whilst her beautiful face was aflame, and those deep blue eyes seemed to dart sparks of love as she regarded me. Imperceptibly I was drawn between her legs, and my tool throbbed against her belly.

'There is only one away, Percy, to cure that stiff thing of yours; let me put it somewhere for you, my dear.' I was passive in her hands, and she presently placed the head of my prick just inside her moist warm cunt, for she had been spending in anticipation. The effect was electric as far she was concerned, her bottom gave one big upward heave, and I felt myself at last buried to the hilt inside my stepmother. 'Mamma, Mamma, where have you put it? It feels so warm and nice.'

'Oh, my boy, my Percy, I must have you. Push it all into me, dear. I must teach you. You will find it delicious to be cuddled in that way: Ah, my love, my boy, let me feel your soul flow into mine. Let me make you feel what real love is like'

'Mamma... mamma, darling, how nice! What are we doing to each other?'

'Making love, Percy dear. Don't you like it?' She pressed closer and tighter in her arms every moment, whilst her hot, swimming cunt sucked me in ravenously at each thrust I gave.

'Making love is nice. May I do it to you often, mamma?'

Manual Of
Classical Erotology

The tribads, also called frictionists from the Greek term 'I rub' are women with whom that part of the genital apparatus, which is called the clitoris, attains such proportions that they can use it as for fornication. The clitoris, a very sensitive carbuncle (a small fleshy cone) capable of movement gets into erection with all women, not only during the coitus, the delights of which it is said to enhance immensely by increased titillation, but also in consequence of mere amorous longing. With tribads, either by a freak of nature or in consequence of frequent use, it attains immoderate dimensions. The tribad can get it in erection, enter a vulva or anus, enjoy a delicious voluptuousness, and procure if not a complete realization of cohabitation at least something very near to it with the woman who plays the passive part. What more is there to say? She plays the man's part with the omission of the ejaculation of the semen, not that this sort of coitus is an altogether dry affair, as women are in the habit of emitting their liquid during the joys of love.

This depravity of voluptuousness, whether caused by the warmth of the climate or by a peculiarity of the soil or waters, or their reasons unknown to us, was especially common with the women of Lesbos; this is attested to all the old writers. Lucian writes in his Dialogues of Courtesans: This is one of those tribads, as they are to be found in Lesbos, who will have nothing to do with men, and do the men's business with women. If such things were an every day occurrence with the Lesbian women, we must believe that they were pushed to them by natural instigation, and to allay an intolerable prurience. Who has not heard of that most celebrated queen of all tribads, Sappho, herself a Lesbian? Some authors, Maximum of Tyre the first among them, have with the best intention tried to exonerate her from his infamous vice, but hear her in Ovid (and he represents the Ancients in sentiment and feeling) repudiating her would-be apologists in Heroides, XV, 15–20: Neither the maidens of Pyrrha, nor those of Methymna, nor all the host of Lesbian beauties please me. Vile to me seems Anactoria, vile the fair Cydno, Atthis is no more so dear to my eyes as once she was, nor yet a hundred others I loved not innocently. Villain! Yours is now what belonged to many women...

Sappho speaks first in general of those that have submitted to her caresses, the maidens of Pyrrha and Methymna; then she mentions by name Anactoria, Cydno and Atthis, to whom Suidas adds Telesippa and Megara: Her favourites, whom she loved well, were three in number, Atthis, Telesippa, Megara, and for those she burnt in impure passion.

These passages from the Ancients are clear enough and do not admit of any doubt; they even assist us in explaining other sentences, which otherwise seem obscure or ambiguous, for instance the masculine Sappho of Horace, Epistles I, XIX, 28: Making plaint against the maids of her country (Odes II, XIII, 25.)

Ovid, Art of Love, III, 331: Sappho should be well known, too; what more wanton than she?

Tristia, II, 363: What was the lore Lesbian Sappho taught, but to love maids?

Martial, VII, 68: Sappho, the amorous, praised our poetess; the latter was more pure, the former not more perfect in art.

Lucian's witty and licentious pen has made famous another tribad, Megilla, in the quoted Dialogue. This Dialogue is not outrageously obscene, for it breaks off just at the moment when things would have had to be said very plainly; nevertheless, the virginal modesty of our Wieland has not dared to translate it into German. The philosopher of Samosata brings Leaena upon the scene, and makes her disclose by what artifices Megilla gained her consent.

Leaena asks Megilla, 'Are you then made like a man, and do with Demonassa as men do?'

'I have not got exactly all that, my Leaena,' answers Megilla, 'but I am not entirely without it. However, you will see me at work, and in a very pleasant manner. I have been born like all of you, but I have the tastes, the desires and something else of a man. Let me do it to you, if you do not believe me, and you will see that I have everything that men have. Give me leave to work you, and you will see.'

Leaena confesses that she at last consented, moved by her solicitations and promises, and no doubt also by the novelty of the thing. 'I let her have her way,' she says, 'yielding to her entreaties, seconded by a magnificent necklace and a robe of fine linen. I took her in my arms like a man; she went to work caressing me, panting with excitement and evidently experiencing the extreme of pleasure.'

Clonarion asks her inquisitively, 'But what did she do to you

Leaena, and how did she manage?'

Leaena eludes the question. 'Do not ask me anything more; these are nasty doings; by Urania, I shall not breathe a word more!' she answers, to the great regret of the reader, who would like to penetrate further this mystery.

Amongst the tribads still to be named is Philaenis, the same, no doubt, who according to Lucian (Amores, Ch. 28; Works Vol. V, p. 88) wrote about erotic postures: Let our women's apartments be filled by women like Philaenis, dishonoured by androgenic loves! However, writers as a rule touch upon these points more lightly than is agreeable to the curiosity of the reader. For the same reason, the too great reserve of Seneca (Controversia, II) is to be regretted, where he says at the end: Hybreas having to plead in favour of a man who had surprised and killed a tribad, described the grief of the husband; on such a subject one must not ask for a too particular investigation.

Much more complete, full and explicit is our good friend of Bilbilis (Martial) who discloses the tribadic doings of Balba in I, 91 so clearly that it could not be done better: As no one, Bassa, never saw you go with men; as rumour never assigned you a lover, as every office about you was fulfilled by a troop of women, no man ever coming nigh you, you seemed to us, I admit, a very Lucretia. But, oh! Shame on you, Bassa, you were a fornicator all the time! You dare to conjoin the private parts of two women together, and your monstrous organ of love feigns the absent male. You have contrived a miracle to match the Theban riddle: that where no man is, there adultery should be!

Surely it is clear enough what Bassa did, in conjoining the privates of two women together. By no means! There are expounders, and very good ones, too, who have quite misunderstood this very easy passage, and have imagined that Bassa misused women by introducing into their vagina a leathern contrivance, an olisbos, a godemiche; we shall speak at the end of this chapter of this kind of pleasure, but it was quite unknown to Bassa, who simulated the man in her own person.

Nothing could be more monstrous than the libertine passion of Philaenis; she did not content herself with introducing her stiff clitoris into the vulva of tribads: Tribad of tribads, you, Philaenis, you are well justified in calling her your mistress whom you work (Martial, VII) or into those of other young girls, and to get a dozen of them under her in a day, but she even pediated boys: Philaenis the tribad pedicates boys and stiffer than a man in one day works eleven girls. (Martial, VII, 67.) In order to leave nothing untasted in the way of virile lusts, she was also a cunnilingue; same epigram, at the end: After all that, when she is in good feather, she does not suck, that is too feminine; she devours right out girls' middle parts. May all the gods confound you, Philaenis, who think it manly work to lick the vulva.

Philaenis, when overmuch in rut, caused herself also to be served by cunnilingues; this is clear enough: When Diodorus, wanting the Tarpeian crowns, left Pharos behind and sailed for Rome, Philaenis vowed that to celebrate her mate's return an innocent maid should lick her, such a one as the chaste Sabine women still cherish. (Martial, IX, 41.) She vowed if her husband returned to have her vulva licked by a young girl, well known for her innocence and chastity. To have it done by prostitutes was, for Philaenis, nothing new; she wanted on that occasion to experiment with a virgin, exactly like men, who always want something new and strange to spur their lust. How rare it was for women to use other women for that purpose appears from Juvenal II, 47–49: There will no other instance be found so abominable in our sex; Taedia does not lick Cluvia, nor Flora Catulla.

But what could you find stronger, more energetic and plainer to enlighten the reader completely on this subject than the following verses (Satire VI, 303–33) where Juvenal's ire against the tribadic orgies in Rome breaks out in words of fire:

At night they stop their litters here, make water here, and flood with long siphons the Goddess' statue, and ride turn and turn about and go through the motions under the eye of the conscious moon; then they make for home. When the morning light returns, you walk through your wife's piss, to visit your great friends. Known are the secret rites of the Bona Dea, when the flute excite their wanton loins, when drunk with music and wine they rush along, whirling their locks and howling, these Maenads of Priapus! How they yearn for instant copulation! How their voice trembles with passionate longing! What floods of old wine gush down their dripping thighs! A prize is offered, and Laufeia challenges the brothel-master's girls, and wins the first place for nimble hips; while she herself is mad for the pleasure Medullina's artful movements give her. Amongst these dames merit carries off the palm from noble blood. There nothing must be feigned, all must be done in very truth and deed – enough to set on fire, however chilled with age, Laomedon's son and old Nestor with his rupture! Then is seen mere lust that will brook not a moment's more delay, women in her bare brutality, while from every corner of the subterranean hall rises the reiterated cry: 'The hour is come, admit the men.' Is the lover asleep! She bids the first young man at hand to snatch up his hood and come at once. Is none to be found? Resort is had to slaves. No hope of slaves? A water-carrier will be hired to come. If he comes not, and men there are none, she will not wait an instant more but get an ass to mount her from behind.

The tribadic orgies were divided into two kinds. In one of

them the Roman dames, giving free course to their lust, defiled the altar of chastity; in the other they celebrated the mysteries of the Bona Dea. You see in the first place the tribads go at night in litters to the altar of chastity, there pass their water against the statue of the Goddess, and having perhaps squirted their urine up to her face, they at all events wet the area all about (their husbands walking right through it in the morning, when they go to see their patrons) and then they ride or allow themselves to be ridden alternately. Other ladies go to celebrate the mysteries of the Bona Dea, well known to the public since the adventures of Clodius. You observe them rousing themselves with the sounds of flutes and trumpets, as also with fumes of wine, to undergo valiantly the joust of mutual love; you see their amorous frenzy, their hair flying in the wind; you note their sighs of longing, and how they piss with excitement. A prize is set, as in the feast of Pope Alexander VI, to be given to the most intrepid tribad. Laufeia calls upon the brothel-girls to let her ride them, and carries off the crown. There is none there of better heart than Medullina, expert in plying her loins and buttocks. There all etiquette ceases, mistresses and servants alike contest for the palm of obscenity; there is no sham, all is tribadic reality. But, after all, finally nature got the upper hand again, the tribad disappeared, and the woman became again a woman, leaving alone tribadism, as a phantom only of pleasure, and not satisfying them. From all parts a cry is raised, 'Now is the time for the men to come in, go and find young men. If you cannot find any, then slaves will do. If they are lacking, bring the first men you can find in the streets!'

On the origin of tribads, Phedrus has a fable:

Another asked the reason why tribads and cinedes were created. The old man thus explained: The same Prometheus, modeller of the human clay, that if it knocks against Fortune is shivered in pieces, once when he had been fashioning all day long separately those parts that modesty keeps hidden beneath a garment, to fit them presently to the bodies he had made, was unexpectedly invited to supper by Bacchus. There he imbibed the nectar in large drafts, and returned late home with unsteady foot; then what with fumes of wine and sleepiness, he joined the female parts to male bodies, and fixed male members on to the women. Thus it is we find lust indulging in depraved pleasures.

The masculine member applied to women is evidently that clitoris of such proportions in erection, that the tribads can use it like a penis; the female apparatus fitted on to a man is nothing else but the posterior orifice, which itches in the case of cinedes, just as the vulva titillates women. Tribads were not wanting in the time of Tertullian; he calls them 'frictrices' in De Pallio, Ch. r: Look at those she-wolves who make their bread by the general incontinence; amongst themselves they are also frictrices. The same author says in the De Resurrectione Carnis, Ch. 16: I do not call a cup poisoned which has received-ed the last sigh of a dying man; I give that name to one that has been infected by the breath of a high-priest of Cybelé, of a gladiator, of an executioner, and I ask if you will not refuse it as you would such persons' actual kisses.

Nor was the trade of tribad out of date in the time of Aloysia Sigaea: 'Nay! Do not think me,' says Tullia, 'worse than others. This taste is spread almost over the universe. Italians, Spaniards, French, are all alike as to the tribadism of their women; if they were not ashamed, they would always be rutting in each other's arms. (Dialogue II.)

More, she quotes herself some examples of the hot transports of tribads in Dialogue VII:

Enemunda, the sister of Fernando Porcio, was very beautiful, and not less so was a friend of hers, Francisca Bellina. They frequently slept together in Fernando's house. Fernando laid secret snares for Francisca; the latter knew that he desired to have her, and was proud of it. One morning the young man, stung by his desires, rose with the sun, and stepped out upon the balcony to cool his hot blood. He heard the bed of his sister in the next room cracking and shaking. The door stood open; Venus had been kind to him and had made the girls careless. He enters; they do not see him, blinded and deafened by pleasure. Francisca was riding Enemunda, both naked, at full gallop.

'The noblest and most powerful mentulas are every day after my maidenhead,' said Francisca, 'I should select the finest, dear, but for you, so fain am I to gratify your tastes and mine.' Whilst speaking she was jogging her vigorously.

Fernando threw himself naked into the bed; the two girls, almost frightened to death, dared not stir. He draws Francisca, exhausted by her ride, into his arms and kisses her. 'How dare you, abandoned girl,' he says, 'violate my sister, who is so pure and chaste? You shall pay me for this; I will revenge the injury done to our house. Answer now to my flames as she has answered to yours.'

'My brother! My brother!' cries Enemunda. 'Pardon two lovers, and do not betray us to slander!'

'No one shall know anything,' he answered, 'let Francisca make me a present of her treasure, and I will make you both a present of my silence.'

The conversation of Ottavia with Tullia, acting as tribad, in the same work (Dialogue II) is still bolder and more to the point:

TULLIA: Pray do not draw back; open your thighs.

OTTAVIA: Very well! Now you cover me entirely, your mouth against mine, your breast against mine, your belly against mine; I will clasp you as you are clasping me.

TULLIA: Raise your legs, cross your thighs over mine, I will show you a new Venus; to you quite new. How nicely you obey! I wish I could command as well as you execute!

OTTAVIA: Ah! Ah! My dear Tullia, my queen! How you push! How you wriggle! I wish those candles were out; I am ashamed there should be light to see how submissive I am.

TULLIA: Now mind what you are doing! When I push, you rise to meet me; move your buttocks vigorously, as I move mine, and lift up as high as ever you can! Is your breath coming short?

OTTAVIA: You dislocate me with your violent pushing; you stifle me; I would not do it for anyone but you.

TULLIA: Press me tightly, Ottavia, take...there! I am all melting and burning. Ah! Ah! Ah!

OTTAVIA: Your affair is setting fire to mine, draw back!

TULLIA: At last, my darling, I have served you as a husband; you are my wife now!

OTTAVIA: I wish to heaven you were my husband! What a loving wife I should make! What a husband I should have! But you have inundated my garden; I am all bedewed! What you been doing, Tullia?

TULLIA: I have done everything up to the end, and from the dark recesses of my vessel love in blind transports has shot the liquor of Venus into your maiden barque.

Leo Africanus, in his Description of Africa (p. 336, edition Elzevir, of 1632) mentions the tribads of Fez: But those who have more common sense, call these women (he is speaking of witches) 'Sahacat' a word which corresponds with the Latin 'fricatrices', because they take their pleasure with each other. I cannot speak more plainly without offending decency. When good-looking women visit them, these witches fall at once in hot love with them, not less hot than the love of young men for girls, and they ask them in the guise of the devil to pay them by suffering their embraces. So it happens that very often when they think they have been obeying the behests of demons, they have really only had to do with witches. Many, too, pleased with the game they have played, seek of their own impulse to enjoy intercourse again with the witches, and under pretence of being ill, summon one of them or send their unfortunate husbands to fetch her. Then the witches seeing how matters stand, asseverate that the wife is possessed by a demon, and can only be liberated by joining their association.

You ask whether tribads are still to be found in our day? If there are none now, there certainly were some in existence in Paris only a short time before the Great Revolution, if we are to trust the author of Gynaeology (III, p. 428) there was a veritable college of tribads in Paris who went by the names of Vestals, holding regular meetings in particular localities. There were a great many members, and of the highest classes. They had their statutes with respect to admission and the affiliated were divided into three degrees – aspirants, postulants and initiates. Before the postulant could be admitted to the secret of the order, she had to undergo for three days a difficult probation. Shut up in a cell covered with lewd tapestries, and ornamented with carved Priapi of magnificent proportions, she had to keep up a fire with I do not know how many ingredients, and arranged in such a manner that it would go out if there was taken too much or too little of any of the materials. On the four altars of the temple, which was adorned with statues of Sappho (of the Lesbians she had loved) and of the Chevalier d'Eon, who for so many years successfully dissimulated his sex, and with splendid hangings, perpetual fires were burning. Kept English women, too, did not recoil at tribadism as the same author states (III, p. 394). He affirms that not long before the close of the last century, confederacies of tribads called 'Alexandrine Confederacies' were still in existence in London, though in a small number only.

Enough now of those who are, strictly speaking, included under the name of tribads; but the word has a more extended signification. The term is also applied to those women who in default of a real mentula, make use of their finger or of a leathern contrivance, which they introduce into their vulva, and so attain enjoyment. Germany, I have lately heard, has been ringing with complaints about this abuse. As regards the leathern engine, called by the Greeks olisbos, the women of Miletus, above all others, made it their instrument of pleasure. Aristophanes, in the Lysistrata, 108–110: For since the day the Milesians left us in the lurch, not an olisbos have I set eyes on, eight inches long, that might give us its leathern aid...

Cratinus says: Lewd women will be using the olisbos... and Hesychius quotes the same passage. If you ask whether modern women, who have suffered the wrong of seeing their beauty slighted, actually have recourse to this leathern substitute, Aloysia Sigaea (Dialogue II) shall answer you: The Milesian women made for themselves imitations in leather, eight inches long and thick in proportion. Aristophanes tells us that the women of his day habitually made use of such. And to this very day Italian, Spanish and Asiatic women honour this instrument with a place in their toilet apparatus; it is their most precious possession, and one very highly appreciated.

It is an undoubted fact that the Roman matrons cherished a species of inoffensive snake, the cold skin of which served as a refrigerator in summer, Martial, VII, 86: If Glacilla winds an icy serpent around her neck...' Lucian Alexander, Works, Volume IV, p. 259: In that country one sees serpents of an enormous size, but so quiet and mild that they are fondled by women, sleep with the children, do not get angry on being trodden on or handled, and suck the nipples of the breast like a nursling.

This being so, our eminent Bottiger was probably right when he wrote on page 454 of his Sabina, a profoundly scientific work in German, that very likely snakes were used as instruments to satisfy the lubricity of amorous women. You may understand now what happened or what might have happened to Atia, the mother of Augustus, of whom Suetonius wrote: I read in the treatise of Asclepiades of Mendé called the Theologumena, how Atia the mother of Augustus, having gone at midnight to the temple of Apollo, to assist at a solemn sacrifice, fell asleep, and so did the other women present; how a serpent suddenly glided close to her, and after some little time withdrew again, and how on waking she purified herself, as though she had left the arms of her husband. (Augustus, Ch. 94.)

There would be nothing surprising in the fact that a serpent of that sort should have investigated even without incitation on Atia's part, a certain locality which was well known to it by the lubricity of other women, and that Atia felt on awakening the very same sensation as though she had undergone real coitus.

The Dialogues Of Luisa Sigea

OTTAVIA. Thy bed contains us now, the same bed in which thou hast so often desired that I should pass the nights, when thy husband Callias was absent, not merely with thee, but even within thy embraces.

TULLIA. I have occasionally spent sleepless nights, because thy love, with which I have been wasting myself away, having entered all my veins, has consumed me as fire.

OTTAVIA. Thou didst love me? And thou lovest me no more?

TULLIA. I do love thee, cousin, and I am dying wretchedly.

OTTAVIA. Thou art really dying, thou for whom I would lay down my own life to save thine? What sadness of mind is this? For I have no reason to doubt but that thou art in good bodily health.

TULLIA. As thou lovest Caviceo, so I love thee.

OTTAVIA. Speak clearly: what enigmatical discourse is this?

TULLIA. But thou also lay first aside from thee so comely, so handsome, so tender, whatever modesty is in thee.

OTTAVIA. When thou didst wish me to get into thy bed

stark naked (and I have done so), such as I am to enter it, thou toldest me, the moment I am to be delivered to Caviceo's enjoyment, did I not sufficiently divest myself of all shame?

TULLIA. Indeed the Queen of the Lydians formerly said: 'I have taken off my tunic and at the same time laid aside all shame.

OTTAVIA. I have under thy exhortation overcome my timidity, and under thy guidance mastered myself.

TULLIA. Give me a loving kiss, oh fondest of maidens.

OTTAVIA. Why not? As many as thou wilt, and as thou wilt.

TULLIA. Oh divinely shaped mouth! Oh eyes brighter than light! Oh type of Venus.

OTTAVIA. And thou removest the blankets? I know not what I should fear, what I should beseech of thee, wert thou not Tullia. Here I am stark naked: what else dost thou require?

TULLIA. Oh ye Gods! How I should like ye would grant me the power of playing the role of Caviceo!

OTTAVIA. What's that? Shall Caviceo lay hold of my paps, as thou dost now? Shall he accumulate kisses upon kisses incessantly? Shall he attack my lips, neck and breasts with similar bites?

TULLIA. These will be, my soul, the preludes to the fight, and the courses at the flowing banquet of Venus.

OTTAVIA. Hold off, thou art running thy hand over my whole person, thou art now thrusting it lower down. Why art thou fondling my thighs? Ah! Ah! Ah! Tullia! Pray, why art thou fumbling that spot? Nor dost thou remove thy piercing eyes from it.

TULLIA. I am viewing this field of Venus with curious longing; it is neither wide nor spacious, but full of the sweetest delights; inexhaustible Venus shall herein waste away the force of thy Mars.

OTTAVIA. Thou art not mad, Tullia? Oh, wert thou Caviceo, I should be no longer in safety, for astraddle on me as thou art, why dost thou want to inspect all my members behind and before? There is nothing in me that surpasses thy own beauty. Take a peep at thyself, if thou wilt see something thou mayest both love and ought to extol.

TULLIA. I would be silly and not modest, were I to deny that I am gifted with some beauty; I am, moreover, in the prime of life; I have just passed my twenty-sixth year, Callias has had but one child by me. If any pleasure may be afforded to thy senses on my part, enjoy it; I do not oppose it.

OTTAVIA. Nor I either. Enjoy me as much as ever thou mayest, I consent to it. But I am well aware that no pleasure can accrue to thee from a maiden as I am, nor to me from thee either, even though thou really wast as a marvellous garden of all delicacies and attractions.

TULLIA. Thou hast indeed a garden, wherein Caviceo will feed on the most delicious fruits.

OTTAVIA. I have no garden which thou hast not likewise abounding in the same fruit. Now, what is it thou callest a garden? Where is it situated? What are these fruits?

TULLIA. I perceive thy roguery. Of course, thou who retaliatest on my garden was as well acquainted with thy own, as I with mine.

OTTAVIA. Perhaps thou designated by this word that spot which thou art clutching in thy right hand, teasing with thy fingers and tickling with the ends of thy nails, to excite a desire in me?

TULLIA. That's so, cousin. Having no experience of it, thou ignorest its use, but I shall try and make thee know it.

OTTAVIA. Should I learn it exclusive of my marriage, I would not be chaste, nor worthy of thy love, being then so unlike thee. But tell me, what would that use be? First of all, stretch thyself in bed, because, seated up as thou art, thou art only causing both of us inconvenience.

TULLIA. I shall endeavour to satisfy thee. Now prick up thy ears: for the more attentively thou listens to this discourse, so much the more easily and frequently will Caviceo erect. May Venus grant it! Accept the omen, Ottavia.

OTTAVIA. I do accept it. Thou art in roars of laughter? I do not really see what harm there is in these words.

TULLIA. But thou shall feel what delights I wish thy garden through this omen.

OTTAVIA. Thou art speaking to one deaf.

TULLIA. Venus grant that thou mayest hear and comprehend! This garden of thine, which I hope may never lack the flowers and fruit of Venus, in spring or winter, is that spot, cousin, which a moss veils, with thee it is down, under the hillock of the lower belly; they call it the pubis. This down is a sign that, in the girl it first begins to bloom, her maidenhead is fit for a man and ripe for Venus. The Latins called it cymba, navis, concha, saltus, clitorium, porta, ostium, portus, interfemineum, lanuvium, virginal, vagina, facandrum, vomer, ager, sulcus, larva, annulus. Julia, the daughter of Augustus, was wont to say that she bore Agrippa children, resembling her husband as near as possible, because she never conveyed travellers in her bark unless it was already full. I hope, cousin, that thou wilt come from my embraces tonight more enlightened than if thou had been sleeping upon the Parnassus, so that thou canst make love also in Greek; thou hast learned it out of Juvenal.

OTTAVIA. I would rather be instructed like thee, cousin,

than satiated with voluptuousness. When I consider how young and learned thou art, I should like thou wert Caviceo. How gladly would I then lay before thee all the fineries of my person!

TULLIA. Dear maid, hug me, me who am mad in love with thee. Allow my eyes and handlings a free scope, everywhere it is possible. Caviceo will lose nothing thereby, nor thou either. Unhappy me! How vain are my efforts, accordingly as I advance! How madly I love thee!

OTTAVIA. Appease thy love and yield to that passion of thy soul. That which is thy desire is mine also.

TULLIA. Therefore, bestow this garden of thine upon me, that I may be its mistress, withal it would be useless to me, as I have no key to open its gate, nor hammer to strike it in, nor foot to enter it.

OTTAVIA. To be sure I present thee with it, being myself wholly thine. Do I own any right which is not also thine? Thou art falling upon me: what does it mean?

TULLIA. Pray do not draw back; open thy thighs.

OTTAVIA. So I have. Thou hast me now all to thyself: thou art pressing thy mouth against mine, thy bosom against mine, and thy womb against my womb: would I could entwine 'round thee, as thou entwines 'round me.

TULLIA. Lift thy legs higher up, set thy thighs over mine. I make thee acquainted with a new Venus, as thou art a new hand. How nicely thou givest in! Could I but command as well as thou obeyest!

OTTAVIA. Ah! Ah! My Tullia, my darling, my lady, how thou art thumping me! How thou art shaking me! Would those candles were extinguished; I am ashamed, having this light witness of my submission.

TULLIA. Look to what thou art about. Every time I bounce

down, thou bounce up; imitate me in putting life into thy buttocks; heave them as high as thou canst. Art thou afraid of losing mettle?

OTTAVIA. Thou art truly worrying me by these repeated shocks; thou art smothering me. Could I bear such a savage assault from anybody else?

TULLIA. Hold, squeeze tighter, Ottavia; receive... lo, lo it is spilling... my heart is burning. Ah! Ah! Ah!

OTTAVIA. The garden is setting mine on fire, withdraw!

TULLIA. Cheer up, my goddess, I have been to thee a husband! My spouse! My wife!

OTTAVIA. Would to God thou wert my husband! What a loving wife thou wouldst have! What a fond husband I should own! Indeed, thou hast even watered my garden with rain, I feel all wet by it; what filth hast thou spilt over me, Tullia?

TULLIA. Of course I have finished the job and love has, with wild impetuosity, cast the Venereal sap from out the dark well in my bark into thy virginal skiff. But has ever keener voluptuousness tickled thy senses, to thy innermost bowels?

OTTAVIA. Truly, I beg to observe I have experienced hardly any voluptuousness from what thou hast just done me. I was somewhat troubled on feeling thee so over transported, and a few sparks of thy flame lit up that spot, which thou wast bruising by thy frequent bounces. But these rather pointed out the conflagration than consumed. Now, do tell me, Tullia, does this humour of thine also usurp other women's souls, causing them to loathe after, and assail, little girls?

TULLIA. Unless they are stupid and have hearts of stone, they loathe after, and assail, them. For what is more charming than a rosy and refined young lady, such as thou art thyself? Thus Iphis, before she was changed into a boy, burnt for Ianthe:

Iphis loves she despairs of enjoying, and this but increases her flames, so a maid burns for a maid, and scarcely retaining her tears, 'What solution awaits me?' she said, 'me whom an incomprehensible and strange love, a new Venus masters. Had the Gods wished to spare me, they should have doomed me to perish. Since they have not willed my death, they might at least mete me out a flame compatible with nature.

Neither a father's harshness, nor herself is opposed to thy request,

And still thou must not enjoy her: and however things may turn,

Thou canst not be happy, even though Gods and men set to the work.

Today again my vows were all hear,

And the propitious Gods have given me whatever they could.

What I wish for, both father, Ianthe, and my future father-in-law wish for;

But nature, being more powerful than all these, is unwilling;

She alone is noxious to me. Lo the longed for time comes

And the wedding-day at hand; and Ianthe shall be soon mine:

No, it shall not be; we shall be thirsty in the midst of waters.

Oh nuptial Juno and thou Hymen, why do ye come to these solemnities?

Who shall lead as bridegroom, both of us being brides?'

I must indeed acknowledge, Ottavia, we are nearly all of us great libertines. Dost thou hear the Petronian Quartilla? 'May I incur the wrath of Juno, if ever I remember I was a maiden. While as yet a mere child, I got corrupted with my playmates, and then, accordingly as the years succeeded one another, I became attached to grown up youths, until I have finally arrived at the present age.'

OTTAVIA. Up to this day, and thou art well aware of it, Tullia, I have been leading a chaste life in body and soul. Thou callest me a simpleton and a fool. But I already feel tainted with lust, and the desire of Venus. I am extremely grateful to fiery Venus that my wedding day is almost at hand; because I really think that, when men sleep with us, it is only in their embraces we can obtain a true and solid voluptuousness.

TULLIA. Thou reasonest well and thou shalt learn so next: May the Lampsacian entertainment make thee happy! But the swelling out of the belly, child-bearing and delivery usually follow the over free sports of men with us, and 'turgentis verbera caulae'. Outside of marriage this passion which invites and urges little girls unto complete coition is fraught with dangers and misfortunes. On the contrary, everything gets on free and joyfully under Hymen. The newly married girls cover their heads with the same veil as they also cover all the crimes of their lust; under this veil, they conceal themselves the more easily from the sharp eyes of the law and the public. Therefore, Ottavia, maidens and those leading a single life must seek by another way that voluptuousness, towards which thou beholdest all species of animated beings, as Lucretius says, borne by an impetuosity which nothing, save the force of Venus, can soothe. It is then nowise strange that a maiden should be loved by a maiden: since even the greatest of Heroes formerly found, in their own sex, stimulants of their lust.

OTTAVIA. But thou who hast tasted a man art not a maiden; thou art free to enjoy entire pleasure. How is it thou art in love with me? That thou art seeking pleasure in that way by which Venus outwits Venus?

TULLIA. My friend, Pomponia, at first (for I will keep no secrets with thee) began thus, some years ago, to strain herself freely though licentiously with me, as we were very intimate with each other since infancy: no woman was ever more lascivious or artful at the same time. My soul abhorred such a thing from the beginning, but by little and little I became accustomed to what I used to call a torture. Pomponia would set me the example, not only accommodating the enjoyment of her person to my petulance, but also ordering me, showing herself an exceedingly mild courtesan towards me, and a procuress towards herself. When I had at length made a long practice of this enjoyment, I could hardly get on without it. But, my darling Ottavia, since thou hast driven thy countless darts through my heart, I have been so transported with thy love, I am so inflamed with it still, that beside thee I look contemptuously on all things else, even my own Callias; and I fancy every pleasure reposes within thy embraces. Do not consider me on this account worse than others. For this caprice is rooted in almost every part of the earth. The Italian, Spanish and French women love one another: and were they not held back by shame, they would all rush headlong one against the other in rut. Formerly this custom was familiar especially among the Lesbians; Sappho enhanced this name, and thus dignified it. How often have Andromede, Athis, Anactorie, Mnais and Girino, her doties, worried her loins! The Greeks call heroines of this kind, tribades; the Latins style them frictrices and subagitatrices. But Philaenis is looked upon as having invented it, because she hopelessly abandoned herself to this pleasure; and as having by her practice, for she was a woman of high renown, advised the women and little girls about her of the use of voluptuousness unknown up to her time. They called them tribades, because they tread and get trodden; frictrices, from the rubbing together of bodies; subagitatrices, from the more violent movement.

OTTAVIA. Faith! Thou art saying queer things, but they are at least as funny as absurd. Consequently thou shalt have already gained the reputation both of tribade, frictrice and subagitatrice: but what name wilt thou give me?

TULLIA. My tender, sappy, lovely Cypris. At least I have meddled with nothing whereby thy integrity might be lessened, by which I might have broken in this little door of thine, in order to gather the flower of thy maidenhead.

OTTAVIA. How couldst thou, eh?

TULLIA. The Milesian women were wont to make themselves leather mentules eight inches long and broad in proportion. Aristophanes informs us that the women of his time were wont to use them. Even nowadays among Italian, especially Spanish as also Asiatic women, this tool plays a considerable role in the female boudoir, as being their most precious piece of furniture: it is held in the highest esteem.

OTTAVIA. I don't understand it or its use.

TULLIA. Later on thou shalt; but let our conversation turn to something else.

Tips To The Maidens

It was a beautiful May morning in Paris as Clara walked to the quarters of her new governess, Donna Maria. The governess had been affectionate but firm in the month Clara had been in her charge. This morning, Clara was excited because Donna Maria had said she had a surprise for her.

When Clara entered Donna Maria's boudoir, she saw on the table a full set of undergarments beautifully decorated with silk ribbons, together with pretty stockings, all marked with initials CL.

At their sight, she could not refrain from exclaiming, 'How pretty.'

'They are yours.'

'Mine?'

'I made them for you during my spare time.'

'Oh, thank you, dear,' she said, embracing the governess rapturously.

'What else could your Maria do for you?' She accentuated that phrase so that Clara was deeply moved.

Still closely embraced, she said caressingly, 'Thanks again, dearest Mary.' And moved by the same wish, they kissed each other with lips open and trembling, notwithstanding their saliva did not mix.

Clara, out of respect, and Maria not wishing to offend, were restrained from proceeding to extremes. Lustfulness, however, had been aroused and was raging in the veins of these women.

'So they are all for me?'

'Yes, and everything I have is yours, darling.'

'Will the chemise fit me?'

'They were made to measure.'

'But how do you know, not having tried them on me?'

'I kept it a secret or they would not have been a surprise.'

'That's true, I must try them.'

'Yes, honey. Then go to my chamber and undress, but hurry and hurry and before trying on the corset, call me up.'

Clara took the garments with her and entered the adjoining room.

When Maria was left alone, she exclaimed rapturously, 'Mine! She's going to be mine.' Educated in a French convent, her teachers had soon taught her all the pleasures of love, not teaching her the horror of man but fear of the consequences of carnal contact between the different sexes. Pleasure without dishonour was the motto of their teachings and Maria had enjoyed these pleasures all her life without losing her material virginity.

Maria seated on a sofa facing a mirror, strained her ear to catch the sounds of the undressing girl and, knowing that eloquence and hardiness develops along with lustfulness, wanted to be ready to receive the virgin in a befitting manner. So she lifted up her skirts, letting out a pair of beautiful legs clad in handsome silk stockings. She smiled at the reflection of her own beauty, and a few seconds later slid towards one end of the sofa, reclining her head and entering her finger, wet with saliva, in the mossy and beautiful grotto of love that showed under the silky and curly hair.

Soon she was agitating her clitoris and the smile dissolved in pleasure. Her eyes roamed about the room ravishingly and she murmured coaxingly, 'Clara, Clara, darling... do you want... it's yours... take it... my honey... come on, have it all!' Feeling the crisis approaching, she restrained herself, murmuring, 'I am a thief... this is hers and I mustn't throw it like that.'

At length her desire overcame all power of restraint and Maria unheedingly continued the friction, desiring only to spend. She was nearing the convulsion of pleasure and exclaimed loudly, 'This is dying of pleasure... Clara, come darling!'

'I'm coming,' replied the girl from within.

'Ah...' Then she lowered her skirts and calmed by the operation, laughed and said playfully, 'Well, aren't you through yet.'

'Here I am,' said Clara, entering the boudoir. 'Don't look at me, I'm ashamed.'

'You darling.' Clara was dressed in a fine chemise and blue stockings. She was beautiful and provocative. The eyes of Maria shone with desire. 'How pretty you are!'

'And you, how handsome.'

Instinctively they embraced each other.

'Leave the corset on the chair.'

Clara obeyed her.

'Sit down here on the couch. I don't get tired admiring you.' Maria knew perfectly well that nothing provoked people more than talking audaciously; if Clara became hot, her victory was a matter of an instant. And if she was not hot, it was of the utmost necessity that she should be heated and that was what Maria was going to do. 'Are you pleased with my gift?'

'Very.'

'Does the chemise fit you?'

'Perfectly; it fits me like a glove.'

'I think the decolletté is a little too wide.'

'No.'

'Yes, look, the bosoms show too much. How pretty and round they are...' She began to kiss them whilst Clara lowered her eyes letting her do as she pleased. 'What have you here?'

'Where?'

'On this nib, looks like an insect bite.'

'I don't know.'

'What a pity, you must take care of it... a little saliva will do it good...' She began to suck quite innocently, the right nib, whilst affectionately titillating the other breast.

Clara began to experience an unknown pleasure, rolled her eyes wildly and pressed her lips tightly together, breathing very hard.

Maria, noting everything, was gaining ground rapidly and increased with her caresses the nervous excitement that had overtaken Clara. 'Poor little thing, to have such a pretty nib hurt. It looks like a fresh strawberry. How sweet. Recline yourself, dearie, you'll feel better.'

Clara obeyed passively, sighing.

Maria thought the time had come to play her last and strongest card and discreetly put her hand under Clara's chemise looking for the hairy mount of the beautiful girl.

Clara instinctively opened her legs wider.

This was sufficient for Maria. Her hand went directly to the cleft, which was moist with spend, and began to play with her clitoris, naming it caressingly Love Nest, Happiness, Paradise, and so forth.

Clara could not say a word. She only murmured brokenly, 'My God, what ails me?' Suddenly, after a heavy sigh, she said, 'How foolish we have been. Education has sealed my lips too long! And bashfulness has blinded me.'

'How many hours of pleasure have we lost?'

'Don't stop... this is heaven! Maria, do you love me?'

'I adore you. And you?'

'I worship you. Will you always be mine?'

'All my life.'

'Swear it.'

'I swear.'

'And so do I. Oh, Maria, darling, I'm spending... all... my life...'

'Wait a moment.'

'I can't,' said Clara, writhing with pleasure.

'Go on then darling, do go on.'

'Oh, honey, this is a paradise on earth... what happiness...'

From that moment you could only hear the breathing of the two, almost suppressed by the intensity of pleasure and the inarticulate groans of happiness. And this was only the preface of the enchanting scene which was to take place between these two happy girls.

We must necessarily return to Maria's room, where we left Clara. The disordered bed clearly proved that love had fought strenuously there. Maria was undressed except for her chemise and her eyes shown with pleasure.

Clara was lying on the bed on her back and with her legs open. Under her buttocks she had a pillow.

Maria jumped on the bed and, blind with passion, placed herself over Clara, gathering up her chemise and revealing the most splendid buttocks you could dream of. 'Let's put our breasts together.'

'Tongues are much better.'

The two lovers were caressing each other madly.

'For more than eight years I have hoped to possess you,' said Maria.

'I have had the same feeling for the past two years.'

'I know everything and I'll teach you all the pleasures. Do you really love me?'

'Madly. And you?'

'Blindly. Swear that you will belong to no other woman?'

'I do.'

Uproarious love followed these words and sighs were audible. The swaying increased gradually. 'Do you feel me?'

'Yes.'

'Where?'

'Over my clitoris... go on...'

'I feel you also, don't stop.'

I could overhear no more, the sighs drowned everything.

Suddenly the pleasure of dissolution made their bodies rigid, and, for that morning, all was over.

The Romance Of Lust

When night came I was all curiosity to know how my dear mistress had carried on matters with Lizzie. She told me that Lizzie had been somewhat nervous at first, but she had spoken kindly to her, told her how her amiable and loving conduct after her first whipping had won her affection; that she did not mean to be so severe as on the former occasion, but that discipline must be kept up.

'So come, my dear girl, drop off your frock, as I shall mine, that the bundle of clothes may be out of the way, as well as to avoid their being creased.'

Seeing that Lizzie still trembled a little after she had dropped her gown, she took her in her arms and, kissing her lovingly, desired her not to be afraid, she would not punish her much. 'Lift up all your things, my dear, and let me see if any marks of the former punishment remain.'

Lizzie had a very prominent and very promising bottom. Miss Frankland felt it all over, and admired loudly its form and firmness, declaring it was quite beautiful to look at, and how womanly it was growing.

'Turn around and let me see if you are as womanly in front… upon my word, a well-formed mount with a charming mossy covering.'

Her hand wandering over her form excited Lizzie, whose face flushed and eyes glistened with rising desires. Miss Frankland herself became moved, but proceeded at once to lay her across her lap, and began with gentle switches, just sufficiently sharp to attract the blood in that direction, which, of course, acted with double force on all the already excited erotic organs. Lizzie began to wriggle her bum in all the lasciviousness of lust under the excited gaze of Miss Frankland, who seeing how matters were going on in her favour increased the force of her blows, but only sufficiently to still more lecherously excite her patient, until, driven to an excess of lust, she cried out, 'Oh, my loved Miss Frankland, I am dying with pleasure, do embrace and caress me.'

Miss Frankland lifted her up and drew her to her bosom and lips, and while sucking her tongue, slipped her hand down and found Lizzie's quim wet with her flowing spunk and her little clitoris stiff with the erotic passion that was consuming her. She frigged her until she spent again while their tongues were in each other's mouth. As Lizzie spent, Miss Frankland shoved a finger up her cunt, which of course met with no resistance, but as Lizzie possessed in perfection the art of nipping, she was sufficiently tight to leave a doubt of anything but finger fucking.

'Ah, you little puss, you have been playing with this before now, tell me the truth?'

'I will tell you everything if you will only play with me again. Ever since you flogged Mary and myself, we have both been so often burning down there, and have found out that feeling it, and pushing fingers in, was so nice, although at first we often hurt ourselves. But you do it so much better, Miss Frankland!'

'I shall do it much better, my darling, with what I have got

down there. Look here!' And lifting up her petticoat and chemise she exposed, to the absolute astonishment of Lizzie, her
extraordinary mass of hair, and her fiery red clitoris glowing and
sticking out of it black mass of curls.

'How beautiful!' cried Lizzie. 'I declare, you have got a doo-
dle, for which I have been so longing. I must kiss it.' Stooping
down, she took it in her mouth and sucked it.

'Stop, dear Lizzie, we shall both enjoy it.' Taking the cushion
from the chair, she lay down on her back on the floor, telling Lizzie
to turn her face the other way and to kneel down across her body so
that both their mouths could adapt themselves to each other's quim.

Lizzie told me afterwards that she took care to show no previous knowledge, but to let Miss Frankland apparently initiate
her into all the ceremonies of gamahuching.

Miss Frankland glued her lips to dear Lizzie's charming quim,
while Lizzie took her extraordinary clitoris into her mouth. After a
few ardent caresses, Miss Frankland pushed a finger up Lizzie's bottom-hole, and then paused an instant to tell Lizzie not only to follow her example in that respect, but to use her other hand in her
quim while sucking her clitoris. Then, both adapting themselves as
prescribed, they gamahuched on, until both could no longer move
from the excessive raptures produced by their profuse discharge.
After this first bout, Lizzie became curious to see all the wonderful
hair-covered organ and limbs of Miss Frankland, who gratified her
to the utmost extent of her wishes. Nor did she leave this inspection
entirely to Lizzie, but reciprocated it. Undoing her dress above, she
uncovered the charming budding beauties of Lizzie's bubbies, and
began sucking the nipples. Their mutual caresses and handling very
quickly re-fired these hot and lecherous women.

After a little renewed gamahuching, until both were wild with
excitement, Miss Frankland proposed to put her clitoris into

Lizzie's quim; told her to kneel down, and kneeling behind her, she sheathed it with ease in the hot and juicy folds of Lizzie's beautiful cunt. Passing her hand under Lizzie's belly, she frigged her clitoris until again nature gave down her delicious tribute, and they sank in all the voluptuous languor that follows. A third time they renewed their salacious and lascivious raptures, and then resumed their dresses so as to be ready to receive us. Miss Frankland begged Lizzie to keep her counsel and not reveal, even to Mary, what had passed. But Lizzie urged Miss Frankland to admit Mary into the new mysteries she had just herself been taught, and said she could assure her that Mary had a far more beautiful body than hers, and would like it quite as well as she did.

'Well, my dear, I shall think of it, and find an occasion to flog her, as I have done you.'

'Oh, that will be jolly!' cried Lizzie. 'She will like it just as much as I do. It is so nice. You must flog me every day, dear Miss Frankland. I loved you from the first, I adore you now.'

The embraced most lovingly, but our return put an end for the present to any further conversation.

The superb Frankland, now my guardian's wife, also came alone to my chambers, and we had a renewal of all our wildest experiences. She told me it was such a comfort to her, for although her husband, Mr. Nixon, was very loving, and did all he could, still it was nothing but exciting her to long for others, especially for me.

Pressing her enquiries, I acknowledged my intrigue with the Benson and Egerton. This evidently excited her lust, as I could see by the wild sparkle of her eye. My praises of these two ladies, and my saying how glorious it would be for her to make a fifth, and my description of the exquisite body and the tribadic tendencies of Mrs. Benson, fired her wild imagination and woke up all her tribadic lusts, and it ended in her begging me to give a luncheon at my chambers to the Benson and the Egerton, that she might be introduced to them.

The little luncheon came off most agreeably. The ladies all took to each other most warmly. Seeing which, I boldly broke the ice, and telling the Benson and Egerton that dear Mrs. Nixon was my first initiator in love's mysteries, and as had both of them, the wisest thing we could do would be to throw away all restraint and have a jollification all 'round.

'Ah, now,' said I, 'that is just the thing, you are at once put at ease, then let us do it with ease; strip is the word, and let us have it luxuriously.'

They laughed, kissed each other, and said the dear must have way, and all at once proceeded to undress.

The glorious and wonderfully hairy body of the Frankland perfectly astonished them, and raised their tribadic passions to fever heat, especially the Benson, who threw herself on that glorious form in an ecstasy of delight, more especially as the Frankland's passions being excited, her long red clitoris stood out from the dense black mass of hair, which covered not only her belly and mount, but all down and around her cunt. Nothing would satisfy the Benson but an immediate mutual gamahuche, for with true tribadic instinct, these two beautiful and libidinous women divined their mutual letch for that particular lascivious inclination and at once proceeded, one on the top of the other, to wildly gamahuche each other. The Frankland, who at first was under, was now above, and as she knelt and pushed out her stupendous arse to bring her cunt over the Benson's mouth, the sight of its hairy arsehole roused my desire.

The Benson was madly stimulated by the sight of the Frankland's superb body; her long red clitoris appeared only to be more excited and stirred the whole soul of the adorable Benson. She threw herself in reverse upon the Frankland before she had time to raise herself, seized with her mouth the wonderful clitoris, and then with fingers up arsehole and cunt worked furiously. The dear Frankland responded on the fine clitoris of the Benson. We ran off two bouts in this delicious position, and then with more regulated passions rose to form more general combinations.

We all laughed at her odd choice, but agreed at once, especially the Frankland, whose greatest letch was to fuck very fair young women with her long and capable clitoris. A fairer creature than the lovely Egerton could not be found. The Frankland admitted that in her inmost heart she had longed thus to have the Egerton from the moment she had first seen her, and her delight and surprise at finding the dear Egerton had equally desired to possess her, fired her fierce lust with increased desire.

I had aided the Frankland by using a double dildo, which at once filled both apertures. This excellent instrument was an invention of the Frankland, which she had suggested to a Parisian dildo maker, and had had it made in two or three sizes. It became very useful in our orgies, as from disparity of numbers an odd couple were left out, when the double jouissance was in operation, and then the two outsiders, with tongues and dildos, could gamahuche with great satisfaction.

During our tribadic junction, the Egerton was fucked by the Frankland in the arse, and then she sodomised the Benson to their mutual satisfaction. We all rose, purified, and refreshed with wine and biscuits, while discussing what our next move should be.

Passion's Evil

T was midnight struck and the Countess Gamiani's apartments were once again resplendent with the glitter of crystal, of sparkling lights. The minuets and the quadrilles waxed yet more lively, and dancers were whirled away by the sounds coming from an orchestra playing wine-sweet music. The ladies were marvellously arrayed; necklaces, jewels, shone.

Gracious, lavishing her attentions everywhere, the mistress of the ball seemed to be enjoying the success of an assembly prepared and announced at great expense. She was seen to smile agreeably at all the flattering comments, at all the usual prattlings everyone effused in her presence.

Frozen within my habitual role of the observer, I had already acquitted myself by delivering more than one remark, and that dispensed me from having to accord the Countess Gamiani the merit it was generally supposed she possessed. I had early judged her a lady of consequence in society. It remained for me to dissect her moral character, to turn the scalpel towards the heart's innermost regions. And something, I knew not what, something strange, something unfathomable impeded me, checked my examination. I sensed an infinite difficulty in sounding the depths of this woman's existence; her conduct explained nothing.

Still young, provided with an immense fortune, attractive according to those standards that enjoy the most general acceptance, this woman, lacking close kin, having no devoted friends, was, so to speak, individualized in the world. What she spent on her living alone seemed, by all appearances, capable of being shared by more than one other person. Many tongues had sung her eulogy, and each had ended by speaking ill of her; but, in the absence of proof, the Countess remained impenetrable. Some designed her as a Fedora, a heartless, inaccessible woman. Others figured a profoundly wounded soul which bade her wish to avoid cruel deceptions.

I was eager to have done with my doubts. I taxed all my logic's resources, but in vain, there was no arriving at a satisfactory conclusion. Vexed, I was about to abandon my speculations when, from behind me, I heard an elderly libertine raise his voice and utter this exclamation, 'Bah! The woman's a Lesbian.'

The word came as a bolt of lightning; everything fell together, made sense, no further contradictions were possible.

Lesbianism! Ah, the word rings strangely in the ear, then rouses up in you I have no idea what confused images of delights and lusts unheard of; voluptuousness carried to its last degree. ''Tis lewdness raging, mad, furious lubricity, the horrifying love play forever unachieved, never fulfilled'.

All efforts failed to rid me of these ideas; in a trice they had set my imagination in a riot. I could already see the Countess naked in the arms of another woman, her hair dishevelled, her frame quivering, breathless, exhausted, yet tortured by yet another pleasure broken short, aborted. My blood was afire, my senses groaned, I slipped back upon a sofa as if stunned.

The emotion once passed, I began coldly to calculate what I had to do in order to surprise the Countess in her games; I had to see them at any price.

I decided to watch her during the night, to conceal myself in her bedroom. The windowed door of a dressing room stood opposite her bed. A glance assured me of all the advantages the position offered, and concealing myself behind some dresses arranged on hangers, I patiently resigned myself to waiting for the hour of the Sabbath.

It was shortly after I was nestled in my hiding place that the Countess made her appearance, calling to her chambermaid, a young girl whose skin was dark, whose figure, lines and shape were inviting. 'Julie, I'll not need you tonight, so go to bed, and if you hear noise in my room, don't be disturbed. I wish to be alone.'

Her words gave fair promise of a drama. I applauded my audacity.

Little by little the voices in the salon grew faint. The Countess remained alone with one of her friends, a Mademoiselle Fanny B, and it was not long afterwards both found themselves in the room and before my eyes.

FANNY: What a wretched inconvenience! Rain pouring down and no carriage!

GAMIANI: I am quite as sorry about it as you are. It is a great pity. It just happens that my own carriage is at the harness maker's.

FANNY: My mother is certain to be worried.

GAMIANI: Don't fret yourself, dear Fanny, your mother has been notified, she knows you are to spend the night with me. I offer you my hospitality.

FANNY: Indeed, you are too kind. I shall prove a nuisance

to you.

GAMIANI: Rather a real delight. We'll make an adventure of it, a diversion... I don't want to send you off to sleep in another room all by yourself; we'll stay together.

FANNY: Why? I'll interfere with your sleep.

GAMIANI: Nonsense, you're too ceremonious. Come and let's be like two young friends, two schoolgirls.

A gentle kiss lent support to this effusion of tenderness.

GAMIANI: I'll help you undress, for my maid has gone to sleep. But we can do very well without her. Why, what's this! See how she's made! Happy girl! I admire your figure.

FANNY: Do you find it agreeable?

GAMIANI: Ravishing!

FANNY: You wish to flatter me.

GAMIANI: Oh, marvellous! What whiteness! 'Tis quite enough to make one jealous.

FANNY: As for that, I must say something, for in all frankness, you are fairer than I.

GAMIANI: But my child, you don't think so? Then do as I and take everything off. What is this confusion? One would fancy you were in the company of a gentleman. There, look into the mirror... As Paris, you would cast away the apple, rascal! She smiles to see herself so lovely, and indeed you do deserve a kiss on the forehead, on your cheeks, upon your lips... she is beautiful everywhere, everywhere...

The Countess' mouth, lascivious, ardent, strays over Fanny's body. Disconcerted, trembling, Fanny allows everything to be done, understands nothing. 'Twas a most delicious couple, full of voluptuousness, of grace, of lascivious abandon, of timorous modesty. One might have said this was a virgin, an angel, in the arms of a transported bacchante.

What beauties surrendered to my gaze, what a spectacle was this, how fit it was to arouse my passions!

FANNY: Oh, what is it you are doing? Leave me, Madame, I beseech you…

GAMIANI: No, ah no, no, my Fanny, my life, my joy! You are far too lovely See yourself, do! I love you! I love you as love itself! I am wild to have you!

The child's struggles were fruitless, kisses stifled her cries. Pressed, hugged, arms twined about her, her resistance was useless. The Countess, clasping her fiercely, bore her to the bed and cast her down upon it as if it were a prey flung down and to be devoured.

FANNY: But what is it ails you? Oh, God! Madame, it is dreadful! I'll scream… take your hands away… you terrify me…

And more animated kisses, kisses more insistent replied to her outcry. The arms squeezed tighter, the two bodies formed but one.

GAMIANI: Fanny, give yourself to me, entirely to me! Come hither, my life! I say, 'tis pleasure… oh, how you tremble, child, yield to me…

FANNY: It is bad! It is wrong! You are killing me… ah, I am dying…

GAMIANI: Yes, squeeze me, my little one, my love, squeeze tight, and tighter still! How beautiful she is in her pleasure!

Lascivious… you enjoy it, you are happy… Oh, God!

It was a curious sight. The Countess, fire flashing in her eye, hair in disorder, was flinging herself, writhing, upon her victim whose senses, too, were afire. Both fought, grappled, stiffened and clutched each other, held fast. They met in shocks, in jolts and leaps, stifled their cries, their sighs with passionate kisses. The bed creaked beneath the Countess' furious blows.

Soon exhausted, stricken, Fanny's arms relaxed. She lay pale and motionless, like a glorious corpse.

The Countess was delirious. Furious, bounding, she cast herself into the centre of the room, rolled upon the rugs, exciting herself by striking luxurious poses, adopting madly lubricious postures, with her fingers provoking all pleasure's excesses.

The sight of her entirely drove me out of my mind.

For an instant, disgust, indignation, had dominated me; I wanted to declare my presence to the Countess, to overwhelm her with the weight of my scorn. My senses were, however, stronger than my reason. The flesh rose in superb, vibrant triumph. I was beside myself, as one insane. It was upon the lovely Fanny I hurled myself, naked, flaming, purple, terrible.

She had scarcely time to realize that this was a new attack when, already victorious, I felt her supple and delicate body tremble, agitate itself beneath mine, reply to each of my strokes. Our tongues touched, burning, stinging, our souls melted and fused into one. Fanny cried, 'Oh, great God, they are putting me to death! Upon which the lovely creature became rigid, sighed and then fell back as she inundated me with her favours.

'Ah, Fanny!' I declared. 'Wait… ah, there, 'tis yours…' And I in my turn thought that what issued from me was my very life's breath and soul.

What extravagance... annihilated, lost in Fanny's embrace, I had felt nothing of the Countess' frantic assaults. Brought back to her senses by our cries, our gasps, beside herself with fury and envy, she had thrown herself upon me in an endeavour to tear me away from her friend. Her arms clasped me, she shook me; her fingers dug into my flesh, her teeth bit me.

That double onslaught of two bodies sweating from rapture, both ablaze with lust, revived me again, renewed my desires. Fire seared me through and through. I remained held fast in Fanny's potent grip. Then, without in any way giving up my position, in this unearthly disorder of three seething, entwined bodies tangled one with the other, I succeeded in laying firm hands on the Countess' thighs and in wrenching them apart and in drawing her loins down towards my head. 'Gamiani, be mine! Move forward, extend yourself, steady, upon your arms.'

Gamiani understood me, and I was able to ply my active, devouring tongue over her most fiery parts.

Fanny, insensate, lost, amorously caressed the palpitating breast which quivered above her.

An instant of this and the Countess was vanquished; she was finished. 'What is this fire you light in me? 'Tis too much... I ask for quarter... Oh, what a game of lust! You will have me slain... God! I am stifling.' Her body fell heavily to one side, an inert mass.

Fanny, yet more exalted than before, casts her arms about my neck, twines herself about me, squeezes me, locks her legs around my waist.

GAMIANI: You've not forgotten the atrocious ordeal my aunt made me undergo in the interests of her lechery. I had no sooner realized the horror of her conduct than I put myself in possession of some documents which were the guarantee of my fortune. I also took some jewels and some money and, profiting from a moment when that worthy lady was absent, I left to seek refuge in the convent of the Sisters of Redemption. No doubt touched by my youth and my apparent shyness, the Mother superior gave me the warmest possible welcome, which was calculated to dissipate my fears and help me overcome my embarrassment.

I related what had happened to me, I asked asylum and requested her protection. She took me in her arms, hugged me affectionately and called me her daughter. After that she described the sweet tranquillity of life in the convent. She added fuel to my hatred for men and ended with a pious exhortation, which seemed to me language that could only have emanated from a divine spirit. In order that the abrupt transition from worldly life to that of the cloister be rendered less extreme, it was decided I would remain close to the Superior and would sleep each night in her cell. Things went splendidly; by the second night we were chatting together in the most familiar way. In bed, the superior began to toss and turn. This continued a long time; she complained of being cold and besought me to lie with her and avail her of my warmth. I found her absolutely naked. 'One sleeps more soundly,' she explained, 'when unencumbered by a nightgown.' She suggested I remove mine and I did so to please her. 'Oh, my little one,' cried she, fingering me, 'your skin is burning... and how soft it is! The barbarians who dared molest you in that way! You must have suffered atrociously. Tell me just what they did to you. They beat you, you say?' I repeated my story in all its details, emphasizing those which seemed to interest her the most. She took such a keen pleasure in hearing me speak that she was soon quivering in an extraordinary manner. 'Poor child! Poor child!' she reiterated, clutching me with all her strength.

I knew not how it came to pass but I gradually found myself lying on top of her. Her legs were wrapped around my waist, her arms surrounded me. A tepid, penetrating warmth spread through my frame. I felt an unknown ease, a delicious comfort which communicated to my bones, to my flesh. I cannot tell you what love-sweat which flowed in me with a milky sweetness. 'You are kind, you are very good to me,' I said to the Superior. 'I love you, I am happy here beside you. I never want to be away from you.' My mouth glued itself to her lips, and with much passion I continued: 'Oh, yes! I love you so much I feel as if I were dying of love… I don't know… but I feel…'

The Superior stroked me slowly. Her body squirmed, wriggled, but sweetly, beneath mine. Her stiff woolly fleece brushed mine, stung, pricked me sharply, roused up a perfectly divine tickling sensation. I was out of my mind from this devilry. I shivered so much my whole body quaked. The Superior flung me a violent kiss; I stopped bolt still. 'Oh, my God!' I cried, 'no more… ah…' and never did dew fall more abundantly, more deliciously after any love-combat that ever there was.

The ecstasy passed, yet far from exhausted, I flung myself with redoubled zeal upon my companion; I ate her alive with caresses. I took her hand and conveyed it to the place she had just so powerfully irritated. The Superior, seeing me thus, forgot herself altogether and began to behave like a bacchante. Our ardour, our kisses, our bites competed vigorously. Oh, what agility, what suppleness were in that woman's limbs. Her body curved, arched, straightened with a snap, rolled; it drove me mad. I was no longer in control of myself. I had scarce enough time to return a kiss, so thickly did hers rain down upon me, covering me from head to foot. It seemed as if I were being eaten, devoured in a thousand separate places! That incredible activity, that tempest of lubricious fondlings put me in a state I cannot possibly describe. Oh Fanny, could you only have been there to witness our assaults, our outbursts! Had you but seen us two, furious, panting, you would have been able to understand all that may occur when two women in love are under the sway of their senses. In an instant my head was gripped between my wrestling-companion's thighs. I divined her desires. Inspired by lust, I fell to gnawing upon her most sensitive parts. But I ill complied with her wishes. Quickly, she eluded me, slid out from under my body, and suddenly spreading my thighs, she immediately attacked me with her mouth. Her pointed, nervous tongue stabbed at me, sounded me like a plummet, or a needle one thrusts and rapidly withdraws, or a dagger. Her teeth closed upon me and seemed about to tear me. I began to fling about as if I were doomed. I thrust the superior's head away, I dragged her by the hair. Then she let go: she touched me softly, injected saliva into me, licked me slowly, or mildly nipped my hairs and flesh with a refinement so delicate and at the same time so sensual that the very thought of it makes me come this minute with pleasure.

Oh! What delights made me drunk! What a rage held me in its grip! I screamed and shouted unendingly; I fought, fell stricken, was raised up, it began again, and always the swift-moving, sharp-pointed tongue found me, ran stiffly into me. Two thin, firm lips took my clitoris, pinched it, kneaded it in such a way I thought I should die. No, Fanny, it is not possible to feel that, to enjoy oneself that way more than once in a lifetime. An indescribable nervous tension, the blood pounding in my swollen arteries, what heat in my flesh, what fire in my blood! I was burning, I tell you, I was liquefying, and I felt an avid mouth, an insatiable mouth, aspire after my life's very essence. I assure you that I was dry and I ought to have been drenched with blood and oily fluid. But how happy I was! Fanny! Fanny! I can restrain myself not another second! As I speak to you of those excesses I think I can again feel those same consuming titillations finish me... quicker... harder... good, ah, good... ah, I am dying...

Fanny was worse than a famished she-wolf. 'Enough! Enough!' Gamiani repeated. 'You're sucking me dry, you devilish creature! I'd have sworn you were less skilful, less passionate. Ah, but I see what we have here. You're developing. The fire is in you.'

'But how could it not be?' asked Fanny. 'One should have to be deprived of blood and life to remain insensible with you. Tell me, then, tell me, what did you do next?

GAMIANI: Now wizened by experience, I repaid in kind and with interest, I set about the ruination of my ardent companion. Thereafter nothing hindered us, all restraint was banished and I soon learned that the nuns of the convent of Redemption were given to collective worship of the senses' fury; that they had a secret place where they assembled for their orgies and there they sported at their ease. The service opened at the hour of Complines and was finished by that of matins.

The Superior next proceeded to unfold her philosophy. What I heard appalled me to such a pint I beheld her as a Satan incarnate. However, she reassured me, murmured a few compliments in my ear and above all diverted me by relating how she lost her maidenhead. You'd never guess to whom it was that priceless treasure was given. The tale is a strange one and is well worth the trouble to tell.

The Superior, whom from now on I shall call Sainte, was the daughter of a ship's captain. Her mother, an intelligent and reasonable woman, had brought her up in all the principles of our sacred belief, which by no means prevented young Saint's temperament from developing at an early age. When she was twelve she was rocked by intolerably fierce desires; these she sought to satisfy by every one of the most bizarre means a roving imagination could devise.

The unhappy girl laboured over herself every night. Her untaught and inadequate fingers spoiled her youth and ruined her health. She one day clapped eyes on two dogs in the act of holding amorous commerce. Her lewd curiosity led her to observe the mechanism and action of either sex; she studied the matter closely and henceforth had a better idea of what she was lacking. Wiser now, she was also the more tormented. Living as she was in an isolated house, surrounded by elderly servants, never seeing a man, how could she ever hope to come upon that living arrow, so red and so swift, which had seemed so very wonderful to her and which she supposed must similarly exist for women. My nymphomaniac racked her brains; it finally occurred to her that the gardener, a strong young man who came three times a week to take care of the grounds, might well be the solution to her problem. She went to the window to watch him pull weeds. She examined him at considerable length, observing his broad back and manly figure. Enticed, she went into the garden with some water for him.

The gardener drank the water gratefully. As he returned the glass to her and thanked her, his grey eyes peered into hers. She noticed a swelling within his pants. Saint's heart leapt for joy at this manifestation of interest. The gardener drew near. They embraced. Without a word he led her to some nearby bushes. As soon as they were hidden Sainte untied the fly of the gardener's trousers. His prick sprang out.

Sainte gasped in pleasure. She had at last found what she had always been seeking, that about which she dreamed every night. Her ideal was there before her eyes, very real, very palpable. Better still, the unspeakable jewel was springing erect in a more solid, more ardent, more threatening fashion than she had ever visualized in her most randy moments. She grabbed it and stroked it, wondering how something so hard could be so smooth.

Driven as if by madness, Sainte forced the gardener down, took off her dress and joined him.

The gardener grasped her full breasts. With his other hand he fingered her already gushing cunt. Sainte continued to fondle the man's prick, until it had risen to eight honest, well pronounced inches. At first, this extravagant wealth terrified our maiden. Nevertheless, urged on by desire, she moved downward to have a closer look. She kissed it, and curious to see what the single creamy drop that formed at the head tasted like, licked it. The man trembled and pulled Sainte to him.

Suddenly, Sainte became frightened. She was about to retreat when a final glance at the man's flamboyant bait reawakened every one of her desires. She became emboldened at once, with a resolute air lifted her skirts and bravely walked backwards, her back bent, her behind aimed at the redoubtable point. The battle is engaged, blows are struck, and the weapon rises gloriously to the level of a god. Sainte is penetrated, de-virginized, satisfied! Her joy, her transports explode in a song of oohs and aahs, but the lass sings with such gusto her mother overhears the tune, comes running and surprises her daughter very nicely pegged and buttered, writhing and dancing away, struggling skewered on the blade and ejecting her soul!

FANNY: Superb farce.

GAMIANI: To cure the poor girl of her wicked ways, she is installed in a convent.

FANNY: 'Twould have been better to have let her bump bellies with a jungle full of monkeys.

GAMIANI: You'll soon see how right you are. My temperament willingly adapted itself to a life of feasts and pleasures. Very joyfully, most willingly I consented to be initiated into the mysteries of monastic saturnalias. My admission having been accepted by the chapter, I was presented two days later. According to the rules, I arrived naked. I took the required oath and to complete the ceremony I courageously prostituted myself to an enormous wooden Priapus, a simulacrum with dimensions comparable to a smith's forearm. I had no sooner finished that painful libation when a band of nuns descended upon me with all the impetuosity of a tribe of cannibals. I lent myself to every caprice, I struck the most lubricious attitudes possible, and finally I ended with an obscene dance and was proclaimed victorious. I was exhausted. A little nun, a very lively little nun, wide awake, alert and more refined than the Superior, conducted me to her bed; she was by far the most thoroughgoing nymphomaniac Hell has ever bred. I conceived a true carnal passion for her and we were almost always together during the vast nocturnal routs.

FANNY: Where were those assignations held?

GAMIANI: In a spacious hall that art and the genius of depravity had been pleased to decorate in the most lavish manner. One arrived there by way of two doors closed off in the

Oriental fashion by rich draperies edged with gold fringe, ornamented with a thousand curious designs. The walls were hung in dark blue velvet framed by lemonwood wainscoting most artfully carved. Large mirrors set at equal distances, rose from floor to ceiling. The nude groups of delirious nuns were reflected, during the orgies, in a thousand forms or rather seemed to spring out, glittering and alive, from between the tapestry-covered panels. Cushions, hassocks, pillows, couches took the place of chairs and better served lust's frolicking and lechery's postures. A doubly thick rug, made of delicate material and delightful to the touch, covered the floor. Woven into the carpet, with an amazing magic of colour, were twenty amorous groups in lascivious attitudes, all very suitable to whet jaded desires, revive surfeited appetites. Elsewhere – in paintings, upon the ceiling – the eye discovered the most eloquent representations of extravagance and abandoned debauchery. I shall always remember a hot-blooded Thyade tormented by a Corybant. Never could I glance at that picture without immediately feeling pleasure stir in me.

FANNY: That must have been delicious... to see all those things!

GAMIANI: To that luxury of decoration add the intoxication of perfumes and flowers. A steady temperate warmth, a tender, mysterious illumination provided by six lamps of alabaster, sweeter than an opal's reflection – all that gave birth in one to I don't know what vague enchantment, mingled with a troubling desire, with a sensual daydream... It was the East, its luxuriance, its poetry, its careless, unstudied voluptuousness. It was the mystery of the harem... its secret delights and, above all else its ineffable languor.

FANNY: How sweet it must have been to spend nights of

drunkenness there with one's beloved.

GAMIANI: Doubtless love would willingly have taken up its abode there had it not been for the noisy and filthy orgy which, every night, transformed the place into an ungodly stew, a nest of horrors.

FANNY: How did that happen?

GAMIANI: The midnight hour would sound and thereupon the nuns would enter; they were clad in a simple black tunic; it emphasized the whiteness of their skins. Everyone had bare feet, loose-floating hair. A splendid service was soon laid; it happened as if by magic. The Superior gave the signal and one did what one wished. Some remained seated, others reclined upon pillows. Exquisite meats, warm, stimulating wines were consumed in a flash; everyone had a terrible hunger. Those women's faces, worn by excess and abuse, cold, pale as daylight, would take on colour; would gradually become flushed. Bacchic incenses, aphrodisiac philtres injected fire into the body, trouble into the mind. Conversation waxed lively, became a confused humming and always ended in obscene remarks, delirious provocations, wrapped in song, laughter, outbursts, the crash of glasses and the bursting of wine bottles and decanters. The most feverish nun, she in the greatest haste, would suddenly fall upon her neighbour and bestow a violent kiss which had the effect of galvanizing the entire assembly. Couples formed at once, became entangled, twisted in frantic embraces. One would hear the sound of lips being applied to flesh or meeting each other with fury. Then stifled moans, sighs, would begin to resound through the room, anguished groans and cries of ardour or prostration. Soon cheeks, breasts, shoulders would appear no longer to suffice as objects for the unrestrained kisses. Dresses were lifted or tossed aside. Then one beheld a unique spectacle, nothing but female bodies, supple, gracefully interlaced; their nakedness interwoven, stirring, pressing, straining, moving with skill and adroitness, with consummate impetuousness and refinement and lust. If the excess of pleasure were not precisely to impatient desire's taste, someone would detach herself for an instant in order to recover her breath. She and her partner would regard one another with smouldering eyes, and they would fight to achieve the most lascivious poses, the most enticing gestures or look. She of the two who triumphed through seduction and debauch would suddenly see her beloved melt, fall upon her, fling her over, cover her with kisses and sucks, eat her with caresses, devour her even to the centre of the most secret pleasures, at all times placing herself in such a way as to be able to receive the same attacks. The two heads would become buried between thighs, there would now be one body only; one agitated, convulsively tormented body whence a low, throaty gasp of lubricious joy would escape, to be followed by a double scream of happiness.

'They're coming! They're coming!' Those doomed nuns would immediately cry up in chorus. And they who were made to do the like would leap wild-eyed upon each other, more furious than beasts let free in an arena. Eager to know pleasure in their turn, they would undertake the most strenuous enterprises. By dint of leaps and starts the groups used to crash against each other and would fall pell-mell to the floor, panting, finished, tired or orgy, exhausted from lust: a macabre confusion of nude women, swooning, gasping, heaped together in the most ignominious disorder upon which often, the first glow of daybreak would shine.

FANNY: What madness!

GAMIANI: They didn't limit themselves to that; their

caprices were infinitely various. Deprived of men, we were on that account only the more ingenious at devising new stunts. All the priapic instruments, every one of antiquity's obscene tales and those of modern times was well known to us. We had gone far beyond them. Elephantis and Aretino had no such imaginations as we. It would take too long to enumerate our artifices, our stratagems, our potions marvellously compounded so as to revive failing strength, waken the desires and satisfy them. You will be able to judge the thing by the extraordinary treatment to which we exposed one of our number in an effort to needle her, prick up her desires. She was first of all plunged into a bath of heated animal's blood to quicken her vigour. Next, an aphrodisiac potion was administered, after which she lay down on a bed and every inch of her body was massaged. Next, she was put to sleep by hypnotism. As soon as she had fallen into slumber, her body was adjusted in an advantageous position and she was whipped till she bled, she was pricked with pointed instruments as well. The patient woke in the middle of the process. Entranced, wild-eyed, she lifted herself up, stared at us with an insane expression and straightway entered the most violent paroxysms. Six persons had trouble keeping her under control. Only a vigorous tonguing was able to pacify her. Her fury burst out in torrents. But were it to happen that relief did not come, the wretched one's state would worsen and in all probability she would cry out for a man.

FANNY: What, a man? Mercy! Where did you find one?

GAMIANI: Yes, my dear, a man. We had two knaves who visited, both very nicely furnished and each very docile. We wished to cede in nothing to those Roman ladies who employed male servants to service them in their saturnalias.

The first time I was put to the test, I was delirious from wine.

Defying all my sisters, I flung myself upon the table used during this particular ceremony. The knave was immediately hoisted into position and dressed before me. His awe-inspiring shaft, warmed by the nuns' handlings, thudded heavily against my flank. I took his colossus in both hands, placed it at the aperture and after several moments of fondling I strove to insert it. My movements helping the business, and my fingers and a dilating ointment as well, I was soon mistress of at least five brave inches. I wanted to push some more but I lacked the strength and fell back. It seemed as if my skin were being ripped, as if I were being split asunder, quartered; the pain was numbing, stifling; with it was mixed a fiery irritation, titillating and sensual. Constantly in action, the knave produced a friction so vigorous my entire spinal column was rattled. His spermatic ducts opened wide and gushed their contents. The burning liquor quivered for an instant within my loins. Oh, what joy! And how I came! I sensed it race out in spurts and flaming jets and fall drop by drop to the depths of my vagina. I was streaming with love. I emitted a prolonged cry of enervation and was succoured. By means of my lubricious capers I had gained an additional two inches of meat; all measure had been exceeded, all records eclipsed, my companions acknowledged defeat.

Exhausted, aching in all my limbs, racked with pain, I thought my pleasures over when the intractable rod stiffened more brilliantly than before, sounded me, pierced me and nearly lifted me from my resting place. My nerves became swollen, my teeth locked and grated, my arms strained at my two cramped thighs. All of a sudden, a violent bomb-burst of a jet broke forth and inundated me with a hot and gluey rain, so strong, so abundant it seemed to overcharge my veins and bolt to my very heart. My flesh, relaxed and eased, permitted me to feel nothing but poignant felicities which stung to the bone, the marrow, the brain and the nerves, dissolved my joints and put me into a burning deliquescence... delicious torture... intolerable voluptuousness that unties what binds life together and causes you to die in drunkenness...

FANNY: What transports you provoke in me, Gamiani? I'll soon be able to contain myself no longer... Well, how was it you finally got out of that devilish convent?

GAMIANI: It happened thus. After a great orgy, we had the idea to transform ourselves into men with the aid of an artificial penis: to impale each other in such a manner we would be joined into an unbroken line, and then to have a dance. I formed the chain's last link; I was, that is to say, the only one who rode horse back but had no rider. What was my surprise when I felt myself assaulted by a naked man who had, I've no idea how, got into our midst. I cried out in fright. The line of nuns broke at once; they all rushed up and fell incontinently upon the unfortunate intruder. Each wished in reality to conclude a pleasure begun by a bothersome artifice. The too much toasted animal was soon drained dry. You should have seen his state of prostration and torpor; his device was flabby, it dangled, all his virility was in the most negative demonstration imaginable. I had much difficulty getting a spark from him when my turn came to taste the prolific elixir. I succeeded nevertheless. Lying prone upon the dying fellow, my head lodged between his thighs, I put such skill and deftness into sucking the sleeping Monsieur Priapus that he woke flushed, rubicund, vivacious and fit to give pleasure. Myself caressed by an agile tongue, I soon sensed the oncoming of an incredible pleasure, and I finished it by taking my seat gloriously and with delight upon the sceptre I had just made mine by the right of conquest.

Kate Percival:
The Belle Of The Delaware

have not yet given a description of myself to the reader and it is nothing but right that I should do so. At the age of eighteen my charms were well developed, and although they had not attained the ripe fullness which a few years latter was the admiration and delight of all my adorers, still I possessed all the insignia of womanhood. In stature I was above the medium height, my hair was a dark auburn, and hung in massive bands on a white neck. My eyes were a deep-blue and possessed a languishing voluptuous expression; they were fringed with long silky eyelashes and arched with brows so finely pencilled, that I have often been accused of using art to give them their graceful appearance. My features were classically regular, my skin of dazzling whiteness, my shoulders were gracefully rounded and my bust faultless in its contours. My more secret charms I shall describe at some future time when I shall have to expose them to the reader's gaze.

I have said that up to the age of eighteen I had never experienced the slightest sexual desire. The spark of voluptuousness, which has ever since burnt so fiercely in my breast, was destined to be lighted up by one of my own sex. Yes, dear Laura, it was you who first taught me the delights and joys of love; it was you who first kindled that flame of desire that has caused me to experience twelve years of delirious bliss; it was to your gentle teaching, sweet friend, that I owe my initiation in all the mysteries of the Court of Venus; it was your soft hand that pointed out to me that path of pleasure – and all the delight shown on the wayside. The incident happened in this wise:

About three months before I left school, we were told one morning that a new music and French teacher would take her abode in B. Seminary the next day. We were all extremely anxious to see her, and at the expected hour she made her appearance. Her name was Laura Castleton, and her father lived in St. Mary's County, MD. She was a brunette, about twenty years of age, and one of the most beautiful girls I ever saw. She was nearly as tall as myself, but considerably stouter, her body was moulded in a most exquisite manner, and although her eyes were very black and her hair like a raven's plume, her skin was white as alabaster. Her teeth were as regular as if they had been cut out of a solid piece of ivory, and her hands and feet were fairy-like in their proportions. I was the eldest girl in the school and Laura immediately made me her companion. She was exceedingly intelligent, well educated and well read. I was soon attracted to her, and we became inseparable. We would pass all our spare time reading to each other or in conversation on literary subjects. I agreed to love her with my whole heart, and was never happy except in her company.

'Laura,' said I to her one day when we were walking on the playground with our arms 'round each others waists, 'why cannot we sleep together?'

'Would you like it, Kate?' she replied, bending her black eyes upon my face with a peculiar gloom in them which sent the blood rushing to my cheeks – but why and wherefore I did not know.

'Indeed I would, Laura. It would be so nice to lie in your arms all night.'

'Well, darling, I will ask Mrs. B., I have no doubt but she will give her consent.'

The lovely girl drew me towards her, and gave me a warmer kiss than she had ever before bestowed upon me. The contact of her easy lips to mine sent an indefinable thrill through my body which I had never experienced before. In the evening she informed me that she had spoken to Mrs. B., and that the latter had consented that we should sleep together. I was overjoyed at this news, and longed for night to come, that I might recline in my darling's arms.

At last the bedtime hour arrived, and I followed Laura to her chamber. She put the lamp on the dressing table and, kissing me affectionately, bade me undress myself quickly. We began our toilette for the night. I was undressed first, and having put on my nightgown, I sat down on the side of the bed and watched Laura disrobing herself. After she had removed her dress and her petticoats, I could not help being struck with her resplendent charms. Her chemise had fallen off her shoulders and revealed to my gaze, ivory shoulders, beautifully rounded, and two globes of alabaster reposing on a field of snow. She appeared to be entirely unaware that I was watching her, for she sat down on a chair exactly in front of me, and crossing one leg over the other, she began to remove her gaiters and stockings. This attitude raised her chemise in front, and allowed me to have a full view of her magnificently formed limbs. I even caught sight of her voluptuous thighs. Laura caught my eye.

'What are you gazing at so earnestly?' she asked.

'I am gazing at your beauties, Laura.'

'One would think that you were my lover,' returned Laura laughing.

'So I am, dear, for you know I love you.'

'You little witch. You know well enough what I mean. But if you want to admire beauty, why not look in the glass, for I am not near as beautiful as you are, dear Kate.'

'What nonsense, Laura,' I replied, 'but come let us get into bed.'

So saying, I jumped between the sheets, and was followed almost immediately by Laura, who first, however, placed the lamp on a chair by the bedside. She clasped me in her arms and pressed me to her breast, while she kissed my lips, cheeks and eyes passionately.

The warmth of her embraces, and her glowing limbs entwined in mine, caused a strange sensation to steal through me. My cheeks burned and I returned her kisses with an ardour that equalled her own.

'How delightful it is to be in your arms, dear Laura,' I exclaimed.

'Do you really like it?' she replied, pressing me still closer to her. At the same time our night dresses became disarranged, and I felt her naked thighs pressing against mine.

Laura kissed me again with even greater warmth than before, and while she was thus engaged she slipped one of her soft hands in the opening of my night chemise, and I felt it descend on one of my breasts. When I felt this, a trembling seized my limbs, and I pressed her convulsively to my heart.

'What a voluptuous girl you are, Kate,' said she, moulding my breasts and titillating my nipples. 'You set me on fire.'

'I never felt so happy in all my life, Laura. I could live and die in your arms.'

I now carried my hand to her globes of alabaster, and pressed and folded them, imitating her in all her actions. Nay more, I turned down the bed cloths and unbuttoning her night-dress in front, I exposed those charming snowy hillocks to my delighted gaze. The light of the lamp shone directly upon them, and I was never tired of admiring the whiteness, firmness and splendid development of those glowing semi-globes. I buried my face between them, and pressed a thousand kisses on the soft velvet surface.

'Why Kate, you are a perfect volcano,' said Laura, trembling under my embraces, 'and I have been labouring under the delusion that you were an icicle.'

'I was an icicle, darling, but now I have been melted by your charms.'

'What a happy man your husband will be,' said Laura.

'Happy? Why?'

'To enfold such a glorious creature as you are in his embrace. If you take so much delight with one of your own sex, what will you do when clasped in a man's arms?'

'You are jesting Laura, do you suppose for a moment that I will ever allow a man to kiss and embrace me as you do?'

'Certainly, my love – he will do a great deal more than I do.'

'More? What can you mean?'

'Is it possible, Kate, that you do not know?'

'I really do not know. Do tell me, there's a dear girl.'

'I can scarcely believe it possible that you are eighteen years of age – a perfectly developed woman – and that you know nothing of the mysteries of love. Are you not aware, darling, that you possess a jewel about you that a man would give half his life to ravish?'

'You speak in riddles, Laura. Where is this jewel?'

'Lie perfectly quiet and I will show you where it is.'

My cheeks burned and I was all in a glow, for I had pretended to more ignorant that I was in reality. Laura fastened her lips on my breast and placed her hand on one of my thighs. She then slowly carried it up the marble column, and at last invaded the very sanctuary of love itself. When I felt her fingers roaming in the mossy covering of that hallowed spot, every moment growing more bold and enterprising, I could not help giving utterance to a faint scream – it was the last cry of expiring modesty, and I grew as hardy and lascivious as my beautiful companion. I stretched my thighs open to their widest extent, the better to second the examination Laura was making of my person. The lovely girl appeared to be strangely affected while she was manipulating my secret charms. Her eyes shot fire, her bosom heaved, and she began to wiggle her bottom. For some time she played with the hair that thickly covered my mount of Venus. Twisting it 'round her finger, she then gently divided the folding lips, and endeavoured to penetrate into the interior of the mystic grotto, but she could not effect an entrance and was obliged to satisfy herself with titillating the inside of the lips. Suddenly, flows of pleasure shot through my entire body, for her finger had come in contact with the peeping sentinel that guarded the abode of bliss, an article which until that moment I had not known I possessed. She rubbed it gently, giving me the most exquisite pleasure. If the last remnant of prudery had not taken flight before, this last act would have routed it completely. With a single jerk I threw off the bed-clothes, and thus we both lay naked the waist down.

'How magnificently you are formed, dear Kate,' said Laura, examining all my hidden charms by the aid of the lamp. 'What glorious thighs, what a delicious bijou, what a thick forest of hair, and what a splendidly developed clitoris. Now, sweet girl, I will make you taste the most delicious sensation you have ever experienced in your life. Let me do with you as I will.'

'Do what you like with me, darling. I resign myself entirely in your hands.'

Laura now commenced to gently rub my clitoris with her finger, while she kissed my breasts and lips passionately. I soon began again to experience the delicious sensation I had before spoken of; rivers of pleasure permeated through my system. My breasts bounded up and down, my buttocks were set in motion from the effect of her caressing finger, my thighs were stretched widely apart, and my whole body was under the exquisite influence of her scientific manipulations. At last the acme came, an overwhelming shivering seized me, I gave two or three convulsive heaves with my buttocks, and in an agony of delight I poured down my first tribute to the God of love.

For a quarter of an hour, I lay in a complete state of annihilation, and was only recalled from it by the kisses of Laura.

'Darling Kate,' she exclaimed, 'you must give me relief or I shall die. The sight of your enjoyment has lighted up such a fire within me that I shall burn up if you do not quench it.'

'I will do my best, dear Laura to assuage your desires. You have made me experience such unheard of delight that I should indeed be wanting in gratitude if I was not to attempt to make you some return.'

I rose up, and, kneeling across her, began to examine at my ease her lovely Mons Veneris. It was a glorious object, covered over with a mass of black silky hair, through the midst of which I could discern the plump lips folding close together. I placed my finger between them and felt her clitoris swelling beneath it until it actually peeped its little red head from its soft place of concealment. I now advanced one finger and found that it entered her coral sheath with the utmost ease, at the same time it was tightly grasped by the sensitive folds of her vagina. I began to move it in and out, while I kissed her white belly and thighs.

'Stop, darling,' said Laura, rising up and going to a drawer. 'I will contrive something better to bring on the dissolving period. You are rather a novice as yet in the art of procuring enjoyment.'

She took from the drawer a dildo, which she fastened securely around my waist, and, making me lie on my back, she leaned over me and guided it into her sensitive quiver. She then commenced to move herself rapidly upon it. It was a delicious sight to me, I could see the instrument entering in and out of her luscious grotto, while her features expressed the most entrancing enjoyment, and her broad white bottom and breasts shivered with pleasure. Her motions did not continue long, however. In a few minutes she succumbed and the elixir of love poured down her white thighs. The voluptuous sight before me, and the rubbing of the dildo on my clitoris caused me to emit again at the same moment that she did, and we both sunk exhausted on the bed. I shall not detain the reader with all the exquisite enjoyments I experienced for the next three months in my lessons with the beautiful Laura, suffice it to say that we exhausted every method two young girls of ardent imagination could propose. At last the time approached for us to separate, and with tears and embraces we bade each other adieu.

I returned home, and it was several years before I saw the sweet companion of my school days again.

Amy Denmead's History

was born in Philadelphia. My father was a successful merchant, doing business there. We lived in a large house in the upper part of Chestnut Street, and my father's wealth procured me every luxury that the heart could wish for. I never knew my mother for she died when I was quite young. My sister was married to you, Herbert, when I was eighteen-years-old. My ideas up to that time were very vague regarding the sexes, but I was soon destined to be fully enlightened.

I felt very dull after my sister had gone away, and my father proposed that I should write and ask my old school fellow, Florence Maltby, to come and stay on a visit with us. I cordially agreed to this proposition for I loved Florence and had not seen her for several years, although we kept up a constant correspondence.

Florence accepted my invitation, and on the day agreed upon, she took up her abode with us.

Miss Maltby was a beautiful girl about twenty-years-old and her hair and eyes were black – in fact, she was a decided brunette. She was fiery, impulsive, and amorous. We had a thousand things to converse about, and in a few hours all our old friendship was re-knit, and we became more intimate than ever. Of course, we slept together.

For two or three nights nothing occurred of special moment. I noticed however, that Florence would kiss me with a great deal of warmth, and press me tenderly in her arms when we were in bed together, but I thought nothing of it.

One night, about a week after she had been an inmate of our house, when we retired to our chamber, instead of undressing as usual, Florence seated herself on the side of the bed and watched me in the process of disrobing. I had unhooked the front of my dress, and it had fallen off my shoulders, and my chemise being open in front allowed my two breasts to be seen; nay even a portion of the white plain below was visible. Florence no sooner saw this than her eyes brightened and she ran up to me and began to mould my bubbies. Although this action some-what surprised me, I made no resistance, and to tell the truth the contact of her soft hand on my breasts was very agreeable.

'What delicious breasts you have, Amy,' said Florence, 'how well formed they are, and yet how large! See how stiff the rosy nipples stand out from this field of snow! Oh, how I love to kiss and press them!' And she buried her head between the two semi globes. 'And then your belly, how soft and white it is,' she continued, passing her hand over it, 'how happy will the man be who presses that belly to his own.'

'Oh, fie, Florence, you should not talk in that manner,' I replied, my face flushing with the fire kindled in me by her las-civious touches. 'But you exaggerate my beauties. It is true my breasts are a little larger than yours, but they are not one bit more handsome, more firm or more elastic. Come dear let us compare them, for I do not see why I should not be gratified as well as yourself.'

I now unhooked Florence's dress behind and pulled it down to her waist. Her two semi-globes were completely exposed. They were beautifully formed – firm, elastic and standing boldly out from her chest. I pressed and caressed them, sucking the rosy nipples, which stood out stiff with desire.

'You naughty girl,' said Florence, 'you will devour me. Your kisses send a fire through my veins, and these delicious globes, too…'

'Could it be possible to see prettier bubbies than these?' I interrupted. 'Just see how stiff the nipples are, and then you talk of my belly, look at yours. How deliciously smooth! How beautifully white.'

'Come, darling,' said Florence, 'let us rub our breasts together, I am sure it will give us mutual delight.'

'I will do anything you wish, Florence, for I feel a strange fire burning in me. Come love, come.'

We pulled down our clothes as low as possible so as to leave us a clear field. We then brought our chests together in such a way that our breasts rubbed against each other. To show how amorous we were, I need only say that this strange action gave us great delight.

'Is it not exquisite?' said Florence, 'The sensations of your breasts against mine fires my blood.'

'I experience the same feelings.' I returned. 'Oh, it is charming.'

'Amy,' said Florence after a few minutes repose, 'do you know what I would like to do?'

'No. What?'

'I should like to explore your more secret beauties.'

'With all my heart,' I replied, 'if you will allow me the same privilege.'

'Willingly, I should love it,' returned Florence.

'Come then, darling,' I exclaimed, 'I am ready, do with me as you like.'

'Dear girl, how good you are!' returned Florence. 'Lay down with your belly on the bed, that I may admire and manipulate your beauties... that's right, darling.'

I threw myself on my face on the bed. Florence came behind me, and lifting up my petticoats, exposed my bottom to her gaze. Of course she saw also the pouting lips of my bijou at the bottom of the fleshy cushions, faintly overshadowed with hair. She moved my thighs slightly apart, by which movements the lips of my sheath were slightly separated, revealing a line of coral between them. Florence absolutely threw herself on my bottom and devoured it with the most lascivious and ardent kisses.

'Does that position suit you, dear Florence?' said I, with my face buried in the bed.

'It is charming... delicious,' said Florence, moulding and pressing my buttocks. 'Great Heavens, Amy, how the sight of your beauties fires me! What magnificent buttocks, how white and firm, how well developed...' And again she bent down and smothered them with kisses. 'I should never be tired kissing your lovely bottom,' she continued, 'and the edges of that dear little cleft I see between your thighs... how inviting it looks. How beautiful it is shaded with silky down. Oh, I must, I must!' And she put her finger between the lips of my sheath and titillated my vagina. 'How charming, how delicious,' she repeated. 'Amy, I am in a blaze; my slit is on fire. How deliciously tight your vagina clasps my finger, and what a delightful warmth is there.... there! Now I have your clitoris! How stiff it is!'

'Dearest Florence,' I exclaimed, wiggling my buttocks, for

the in-and-out motion of her finger was more than I could bear, 'your touches and titillations are bringing on a crisis. Stay the motion of your finger or I shall come. There... there... there it is! Oh, I die! I die!'

During this last speech of mine, I moved my buttocks up and down, imitating the conjugal act, Florence all the time continuing her manipulations until the crisis came and I fell motionless on my belly.

'Come, Amy,' said Florence, withdrawing her dripping finger from my sheath. 'For Heaven's sake give me relief or I die.'

I rose from my recumbent posture, and seizing Florence by the waist, pushed her on the bed. She fell on her back. I threw her petticoats over her head. This action revealed all the lower portion of Florence's body, and a beautiful sight it was. Two magnificently developed thighs lead up to a charming grotto covered with black hair, between the pouting lips of which could be seen her clitoris stiff with intense desire. I admired for a moment Florence's beauties, and then commenced my manipulations. First of all, I stroked down her belly, implanting kiss after kiss upon it. I then played with the hair covering her Mons Veneris, twisting my finger in and out of it. I then divided the lips of her sheath, and titillated her highly excited clitoris.

'Great Heavens, Florence,' I exclaimed, 'what a beautiful bijou yours is! What delicious pouting lips! What a forest of black hair, and then your clitoris, how finely developed! Let me kiss it! Let me suck it.' I now stooped down and inserted my tongue between the lips of Florence's ruby passage, and titillated her clitoris with the tip of it. 'Great God, how delicious,' I exclaimed. 'I feel ready to come again. I do, indeed, darling.'

'Amy, darling, keep on, keep on,' said Florence, almost crazy with delight. 'Pass one hand behind and press my buttocks.'

I did as she desired, and advanced one finger in the narrow canal adjacent to the legitimate road and kept time with my tongue and finger.

'There, that's it!' she continued. 'I am coming. Oh, now, now! There! There! There!' She opened her thighs to the widest extent and lifted her legs high in the air. A convulsive shudder ran through her frame, and she discharged profusely, appearing to be perfectly annihilated by the deliciousness of her sensations. I threw myself by her side on the bed. After a long pause we both rose and kissed each other tenderly.

Such was my first initiation in the sports of Venus. Florence remained with us some months and scarcely a day passed that we did not enjoy the pleasures of the gods. When she left us, I was for a time disconsolate, but, soon after, I received an invitation to visit my sister.

Love And Saftey

I shall now pass on to the second head of Part I, namely Tribadism, from the Greek tribo, or the pleasures of women with women: Tribadism, which has solaced so many passionate women in the world, and has given them the opportunity of safely gratifying their passions without incurring the risk of letting the world know too much. Tribadism and tribades, whose frolics and lascivious caresses and gambols have been sung by so many poets and poetesses, from the Sappho and her Lesbian girls to our own time. The magic word combines in itself all the love sports, frigging, and gamahuching, with fingers, with dildos, and with tongues, that from the youngest girl to the most matured woman, our sex can enjoy together. Among the Greeks, Sappho is the best known tribade of antiquity, who passed her days with the girls of Lesbos. Then, after a long time through the ages, we come to Messalina, whom Juvenal describes as frigging her companions in wild orgies, until quivering with pleasure they fell back in the last agony of bliss with the cream of life flowing down their streaming thighs. Then down to modern times... how many famous queens, courtesans, women of all ranks have been Anandrynes as Mirabeau calls them (a Greek word signifying 'without man') or Fricarelles, as old Brantome termed them, i.e., friggers or rubbers. Or as the author of the Diable Au Corps has it the 'rubbers together' from the practice of girls lying upon one another and rubbing the lips of their cunts, and the mossy curls against each other until the last moment came, and both mutually spent. Their name is legion.

For our present purpose, it will be sufficient to consider all the various methods practised in our day and time; they are many, for the nineteenth century has made it very popular from the example set by me, the Empress of Austria, by ladies of the highest society in Vienna, Paris, London, and other towns, and by so many illustrious singers and actresses, such as Christine N. Oceana, the fair Mrs. L., and by so many sweet courtesans who find in this an exciting change from their usual erotic sports.

I shall only treat here of those forms of tribadism that leave the maidenhead unharmed. The others (which though of course absolutely safe in accordance with my plan) slightly take away that useless and unusual appendage. By this method, Tribadism can then be practised without the slightest injury to the virgin: by mutual frigging; by rubbing the cunts together in various delightful postures; by rubbing (in other sweet positions) the nipples of the breasts within the soft and juicy folds of the quim; and lastly by the gamahuche, the French word for tongue frigging, either first one and then the other, or by lying reversed so that each may gamahuche the other at the same moment, and which perhaps affords the greatest pleasure that can be had by any means whatever. The last methods, by dildos and other instruments, I shall describe in due course.

Before we commence the recital of so many charming subjects let us drink to Sappho.' Champagne, cool and sparkling, was soon passing around the hall in silver cups, the little blocks of clear ice tinkling against the lips of the fair drinkers, and the fair Asturian resumed her place and theme:

'From the youngest school girl upwards, all girls and women have, as we have seen, delighted in sweet but solitary amusements, plunging the (at first) timid finger into the sweet little slit where Cupid lives, and it always forms their delight through life. But the next step is the natural desire to vary what the French call 'the hand-play' alone, by teaching it to, and partaking of it with, a friend. So we find in almost all schools and convents for our sex that the little rogues will sleep together and, clasped in each other's arms, pass their middle finger into that rosy and pink-lipped slit of each other that they soon found out was so sweet to their own.'

'Come here, my little darlings,' said the Empress to two sweet little things with rosy cheeks and ebony and golden hair respectively. 'Come here!' And soon she stripped off the thin muslin and pink silk girdle from them as they advanced. 'Come and stand here by me. See their lovely little forms, and small undeveloped bosoms, see where the little cleft half hides itself between their thighs. Come, my pets, you must show us that pretty little game I found you playing at in bed this morning.' Here the two sweet children threw themselves on the experimenting couch, and soon each had a little pink finger in the pouting slit of the other, and the motions of their pretty bottoms and widespread thighs showed the crisis was coming, which it soon did as they fell apart from each other with murmurs and coos of pleasure. And the rosy little cunts showed the clear drops of their virgin spunk on the soft inner lips, glistening like beads of dew on rose leaves. 'Capital,' said the Empress, who with her hand under her robe was frigging herself and following all their motions, as indeed were the audience; flushed faces and quivering limbs were seen everywhere.

They tripped away and she resumed:

'So in schools and in convents, there the middle-aged and voluptuous nun takes her greatest pleasure in initiating the blushing and bashful novice in all the delights of tribadism, such as I have enumerated above. And here I may say that, charming as the sports of those about the same age are, you will find a peculiarly poignant pleasure in a great difference of age. Imagine how exciting it is for a woman of, say, fifty, well-formed and knowing all things, how exciting it is, I say, for such a one to clasp to her full-formed and mature bosom the slender frame of some sweet girl, to press the thick black forest of her curls, and the full lips of her cunt, against the smaller cleft of a lovely girl; to watch her first delight at the sight each of the other, to see the young woman stiffen herself out, and grind her pearly teeth in the ecstasy of a spend, while she herself is lost in lustful delight at feeling her companion's little hand wet through with the flowing spunk that follows her motions to and fro in the fully developed quim of her partner, drenching the thick curls through. It is this pleasure which makes so many mothers teach their daughters this exquisite bliss, so that they became the closest confidantes and friends with no silly concealments about their mutual little love affairs, in after life. And so many sisters, the elder teaching the younger, feel a more than sisterly love as they dissolve in each other's arms. And this mutual confidence has often induced the one that is freshly married to take the greatest pleasure in initiating her sister into the secrets of married life, by performing all things in her presence, with her husband, and even taking pleasure in allowing her husband to initiate the novice as well, in a charming trio. I once knew two sisters who, being both married, went all four for a six-month tour of the Continent, and on reaching Brussels changed husbands and so travelled the whole tour, reassuming their own partners again at Dover, on their return, no one the wiser. Ye, Gods, what parties of four they must have had!'

'To return to the subject... another charming way, called Klitorizing, is for two to lie on each other, and then pressing and clasping close to open with the hands the lips of their quims, so that they may, in squeezing together, be pushed quite into each other. In this way, they can rub together till the warmth, the friction of the hair and lips, and button, and their mutual kisses bring on such a spasm of delight, that the curls of each will be drenched and soaked with the flood of love, which they can pour down again and again, till, weary with pleasure, they fall apart and sleep. This may be varied by a similar pleasure, by each lying a different way on the bed, and opening the thighs widely, first pass close to each other, each with a leg outside, this brings the lips of the quims in contact, then each frigging herself with a finger at the approach of pleasure, can see the other spend, and feel the contractions and quivering of her cunt and the motions of her belly. The next method is one that is not often tried, but is very satisfactory; some women have full and protuberant breasts, and prominent nipples; now the nipple is one of the most sensitive points next to the quim. You should never frig a woman without tickling her nipple with your tongue, for she will have twice the pleasure and come twice as soon; I have known women to spend with pleasure by having the nipple sucked and tickled and nothing else. Mothers frequently come when being sucked by the child, especially if they assist with their finger; and husbands frequently also give their wives heavenly pleasure, and drive them half-mad with lust and lasciviousness by placing them in such a position that they can fuck them while the baby sucks the milk from their breasts. The gentle titillations of its tongue make an electric response to the strokes of the man's prick as it passes to and fro in its warm and glowing sheath.

Having shown the exquisite sensitiveness of the nipple, I will proceed to show how, with a woman such as I mentioned above, a charming sensation may be experienced. Let her lie down on her back on a bed, and let her companion kneel over her, facing her, and sink down so that the nipple, raised up firm and hard (a nipple stands like a prick) by tickling with the tongue, may be embedded in her quim. Now, by a series of sweet motions, and twisting of the bottom of the uppermost, and the use of the finger of the under-most in her own quim, the pleasures will be heavenly. The one underneath will be frigging herself with her own finger and feel the titillations of her friend's cunt, and its motions and contractions on her nipple, and can see the approaches of pleasure as the curls, ebony or gold, and the red lips rub and move on her bosom. And the darling above can feel the nipple like a little prick rubbing her button and the swell of the bosom pressing against her thighs. She can see, too, the flushed face of her loved friend with her pretty eyes turned up in the ecstasy of delight, her tongue just appearing through the pearly row of teeth, and feel the vibration of her whole frame as they both spend, the bosom streaming with the sweet and pearly discharge of the cunt about it. This scene must be illustrated.'

The illustration did justice to the above description; therefore, it need not be detailed very carefully. Suffice it to say that the actresses in it were a magnificent woman with a bosom of great volume, and with well-developed brown nipples, who under the caresses of the other – a lovely girl of eighteen – soon erect and stiff. The scene was carried out exactly as described above, and with such a picture before their eyes, we need hardly say the fair audience accompanied them in a similar manner to the blissful end, each in her own way. But it is needless to say that, observing the delicious excitement the woman showed as her nipple was sucked in and titillated by the cunt above her, the old saying recurred to their minds that, 'with one's tongue on a woman's nipple, and a finger on the pink button of her quim, one could make her so randy that she wouldn't stop if the angel Gabriel, and her father and mother, were all to walk into the room together'.

The Empress of Austria, with sparkling eyes and heaving bosom, resumed her lecture:

'I now come,' she said, 'to one of the most heavenly methods of all, practised by old and young, by all ages, by both sexes, in any combination, giving a pleasure that outlasts all others, and is as sweet and easily practised by a child, as by an old man or woman. You know to what I refer – the gamahuche. The derivation of the word is hard to find, but it means the procuring of mutual pleasure by two girls, or a girl and a man (and in Turkey and other places, I am sorry to say, of men and pretty boys together) by the lips and tongue, and so obtaining (whether we be of one sex or the other) a pleasure which is, in the opinion of most, equal if not superior to the most perfect fuck, without at the same time running any danger, either to virginity or reputation. From the earliest times, and more especially among the Greeks and Romans, this heavenly pleasure has been popular. Its various forms were all described and practised, but the modern word gamahuche combines and signifies all those forms, i.e., to quote the Latin form cunnilingus, meaning he or she who delighted in licking the quim of lovely women, darting their tongues into the rosy folds till the quivering and writhing form was dissolved in pleasure. Irrumatio, meaning the soft sucking of a man's prick by a woman, the passing of the tongue 'round the rosy head till the supreme moment. Fellatores, what they called those men and women who practised this.'

'Amongst tribades and women who love their own sex, these forms have always been the end of all, the quintessence of pleasure, and all who have tried it have (even those to whom fucking is a common thing) declared it the acme of lasciviousness. Let us, therefore, devote a short time to the delicious delirium of gamahuching among ourselves and own sex as connected with men. One of the greatest advantages of gamahuching is that no woman is too young or too old to taste its delights. Take a sweet little darling, lay her across the bed, open her pretty legs wide, and kneeling between them tickle the pink slit of her cunt with your tongue, just on the button, and soon you will see her head thrown back, and her bottom moving up and down, and her thighs stretched out rigidly in the ecstasy of a first spend – and this when the rougher touches of a finger might cause more pain than pleasure. How many sisters have mutually experienced this pleasure from each other! How many schoolgirls! Many a mother has thus initiated her daughter, by a sweet kiss like this, watching the quivering side-to-side movements, the trembling hips, the heaving bottom; hearing the sighs of love whilst two of her fingers, buried in the rich hairy gap of her own matured cunt have, by their rapid and experienced motion, brought down the flood of pleasure, at the same crisis, and so secured her daughter's love.'

'And however old a woman or man is, the magic tongue will assuredly produce its effects. What raptures many a dame of sixty or sixty-five has experienced from the well-paid caresses of a lascivious and knowing waiting-maid drawing forth the torrents of spunk from between the fat thighs of her mistress, who thus experiences the pleasures which she is too old, perhaps, to attract men to share. We must divide gamahuching into the single and double gamahuche. The single is when one is passive, the other active, and then the reverse, each in her turn. The double gamahuche (the French call it 'the great game') is where the two women or girls lie, one on the other, each with her head buried between the other's plump thighs, each with the active tongue tickling the button or darting as far as possible into the cunt; licking and rolling the inner lips and the sides of the outer one rubbing the hair; their bodies mutually clasped 'round each other, rolling to and fro in the agony of delight, till with a shuddering spasm of lust they inundate each other's pretty lips with a flood of spunk they mutually shoot forth. Such is the great gamahuche, which we will consider and show examples of in a short time.'

'To go back for a moment, however... the simple gamahuche is one often practised when one is instructing the other, and where circumstances perhaps render it inconvenient to be naked, which both should be to enjoy the great gamahuche properly. I will tell you of a little inimitable description from the Diable Au Corps by Andrea Nerciat. The Marquise and her waiting-maid, Nicole, are about to instruct Philippine into this charming sport, and it is thus told...

The Marquise seizes Philippine by the shoulders and pushes her back so that she falls crossways on the edge of the bed. Nicole, an old hand at it, and spurred on by her own lustful desires, finishes putting her in the proper position, and puts her hand under the thighs thus exposed while the Marquise takes on herself the task of pulling up all her clothes above her navel. Every charm that Philippine possesses is at the mercy of the lovely Marquise and Nicole, and the burning lips of the latter soon find their way to the centre of attraction with its pink, plump lips, and thick curls of ebony hair. Her tongue soon finds the magic spot, the Marquise tickles the nipples of Philippine's breasts with her tongue and finger, and Nicole follows up her lead with all her power and love. Philippine – by her sighs, by the hurried undulations of her breasts, by the tremulous movements of her bottom, and by that slight internal sound that experts know so well – shows the extreme pleasure that she feels, till that supreme moment when, stiffening out her whole body in one convulsive thrust upwards, she spends and falls back again. Nicole rises up, her rosy lips covered with the pearly drops of liquid pleasure that are now seen trickling down Philippine's thighs and hanging like dew on the curls of her cunt. Nicole's finger coming forth from her petticoats, slippery with moisture, shows that she has accompanied her greedy pupil to the end.'

The murmurs of pleasure through the hall, and the many pairs of hands mutually missing from sight, showed how much this extract pleased the Empress's audience.

'There are many positions for the single gamahuche. We will organize three groups, showing you the three most convenient forms of it.'

Six lovely girls and women stepped forth amidst the applause and excitement of the audience. The first couple were two of about the same age. One disposed herself on the edge of the couch, so that her legs hung over the side. The other girl knelt between, and inserting a finger in her own cunt soon had her lips and face buried in the quim of her lover. The Empress herself, attending to this central group, tickled the nipples of the victim's breasts.

Of the other couple, a fine stout, fat woman of about forty-five leant over a chair with its back towards her. The other, a girl of about eighteen with red hair and curls of burnished red upon her little quim, sat on a stool between her legs, widely straddled apart. Thus the bottom of the elder was just over her face, and she and all the audience had a view of a magnificent bottom with its corrugated brown hole surrounded by little ringlets of black hair, and pressed out between her thighs the thick lips of her enormously developed cunt. The girl, thus conveniently placed, pressed her face against the red flesh of her quim, and darted in her tongue. The outrageously lustful passions of the elder woman soon showed themselves, convulsive tremors shook her frame, and her cunt opened and shut on the girl's tongue. The latter was frigging herself furiously as she proceeded with her task, and the elder woman supplemented her efforts by frigging herself on the button in front. Soon the crisis approached; we heard her murmuring, 'Prick, cunt, fuck!' till at last, with a spasmodic contraction of the cheeks of her bottom, a flood of spunk, creamy and thick, shot out like a man's over the face and bosom of her 'lover' and ran down her thighs while the girl spent on her own finger.

The third couple needs little description. The first woman laid herself flat on the bed, on her back, with her head on the pillow. The other knelt astride of her face, with her own face towards the feet of the first. By this method, her pretty bottom, with its snowy hemispheres, was just in front of her friend's eyes, whose lips and tongue were busy with her cunt. By slightly stooping forward, she could frig with her hand the lascivious quim in front of and below her, and clearly visible between the side-spread thighs.

The three couples soon exhibited these phases of gamahuching and retired amidst applause. And as each successive step in useful knowledge was placed before the audience, by precept and example, we could see the blaze of sensual passion rising higher and higher. Fully developed women, with their mature charms, were all occupied in exciting themselves or each other, while the silver cups of cool concoctions passed rapidly 'round.

An extract from the Pearl Annual in the form of a leaflet was then handed to each lady to further illustrate the subject:

My Last Night at School

The night before leaving Madame Minette's, I slept with Miss Sappho, who was much grieved at the idea of my departure.

We retired to bed, entirely naked, and after hugging and kissing each other, till we were almost delirious from the intensity of our feeling. I then asked her to kneel on the bed and lean forward till her elbows touched her knees. How lovely those superb buttocks appeared in this position! I kissed them madly. Then, gently pulling her thighs apart, I separated the cheeks of her bottom and saw the lovely little pink hole, which perceptibly throbbed as I gazed. I perforated it with my finger, pushing it backwards and forwards, as she swayed to and fro, uttering low moans of enjoyment. I then parted them still further, and saw the innermost part of the delicious cunt, which was delightfully moist and sensitive.

'Gamahuche me, darling,' said she, 'or I shall die.'

Instead of complying, I took up a birch, and commenced to flagellate that lovely bottom, tickling the inside of her thighs, and even the lips of her cunt.

She again commenced to move, and I saw the cheeks become rigid, and every muscle seemed strained to the utmost. Then her whole body appeared to throb, and I saw the spend trickling down between her thighs.

Before I could place my mouth on the beloved spot, to suck out every drop of the divine liquid, I fell to the floor in the agonies of emission, my sensations being so overpowering that I fainted.

When I recovered my senses, darling Sappho was seated across my loins, facing me, and frigging herself under my eyes. I begged her to kneel over me and frig herself with one of my nipples instead of her finger.

The darling girl complied, while I bit her belly, and passing one hand behind her inserted a finger in her bottom-hole, the effect of which was the inundation of my nipple by her copious spend.

She then lay behind me, with her head towards my bottom, and raising one of my legs as high as she could, she literally took the whole of my cunt in her mouth, and sucked me till I howled aloud with rapture.

After this we fondled each other till our desires were again aroused. She then fastened on a dildo, and lying on my belly, fucked me with deep and long-drawn luscious thrusts, which speedily caused me to spend again, as I clung to her with a super-human embrace.

I then took the dildo from her, and lying with my head on her thigh, took it in my hand, and fucked her in return, till she was utterly exhausted. We then fell asleep in each other's arms.

You shall now see,' said the Empress, 'the final scene of the 'double Gamahuche. I myself will show you the method with my own favourite Lizette of the Viennese Circus, and I flatter myself that no woman better understand this, the crowning pleasure of Tribadism.'

Loud applause followed, and six naked girls wheeled forward the voluptuous spring couch to the front of the dais, so that it stood sideways to the audience. The naked girls hastened to disrobe their splendid mistress, and she stood naked before all eyes. Her figure was tall, her breasts were spheres of ivory, with rosy pink nipples standing out finely, a few little ringlets of hair growing around the nipple, a sign of lust. Her waist, her feet, her legs and her thighs were all of lovely contours and fully developed curves. Her cunt was overshadowed with thick curls of ebony hair, which ran up in that rare but beautiful manner as far as the navel, after the manner of the Italian women. Lizette, as naked as her mistress, had glowing dark-red auburn hair, and her quim was quite covered with red curls of surpassing beauty and colour. And whatever individual taste may be, there is no doubt that for sensual passion, for furious lust and perfection in bed, nothing equals those redheaded women. There is no sport of love in which they are matched, not even by the black, ebony-haired and pale-faced ones, the next best colour for lasciviousness. And now appeared before all that beauty which had so enslaved her mistress, namely her magnificent button. Usually the size of the top of a finger or thumb in most women, Lizette possessed (as do so many Spanish and Italian women) one the length of four-and-a-half or five inches. It stuck, excited as it was, straight out like a miniature prick. Unable to restrain herself at the sight, the Empress gave them, quite impromptu, a preliminary to the double gamahuche in the shape of a button-fuck. This has been one of the great delights of Tribadism with those who are lucky enough to find a woman with it sufficiently developed. Throwing herself back, she drew Lizette on her, and clasping her close in her arms pressed their quims close together, the ebony and gold in contact. Then crossing her legs over her back, as with a man she guided the stiff and rosy button into her cunt. So excited were they that after a few frantic pushes and pulls we saw the spending trickling over their thighs. Then, without a moment's delay, the double gamahuche began.

Lizette reversed herself on her imperial mistress, and mutually, with the face of each and her tongue buried in the thick juicy lips and thick curls of the other's cunt, they began to titillate the inmost recesses of them with their tongues; the Empress was sucking the button of Lizette while she was forcing her tongue, like a miniature prick, into the full-fledged cunt before her. Soon the hands and fingers helped; a finger of each was pushed gently in and out of the corrugated holes of their bottoms and another in the passage wet and slippery of their cunts. Their words grew thick, and their bodies trembled with mad lust. The audience was electrified. Then, with one passionate clasp and heave, their bodies stiffened out in the agony of spending, and the pearly drops of each oozed from their quims over their crimson lips and flushed faces. They rose amid shouts of delight, and the Empress, having re-attired and refreshed herself, and Lizette, resumed her lecture as the iced cups and soothing cigarettes went around:

'So much,' said she, 'for the dildos for use alone. The other forms require another, either man or woman or both. First there is the dildo well described above. I think it would please you to see into what a splendid man it transforms me, and my dear Lizette shall be the Eve to my Adam.'

Lizette swiftly stepped from behind the Empress, bearing on a gold salver a magnificent dildo as described above in the advertisement.

Kneeling before her mistress, she fastened one of the silk straps around her waist, and the four others, two meeting around each magnificently formed thigh, whose great smooth marble curves, as the poet observes, were the observed of all observers. Thus fastened, the artificial prick stood boldly forth from among the curls of the stomacher, and the lovely Empress looked like the Hermaphroditus of old, sculptured in the South Kensington Gallery, with the face and flowing look of a lovely woman, but the prick and balls of an Apollo.

Lizette approached, and squeezing the ball that hung between her mistress's thighs, dipped the ruby head into a jug of boiling, or nearly boiling, scented soap and water. It immediately filled and Lizette, frigging herself madly, threw herself backwards on the sloping couch and opened her thighs widely, showed the glorious bush of dark red hair that shaded her lovely cunt. In dying accents, she called out, 'Come, my darling mistress, come.'

Nor did the Empress delay. Throwing herself on her favourite, she separated the moist lips with one hand, and with the other guided the tip into its sheath. Then with one mad plunge she drove it to the hilt, till the real curls of glowing red and the false ones of jet black were intermingled. Lizette gave a short, gasping sob of utter bliss and bounded up to meet the stroke. Active as a man, and with his exact motions, the Empress drove on and on, in and out, fast and furious, frigging herself with one finger under the stomacher of the dildo. Lizette's eyes turned upwards, her head fell back. 'Now... oh, now, my darling!' she murmured, and the boiling injection was shot up into pretty Lizette's womb, meeting the flood of spunk, scarcely less hot, that streamed from her cunt. At that moment, the Empress spent, and she fell weary and lifeless on her sweetheart's belly, the dildo buried to the hilt in the cunt that still nipped it with convulsive throbs. They say 'Imitation is the sincerest from of flattery', and if so, the Empress and Lizette must

315

have felt flattered, for while the above scene was taking place, dildos had been distributed to every pair, and the fair audience were in pairs imitating the sweet example.

The Empress, recovering, resumed her lecture once again:

'There are also several other kinds of dildos. There is another double one without a ball, i.e., straight with two heads, so that two girls can each simultaneously enjoy the magic touch. Again, there is one with two heads, one large and one small. The large head penetrates the quim and the other (conveniently placed) perforates the little bottom-hole with double friction. And once more is this doubled again with four heads, two large and two small, so that when two women have it between them they have each one in the cunt and one in the posterior aperture. The effect of this is maddening. And lastly, there is one very peculiar dildo described in the Diable Au Corps which is made to fit the chin of a lady or gentleman, so that when kneeling between a girl's soft thighs, he or she can insert it, and not only give her the pleasure of a prick, but see the effect as she approaches spending immediately under his or her eyes. So much, my dears, for the dildo or artificial prick.'

Parisian Frolics

Mme. de Liancourt accompanied me one day when I had arranged to meet Martha. As soon as we discovered the latter, she went forward by herself to meet her while I slipped off to her chambers. Mme. de Liancourt told Martha that the latter's husband was suspicious, and was endeavouring to have a watch kept on her, and that this was why I had not come to the rendezvous – I had asked her to come instead to explain, and to bring her to where I was awaiting her. After a little hesitation, Martha consented to accompany her to the Rue de Suresnes.

Presently (hidden in the small boudoir) I saw them come in and pass into the bedroom.

'You're quite safe here. You're in my own rooms. Here you can bill and coo as much as you please with your lover!'

Martha coloured to the tips of her little ears. 'But, Madame, Monsieur R. isn't my lover! We have never…'

'Really? My child, you have done well to tell me this, and you need fear no indiscretion on my part, for I also have a lover! The danger you were running has made me take an interest in you, and this is why I gladly brought you here at the request of Monsieur R. Really, it was almost heroic of me to do so, for there are not many women who would go out of their way to bring to a mutual male friend another woman younger and prettier than herself! But it is so, dear, for you are certainly prettier than me!'

She kissed Martha. Then she invited her to take off her wraps and to make herself at home. But when she observed that Martha remained fully dressed with the exception of her mantle, she said to her, 'Don't be afraid, dear, do make yourself at home and do as I do. You mustn't remain as you are and receive your lover, for men like to see their sweethearts in some deshabille when they come to visit them. Besides this, I have to change my dress for my evening's engagements. It will be pleasant to take advantage of this and see how some of my dresses will look on you. An excellent idea, for should any one have followed us here and finds us so engaged, it will completely throw them off the scent!'

I admired the cleverness of this argument.

Mme. de Liancourt rapidly divested herself of her dresses, corset, and petticoats till she had on her chemise only. Then she proceeded to reduce Martha to a similar condition of undress, in spite of the latter's hesitation, especially as to removing her corset, as she alleged that she should keep this on if she was to try on any dresses. This Mme. de Liancourt would not agree to.

'You wear very pretty underclothing, dear. No doubt you study his tastes in such details?'

This was a good guess, for Martha had put on the corset we had bought together, also the lace petticoats and the delicately trimmed chemise. How delicate is the female instinct in the matter of attracting the male amorous desires!

'I do not know whether my dress will fit you, dear,' continued Mme. de Liancourt. 'I think I am bigger than you are in the bust!' Under this pretext, she threw open her chemise and exhibited her breasts, which she set to work to compare with those of Martha, after having first unfastened and opened the latter's chemise. 'What deliciously white and firm little bubbies you have, dear! I expect you have often been complimented on them. Your lover is a very fortunate man. Of course, I don't mean your husband, for if the latter saw you thus, I suppose he would try to spoil these little darlings, where as your lover would know how to show his appreciation of them by his caresses.'

'Suppose he should suddenly turn up and catch us as we are!'

'I should rush off into any corner that I could!' replied Mme. de Liancourt with a smile she endeavoured vainly to repress. She added, 'But at a ball, we women show quite as much of ourselves as you and I are now doing! I, at all events, have my dresses cut low enough to let my nipples be seen! Besides, it is only a woman with a bad figure that objects to be found naked or practically so. I'm not one of that lot. See?' With a touch, she caused her chemise to fall to her feet, and stepped forward out of it in all her glorious nudity, the effect being heightened by the contrast caused by a triangular patch of tawny golden hair at the junction of her belly and thighs, and her black silk stockings with their rose-tinted garters worn above the knees! 'This is how I meet my lover!' she said.

Martha became scarlet.

'How you are blushing, dear! Is it because of the sight of me standing naked? If so, you remind me of one of my girlfriends who declares that the sight of me naked excites her much more than the sight of a naked man would. Every time she comes to see me, she insists on my undressing completely in front of her!

Then you should see how she kisses and embraces me just as if she were playing with a naked man! Then she will go and do a thousand-and-one improper and indecent things to me, which at first used to make me feel horribly ashamed, but which now I really like – even to the length of paying her back in the same coin! Oh, it's lovely! And mind you, we're not deceiving our husbands! Strange, but true, isn't it, eh?'

She kissed the blushing Martha, and continued: 'Ever since, I have had lovers and enjoyed them. I still recollect how delicious those tête-à-têtes with my girlfriend were! We used to caress and kiss each others breasts, like this...'

'Oh! You're biting me!'

'Doesn't your lover do this to you? See how your pretty little nipples are stiffening and standing out!'

'Oh, Madame, you're tickling me! Oh! Take away your hand! Oh! What are you doing? No! No! I don't want it!'

Mme. de Liancourt had seized Martha and was passionately clasping her against herself, holding her tightly with one arm around her waist while she slipped her other hand between Martha's thighs. The latter, utterly surprised by this sudden attack, could only struggle feebly.

'Oh, but Madame, what... are you going... to do... to me?'

'Make love with you, darling! I'm gone on you! Don't you know how one woman can adore another? How two women can mutually prove their love for each other? Let me show you! But you surely must know all about it! At school, didn't one of the bigger girls take charge of you, and teach you... this? You're blushing now. Oh, you little humbug! No one never forgets that sort of thing! Your girlfriend must have had a sweet time! Come, dear little humbug, what was it you used to do together?'

'Really I don't know!'

'Really and truly? Well, I know. Come, you'd like to do it again, wouldn't you, with me?'

'No! No! Suppose he came in!'

'He can't without our hearing him. Come, you pretty little coward, come. Place yourself against me. Take off your chemise. You can have a dressing gown if you like.' She gave Martha one. 'No, don't fasten it; leave it quite open. I want to have a good look at you. Your breasts, your belly, your hairs... oh, how they curl and cluster!' Suddenly, she knelt and applied her lips to the dark triangular patch that luxuriated at the end of Martha's stomach, the latter still offering a shamefaced resistance.

'No, no!' she cried, squeezing her legs closely together.

It had been decreed and registered in the Book of Lesbian Venus that Mme. de Liancourt should sacrifice yet another victim on the altar dedicated to tribadic love. I didn't think it was advisable to intervene. I felt sure that my turn would come before long. In the meantime, here was Mme de Liancourt preparing for my delectation the most charming spectacle one could desire, one which the famous Regent would gladly have had performed before him at the Palais Royal.

Martha, now half-willing, but still half reluctant, passively allowed herself to be placed on the sofa. Mme. de Liancourt seated herself at Martha's side, passed one arm around her, and slipped her other hand between Martha's thighs while she passionately kissed her, darting her tongue into Martha's mouth. Her finger, directed by both art and passion, soon produced the desired result. Martha's breath began to come brokenly, her eyes half closed, her bosom and breasts heaved agitatedly. At this moment, Mme. de Liancourt, no longer content to play only the part of the communicator of pleasure, caught hold of one of Martha's hands and gently conducted it to her own cunt with a mute demand for reciprocity. And Martha did not draw it back. She recognized the silent request, and her gentle little hand began to do its untutored best.

What a charming picture the pair made! What a glorious group worthy of Fragonard or of Boucher! I would have paid gladly a long price for a series of photographs representing them thus. Both girls intertwining their lovely white thighs and slender legs, and then separating them only to interlace them in some other way in the midst of a storm of kisses and broken ejaculations, principally from Mme. de Liancourt, who by now was simply mad with lust, her hips and haunches quivering, her body rapturously becoming more and more rigid!

'Martha! Oh, darling! Keep on! Oh! Keep on! You're doing it beautifully! Oh! Oh! I'm coming! Oh! Oh! I'm spending! Ah! Ah!'

A moment of silence followed this ecstatic crisis, Mm. de Liancourt still keeping her hand on Martha's slit.

'How wet you are! You've also spent, you naughty thing! Darling, we've done it together! Wipe yourself.' She gave Martha a handkerchief. 'Now, wasn't that good?'

'Yes…' replied Martha, timidly.

'Then let's do it together!'

'If you like…'

Immediately, our two lascivious heroines recommenced their lubricious caresses. Martha extended herself flat on her back on the sofa. Her seducer, bending over her, looked her all over and felt and handled her as the spirit willed in her. Freshly aroused in her new lust – as was manifest from the agitation of her bosom and breasts – Martha's hand, without invitation, stole to Mme. de Liancourt's cunt and resumed its loving ministration. She had caught the fancy, she, so timid with me; nevertheless, she began to protest when, after having tenderly sucked her breasts, her mistress in lesbian pleasures carried her lips lower down. 'No, no, not there!' she panted, trying to raise herself.

'Yes, yes! I wish it! Let me kiss your sweet cunny with its pretty hair! I'll do it just as well as your lover can!'

'But he has never... kissed me there!'

'Then he doesn't know his duties as your lover! So much the better for me! I shall now be the first to do it to you. You'll see how delicious it is. I used to be just like you at first, but now I simply adore this way, and you'll always do it this way in future whenever you get a chance! So, let me arrange you... open wider these pretty thighs.' Then, in the twinkling of an eye, the desired spot was covered with her lascivious and skilful mouth.

'No! Not there! Not down there!' panted Martha as she felt Mme de Liancourt's tongue wandering over her cunt, still virgin to such treatment and to the accompanying sensations. For response, she was dragged down to the foot of the sofa, her thighs widely pulled apart, as Mme. de Liancourt, falling on her knees between them, murmured almost unconsciously, 'Oh, what a lovely sweet fresh little cunny... oh, the beauty!' Then, like the swoop of hawk on a chicken, her mouth attacked it and remained there as if glued to it. Completely defeated, Martha fell on her back again and resigned herself as best she could to abandon herself to the voluptuous sensations that now were thrilling through her, induced by the ardent tongue of her passionate friend. Some minutes thus passed.

At last Mme. de Liancourt raised herself, red, flushed, panting, almost delirious. 'Together? Will you?'

'What?' gasped Martha.

'This! Let's do it together! Will you?'

'If you wish it... but... how?'

'I'll show you, darling! Now watch!' She got on the sofa, turned her bottom towards Martha's head, straddled across Martha, and then placed herself astride her face, her belly resting on Martha's breasts, and her cunt seeking the same lingual caress that she was recommencing on Martha's, which was now lying below her lips. Her thighs hid half the face of my sweet little mistress, and I could only see a bit of her forehead and her pretty hair emerging from between Mme. de Liancourt's buttocks. As the latter wriggled and waggled her charming globes of flesh in lascivious undulations, I noted that Martha had accommodated herself to her position, and that her mouth, as docilely as her hand, comprehended and daintily executed the delicate function demanded from it.

As for Mme. de Liancourt, she was simply mad with passionate lust. What a strange thing it is that a woman can thus procure for herself such keen and ecstatic enjoyment in thus caressing another woman. I was splendidly placed for contemplating both her and the object of her delirious worship. I saw her face in profile, her chin resting on the hairs, her mouth poised on the lips of Martha's slit between which her tongue was playing. These secret charms of Martha, hitherto unknown to me, made me envy Mme. de Liancourt both her place and the game she was playing. Time after time, I was on the point of bursting out of my hiding place and planting my mouth on the sweet spot she was attacking. Our convention would have authorized the act, but I refrained; the charm of the spectacle fascinated me.

Sometimes, Mme. de Liancourt seemed as if she wanted to get the whole of Martha's cunt into her mouth. Sometimes, she amused herself by administering little touches to the clitoris with her tongue. Then she would pass her tongue right along the tender slit from top to bottom. Sometimes, she would, with her fingers, separate the sensitive lips and thrust her tongue between them as deeply as she possibly could. Frequently she stopped, inspected attentively the sweet object of her admiration with eyes blazing with lust unsatisfied, and then ejaculated frenziedly in her passionate adoration, 'Oh, this cunt... this sweet cunt... this delicious darling cunt!' She would shower kisses on it, and how Martha must have revelled in bliss! I would have liked to have been able to watch her face. She evidently was acquitting herself most satisfactorily in reciprocating Mme. de Liancourt's attentions, if one might judge by the plunging and joggings of the latter's body as she brokenly exclaimed, 'Oh... oh... you do it well! I can feel your tongue! Now, do you feel mine? Wait... I'm going to shove it right inside this sweet cunt... as far in... as... it will go... there!'

It is impossible to indicate the accent of these words as pronounced by a mouth the tongue of which was endeavouring to talk and lick at one and the same moment! What a terrible state of nervous excitement must have possessed Mme. de Liancourt, a woman so reserved and correct in ordinary life, especially in language. But the ecstatic crisis was fast approaching; her breathing became more and more broken.

'Martha... oh, Martha, oh, darling... I'm coming! Ah! Ah! I'm spending! Are you? Spend... together... together... Wait a moment... now! Now! Oh, I'm spending... again! Spend also! Spend!'

Their bodies stiffened, constricted, and I heard a deep sigh of unspeakable pleasures. They had finished.

Mme de Liancourt slowly slipped off her position, and then proceeded to give her pupil kiss after kiss of approbation and satisfaction. 'Darling, your face is all wet with what you have drawn out of me! And I've drunk you! Use my handkerchief.

How flushed and red you are. Now, wasn't it good?'

'Oh, yes, much better than I could have believed!'

Was it not now the time for me to put in an appearance? But what could I do with two women whose lust had thus been satiated? Nevertheless, I decided to show myself, and opened the door, regretting that I had delayed so long.

Two Flappers In Paris

N ow,' said she, 'if you will allow me, I will introduce to you to my assistants.' And turning to Evelyn and Nora, she went on, 'You will have before you, young ladies, the pick of the beauty and grace of Paris. I make a point of gathering 'round me only girls who are really beautiful, well educated, and of charming disposition and character. They are well trained and full of tact, and I can assure you that you will in no way suffer by making their acquaintance, but quite the contrary.'

My two little friends bowed somewhat nervously.

I pressed them to me affectionately and whispered, 'Even if they are all this, you surpass them a hundred fold!'

A fond look from each of them seemed to thank me, and Madame conducted us to the drawing-room.

Here there was none of that bad taste that is so often to be seen in houses of this description. The temple of the Rue Ch. is an abode of good style. There are not too many mirrors and too much tawdry gilding about. All the furniture and fittings are of the best class and seem designed to set off to the best advantage the pretty faces and the sparkling eyes that are to be encountered there.

The Drawing Room was already occupied; we found there about a dozen of the young women of the establishment. Or rather, I might say of the girls, for the eldest of them was not more than twenty-five, and some of the younger ones seemed, as indeed I knew them to be, just twenty-one, which is the youngest at which a girl may legally enter a Bordelle in Paris. They rose to meet us as we entered. They were all charmingly dressed and showed not the slightest signs of being what they really were. One would have taken them for society girls who had met together at a friend's house for a little gossip and music. And indeed, one of them was seated at a fine Erard Grand, which, draped with rich material and half surrounded with little palm trees, occupied one corner of the room. She was just finishing the last bars of the adagio of a sonata as we entered, and it was evident by her touch and execution that she was a first rate pianist.

Among the first of those who came to meet us was my little friend Rose, of whom I have spoken. Next to her was her special friend Marie, with whom Rose always liked to 'work' JUST in case, as often happened, a visitor wished to be 'entertained' by two girls at once.

Madame R. introduced the girls to us singly, and announced us as her good friend 'whom they all knew' and his two nieces. 'And now, girls,' said Madame, 'perhaps you will entertain us with a little music and dancing. I am sure these young ladies will be surprised and delighted with the way in which you dance the Italian dances, for example. Blanche, will you play us something?'

'Certainly, Madame,' replied the girl who had been at the piano. 'An Italian waltz, perhaps? Something dreamy?'

'Yes, that's it,' I approved smiling, 'something dreamy.'

'Very well,' said Blanche with a merry laugh, 'I will play you Surgente di Amore and The Springs of Love.'

'No,' said Madame, 'let us proceed by degrees. Begin with Tesoro Mio, and then you will give us Io T'amo, and finally will come Surgente di Amore.'

The programme being thus arranged, Blanche took her place at the piano, five couples of dancers were formed, and the impassioned strains of the celebrated waltzes Tesoro Mio and Io T'amo regulated the beautiful dance, quite proper at present, but highly voluptuous. In Io T'amo, especially towards the end, the sensuous nature of the waltz became more noticeable. Rose and Marie especially were dancing with delightful skill; it really seemed they understood the most refined shades of voluptuousness. Instead of continuing to turn around and around in the waltz as their companions did, they seemed to sway from side to side with a delightful undulating motion of their bodies and of their splendid bottoms, while face-to-face or side by side, with their heads thrown back, and their nostrils palpitating, their open lips seemed to invite hot burning kisses.

I was seated on a sofa with, of course, Evelyn and Nora on each side of me, and Madame was seated near us. I could feel my two little companions vibrate in unison with Rose and Marie, whom I had pointed out to them as the couple most deserving of their attention. How could I longer restrain the intense ardour that was devouring me? The charming freshness of Evelyn and Nora, and their sweet confidence in me, simply drove me mad. I could feel their virgin modesty was intensely excited, and I thought with delight of their sweet young bodies, never yet stained by look or touch, which were experiencing such strange sensations – sensations I knew were to be so much more acute in a few minutes time. 'It's pretty, isn't it?' I asked softly.

'Oh, yes!' said Evelyn, trembling. Her lips were slightly parted over her beautiful teeth and her nostrils quivered as though inhaling some rich perfume.

Nora whispered, almost touching my cheek, 'It's only today for the first time that I realize what dancing really is!'

'You darling, you would like to dance too, wouldn't you?'

'Oh, no, I should be afraid!'

'No, you wouldn't be afraid, nor would you Evelyn, would you?'

'Oh, no, not a bit,' said Evelyn eagerly, 'but I should like to dance with Rose, if I may.'

'Certainly you shall dance with her, and you, Nora, with Marie, and all the others, except the pianist, shall leave the room if you like.'

'Oh, yes, yes, that's just what we should like!'

The dance was drawing to a close, and a most voluptuous one, although Rose and Marie had not given one another the supreme embrace, following the directions of Madame.

I whispered a few words in the good lady's ear.

She got up and spoke for a moment to the girls who all retired with the exception of Rose, Marie and Blanche.

When we were alone, I said to Rose, 'I shall be very much obliged if you will have a turn with Evelyn, Rose, and you, Marie, will take charge of Nora. They are charmed with you and are delighted with your way of dancing.'

'Oh,' said Rose, 'that's nothing. We will show the young ladies something much nicer than that! Now, Blanche, play us the Surgente di Amore!'

And Blanche began to play it.

At first, things did not go too well, especially with Nora, who was less quick than Evelyn in accommodating herself to the new measure. But soon, I had the intense pleasure of seeing my two nieces dancing as gracefully and, I might almost say, as lasciviously as their delighted instructress.

Soon the style changed.

Up to this point, Rose and Marie had held their partners in the usual way, but now, placing their arms more firmly around their waists, they pressed their trembling bodies more closely to their own. And then, indeed, the dance became almost maddening in its refined lasciviousness. Of course, Rose and Marie were past mistresses in the art and seemed to take a real pleasure in initiating the two charming flappers. Pressed close together, a thigh was now advanced and inserted between those of Evelyn and Nora, their bodies and breasts seemed to form one, and the warm breath of the partners was mingled. Slowly, in this position they revolved for a few moments, and then it became evident that the voluptuous waltz had justified its title and that (for the first time, as I supposed, in the case of my little friends) the springs of love were opened.

The happy climax was reached just as the last strains of the dance were dying away. Rose and Marie, at the critical moment, had led their partners in front of Madame and myself as we sat on the sofa. I saw suddenly, and at the same moment, Evelyn and Nora fall forward and collapse in the arms of the two girls. Their knees seemed to bend forward, their loins were arched in, their thighs gripped as though in a vice. The thighs of their partners, and the convulsive jerks of their bottoms plainly visible under their thin dresses, left no doubt that the sluices were opened and that the tide of love was flowing freely. They would have certainly fallen if Rose and Marie had not supported them and half carried them to a seat, where they remained for a few moments as though dead; however, they soon recovered and seemed a little ashamed of their weakness.

I went and took them by the hand and led them to the sofa where I had been sitting. 'What has happened?' I asked smiling. They were equally unable to find an answer, so I came to their assistance. 'Don't try to put me off with some fairy tale,' I said gaily.

'I will explain to you what has happened.'

Rose and Marie were talking together at the end of the room, and Madame had gone up to the pianist to congratulate her on the success of her playing.

'Dancing undertaken in a certain manner,' I said, 'is naturally conducive to pleasure in the sense that it excites those parts of the body which are the seat of the novel sensations you have just experienced. Do you know the parts that I mean?'

Silence.

'You know,' I continued, 'that these are the central parts of the body – the loins, the lower part of the belly, the thighs, the bottom, and that all nervous sensations are cantered here. But when the dance is conducted as it was just now, when the bodies touch – still more when it is a man and a girl who are dancing together – when the belly of one is pressed against the belly of the other, and when the thigh of one is inserted and rubs against the thighs of the other and the lower part of the belly, thus exciting the treasures which are hidden there...'

'You are driving me mad!' sighed Nora.

'Don't interrupt, Nora,' said Evelyn with a quick and tender glance. 'Go on, all this is most interesting!'

'Then there takes place what has just occurred to both of you, a prolonged and infinitely delicious spasm, and which, with certain variations, is always produced when one spends, as it is called; that is to say, when one enjoys the sensation which you have just experienced. Evelyn, dear, tell me openly exactly what you felt.'

'For my part,' said Evelyn softly, 'what had the great effect on me was the rubbing... How shall I explain it?'

'Of the thigh?'

'No... of the belly. It seemed to me that my very being was attracted by Rose's belly... I seemed to feel it naked under my dress!'

'There's nothing peculiar about that, darling. I have often felt that remarkable attraction myself.'

'But how can you feel, you, a man, what we girls have just felt, as you are not made as we are?'

'Pleasure is all one. Men and women feel it equally and just in the same way. You have, however, one great advantage over us. Your pleasure, otherwise called your spending, is much more prolonged than ours and does not take out of you nearly so much.'

'Really?' I could see that this piece of information interested the two dears immensely. 'You will think me very inquisitive, but I should like to know how it was that you experienced what you were talking about... the belly.'

'I have often experienced it,' I said. 'My governess was a strict disciplinarian and she often used to whip me. Now, she had a way of turning the punishment of a whipping into a delightful pleasure for me. When she whipped me she used to take down my trousers and turn up my shirt, and then used to place me across her knees, from which she had removed her skirt and petticoat. Thus my bare belly seemed to be pressed against hers and caused me such pleasure as to quite outweigh the smarting of the birch. I enjoyed this all the more because a whipping in itself has peculiarly erotic effects.'

'Erotic?' asked Nora.

'Yes, darling, erotic means having relation to sensual love.'

'Really? And so a whipping raises a sensation of love? Oh, how funny! I should never have believed such a thing if you hadn't told us!'

'But it's true all the same, you dears, and you will be able to test it for yourselves before long... and I can assure you that you will be surprised at the results.' I noticed that Evelyn was making a curious little grimace. 'What is it, Evelyn?' I asked softly.

She blushed deeply, and murmured, 'I should... I should like...'

'And so should I,' said Nora naively.

I was amused at their embarrassment, and insisted, 'You would like what? Come, out with it!'

'I should like to go for a moment to... to a bedroom.'

'Oh,' I said.

'Please!'

There's nothing to blush about in that. I'll bet that, as they say in French, you've done pipi...'

The two little darlings hid their blushes in their hands.

'Of course that's it,' I continued. 'Well, my dears, don't be alarmed. You require certain ablutions, no doubt, but you have not done pipi. What has happened to you is what always happens when one enjoys the supreme pleasure. There has been what is called an emission of love-juice. In the man, this juice – shot out by the devil into the hell of a woman – is the liquid of life, the liquid in which reside the elements of a baby. Now, go with Rose and Marie and they will conduct you to a place where you will find everything you require.'

At a sign from Madame, to whom I had hinted the requirements of my little friends, Rose and Marie came up to them and led them from the room.

Blanche had already retired and I was left alone with the good lady of the house. I took advantage of this to thank her for the complete success of the first part of the programme.

'The second part will be much more pleasant for you,' she assured me. 'Everything is ready and Rose has received all necessary instructions.'

Crimson Hairs:
An Erotic Mystery

Quite another drama with an entirely different outcome was played at the same time just a floor below, in Bertha's and Edna's flat. Bertha had started something. Already, during their dinner and during the short walk they took together in the neighbourhood in order to get some air, Bertha had started to speak about resurrections, ghosts, haunted houses, dead men wandering around who could find no rest, Frankenstein murderers, and bloody deeds. They were lying now in their twin beds, close to each other, and a creeping fear seemed to have taken possession of the resolute Bertha, who never before had shown signs of superstition or inclination for supernatural mysteries. The light was turned off, but in a whispering voice the conversation kept on.

'In my grandmother's house, out on the farm,' Bertha's voice was very unsteady, 'they fed an old woman until she died. There was a mysterious story about that feeble old creature. She had been married and had a lover besides, to whom she promised she would be true and not allow her husband to touch her. Of course, that promise was made only to pacify his jealousy. One

341

day, in the public inn, the husband had bragged about her and told in his uncouth way how his wife laid him every Sunday morning. The lover had been present. The next time she was with him, just after he had taken his tool out of her, he took a knife and cut the veins in both his wrists. He bled to death before her eyes, mocking her that she should not forget him on Sunday mornings. It had haunted her and in the end betrayed her. At first she had been able to suppress it. But after some months, every time her husband had given her a poke, she became hysterical and pleaded with him not to cut his veins. Those bloody wrists and the pale, dying face of the man who loved her had all the time terrorized her when her husband touched her.'

'What a nightmare!'

'Of course, finally the farmer caught on and she confessed. He threw her out and she became feeble-minded. My grand-mother, being an old friend of hers, took her in.'

'Oh, please, Bertha, don't scare me. Suppose a picture of that should haunt me when a fellow kisses me the next time?'

'Only kisses? Darling, is that enough? We never discuss such things, it is better so, but I… never mind.' After a pause, she added, 'You know, they say when they hang a man he gets stiff all over, even down there below, and just at his last moment, he shoots his fluid. Now, when you catch that stuff and insert it into a woman they say she can get a baby.'

'Naturally. Why not? The man having been in jail for quite some time before the execution, he should have a good load.'

'I wonder… I could just imagine, you know, that dead man in the cellar there; what a horrible expression he had on his face. Now, his sperm – so useless shot into the air – don't you think it is going around, I mean like a ghost, and looking for a woman's womb?'

'Don't make me think of it; it's creepy.'

'Poor darling, are you afraid? I am, a bit. Come, move over here to me, I'd like to have you close to me.'

Edna hurried over to Bertha's bed. She nestled herself to her girlfriend and put her arms around her, whispering, 'What is the matter with you today, darling? You seem to be so strange. Now hold me tight and be a good girl and let's sleep. I've got to run around tomorrow and hunt for a job again.'

On Bertha's face was a smile. Her hand, which was not soft or weak, moved over the slim figure in her arms and rested with a firm hold on the small behind. She turned around a bit, and moved until she managed to get her sturdy legs between Edna's and felt the other girl's love nest – not a soft and juicy cunt, but rather bony, because it was not bolstered with flesh. But it gave a thrill, and her long desire for it, a desire kept secret, began to dominate her. She shivered, though not for fear as Edna might think, for she murmured, 'Poor darling.'

Bertha was still mindful of Edna's lingering kiss in the evening when she had come home. She now took her friend's blonde head in both her hands and kissed her, a long, lingering, sucking kiss. Edna answered, of course, but not with so much ardour. She had abused herself too much that afternoon. She was weak and felt more like relaxing than exciting her nerves again. There was no stopping Bertha. She was not a beginner, anyway, but for a long time had been on a starvation diet since her last girlfriend had gone away to be married. Now she progressed rapidly. Rolling herself on top of Edna, and seeing to it that her leg did not lose contact with the right spot, she then rubbed herself in slow motion on the other girl's thigh and soon felt jolly warm in the bottom. Her more direct hand slipped toward Edna's love nest and she fingered her through the silken pyjama trousers with great insistence. This woke Edna up to the fact that something more was going on than just sisterly huddling. She kept still in amazement. Bolder every minute, Bertha soon fumbled with the button on her pyjamas, and before she realized it, her pants were rolled down to her knees and an apt finger was playing not too tenderly with her clitoris.

'How would you like it?' whispered Bertha, her breath husky and jerky, 'how would like it if this was a big strong prick, just piercing you through and through, you little pig?'

'Bertha! What has come over you?'

'Oh, you little bastard, you are all wet, aren't you?'

The finger was working laboriously and Bertha's behind moved in stronger and stronger rhythm, though in this position her pussy had no point of resistance to rub against. Throwing her full weight on Edna and kissing her to exhaustion, Bertha let go of the blonde pussy for a moment and nervously removed her own pyjamas. Then she moved to the great attack. She changed position in bed so that her own bare behind came next to Edna's head on the pillow, and then almost threw her girlfriend on top of herself, panting, groaning with passion, and in such a state of wild strength that the more delicate Edna became a helpless puppet. Bertha's legs opened wide. Her fingers buried themselves in Edna's blonde hair and pressed her mouth down on her open cunt. At this moment Edna found her resistance again and struggled to get away.

'Lick it, you bitch. French me, you stupid ass! Get to it or I'll make you do it, you yellow swine!' Bertha's thighs encircled her head from the sides, and her crafty hands pushed it down. Edna felt suffocated. 'If you want to survive this night, you must lick me for hours and hours or I'll tear you to shreds.' Bertha's love nest pressed firmly against Edna's mouth. Edna wanted to get out of this, but the physical and moral strength of the other girl were too much for her. The bed creaked under them. Timidly, Edna gave in a little and lightly kissed the thin lips touching her mouth. 'Coming around at last! Get to it, baby.' Bertha gave her more room by relaxing the pressure of her hands and stroking her slim back. 'For what am I keeping you here anyway, feeding and housing you, you blonde vixen, if I could not make use of your pointed tongue, you ungrateful brat?' The last words were spoken as if to herself, as if her feverish passion had pressed that remark through her teeth. But Edna had heard it, and a violent struggle on her part was the consequence.

'Let me go, for heaven's sake, let me go! I want to get out of here!' She twisted herself around and came near to freeing herself from the grip of the stronger girl.

Bertha was in earnest now. Pushing Edna's head back in the position she wanted, she sunk her teeth firmly into the flesh of Edna's leg and the girl gave a muffled cry. Releasing her again and letting go of her leg, Bertha's voice came with firm and commanding energy, 'Suck my pussy! For an hour, I tell you! And if you don't, you'll see what happens to you! Go on!'

Edna was overcome with fear. Her whole body ached. She was scared and all clear thoughts had left her. She was almost hypnotized. Timidly, her tongue began its work. She licked along the lips. She kissed the black hair around the hole. Bertha's left hand remained caressing her head. Her right hand went between Edna's legs. The finger pushed deeply into her vulva and stroked firmly up and down. It was not such a bad feeling that crept along Edna's spine. Before she knew it her tongue had found the clitoris, fully swollen as she sucked it. She went down to the vulva and inserted deeply her long and point-ed tongue; letting the tip go around in circles. The more she stuck her tongue out, the more she felt the choking and swelling in her throat, the more excited and hot she became. She had never Frenched a girl before. Men, of course, had done it to her and given her heavenly pleasure, but she had not experienced herself the excitement which flows in waves through the body of the Frenching person. Rapture took possession of her. No woman experienced in tribadism could have given Bertha a better treatment, and she did not take it impassively. On the contrary, she began to heave her bottom up and down, she wriggled and groaned, and it was now Edna who had to take hold of her friend and keep her still, in order not to lose contact with her field of operations.

Bertha had said, 'Lick me for an hour' and she had said a mouthful. For, soon enough, the crisis came. Suddenly, she was still, and then she moved her bottom high up in the air, shaking Edna off for good. Her muscles contracted, her cunt opened and closed, and she fell back exhausted, tired to the bone.

Edna lay somehow on top of her and neither one moved for several moments, until the heavy breathing subsided. Finally, Bertha slipped away from her friend who was entirely apathetic, straightened her out in the bed, and then lay down beside her, embracing and stroking her tenderly. Edna's nerves gave way. She cried softly as Bertha's hand caressed her in a sisterly way.

'Thank you so much, little sweetheart,' Bertha whispered. 'That was awfully sweet of you. Now, now, don't cry. I am sorry if I was a little rough with you. But I wanted you to do it to me for such a long time, you're such a darling. Come… come now… do you want me to do it to you?'

Edna made no move; did not stir. Bertha did not hug her or move her hand toward Edna's spot. At bottom, she did not like to go down on girls, though she had done it. She wanted the other girls to do it to her, and she had always been the one who always 'washed the lipstick from her pussy' as she expressed it. This kid was a bit weak and hysterical, but she felt that she would come around by herself after a time, and then she would have a comforting lover in her bed. Meanwhile, she displayed a tender disposition and soothed Edna's nerves with soft words. She promised her for the next day a new pair of shoes and a dinner party with wine in a speakeasy, because she was to receive a small bonus tomorrow and they would have a good time together. This was not without result, for Edna nestled closer. Finally Bertha joked with her, 'You know,' she said, 'if you do not want me, I'll get you a nice young man with a good love instrument to give you a swell time. How is that?'

'I would not mind,' whispered Edna, 'I believe that's what I need.'

Bertha laughed merrily. 'That's settled then. You just look out. I'll tell you who I'll get for you, Dr. Carr. He is rich and can take care of you and certainly he'll be the one who can produce a long, stiff shaft.'

With that, both girls broke out into a loud laugh. It was common gossip that the Doc was queer, and both girls had always looked him over with a shy smile.

Bertha got out of bed and went to the bathroom 'to wash off the lipstick' and to give herself a douche. She liked that.

Edna heard her tinkering around. Without thinking about it, her own finger went down to her cunny. She rubbed the spot firmly and swiftly for a moment only. She came at once.

When Bertha returned and kissed her tenderly on the forehead, she was already breathing slowly, and she fell asleep like a child.

School Life In Paris

My Dearest Ethel,

My first week at school has been very exciting – and remarkably different from life in the provinces. I arrived on a Sunday. The Madame of the school was very helpful and introduced me to the five girls I was to room with.

In the evening, after dinner, the five senior girls asked if they might go to bed early, as they were rather tired – a permission which Madame readily granted, with a smile, and suggested to me that I had better go too. When I had been in my room a little while, all the five girls came crowding in, which I knew was contrary to rules, but they evidently had something in mind, so I said nothing. After a few remarks which I did not understand, one of the girls said to me, 'Have you ever heard of Lesbos?'

I replied that I had not.

'Well,' she said, 'we five are the Lesbian Society, and as you are on this floor, we want you to join.'

Having expressed my willingness, they told me to undress, and that they would return in a quarter-of-an-hour to proceed to my initiation. When they came back – this time in their dressing gowns – I was already in bed, in my chemise de nuit.

They came into the room very quietly and locked the door; then one of them said, 'We are now going to initiate you into the mysteries of Lesbos.' As they said, this they all threw off their dressing gowns, and I then saw, to my great astonishment, that they had divested themselves previously of everything else, so that they were now in a perfectly nude condition. Approaching me, they pulled back the bedclothes to the foot of the bed, so that I lay exposed, with nothing on but my night-dress. Then they began very gently to remove this also, and I let them do so, wondering what would happen next. Presently I myself was lying stark naked on the bed.

When they saw me in this state, they all gazed upon me with such eager eyes that I felt almost as much shame as I would have if they had been men, and felt myself blushing violently all over, as they proceeded to discuss my appearance in what I must admit were very flattering terms.

'What splendid round plump breasts!' said one.

Others added, 'Did you ever see such big voluptuous thighs?'

'Ah, but look at the 'pussy in between them!'

'What an exquisite coral-tinged cunnie with its plump sensuous lips and soft curling fringe of silky hair!'

As they said this, I felt my legs gently pulled apart, and I thought it best to submit, the more so as I was now rather curious to see what they would do. After they had succeeded in opening my legs, two of the girls, coming one on each side of the bed, bent over me and began to kiss the points of my titties, which stood up under the clever workings of their tongues, and they did it in such a way as to soon send a voluptuous thrill all over my body. Two more of them now placed their hands under my back, and with experienced fingers proceeded to tickle my spine, thereby augmenting the pleasure caused by the kissing of my titties.

All the time this was going on, the remaining girl, named Bertha – the eldest of us all, who had a splendidly developed figure – was keeping her eyes fixed longingly upon my pussy, which seemed to feel the intense force of her eager gaze. Suddenly, she flung herself upon the foot of the bed, and forcing my legs still further apart, she thrust her head down between them. In another instant, I felt her long and ardent tongue forcing its way between the throbbing lips of my excited cunnie, tickling the top of the entrance to it with steady friction, and from time to time exploring its inmost recesses, so as to stimulate every organ of it to the highest enjoyment of sensual pleasure. The sensation this caused me was so heavenly that it is impossible for me to describe; but I found a little later that there was an even greater intensity of pleasure to come.

As soon as she could feel that all the nerves in my cunt were fully aroused and excited, she made a sign to the other girls, who immediately quickened the action of their tongues upon my titties, and of their fingers upon my spine, while she somehow managed to slip inside my pussie one of her fingers, with which she began to irritate it by rubbing the upper part of the inside of it with as much speed and energy as she could, thereby leaving her tongue free to act continuously on a small spot on the top of the entrance to my cunnie, where it caused me a most delicious sensation.

With all these agencies at work, the thrill of pleasure, which was throbbing through every part of my body, became more and more intense, until I could scarcely bear it and was gnawing my cambric handkerchief, when something, that the other girls called the liquor of love, escaped from my cunnie and I seemed to die away in a swoon of voluptuous enjoyment.

When I came to myself, the girls were all gathered around me on the bed, some of them kissing me, and all congratulating me on the way in which I had gone through my initiation, for they declared that while it was going on, the lasciviousness of my movements and the voluptuous contortions of my body had clearly shown what an intensity of pleasure I was experiencing, thereby proving that I was specially endowed by nature for appreciating the vicious enjoyments of sensuality.

I certainly had never had any idea of the lovely sensations I had just experienced, and I thanked them warmly for the exquisite pleasure they had given me. I then kissed every one of the girls and begged of them to be allowed to do to one of them what Bertha had done to me. They had certainly found in me, as they had hoped, an ardent disciple of Lesbianism, and before we parted for the night, we had all six been swooning away in the madness of pleasure, each having done for another, with tongue and finger, what the eldest had previously done for me.

I am sure you must be very surprised with all I am writing to you and with the naughty words I have been using now and again, but dear, as you are my best friend, I think I ought to tell you all that happens to me, the more so as I am anxious that you should know all about it as I want, on the first occasion, to give you the same pleasures as I have experienced. And how could I describe what is taking place here without using the words I do and which I have learned since I am here? These words and many others even naughtier are used by the girls in their daily speech. Do you remember, dear, how in the old times you and I used to get into bed naked together, and how the contact of our nude bodies seemed to give us rather a pleasing thrill of naughtiness? If I had only known then what I have learnt now, what a perfectly lovely time we might have had together!

Never mind, dearest. When I come back for the holiday I will soon teach you what a skilful tongue and finger can do. I expect that by that time I shall be a real expert, as the Lesbian Club has its meetings in the bedrooms of its members every Sunday night, and I intend to practise as much as possible.

If you have never tried, you can have no idea what a perfectly heavenly feeling these different kinds of tickling in one's cunnie produces. It makes one feel as if all the time one has been ignorant of this pleasure has been simply wasted; however, I am told by one of the girls that the older you are before you begin it, the better it is for your health, and the more intense the pleasure is when it does begin.

In my next letter, I will tell you about the work we do, and how we spend our days, and also describe the next meeting of the Lesbians to which you may be sure that I am looking forward very much.

Since my initiation, I have found myself very much more popular with the seniors, for they were, at first, rather afraid that I meant to be pious, which would have interfered somewhat with their Sunday night meeting. But now that they have made sure that I am ready to be as naughty as ever they like, they have quite thrown off all feeling of restraint, freely showing me the most naughty pictures and most awful books, which they keep locked up in their rooms; and also the letters some of them have received, on the sly, from young men who have fallen victims to their charms in church.

Thanks to all this, I am no longer the innocent little monkey I was when I first arrived here, and though I have not yet seen a naked man, as some of the other girls have, I know now what it is that a man has got which we haven't. I also know the way in which he uses it. So you see that I have, at any rate, learned something already that was not taught at old mother Walker's!

My Dearest Ethel,

I told you in my last letter that I would describe the second meeting of our Lesbian Club, but now I come to think of it, it was very little more that a repetition of the first, with the exception of the fact that being no longer the innocent saint that I was on the first occasion, I was better qualified to play my part as a giver, as well as a receiver, of pleasure. The third meeting, however, was of a very different kind, and well merits a description, which I will now attempt to give you.

The Sunday started well, for being a very fine day we had taken exceptional care with our Church costumes, which, as you may well believe, caused somewhat of a sensation during the service, to Madame's great delight.

When we went to our rooms to dress for dinner, we found that Madame's feeling of satisfaction had shown itself in placing a lovely corsage-bouquet of flowers in each of our rooms; and when we reached the dining room, duly arrayed in our strongly scented bouquets, we found that a still further surprise was waiting for us, for Madame had ordered up a plentiful supply of champagne – a luxury hitherto almost unheard of in the establishment!

Thanks to the fact that Madame plied us, as well as herself, liberally with this fascinating beverage, we were all very lively by the time dinner was ended. I was therefore a good deal surprised when, immediately after dinner, Madame proposed that we should all, herself included, go at once to bed. On Sunday nights, I must tell you, we are let off everything in the way of night toilette, which was the reason why the Lesbians chose that night for their meetings.

When I got to my room, I quickly undressed, but to my surprise, the other girls did not arrive for nearly half an hour. Throwing off their hastily put on dressing gowns, they explained that the reason for their delay was they were waiting to give Madame time to get to bed, so that she might not come and disturb us. They were all crowding around in a naked group, admiring my figure, when to my horror, in walked Madame wearing a lovely pink-and-white opera cloak instead of a dressing gown, and bearing in her hand a birch-rod.

To my surprise, the other girls, on seeing her, did not seem in the least astonished or dismayed, but took her arrival quite as a matter of course.

'What is the meaning of this, girls?' she asked in a severe voice. 'Not only do I find you in Blanche's room, but you are all huddled together naked, which is most indecent.'

Immediately, the girls ran to the bed and bent over it, with their backs to Madame, motioning to me to do the same.

She then applied the birch to our plump cheeks and thighs in turn, but it was done so gently that, without hurting in the least, it made the blood run towards our pussies, making us feel awfully hot and naughty. When we were all writhing, not with pain but with lust, she put down the birch, saying, 'There, that will do for the present.'

Saying this, she threw off her opera cloak and disclosed a costume which amazed me more than anything in the world. It consisted of silk open-worked tights of a deep violet hue, the openwork being so wickedly arranged as to leave her pussy, with its fringe of flame-coloured hair, completely exposed to view. Above the tights she wore a tiny evening-corset of white satin, above which her large rounded breasts stood out firm and high like twin hills of snow. A pair of high-heeled white satin shoes and white satin garters just above the knees completed the costume, except for her hands and arms, which I now for the first time perceived were delicately gloved in white kid, sewn with broad violet stitching at the back to match the tights.

Nothing could have displayed her magnificent figure to better advantage, and I found it hard to realize that this glorious looking Angel of Vice, with the gleam of lust fired by champagne in her eye, was really the staid school mistress whom I had looked upon as a model of propriety and virtue!

From a pocket inside the opera cloak, one of the girls produced a large morocco case which, with smiling permission from Madame, she proceeded to open. The contents consisted of three rods of ivory of various sizes, rounded at one end, while to the other end were attached two rubber balls like small tennis balls.

I was at a loss to imagine what these could possibly be when my friend Bertha exclaimed, 'Oh Madame, you have brought the dildos! How charming of you!'

At this you may be sure I pricked up my ears, for Bertha had several times explained to me the nature of a dildo, which is nothing more nor less than an artificial model of a man's dolly.

The smallest dildo was only about three inches long, not much thicker than my forefinger, and had a much sharper point than the others. This I gathered was nicknamed 'the baby' for it was evidently not the first time the girls had seen and handled these treasures.

The next one, known as 'the school boy' was about half as large again, being covered all along its length with obscene carvings in low relief, the object of which was to cause a greater amount of tickling than a smooth surface would have done.

The third was 'the Captain' which was quite twice as long and more than twice as thick as 'the baby' being covered like the last with carvings, while the balls were of a considerably larger size.

Bertha, after a short consultation with Madame, darted off to the latter's bedroom, whence she returned bearing a kettle, which evidently contained some steaming liquid. Under her arm, she carried another leather case, this time looking like a large pistol case, at the sight of which Madame pretended to be much displeased; but she nevertheless opened it and displayed its contents to all of us, the evident astonishment of the girls clearly showing that this, at any rate, was something they had never seen before.

It was a dildo made exactly like 'the Captain' but of such gigantic proportions that it positively took our breath away. It was at least ten inches long, and quite as thick as my wrist, the balls being about the size of cricket balls.

'Surely, Madame,' said one of the girls, 'no one in the world has a cunt large enough to admit that?'

It gave me rather a shock of surprise to hear her use such a naughty word as 'cunt' in speaking to Madame, but I soon found out that the latter could be the smuttiest of us all when she felt inclined, as it was evident she did on the present occasion; in fact she only smiled at the question and said, 'It comes from South America, where the women are accustomed to being poked by natives who, as I daresay you know, have far bigger pricks than European men.'

'But surely no European girl could use it?'

'That all depends on the way in which it is done,' she answered. 'Of course, if a girl in cold blood were to thrust this into her 'cunnie', she would simply fail to get it in, in the first place, and in the second she would about kill herself if she succeeded. But if the cunt had previously been excited, first of all by Lesbian kisses, and then by an ordinary dildo, you would find, I think, that with the help of some pomade, and a good deal of pressure, the giant, as I have named it, would not only go in, but would cause the most exquisite pleasure to the pussy in which it would undoubtedly be a most amazingly tight fit!'

While she was saying this, Bertha had taken out 'the school boy' and had filled the balls with the hot liquid, which, I gathered, was a mixture of milk and isinglass.

I had forgotten to tell you that each of the dildos had straps attached to them for the purpose of fastening them around a female's body, so as to make her resemble a man. 'The baby' was fastened to one girl, while Bertha made herself into a pretty boy by means of 'the school boy'.

'Now, Blanche,' said Madame, approaching me, 'as we do not allow virgins in this society, we are going to take your maidenhead.'

I was laid on the bed, my titties were kissed as before by two of the girls, while Madame herself, putting her head between my legs, began – with a far more expert tongue than Bertha's – to tickle my pussy. Her tongue several times touched my membrane of virginity, which was to be pierced by 'the baby'.

When Madame had excited me sufficiently, 'the baby' girl, climbing on me as a man would have done, slid the instrument into my cunt, causing me an exquisite sense of pleasure, which made me clasp her towards me with all my force, and in a moment I felt a thrill, half of pleasure and half of pain, and I knew that my virginity had gone.

As soon as Madame perceived this, she signalled to 'the baby' girl to come out of me so as to make room for Bertha, who with the larger dildo penetrated into regions which were now entered for the first time. She gave me the liveliest pleasure, and caused me to come with a feeling of exquisite enjoyment, different from the enjoyment I had felt when the girls had kissed me down there, and which I now experienced for the first time. When she saw that the supreme moment had arrived, Bertha gripped the balls between her legs, and squeezing them again and again, squirted up the hot liquid through the tube in the centre of the dildo, so as to produce exactly the same effect inside my cunt as if a man's sperm were being poured into me.

Madame was delighted to see how much I enjoyed the experience, and assured me that, for her part, she much preferred a dildo to a man, because one can make the dildo spend when one chooses, whereas the man has no choice about when he comes.

The girls were now all begging Madame to let them try to get 'the giant' into her in the way she had explained, and, though she at first resisted, she soon took my place on the bed, where she lay with her legs apart, still in her fancy costume, panting with the anticipation of the voluptuous experience she was about to undergo.

Two of the girls started at once to suck her titties, while I began with tongue and finger to tickle her delicious cunt, and very soon had the satisfaction of seeing that we were causing her to thrill with delighted sensuality.

Bertha and another girl were meanwhile filling the immense balls of 'the giant' with liquid, and getting 'the Captain' ready to be used first.

When I had started Madame successfully upon her voyage of pleasure, I motioned to 'the Captain' girl, who at once got on top of her, and, inserting the dildo, proceeded to work it up and down as knowingly and as quickly as if she had been a man.

I, meanwhile, was aiding Bertha to gird on 'the giant' with the result that, when it was adjusted, she looked like a delicate boy endowed by nature with the most monstrous prick that ever was seen. I smothered the point in pomade, and we then stood and waited by the bed. Very soon it was evident from Madame's lascivious movements that 'the Captain' was rapidly conducting her to the supreme pleasure of coming, and a few moments later we saw that 'the Captain', as he slid in and out of her pussy, was covered with a thick frothy moisture, showing that the flow of sperm had begun. This was evidently the moment for 'the giant', and as 'the Captain' slipped out, I instantly inserted my fingers, so that the sensation of pleasure might not slacken for a moment.

With wonderful speed and adroitness, Bertha took the place vacated by the other girl, and while I held the lips of the cunt as wide apart as ever I could with my two hands, Bertha pushed and shoved with all her force, until to our great satisfaction, the dildo began to move slowly inwards. And then followed the most extraordinary scene that can possibly be conceived. Madame, having already reached the highest pitch of enjoyment to which she had ever attained, could scarcely believe there was still greater delight yet to come. But as Bertha pushed 'the giant' steadily onwards, at the same time working it gently in and out in the proper manner, the distension and irritation of the cunt was so extreme, and the delightful feeling of tickling so immensely in excess of anything she had ever felt before, that her body rocked and swayed in a perfect agony of enjoyment, and her voluptuous movements caused us onlookers to feel as randy as possible. As 'the giant' went steadily further in, Bertha quickened the movement, and finally, pushing it right home, she squeezed the balls repeatedly, sending into her very soul a flow both far hotter and far more plentiful than any man's prick could possibly have produced. As Bertha withdrew the dildo from the palpitating pussy, Madame swooned away in a dead faint, utterly exhausted by the immensely prolonged and artificially exaggerated scene of enjoyment, of which she had been the delighted heroine.

On seeing this, one of the girls ran downstairs and soon returned with some champagne, which speedily revived Madame, and she immediately began to give us an account of the exquisite sensations she had been experiencing. She assured us that from the moment 'the giant' began to make its way in, the pleasure was absolutely heavenly, causing her to come twice before the final injection of the fluid, but that at times the feeling became so strong as to be scarcely bearable.

This recital, in addition to the voluptuous scene we had witnessed, aroused our sensuality to a high pitch of expectation, and Madame herself, having recharged 'the Captain' with liquid and having fastened it on, was very soon on top of Bertha, vigorously poking her, while I did the same to one of the other girls with 'the school boy'. And, as the other three girls were doing the 'trio of the Graces' with mutually tickling fingers, the goddess of sensuality was soon reigning supreme over our naked bodies.

When I was at last left alone in bed, I could not get to sleep for a long time, owing to the heated and excited state of my brain and blood, and as I lay awake, I could not help feeling amazed at the part our dignified school mistress had taken in the proceedings. Later on, however, I found that she had long been an ardent devotee of Lesbianism, and had only become a school mistress in order to have plenty of opportunities of satisfying this entrancing lust.

There, my dear Ethel, you have a full and true account of our third meeting, and if it does not make your hair stand on end, fringe and all, I shall be surprised! I wonder, by the way, if my former letters have made you sufficiently curious to induce you to try the experiment of tickling your own pussy? If so, I have not doubt you have discovered the little button, the incitation and tickling of which causes such exquisite pleasure. At the same time, I can tell you from experience that it is not half so nice to do it to oneself as to get someone else to do it, and I am told that to have it done by a nice boy is the most voluptuous thing of all.

Goodbye, dearest, for the present, and I hope you will not be shocked by this awfully naughty letter.

The Life Of Fanny Hill
Or The Memiors Of
A Woman Of Pleasure

D inner was now set on the table, and in pursuance of treating me as a companion, Mrs. Brown, with a tone to cut off all dispute, soon overruled my most humble and most confused protestations against sitting down with her Ladyship, which my very short breeding just suggested to me could not be right, or in the order of things.

At table, the conversation was chiefly kept up by the two madams and carried on in double meaning expressions, interrupted every now and then by kind assurances to me, all tending to confirm and fix my satisfaction with my present condition: augment it they could not, so much a novice was I then.

It was here agreed that I should keep myself up and out of sight for a few days, until such clothes could be procured for me as were fit for the character I was to appear in, that of my mistress's companion, observing withal that on the first impressions of my figure much might depend; and, as they rightly judged, the prospect of exchanging my country clothes for London finery made the clause of confinement digest perfectly well with me. But the truth was, Mrs. Brown did not care that I should be seen or talked to by any of her customers or her Does (as they called the girls provided for them) till she had secured a good market for my maidenhead, which I had at least all the appearances of having brought into her Ladyship's service.

To slip over minutes of no importance to the main of my story, I pass the interval to bedtime, in which I was more and more pleased with the views that opened to me of an easy service under these good people. After supper, being showed up to bed, Miss Phoebe – who observed a kind of reluctance in me to strip and go to bed in my shift before her now that the maid was withdrawn – came up to me, and beginning with unpinning my handkerchief and gown, soon encouraged me to go on with undressing myself. Blushing at now seeing myself naked to my shift, I hurried to get under the bedclothes out of sight. Phoebe laughed, and it was not long before she placed herself by my side. She was about five and twenty.

No sooner than was this precious substitute of my mistress laid down, but that she – who was never out of her way when any occasion of lewdness presented itself – turned to me, embraced, and kissed me with great eagerness. This was new, this was odd. Imputing it to nothing but pure kindness, which for ought I knew it might be the London way to express in that manner, I was determined not to be behind-hand with her, and returned her the kiss and embrace with all the fervour that perfect innocence knew.

Encouraged by this, her hands became extremely free, and wandered over my whole body with touches, squeezes, pressures, that warmed and surprised me with their novelty rather than either shocking or alarming me.

The flattering praises she intermingled with these invasions, contributed also not a little to bribe my passiveness; and, knowing no ill, I feared none, especially from one who had prevented all doubts of her womanhood by conducting my hands to a pair of breasts that hung loosely down in a size and volume that full sufficiently distinguished her sex, to me at least, who had never made any other comparison.

I lay all tame and passive as she could wish, whilst her freedom raised no other emotion but those of a strange, and, till then, unfelt pleasure. Every part of me was open and exposed to the licentious caresses of her hands, which, like a rampant fire, ran over my whole body, and thawed all coldness as they went.

My breasts – if it is not too bold a figure to call so two hard, firm, rising hillocks that just began to show themselves or signify anything to the touch – employed and amused her hands awhile, till, slipping down lower, over a smooth track, she could just feel the soft silky down garnishing the mount-pleasant of those parts, and promised to spread a grateful shelter over the sweet seat of the most exquisite sensation. Her fingers played and strove to twine in the young tendrils of that moss, which nature has contrived at once for use and ornament.

But, not contented with these outer posts, she now attempted the main spot, and began to twitch, to insinuate, and at length to force an introduction of a finger into the quick itself in such a manner that, had she not proceeded by insensible gradations that inflamed me beyond the power of modesty to oppose its resistance to their progress, I should have jumped out of bed and cried for help against such strange assaults.

Instead of which, her lascivious touches had lighted up a new fire that raced through all my veins, but fixed with violence in that centre appointed them by nature, where the first strange hands were now busied in feeling, squeezing, compressing the lips, then opening them again, with a finger between, till an

'Oh!' expressed her hurting me, where the narrowness of the unbroken passage refused it entrance to any depth.

In the meantime, the extension of my limbs, languid stretching, sighs, short heaves, all conspired to assure that experienced wanton that I was more pleased than offended at her proceedings, which she seasoned with love and safety, uttering such exclamations as, 'Oh, what a charming creature thou art! What a happy man will he be that first makes a woman of you! Oh, that I were a man, for your sake!' The broken expressions were interrupted by kisses as fierce and salacious as ever I received from the other sex.

For my part, I was transported, confused, and out of myself; feelings so new were too much for me. My heated and alarmed senses were in a tumult that robbed me of all liberty of thought. Tears of pleasure gushed from my eyes, and somewhat assuaged the fire that raged all over me.

Phoebe, herself, the hackneyed, thorough-bred Phoebe, to whom all modes and devices of pleasure were known and familiar, found, it seems, in this exercise of her art to break young girls, the gratification of one of those arbitrary tastes for which there is no accounting. Not that she hated men or did not even prefer them to her own sex; but when she met with such occasions as this, a satiety of enjoyments in the common road (perhaps, too, a great secret bias) inclined her to make the most of pleasure wherever she could find it, without distinction of sexes. In this view, now well assured that she had, by her touches, sufficiently inflamed me for her purpose, she rolled down the bedclothes gently, and I saw myself stretched naked, my shift being turned up to my neck, whilst I had no power or sense to oppose it. Even my glowing blushes expressed more desire than modesty, whilst the candle, left (to be sure not accidentally) burning, threw a full light on my whole body.

'No!' says Phoebe. 'You must not, my sweet girl, think to hide all these treasures from me. My sight must be feasted as well as my touch... I must devour with my eyes this springing bosom... suffer me to kiss it... I have not seen it enough... let me kiss it once more... what firm, smooth, white flesh is here! How delicately shaped! Then this delicious down! Oh! Let me view the small, dear tender cleft! This is too much, I cannot bear it! I must... I must...' Here she took my hand, and in transport carried it where you will easily guess. But what a difference in the state of the same thing!

A spreading thicket of bushy curls marked her full womanhood. The cavity to which she guided my hand easily received it; and as soon as she felt it within her, she moved herself to and fro with so rapid a friction that I presently withdrew it, wet and clammy, when instantly Phoebe grew more composed, after two or three sighs, and a heart-felt 'Oh!' Giving me a kiss that seemed to exhale her soul through her lips, she replaced the bedclothes over us. What pleasure she had found I will not say, but this I know, that the first sparks of kindling nature, the first ideas of pollution, were caught by me that night; and that the acquaintance and communication with the bad of our sex is often as fatal to innocence as all the seductions of the other. But to go on...

When Phoebe was restored to that calm which I was far from enjoying myself, she artfully sounded me on all the points necessary to govern the designs of my virtuous mistress on me, and by my answers (drawn from pure un-dissembling nature) she had no reason but to promise herself all imaginable success, so far as it depended on my ignorance, easiness, and warmth of constitution.

After a sufficient length of dialogue, my bedfellow left me to my rest, and I fell asleep, through pure weariness from the violent emotions I had been led into, when nature which had been too warmly stirred and fermented to subside without allaying by some means or other relieved me by one of those luscious dreams, the transports of which are scarce inferior to those of real waking action.

Pauline

Night came, and with it a heavy storm. We retired to rest at ten o'clock, and just then there was a great flash of lightning. My little cousin slept that night in the bedroom of her parents, and I was alone with Marguerite. I was very attentive to everything she did. After bolting the door, she emptied her travelling bag, and carefully put away the contents, not forgetting the bundle containing the black machine and the book; the latter two she took particular pains to hide below some pile of linen. I made up my mind then and there that I would examine these things at close quarters on my own account. But my principal plan was to draw a confession from Marguerite without letting her know that I knew of her recent pleasures.

I thought it would be a nice sensation for me to hear things from her gradually, partly by guessing and partly by persuasion, and my plans were laid accordingly. I had gone to my own bed, and scarcely had Marguerite reached her own when a peal of thunder frightened me that much that I jumped out, and pretending to be much frightened, I begged Marguerite to let me sleep with her, as my mother always used to do when there was a storm.

With many words of comfort, and trying to quiet my nervousness, she took pity on me and took me into her bed; I at once clung 'round her neck, pressed as much as possible against her warm body, and with every flash of lightning I made as if I wanted bodily to creep into her.

Coaxing me in every way, she began to stroke me. She pressed me tightly to her bosom, but with indifference, and not as I wanted it, and I did not know what to do to get more. The warmth of her body caused me a very nice sensation; I kept on pressing my face continually between her bosoms, and in doing so felt particularly happy.

But I did not venture to put my hands where I would have liked them to be, and although I had made up my mind to know, all my courage failed me in sight of the very goal of happiness. Suddenly, the idea came to me to complain of pain between my thighs. I wailed and cried, wondering what could be the cause, until Marguerite put her hand there, which I led first to one place then to another. I told her I felt better as soon as I felt the warmth of her hand, and if she would only rub a little it would cease altogether. I said that so innocently she could not possibly know what I intended. She did rub me as a matter of duty; there was no sympathy or feeling in the process. But when I kissed her as a token of gratitude, when I clung to her tighter and tighter, and when I pressed her hand between my thighs, then I noticed the rise of other emotions. While she was fondling the little growth of soft hair on that interesting elevation with one hand, I felt how she tried carefully to open the lips and to find an entrance, which I am sorry to say was not there, yet she was so careful in doing it that it seemed to me she was rather afraid of hurting me.

But I cannot tell you what pleasure I felt when she kept on groping about, first stroking my little downy hair, then gliding with her fingers across the lips, then slightly pinching them, and I had not the least doubt that those desires which had guided me to her were now beginning to disturb her own mind. But I took great care not to let her feel that the working of her hands and fingers caused me other sensations than the soothing of my pains.

The truth is, I felt very happy. There was such a difference between the touch of her hand to my own that I felt quite warm, and when she again put her finger to the slight eminence, I was electrified, and I told her that there the pains were most severe, and that I must have caught a cold there.

Evidently it gave her pleasure to have a pretext of removing the pains with her hand. Gently she rubbed me up and down, backwards and forwards, and close to the most sensitive point, now and again trying to insert the point of the finger into the slit which had no opening. Of course, whenever she tried to make a hole with the tips of her fingers and it hurt me, and I winced, she would then leave off and return to the delicate part, and that was so nice that I was obliged to kiss her. No doubt she got very excited. On her part she began to be very loving; she pressed me to her bosom and, as if by accident, she lifted her chemise, thus bringing our naked bodies into close contact with each other.

I could feel I had scored another point. Strange to say, she began to complain about pains in the same region. This subterfuge was not very ingenious, but what did it matter to me. She thought she must have caught a cold there, and nothing could be more natural than the friendly offer on my part to remove her pains by the warmth of my hand.

She did not refuse my innocent kindness. On the contrary, she thought it was very good of me, and like a flash of lightning she stretched her legs far apart, making room for my healing powers.

I was delighted to think that I had now reached the summit of my wishes, but I went to work very clumsily on purpose to mislead her, and like a novice I touched the object of my curiosity, and on the first touch I noticed the difference between her and myself.

I touched it, but I did not move my hand, it was resting quietly, there was so much of it that the palm of my hand was scarcely large enough to cover all.

But Marguerite could not stand my passive healing powers. She raised her buttocks, thus pressing her private parts against my hand. Her thighs began to shake, and she then told me her pains were a little lower down, more between the lips, and a little further inside.

To oblige her, and to soothe her pains, I inserted my middle finger as far as possible to find that sore place, and I must confess I felt most happy to render this service to the poor creature. Most minutely I examined this wide opening, the bottom of which my finger could not reach, but I professed the most childish innocence, I put my finger in and left it there.

This inactivity did not please Marguerite; she became restless, and in order to gain her end, she had to become the aggressor. This she was not slow in doing, now my finger played the same part as my father's rod, when my mother placed her opening over it. I held my hand still while Marguerite, sighing, kissing and trembling, raised her belly and with violent and more passionate movements, she pushed her slit against my finger, and with another forward movement my hand was buried in the depth of her belly.

When I began to feel her, the cavity was moist and slippery, then it became hot and dry and hard, but after she had become violent and passionate, it sent forth a stream of hot fluid while she sighed and moaned almost frantically. It felt sticky, and I concluded it was the same cream of delight that I had seen oozing over the hands of my cousin that afternoon. When I withdrew my hand, the folds of her cavity had grown flabby, and

Marguerite lay motionless breathing heavily beside me.

Victory! Partly by accident, and partly by cunning, I had brought about an intimacy which required further development. When Marguerite came to her sober senses, she felt uncomfortable and unsure of how she should explain her behaviour; how best to conceal her lust. From my cool and passive conduct she had every reason to conclude my perfect ignorance. She was considering what she should say, and how to act, that I might not condemn her to my relatives, whereby she might lose her situation. I also thought the matter over. Should I continue to profess ignorance or confess all? In doing the first she might tell me all sorts of things, which I should have to believe whether true or not. I therefore decided to be frank, and when I saw she was sorry for her weakness, I comforted her. I told her all I had seen since the day before, and begged of her to give me a full explanation for everything; I guessed she knew everything. Her sighs and groans of pleasure, the jerking of her body, the balmy fluid which came streaming over my hand, all this told me.

I did not tell her that I had watched her when she slept in my room, and that I knew very well the tricks she was up to when alone. This knowledge I thought I would keep to myself, for I wanted to find out whether she would be candid and truthful. My inquisitive questions put her at her ease, and when I told her about my mother, how lustful I had seen her, how she had sucked the prick of her husband, and how she had called out in a tone of heavenly bliss, 'Fuck me! Fuck me, darling!' and when at the height of her pleasure she said, 'What a grand prick, come, let me have it, and drench my cunt with the golden cream of heaven' my words took a load off her mind, and she was not ashamed to admit to me that next to her religion she knew of nothing more important and more blissful on earth than love – love without reins, and the enjoyment of it by nature's own instruments being brought into the closest contact with each other.

I was now in the right groove to learn everything, and if you think you can find philosophy and knowledge of mankind in my writing, I may say that I can thank Marguerite for having given me the first lessons, she was an experienced teacher.

I got to know exactly how nature had formed both sexes, the process of coition, and with it the transfer of the costly fluid from the male into the female body, the fluid by means of which the human race keeps up its ever increasing army, and the spending of the fluid as the greatest enjoyment on earth. I got to know why society keeps these things so carefully guarded from publicity, and what injurious consequences it might have for a girl who, without regard for health, would give herself up to a life of lust.

She told me how my inexperienced hand had satisfied her desires in the same manner as probably my cousin had satisfied himself when he, with outstretched legs, frigged himself that afternoon, and although she had enjoyed the full pleasures of love in the arms of a good-looking, well-made young gentle-man, she yet could content herself by producing the heavenly sensations without the assistance of the male sex. I also learned she had been delivered of a child, a sorry consequence for an unmarried woman who cannot control her fucking propensities. She warned me to guard myself against getting in the family way if it ever should be my lot to let my cunt swallow the elixir of love from a man to whom I was not married. She thought I might have lots of fun it I were cautious and self-controlling; she knew that from her own experience. She then told me the story of her life to the present day, which was so interesting and instructive that I shall make it my duty to give it to you in my next letter. Many things Marguerite told me I knew by this time, but there was much quite new to me.

It was all very nice to hear her story, but it did not satisfy me. I was burning with curiosity to experience myself that delirium of supreme delight which I had witnessed, first with my father and mother, then with my cousin, and now with Marguerite. While she was speaking, I never moved my hand from that little spot that had given her so much pleasure. I played with her curly hair, which seemed to cover the whole of her cunt, and whenever her story was particularly interesting, I pressed those hairy lips that surrounded the entrance to her voluptuous quim most tenderly; and when she drew the picture of how she had felt when, for the first time, she had given herself up to that young gentleman who had managed to make her a mother in one of his subsequent performances; and when she wanted to explain to me what blissful sensations pervaded the whole body as she felt that wonderful member in its full vigour, hard as wood, with its fiery head penetrated into her belly, and when closely joined to her lover she tasted his balmy fluid intermingling with her own. Then I noticed her story warming up her passions. I felt the convulsions of her cunt in my hand as it grew larger and harder. It seemed to swell, and with one movement, my hand was made prisoner between her thighs. I knew the state she was in, and thinking I could help her, I put my finger as far as possible into that open and expecting crack.

With a deep sigh, she broke off her story. Once or twice I tickled rather violently those fattened lips, which seemed to stick to my hand like leeches, then I suddenly kept still and I told her, 'If you want me to go on, I shall want you to procure me a taste of what I may expect when my turn comes, and what you have described to me so nicely.'

Like lightning, her finger pounced upon my rebellious treasure, and from her fiery kisses, with which she nearly smothered me, I could notice that my desire, thus plainly expressed, had given her immense pleasure.

Withdrawing my finger from her cunt, she embedded her own to make it wet, and then again tickled my belly, and finding the swimming slit, she tried to pierce it. But it was no go; however far I stretched my thighs, and as much as I tried to meet her, she could not manage it. Quite melancholy she told me, 'My dearest, pretty Pauline, I cannot do it. Your womb is thoroughly closed, but don't be vexed, you shall have a taste somehow. Come, dear, and sit across me, put yourself in such a position that my lips can touch your lovely little mussel. I will try and see whether my tongue cannot do for you what your virginity refuses you to enjoy.'

That was what my father did to my mother when she sat across him. You may be sure I did not wait to be asked twice. I reckoned on a feast, and I meant to have it. I put myself in position, and arranged it so that her face was just between my thighs. I felt the tip of her nose between the sealed lips. Now she began to work, in a moment I felt the point of her tongue on that part where her attempt with the finger failed, and gave me pain. At the first touch of dear Marguerite's pointed tongue, which felt slippery, yet hardened through being pointed, there came such an extraordinary feeling over me that I did not know what was happening.

Our blankets were on the floor, we had nothing on, and our naked bodies were everywhere in direct contact with each other. I was resting on my left hand, while my right hand was stretched out far to reach her cunt, to continue the game that she herself had interrupted in order to satisfy me. Now the first imperfect sensation of lust, which I reckoned on when I would be a little older, already filled me, soul and body, with feelings I cannot possibly describe. She moved her tongue up and down; she tickled me on the top where the little hair was thickest; she sucked a little lower down; she then took the lips of my cunt between her lips. Every little bit of it she loved, and then she would smother with kisses the whole of it. She wetted the slit with her spittle, and then went at it again with the point of her tongue like an arrow trying to pierce an aperture; violently she tried to penetrate, and it was such a sweet sensation. I felt wonderfully nice within me and felt something was going to happen that was new to me; I felt the gathering of the juices of joy and with them the climax of the approaching discharge of sweetest secretions.

This moment I cannot describe. Heavenly is not the word for it; seven times and seventy times heavenly cannot convey the acme of such supreme and exquisite delight, and I now knew that in spite of my youthfulness, I could already enjoy the sweetest moments of life's only real pleasures. I thought with gratitude of the lovely figure beneath me, through whose kind offices I was now enabled to taste that draught of bliss, and I made ready to repay her.

I got hold of her hairy mussel, as she called it, put in two of my fingers, then three, then the whole of my little hand. It felt deliciously moist and slimy, and like a hungry wolf gnawing a bone, her cunt greedily devoured my hand to the knuckle of my wrist. We were now both beside ourselves, all our senses were concentrated on one point, and the moment I felt a warmish fluid issuing from my own closed little cavern, my hand was bathed in the elixir of life spasmodically ejected from Marguerite's beautiful black-haired cunt. I trembled and, almost unconscious, sank heavily upon Marguerite, who convulsed with pleasure and kissed me passionately.

After I had regained my senses, I found myself beside dear

Marguerite, carefully covered over, hugging me most tenderly. I had been full of fire and lust, but now I was conscious of having done something out of the way, and felt tired through all my limbs. Although I had the sensation of a soothing moisture between my legs, there was a kind of burning pain on those parts which Marguerite a little while before had handled so fondly. It seemed as if I had committed a crime, and suddenly I began to cry.

Marguerite no doubt knew it would be of no use talking to an inexperienced girl, she therefore said nothing, pressed me fondly to her lovely bosom, and allowed me to have my cry until I fell asleep. The experiences of this night quite altered my whole character. My parents could not help noticing it when I returned to town, and they vainly asked for explanation. My relations with Marguerite had also become very much altered. During the day, we behaved like strangers, but at night, in the most unrestrained intimacy of lusty conversation and lascivious hugging, we passed many hours.

I promised her that I would not allow a man to pour into my belly that most dangerous liquid, but that I would enjoy all that could be had without danger. Only a few days had sufficed to make me what I am now. I had found out that everybody dissembled, even the best and most respected. Even Marguerite, who had entirely given herself up to me, did not show me, nor tell me, of the instrument which I had seen her use, and which could give even more pleasure than either tongue or finger because it emitted the fluid my heart was longing for.

I felt I must have it, and laid my plans to get hold of the key which would lead me to that dear instrument. For five days I had manoeuvred in vain, but at last I succeeded in getting the key, and it was not long before I had got hold of that curious machine. I examined it in every direction; it felt cold and hard. I put its point to the place where I had seen Marguerite make it disappear within her, but in vain. It gave me no pleasure, if anything, only pain. I had no opportunity to warm the milk, and had to content myself by warming the cold hard sausage with my hands.

I was determined to open up the entrance to the source of pleasure even though Marguerite had told me that this operation, even in the arms of a man, was often a very painful one, and that sometimes only after many years of trials, and a great deal of practice, the women began to enjoy the real pleasures connected therewith. If I had to suffer pain, I thought I would sooner suffer it now than later on, and therefore started to try. While I warmed the machine in my bosom, I prepared my little tight slit with a damp finger, and found that the four night's teachings of Marguerite had made a wonderful alteration it its pliability, as I could nearly introduce the half of my little finger, but I could feel quite plainly how the muscle tightened on that part of my finger.

It was clear that this had to be got through. Marguerite had dipped the thing in oil, and so I did the same, then I put the point to the small opening. I twisted and turned until that peculiarly shaped head had penetrated a little more than an inch. It hurt me very much; the tip caused a burning sensation, but my imagination was at its height, so I bore the pain and pressed forward. Then I felt I was splitting something, and a hot fluid was spurting out. To my horror, I noticed blood, and the instrument, at least to the length of four inches, was embedded within me. But there was no sign of the pleasure that Marguerite had been able to give me. Even withdrawing that shaft gave me pain, and I felt altogether wretched until I carefully washed away all traces of blood, but the whole day I felt the burning pain caused by a wound.

The experience I had thus gained was not of a pleasant nature, and I dreaded the coming night when Marguerite would find out what I had been up to. I tried to anticipate all inopportune questions by telling her that I had fallen down some steps and hurt myself. When evening came and we went to bed, she examined me, and then she made the discovery that my maidenhead was gone through the fall, which she seemed to regret very much, not on my account, but that the gentleman who would become my husband would not get my first tribute to womanhood. She was very anxious to get me better, and for that night she thought it would be best if we were not to sleep together, but she would put some cold-cream on the sore place. The next morning I felt very much better.

The next two nights compensated me for the loss of the past one, and now I felt for the first time the full force of fucking propensities caused by the tickling of a stranger's hand, and by its penetration of a woman's cunt. For the first time, I discharged the most copious fluid under the most lustful sensations, and I felt that heavenly bliss that nothing in the world can surpass, and with the last quiver I dropped off into a sweet slumber.

It did not injure my health, nor did it diminish my pleasures in later years, but I must say I was sufficiently strong-minded to keep my feelings within bounds, having noticed how self-abuse affected my cousin's health, and always foresaw the consequences of too much self-indulgence. According to the laws of society, I might enjoy myself, but with precaution, and I was fortunate enough to get my first lessons from a female. Had a young man been near me, and supposing he had enough audacity to approach me lustfully, he would have found in me an easy and most willing victim, and I am afraid I should have been lost in abandoning myself to his desires.

I must now conclude, and before I proceed with my next, I must tell you that after that lusty bout with Marguerite, for the first time I saw in myself the signs of a fully developed woman.

I scarcely think there were ever two females more alike in their temperament than Marguerite and myself. I never thought I should experience the moment of forgetfulness when Marguerite warned me against the attentions of a man, and how unhappy a girl might become by once forgetting herself, and giving way to her natural feelings, but before I continue, I think it best to tell you what I learned from Marguerite during the few nights at the house of my uncle, and later on at other places in her society. She told me the first experiences of her life, which are as follows:

Marguerite was born in Lausanne, of well-to-do parents. She had a first-class education, but at the age of seventeen was left an orphan. Her parents left her a small fortune, and as her habits were not extravagant, she would have been able to live in comparative luxury had she not fallen into the hands of an unscrupulous guardian who managed to rob her of her capital. Because of this she was obliged to earn a living, and she became companion to a very rich Baroness from Vienna, who kept a country house in a charming villa near Morges on the lake of Geneva.

Her duties were few, having to attend on the Baroness only when making her toilette, which she described to me as most elegant and refined. She used to spend several hours over it every morning, and at first the lady treated her rather off-hand, but little by little the situation improved; a kind of intimacy sprung up, and on the whole it became pleasant.

The Baroness began to question her in all directions, whether she ever had a sweetheart, whether she felt as if she would like to have one, and when she found out how perfectly innocent her maid was, the intimacy grew stronger, and in less than a fortnight the Baroness asked point-blank whether she understood anything of the toilette de la motte – the toilet of the cunt.

Marguerite was very innocent, but she knew that the word cunt referred to the hairy slit between her legs, and blushingly looking down she said, 'No.'

The Baroness thought that it was highly necessary she should learn this high art if she meant to remain in her service, because the Baroness was accustomed to these little attentions from her predecessors, and in order to give her a first lesson, she took her seat on the sofa, placed her feet on the back of two chairs, to give plenty of stretch to her thighs. She then gave Marguerite a very nice tortoise-shell comb, which was as soft as it was delicate, and then showed her the way the dressing of the hair on her cunt was to be performed.

Marguerite now saw for the first time a fringe of extraordinary growth. With mixed sensations, she began to comb these interesting curls, at first slightly clumsy, but soon with greater skill, and as the Baroness was a woman of fine build, very handsome, blonde, and with a lovely complexion, it was anything but unpleasant for Marguerite to fiddle about and to view those lovely thighs, and that fat bottom, which had just previously undergone the bathing and a delicately perfumed bath.

Marguerite gave me a most minute description of the charms of this handsome woman; she spoke of it with a kind of veneration and feeling of love, and she confessed to me that, although she at first blushed and felt ashamed, she soon looked forward to these morning-performances with some degree of pleasure.

The Baroness seemed to find great delight in being touched with the brush and comb; slight groans and heavy sighs escaped her lips. Her hips and thighs heaved convulsively, and the crevice, which at the onset was almost hermetically closed, began to open, slowly growing larger and wider and redder, until it resembled a yawning abyss ready to swallow brush and comb.

Then the clitoris, which now looked like a cone-shaped object, began to quiver, and the Baroness expressed herself highly satisfied with her companion's perfect skill in hairdressing.

Seeing the pleasure the Baroness derived from it, Marguerite would try when alone at nights in her bedroom a little bit of hair-dressing on her own account, and although quite inexperienced, she soon found out that nature had hidden on this spot of the female body the source of inexhaustible pleasure, and by way of instinct, her delicate little fingers supplanted the brush and comb and gave the finishing touch to the outburst of the most exquisite bliss. Cunning (like all girls of her age) she calculated the Baroness might also prefer a little fingering, and that the brush was only an introduction to satisfy her desires, and she had calculated rightly; she soon found out where there is lust on both sides, and where the opportunities are favourable, it wants but little to come to an understanding. Yet several weeks elapsed with mutual deceptions.

Both of them expected the first step to be taken by the other. The Baroness was dying for Marguerite to take the initiative, and Marguerite on her part was waiting to be solicited, until at last the latter came off conqueror. She was supplicated to dispense with brush and comb, and to use her fingers for this interesting toilet, and no sooner was the first experiment happily accomplished when the Baroness threw off her mask of reticence, and showed herself in her true colours. There was now no deception; she proved herself a woman, voluptuous, lascivious, and lusty beyond description, and showed by word and gesture that between her legs was the spot that gave her pleasures which, in her agony of delight, she called heavenly, heavenly divine.

She was married to a man who early in life had debauched himself, and who, after two years of married life, became useless as a husband as regards sexual intercourse. Even in these two years, he was only able to create desires, which he could only satisfy with difficulty. As is the case with so many (perhaps with most women) she only enjoyed carnal connection in the second year, and in most encounters he had already finished before she had begun, then leaving her to stew in her own gravy as best she could. This process left her longing instead of being satisfied in a natural way, craving for something that she could not get.

In the early days, the Baroness seemed quite satisfied with those pleasures she could get at the hands of her companion, but as soon as every feeling of shyness and mock-modesty had subsided, the most extravagant scenes of debauchery took place between the woman and the maid, between the mistress and her servant, either at night before retiring to rest, or in the mornings before getting out of bed. Yet during the day there was no sign of intimacy, and Marguerite knew her place.

If at first the gambols were one-sided, it was not long before they became mutual. Marguerite had to undress herself, and lay stark naked on the bed; there was no need to tell me what they were up to; had I not had experience of that myself, the only difference being that Marguerite played the part with the Baroness I had gone through with Marguerite.

The Baroness seemed to have had no end of imaginative ways to create fresh desires, and always knew how to make the most, how to get the greatest pleasure out of every new encounter, Marguerite told me these were the happiest days of her existence.

The Prima Donna

As chance would have it, one day he brought another young lady-pupil with him to be introduced to me, and she stayed behind after he was gone. She was not a very handsome girl, but she had a lovely figure, a pale face with big black eyes, and raven black hair; a regular Italian of medium height, with a splendid set of ivory teeth which somehow particularly fascinated me, whilst her large eyes gave such languishing glances at me. I was drawn to desire a more intimate acquaintance with her.

'How do you pass your time when not studying?' I enquired of the Signora Rosetta.

'Oh, Mademoiselle Pauline, I belong to a charming ladies' club, and between ourselves we have such delightful games as no gentleman could be permitted to join in,' she replied.

'Could you introduce me, and what are the terms?'

'Certainly, and only fifty florins a year; the moderate refreshments we indulge in do not cost much. Ah, you have no idea how we can enjoy ourselves without the men; the stupid things think they are everything to us girls. If you would not object to being sworn to secrecy, I can propose you any time. How would next Sunday suit you?'

This was agreed upon, and on that evening at about seven o'clock she took me there in a carriage. It was only a plain-looking house, the door being opened by a demure looking middle-aged woman who showed us into a quietly furnished waiting room, where Rosetta left me for a few minutes by myself. Presently, I heard several female voices in the next room exclaim, 'Oh, that will be jolly, introduce Pauline at once, we all want to kiss her, she will be a fresh bit.' And, 'Rosetta, it was good of you, we wanted a nice recruit so badly. Won't she have a time of it at first?'

My friend, looking rather flushed, now came and conducted me into what she called the club boudoir, where I was announced before nearly twenty young ladies as Sister Pauline, who would at once take the oath of secrecy.

The president rose from her seat on an ottoman, saying, 'Pauline, I will administer the oath before any of us kiss and salute you as a sister. Here is a bible, which, of course, enjoins us to 'love one another'. Kiss it, and swear never to divulge to any living being outside this club anything you may see, hear or do whilst acting as a member of our society, so help you God, Amen!' This over, she kissed me, as also did all the others present.

'Now,' said the president, 'you must be initiated. Rosetta will prepare Pauline for the ceremony.'

My friend proceeded to divest me of all my clothing, except my boots, hose and garters, and you may guess how, blushing and shamefaced, I stood in front of the lady president, but having been sworn in, I resolved to go through it all with spirit. I guessed they could not teach me more than I had already learned from my dear Felix. But I had yet to find there were more things in the Philosophy of Love than one – or even many – lovers can impart. It is like every other science: life is never long enough to learn all its mysteries.

'We use plain words amongst ourselves,' continued the president. 'With us, a spade is a spade. Do you know the meaning of the words prick, cunt, fuck and gamahuche? Answer freely, Pauline.'

'Yes, I have seen them explained in a private book, but never heard them used.'

'And where did you see such a book?'

'It belonged to my cousin's governess, and I found it one day by chance, so I availed myself of the opportunity to read it.'

'We have a small collection of such books and pictures, for the use of our members when here, but you will learn more by practical experience. You need not tell me, Pauline, but I am sure you have been fucked, so the ordeal of initiation will simply be a pleasure to you. See, this is far better than any man's prick. I shall strap it on, and give you the very acme of delight; such transports as you have never had.'

She was holding out a tremendous glistening imitation of the male organ, which I thought was ivory, but afterwards found was made of specially prepared white rubber, as firm, and yet as soft to the touch, as the live article.

'Oh, my gracious, spare me that,' I said as its proportions (quite ten inches long and as big around as my wrist, with balls to match) so frightened me, I turned my burning face aside and covered my mount with both hands.

Instantly, I was seized by several of the young ladies. They carried me to a sofa that had no back, but merely a rolled head at one end with a good bolster upon which they reclined my head, making me lay on my back. They parted my thighs so that a foot touched the carpet on either side. This sofa was in a corner of the salon standing away from the wall far enough to enable them to walk all around it. Above me, as I gazed upwards, the mirrored ceiling reflected my naked figure, while other mirrors at the side and the foot showed everything to perfection. Next, a thick pillow was placed under my buttocks, and my legs being stretched open, I had a rare view of my own cunt with its profuse auburn hair. curling thickly over my mount, whilst lower down the slightly pouting lips of the entrance to the haven of bliss were only comparatively shaded by a thin growth of the same.

'Isn't she a love?' I heard them whisper one to another, 'I believe she's already spending. A cunt of that colour is always a randy one.'

'I will kiss her!'

'And so will I!' said another.

'Every one of you follow my example, and put your tongues well into that glowing cunt, before I use my Godemiche,' ordered the lady president, 'it will drive her mad to be fucked.'

And so it did. She had a splendid figure, of that ripe period of womanhood, so young, fresh and fully developed that she might be anything from twenty to thirty, nearly six feet tall, every part well fleshed and in proportion, as she knelt down to give me a most fiery ardent kiss. Taking my clitoris between her full, cherry lips, she sucked it deliciously for a moment or two, and then her long tongue darted right into the passage of my vagina, giving me such a thrill that I squirmed and squealed with pleasure as my pent up reservoirs flooded her mouth with my creamy spunk; to her evident delight as she stuck to the spot, sucking till not a drop more would come. Then she rose to her feet with a flushed face and flashing eyes, her dark complexion making her look like a veritable Juno; she had the appearance and mien of a real goddess, which made her a magnificent president for such a society.

That kiss fired me with love for the divine creature who had given it to me, and I longed to return the rapture she had made me experience, but I had no time to follow such thoughts just then. One after another they sucked and tongued me, Rosetta being the next in order, and then she and the president stood on either side of me, so that my hands could just reach their cunts, which my busy fingers probed and frigged rapidly. The next girl, Anita, a glorious blonde after her turn, threw herself over me lengthways, her belly on my bosom with her cunt to my mouth, whilst I could feel that her fingers were holding the lips of my vagina wide open for the others to readily devour my clitty and tongue me. Each one rose from her knees, knelt down and kissed every part of my body she could fix her lips upon, and by the time a dozen of them had their turns, they worked me up to such a pitch of excitement, the spend came from me in regular jets of thick, clotted creamy whilst I screamed in a delirium of ecstasy. Seeing this, the last few only just kissed and put their tongues into me, for fear the strain of emotion might prove too much for me, but the feeling within me was one ardent longing for more, more, more! In fact, my passions gave me such strength they could hardly keep my body on the sofa as I writhed in delight.

'Well done, Pauline,' the president said at last, 'we have not had such a lusciously lustful recruit for a long time. You will never want for friends or lovers amongst us. Now, refresh yourself a little, and I will finish your initiation, which will be equally good.'

I had some wine, and then a delicious cup of very glutinous, hot spiced soup, followed by a cordial, which warmed me all over and made me feel randy. I appealed to the president to give me a kiss, and as she bent over me to do so, my hand seized hold of her grand cunt, my fingers frigging as rapidly as possible for a moment or two. Then, as our tongues were fucking each other's mouths, I felt her give down a torrent of hot boiling spend which drowned my hand and ran all down her thighs. Then the others, who were all naked, pulled her away from me and proceeded to strap on that tremendous weapon, which they had warmed and anointed with oil till it glistened like a cock just withdrawn from a steaming cunt.

I was not afraid of it now, and I fairly panted with desire, heaving up my buttocks as a challenge for it to come on. 'Quick, quick, let me have it at once! You must fuck me at once!' The intensity of my emotion had driven every spark of modesty from my nature; fucking was all I wanted, and must have!

The head of the big dildo was now placed to my ravenous cunt, and being so well lubricated, it passed in a little way, and I bucked up to meet its plunge as she rammed it with all her force.

'Ah! Ah! Oh! Oh! You will split me, indeed you will!' I screamed, in great pain as the enormous thing stretched my poor passage to its uttermost capacity, and yet stuck only halfway in.

'Courage, Pauline, it may be a little difficult, you are more of a virgin than I expected, but I shall soon make you a woman of proper capacity,' she said, holding tightly to my hips, and giving the prick a straighter direction. She pushed firmly, but slowly, and then drawing back a little, gave a sudden plunge which elicited a fearful shriek of agony from me, but landed her battering ram right up to my vitals. Being properly charged, one of the girls behind her touched a spring, which made it shoot into me quite a volume of creamy and thick stuff with a hot gush which had a most delightful and soothing effect upon the parts that had been so fearfully stretched by that dreadful big thing. My eyes had been closed, but this made me open them with a smile, and she at once began a gentle motion of the instrument within me, again stirring up all the ardour of my lascivious temperament. Giving long, slow, in-and-out strokes in my now streaming cunt, she drove me wild. I spent again and again, the thick creamy stuff churning frothily out at each stroke, and squirting out every time she drove the whole length well home.

Rosetta sat across my face so that I could suck her cunt, whilst one girl on each side of me sucked a nipple of my bosom at the same time as they frigged my bottom most deliciously with their fingers.

How can I describe the maddening emotions caused by such fucking and auxiliary excitements? I plunged and squealed till the strength was all out of me and I lay as if dead, simply sighing, 'More! More! Kill me! Let me die!' in almost inaudible whispers.

They gave me more liqueur, and then helped me to dress, all of them also assuming their usual attire.

By direction of the lady president, we were about to select partners for a dance when Anita suddenly announced that she had to bring to their notice a breach of the rules, and ask for proper punishment to be awarded to the offender.

'Who is it?' asked the president.

'No less a personage than your own self, my dear Vanessa, and I hope to have the pleasure of laying it on pretty sharply, as you know the accuser has also to be executioner of the sentences of our court.'

I noticed a sudden, but only momentary, pallor on Vanessa's face as she replied with assumed composure, 'Go on, I must submit to discipline as well as any other, if guilty. I know some few of you dears who have felt my rather heavy hand would just like to see me tied up for once. State your case, please.'

Anita said, 'Our lady president was so carried away by the sight of the beauties and charms of sweet Pauline, that being in a hurry to enjoy them, she quite omitted the usual formality of reading the rules to every new member of our society before proceeding to initiate her.'

Vanessa replied, 'I must plead guilty to that, and trust you will not be too severe.'

Anita went on, 'I have another count against her. She has

accused several of us, without even mentioning names, of having a malicious wish to see her whipped, for which I ask you to impose something extra.'

A moment or two of silence and whispering, and then Rosetta proceeded to pronounce the sentence unanimously agreed upon. Vanessa should receive as many slaps on her bare bottom as there were members of the society, twenty-two, as a punishment for the hint of malice, which equally applied to everyone, after which she would have to receive twenty good strokes of the birch for neglect of the rules, Anita to wield the twig.

Vanessa rose from her seat and two of the young ladies helped to prepare her by removing her dress, skirts, corset, etc., till only chemise and drawers remained. Then, leading her to the same sofa which had done duty for me, they laid her face downwards, tying both ankles and wrists to rings I was surprised to notice in the floor. Then her creamy silk chemise was rolled right up her back, close under the armpits, then her drawers of the same material, beautifully trimmed with embroidery, were unfastened and pulled well open, giving a splendid view of the lovely fresh, plump buttocks, which looked as firm as the cheeks of a fine apple. The legs, or rather the voluptuous thighs, being well apart, disclosed a fascinating scene of the wrinkled aperture in her bum set in a little dark-brown frame shaded by black silky hair, which grew more dense lower down where the eye wandered to the pouting vermillion lips of a glorious cunt still glistening with a moisture from her previous engagement in rogering me with her big dildo.

Eleven of us were ranged single file on either side of her, and the two leaders, Anita and Rosetta, simultaneously each gave a spanking slap on their side of Vanessa's grand arse, slowly followed at intervals of a few seconds by the others, who, in pairs, slapped as hard as they could. The smacks were delivered resounding through the salon, making the grand lady wince and squirm at each double impact of their hands, till as I and another gave the last slaps, her bottom was as rosy as a ripe peach, and we could hear her sob as she tried to bravely bear it all.

'Now you may be sure I shan't give that fine big bottom time to cool or lose its rosy tint. Let me see, the sentence was twenty strokes, so Rosetta, count carefully, and call out 'hold' at eighteen in order that the last two may be real stingers,' she said, swishing the rod in the air over her head so as to let Vanessa hear it whirr through the atmosphere.

'Really,' she continued, 'to think I am going to whip the finest bottom in our society. Well, I must do my duty, however painful, or she may forget herself another time.'

Swish! A smart cut across the right buttock, then swish! another cut to the left. Swish! and number three went well around her hips, eliciting a faint 'Oh! Oh! Oh!' from the victim, whose rosy bottom showed plainly the course of the smarting twigs in red and blue lines where the skin was almost broken.

Four, five and six were smartly laid on, making poor Vanessa fairly groan with agony as her flesh quivered and the muscles of her thighs could be seen to contract with the intensity of her suffering.

How Anita seemed to gloat over her occupation and never hurried in the least, in fact, making the delay between each cut more palpable as she went on. She was a study, quite as much so as the victim – flushed face and blue eyes which seemed almost to scintillate they sparkled so. Then her heaving bosom, of the whitest skin which now showed almost the whole of her voluptuous bubbies, escaped from the confinement of her corsets as they rose and fell at each excited respiration. How I longed to kneel in front of her and gamahuche the luscious cunt I knew she must have beneath her skirts.

Presently, Vanessa's bottom was red with the sanguinary proof of Anita's skill; red marks covered her well-shaped behind while she sobbed and screamed in turn, till at last Rosetta called, 'Eighteen, hold.' By this time the thighs, as well as the broad expanse of Vanessa's rump, were burning from the punishment.

Drawing herself up, Anita paused for quite half a minute, and then, making the birch swish through the air, gave a fearful undercut below the red-streaked bottom so as to touch up the most tender spot of all. The victim gave a thrilling screech of agony, 'Oh, mercy! I shall die if you cut again like that!' and then let our another prolonged cry of agony as the last cut followed, almost on the same spot.

I thought she had fainted, but to my surprise, in a few seconds she besought Anita to give relief by a good fucking with the grand dildo.

This was another ever-to-be-remembered scene as Anita gave her a long drawn-out consolation. I felt my eyes almost starting out of my head so intensely fascinated was I as she fucked furiously, and made Vanessa give such evident signs of the erotic passion it excited.

A general gamahuche followed this scene, and I had the pleasure of playing 'sixty-nine' with the glorious blonde I had been so anxious to suck, whilst she on her part fairly drained every drop I could emit on her lascivious tongue.

My Secret Life

Sarah (who I am sure had then lost her man and was more and more impecunious) used to come home early often ill-tempered and low spirited. Unasked, she then would get into bed with us. She was kind, in an extraordinary degree, to Lizzie, and would kiss her when lying by her side. Sarah's fingers were always on the little one's cunt. She laughed when I found them there, and then used to push her hand over Lizzie and catch hold of me. Sometimes Sarah used to feel Lizzie whilst I was fucking her, and frig herself at the same time. She made no secret about it. 'I must do something. I don't often spend with a man, and I like frigging while you are doing Liz.'

Previously, I had somehow formed the opinion that Sarah liked feeling the cunts of young ones, but thought nothing much about it. One day she was slightly tipsy, and got into bed just as I got out to piddle, then pulling every thing up and showing all her parts she said, 'I'm getting stout, doctor, aren't I?' I felt her bum and belly and just opened her cunt lips. 'I want a fuck, so give me one.'

'I'll try, after I have had Liz again.'

Sarah turned around and, clutching Liz, lifted her on her belly. She began to kiss her passionately, twisting her limbs over her and wriggling her belly up to her so that their cunts were close together, moving as if fucking.

Liz tried to get away. 'Don't now, don't!'

After a few heaves, Sarah let her go, laughing, and turning her rump towards us frigged herself.

I thought of this a good deal, and it increased my desire for knowledge. This form of sexual voluptuousness amongst women now haunted me. I questioned Liz about Sarah's behaviour in bed with her, for she always now slept with her, and no man was ever there. I found that Sarah had a letch for frigging herself, and that with Liz she seemed to find her solace in the absent pleasure with a man. Her taste for the men was diminishing. She had done this almost from the first day Liz came to London. Then I guessed that Sarah did something more. I asked questions and threatened not to see Liz any more if she did not tell me the truth. She disclosed that Sarah pulled her on top of her, and pressing clitoris to clitoris rubbed them together, till Sarah at least had the full enjoyment of that voluptuous friction. It was flat fucking, tribadism – the amusement of girls at boarding schools and convents and perhaps harems.

'Don't tell her,' said Liz. 'She has made me promise not, and says you'd hate me if you knew of it. You won't hate me will you? I don't like her wet thing in mine.'

'Is it not nice?'

'It is a little nice sometimes, but I don't like thinging like that.'

I promised to keep Lizzie's secret. 'You call it thinging, why?'

'Because her thing be against my thing,' said the girl, laughing. 'It's like two snails.'

I roared with laughter at such an illustrative remark, and never heard flat fucking called thinging before or since. Then I began to think about flat fucking, and recollected what in my youth Fred had said, and what I had been told by Camille of women rubbing their cunts together. I had seen two French women doing it for my amusement, as I thought, and to show me how to place themselves like a man and woman in copulation. One woman I recollected had a strongly developed clitoris, and I had not liked it. But I did not believe in women having pleasure that way, and the bawdy sight had passed from my mind. Nor had any clear idea of the truth even arisen in my mind when I saw two servants on each other in the bathroom at my cousin's school, Gabrielle on Violette. I had heard since of women flat fucking, and suddenly recollected a row at a brothel in which the amusement had been referred to.

When I spent my first fortune, I took after longish continence to visiting harlots who let me have them for five shillings, and would let a man do almost anything. One night I went to see a woman and arrived just as she was having a row with a woman who was about forty-five years old. My girl came into the room with me, but was unable to contain herself and left me. I opened the door and heard her and another lodger bullying the woman for getting quite a young girl into her bed. 'You old cat, you dirty, slimy-cunted old bitch, I'll tell them all.' She came back into the room with me and slammed the door. 'The old bitch gets Mary into bed with her!'

'Why does the girl let her?'

'Oh, she's a dirty little bitch, too.'

'Well, I pull you about and you me.'

'Oh, that is quite different.' Perhaps the woman was jealous or it was whores' morality.

I told her I saw no harm in two women doing what they liked to do. I had never given the subject much thought, but now I began to think of the way women could bring their organs together for mutual pleasure, and of various tricks which I had seen women perform, but the subject never interested me fully till now. Then I got some medical books and some French books, and under Lesbos and Tribade and some other words, I got the key to the full mysteries of Sappho and the Lesbians, which added a mite more to my knowledge and admiration of the wonders of the article called cunt.

I kept my promise of secrecy, but often looked at Sarah and longed to question her on this subject. I began to talk about quim-to-quim friction, flat fucking, and explained the word tribadism, a word Sarah had never heard. I let her know that I thought there was no harm in women rubbing their cunts together or gamahuching each other, and Sarah at once, I thought, got more free in her manifestations towards Liz. Sarah was much more often drunk now than previously, just as if she were in trouble. One night she came in when we were in bed, for she did not now always stop in for me, and laid down besides us.

'Get on the top of her, Liz,' said I just to see how far I could go in that direction. 'I like to see you on top of her like a man fucking her.'

Liz refused.

Sarah gave her a kiss and laughed, put one leg out and her arms around her, and rolling on to her back pulled Liz right on to the top of her, kissing her all the time.

'She looks as if she were fucking you,' said I. 'Put your cunts together, pull off your chemises, and let's see you both naked.' I assisted in pulling them off. Liz resisted slightly, but Sarah heaved up her thighs around the girl and grasped her little arse. 'Be quiet Liz,' said I, 'do it with her.'

Sarah suddenly seemed quite excited; her eyes looked wild with lust and she held tight to the girl, heaving up her legs and her heels around Lizzie's calves.

I threw myself on the bed. Between Lizzie's wide open thighs I could see Sarah's black-haired cunt below meeting the mossy cunt of the damsel. I put my fingers there, and begged Lizzie, who was restive, to be quiet. I incited Sarah to get her cunt as close to the girl's as she could, and they were soon so close that I got two fingers up Sarah's cunt, and the thumb of the same hand, with difficulty, touched Lizzie's. Then bawdiness reigned supreme. I was delighted. 'Rub your cunts together,' said I after a minute's fingering.

'We can't.'

'Try. Rub your cunts together and I will give you a sovereign.'

'What do you mean?' Sarah was still holding the girl in her arms.

'Oh, how modest. You know all. Did you never have pleasure with a woman by flat fucking her? Rub away at Liz, hold her quite tight, squeeze your quim up to hers and teach her. She'd like to know everything, and a man can't teach her that,' said I, now wild with lust.

Sarah kissed Lizzie without ceasing; it was one long unbroken sound of osculation, and began heaving her buttocks and wriggling, but I saw she was shamming.

'I am not going to give you a sovereign to be humbugged,' said I, and putting my hand down between both their thighs, I pushed two of my fingers into Sarah's cunt again.

My fingers seemed to stir Sarah's lewdness. Wriggling and kissing Lizzie passionately, she said, 'Never mind him, let me darling.'

Liz, told by me to let Sarah do what she liked, lay quiet, her legs held by Sarah's big legs, who wriggled and fucked while I kept my fingers at work in her cunt as well as I could. There lay the big woman clinging to Liz, twisting and writhing, wriggling and sighing, kissing the girl with passion, thrusting out her tongue, and almost burying her fingers between the girl's buttocks. It was a very long embrace, and neither of them took heed of me now. Liz was obedient, and Sarah's eyes were closed except at intervals. Instinctively, at last, Lizzie grasped Sarah's haunches.

With a sigh, Sarah said, 'Oh, do it, darling... ah... ah... aha!' Sarah relaxed her hold and was quiet. I knew well from the look of her face that she had spent now.

The lasciviousness of the scene and the intense enjoyment of Sarah urged me on. I now lusted for Sarah. 'Get off, Liz. Is your cunt wet? I'll fuck you, Sally.'

Sarah opened her eyes and looked at me, remarking, 'That bugger knows everything.' Then lifting her thighs she again began squeezing Lizzie and rubbing against her.

'I'll fuck you, Sally.'

She took no notice, but writhed as hard as she could, embracing the girl. 'I've only begun,' said she. 'She's a darling.'

Randy to madness, I pulled Lizzie off, and the next instant was up Sarah's cunt. Lizzie lay on her side and my fingers went into her little cunt, feeling, groping the little moist slippery article, until I emitted what sperm was left in me up Sarah's vagina. Then Sarah, with my libation in her, clutched Liz like a fury and got her between her thighs. In vain Liz struggled; the big women held her fast, their cunts met, and Sarah had her Sapphic delight, screeching out so the lodgers below would have heard enough had they been listening. But Sarah in her maddening pleasure forgot all about them then.

After that night, I talked with Sarah about her liking for girls, and about flat fucking. Sarah avoided the subject; she had only done it for a lark and had not wanted anything of the sort, but preferred a prick to any other kind of solace for her cunt. On other occasions, I told Sarah all I had read and knew and that I thought no worse of a woman for having a woman than I did of a man for frigging a man. 'Your cunt's your own, and if two cunts agree to frictionize each other, it is a perfectly legitimate pleasure.' Little by little, she admitted much, but considering that I had spent in and on her in every way possible for nearly four years, I had difficulty in getting her to admit her liking for flat fucking Liz. She never did quite admit it. She had done it once or twice she said, when drunk, but had no taste for it. She liked a good, thick, stiff prick up her. Freely filling her with brandy one night and dosing Liz with Scotch, I got a repetition of the Lesbian game, and completed the evening by fucking both the females.

Innocence Awakened

Old Penwick's bell rang and put a stop to Martha's chat as I turned to Lucia and said, 'Really, Lucia, you must tell me all about men, and wives, and teach me, because I feel like a fool when Martha and you go on so. I don't understand one atom! Though perhaps,' I continued as a bright thought struck me, 'men tickle their wives as you tickled me this afternoon, and that is what Martha meant?'

'I tell you what, Susan, darling!' she replied. 'I won't tell you now, but I'll come to you after you have gone to bed, for I don't want to chat on matters it would be difficult to drop if that old Lady came in suddenly atop of us. I think she has had a little too much to drink and is merry; another time she might speak quite another kind of talk. But come upstairs. I want you to try on my stays, for positively you must leave off wearing such barbarous ones as yours, and we must go to Worcester tomorrow, and see what the shops there can produce, and if we can't get my fancy there I must write to London for some to be sent down for you to try on. Such lovely bubbies as these,' she said laying her two hands on my breasts, 'must not be squashed flat and be displaced, but left free to rise and fall.'

So upstairs we trotted to my room. The first thing Lucia saw on entering was my wet drawers spread on the bed. 'Good gracious, Susan! Why did you leave those things there!'

'Why, what harm if I did?'

'Because if old Mother Warmart should have happened to see them, her suspicions would at once have been roused, and goodness only knows what she would have thought. Very likely that you had been had by a man!'

'Well, Lucia dear, I am sorry, but indeed I never thought there was any reason to hide anything I did. I know you meant no harm. And I am sure I did not, when we had our tickling match.'

'My dear, let me tell you, although all the world does what we did, and a good deal more, too, yet just as our cunnies are covered up from sight so are the deeds done by them. So we will put your drawers away. They are nearly dry, and if they stain at all it will be very slightly. Martha will not guess the truth.' As she spoke, she took up the garment, and held it out in front of her to examine its state of humidity. 'Oh, Lord, what drawers, they are only cut up behind. You ought to have them cut up the waistband in front, too, Susan!'

'Why?'

'Because how on earth could your lover feel you if you had things like this on? Instead of finding a nice charming bush, and a hot little twat ready and eager for his hand and probing finger, this wretched calico would be in his way! And how on earth could you manage an alfresco poke if you wore these drawers!'

'Well, considering I would die sooner than let a man touch me there, I don't see it makes any difference. I am afraid I am extremely ignorant, but I don't know what an alfresco poke means, Lucia.'

'Ah, well, you'll learn, and soon, too. I'll take care of that. But now off with your dress and petticoats. I want to see how my stays will fit you.' So saying, she commenced, with her usual agility, to undo her dress, and before I had got mine half unhooked, she was standing before me in her chemise and drawers only. 'There!' she cried, standing in front of me. 'Look, Susan, do you see how free my breasts are? Nothing to compress them and each in its own little nest. They don't require support, for they are as firm as rocks and hard as marble. Feel them!'

I did. Strange to say, I had never seen a girl's bosom naked before. I had no girl companions, and the only youthful bosom I had ever seen bare was my own. I was immensely moved by the sight of the glowing bosom before me, so white and so beautiful. I put my hand first on one, and then on the other of the exquisite globes, and felt a great pleasure thrill through me as I pressed them. Though not literally hard as marble, they were decidedly firm and elastic, and their shapes were perfect. Lucia was right to consider her bubbies lovely, for they were.

'Kiss them, darling,' said she.

I did so with pleasure. It seemed to me as though some new revelation were opening up to me, for I never should have imagined there could have been anything so delightful in a girl's bosom, had I been asked about it before Lucia exposed hers to me.

'Now, come! Quick! Off with that dress, you dreadful old slow coach!' she cried to me. 'Here, let me help you.' In a moment, she had me in the same state as herself. I saw at once the hideousness of my stays, which were much too high and much too rigid, and which fitted neither breasts, waist or hips. Lucia quickly had them unlaced, and opening the top of my chemise (which she complained of as being too high in the neck) she slipped if off me so that it fell to the floor, and except for my drawers I was naked before her.

'Oh, the little beauties!' she exclaimed. 'The charming, charming little bubbies! How nice! How sound! How firm! Why, Susan, I declare, I should never have thought you had such perfections. Those beastly, disgraceful stays must be burnt! You must never put them on again. Bubbies like these,' she continued, pressing them in her hand and causing me to feel my cunnie tickling all on fire again, 'are not meant to be shut up in a box, but put under a glass case so they may be seen, and their beauty appreciated. What lovely, lovely little rosebuds! Like tiny coral marbles, topping little mountains of snow! I must kiss and nibble them!' And down went her lips first to one, and then to the other, whilst her naughty hand again sought the cunnie she had taught to tickle at her touch. Impatiently, she tried to find the division of my drawers, and at last did so, but so far back that she could not get at what she sought after.

'What beastly drawers!' she cried. 'But I won't be baffled!' She ran to the dressing table, took a pair of scissors, and before I knew what she was at, she had the point through the calico and ripped it down. Throwing the scissors away, she clasped me around the waist with her left arm, and again attacked my bosom with her lips while her hand, having no obstacle to oppose it, took possession of my fleshy motte and throbbing cunnie. She was altogether too delicious for me to wish to oppose her. With the palm of her hand she pressed the rising, elastic cushion above the deep line, whilst her middle finger slipped in up to its knuckle and was completely buried in my rapidly moistening cunnie.

'How nice! What a sweet, sweet, little cunt! How velvety and soft inside! How quickly it responds to my touch! Oh, what Charlie would give to get his prick into such a lovely shrine of love!' She rambled on, moving her finger up and down, occasionally withdrawing it to seek another more ticklish spot between my cunnie's lips near the top, and then pushing it in deep, in and out, until I felt ready to die with the pleasure she caused me. At last she felt a convulsive little throb, which told her that I had very nearly come. She clasped me to her bosom, her breasts against mine, swerving her body a little from side to side so that her bubbies swept on mine backwards and forwards, her nipples catching on mine, and tickling them immensely, while with her lips open and sucking my mouth I felt her moist tongue darting in and out between my teeth. All this takes longer to write than it did to act. I felt myself growing faint with exquisite languor. I could see nothing. One vast pleasure seemed to embrace me on every side. I was all on fire, and suddenly, with a pang of voluptuousness, I spent all over Lucia's hand and wrist.

Keeping her finger still gently moving and gently pressing my motte, she drew back her head, looked at me, and said, 'Now, Susan, was that not a nice one?'

'Indeed it was,' I said, feeling almost unable to speak from an excess of emotion.

'Well, a man would give you fifty times as much pleasure with his hand, and a thousand times more with his prick.' She suddenly left me, ran for my towel, wiped her hand, and then commenced to wipe me gently between my thighs. 'Ah, what a pearl of a cunnie!' she cried. 'What a lovely bush! What a lot of silky hair you have here, darling! What a splendid motte! A regular cushion for love to repose upon, so elastic, yet so soft! Gods, why am I not a man so I might enjoy all these beauties!'

'I almost wish you were Lucia, darling,' I said laughing, 'for I am getting most particularly curious to know what new bliss there can be in store for me. But really, do you know I believe you are making me lose every particle of modesty I ever possessed.' And I laughed again.

'Ah, Susanna, modesty is the veil that covers the cunts of us girls, a useful garment enough when we go abroad into society, and one which no wise woman would care to be without, but in intimate friendship, like ours, it becomes useless, like those wretched drawers of yours and those abominable stays, all absolute bars to freedom and ease. I would not offend against modesty in public, but with you, or my lovers, I think it is a thing to be cast off, and I like to be a natural woman on such occasions, naked as the gloveless hand. Ah, happy thought. Let us strip altogether now, and have a good look at the shapes beneficent nature has given us!'

She threw away the towel, slit first one shoulder, gleaming like polished marble, and then the other, out of her shift, unbuttoned her drawers, and let them fall to the floor, whisked off her garters, pulled off her stockings, and in less time than you could count ten, there was Lucia as naked as she was born, and as beautiful in her nudity as Venus fresh risen from the sea.

I, as usual, was slow. In every step, I was hesitating. A struggle between consciousness and innocence seemed to occur every time I was asked to take a pace more forward on the road to the fulfilment of the sacrifices to love, though I am bound to say that the struggle became weaker and weaker as every forward bound brought with it new and more exquisite enjoyment.

But Lucia could not tolerate slowness. She came and added her nimble assistance, and in a moment I was, like her, in a state of perfect nature; however, a kind of bastard shame took possession of me. Not even before Martha had I been accustomed to being so completely naked as I now was. Instinctively, I put one hand over my motte while with the other hand and arm I attempted to hide my bosom. I felt myself blushing, too, under the keen gaze of Lucia's beaming eyes.

'Oh, the charming, charming Venus de Medici!' she cried, clapping her hands. 'Don't stir from that position, Susan dear! You are lovely, lovely! I want to walk around and observe and admire you from all points of view. Don't stir! Just lift your hand a little bit off your motte... that's it! Ah, I can see in you what that Venus was not permitted by her sculptor to show, the sweetest little cunnie retreating between voluptuous thighs and shaded by the most silky-haired nest I have ever seen.' She chattered on, walking around and around me, putting me into various attitudes and exclaiming, in what sounded like exaggeration, at all the perfect beauties she saw in me. According to her, I had the very finest shape she had ever seen; the most glossy-white smooth skin a girl could possibly have; a bosom for a God to revel in; thighs to clasp a Lazarus with and bring him straight back to life; while my cunnie was an object so perfect in outward appearance that Venus herself would have envied me. All this time I was taking equal stock of her, and of her beauties. Ah, reader, I would I had the pen of a poet that I could do Lucia justice. I only half listened to her ravings about me so absorbed was I in gazing on her, every movement a verse of poetry and every charm a blaze of beauty!

My room was lighted by one high window, and on one side of this window was the press in which I hung my clothes. It had a broad door, and that door was a large mirror fully six feet high. I was a girl of nature. Had I ever bathed near this mirror I should have often seen my naked body reflected in it, but as a matter of fact, it never struck me that it was worthwhile to take the trouble to walk from the corner of my room, where my bath was always placed for me, to look at my naked charms in this glass. I used it occasionally, when I dressed with extra care to go to church, or to go into Worcester or to Malvern, but I was not much given to admire myself in any glass.

I had no idea that I was beautiful and I did not care for my face. But Lucia, who was very artistic in her taste, and no mean hand with brush and pencil, at once saw an opportunity for a pretty picture. She drew the curtains of the window so as to form only a broad chink through which light enough should shine to illumine any object near the window, but not so much as to cause any powerful reflections from the walls, and then she placed us side by side opposite the mirror. I was delighted. I had never seen anything so perfectly lovely as we looked in that glass. Two naked nymphs with the most graceful forms glowing with life showing all that makes beauty most bewitching – rosy cheeks, cherry lips, glistening eyes, necks and arms and thighs of polished marble, breasts looking each a little askance tipped with rosy nipples, skins as pure as snow, but lighted with the faintest rosy tints as of light reflected from a dying sunset sky; forms which shone out against the dark background, sharp, yet softly lined and clear as the light of day. Oh, what a mistake artists make in failing to ornament the soft rising triangle beneath the curve of their beauties' bellies, with the dark curling hair that nature has provided surely to enhance the lovely slope which leads to the entrance of the Temple of Love. The contrast afforded by this dark, bushy little hill, and the surrounding white plain of the belly and the snowiness of the round, voluptuous thighs is really exquisite. And why do painters and sculptors neglect the soft, inward folds which form that deep, quiet-looking line that retreats into the depths between the thighs, half hidden by the curling locks, but plain in nature? I have seen statues and pictures in which all that a man has – prick, balls and bush – are represented with striking fidelity, if partly idealized. Why then should it be indecent to picture woman's most powerful charm? It cannot surely be said that the thing men most prize in her is too ugly to be drawn or moulded!

Lucia was wild over her lovely picture, as she called it. She put herself and me into various attitudes, and admired, as indeed did I, all that the faithful glass reflected. I could not help noticing, however, that her form showed greater maturity than mine, but she told me that there were few girls of my age who could compare with me in that quality, and that in a very short time, some few months, my shoulders, hips and limbs would be as round as hers.

'As for your bosom, Susan, I would not wish to see it one atom more developed. I should like you to keep these exquisite little bubbies just as they are. Let them grow just a trifle firmer perhaps, but not one atom larger. See... a man's hand could hardly completely cover one. They have just sufficient prominence to fulfil the law of beauty, and they look so imploringly at one as though to say, please squeeze me! Please, kiss me! However, your motte I should like to see just a trifle more plump,' she continued, 'another quarter of an inch rise would do it no harm and be more agreeable for a man to feel when he drives home the last inch, or squeezes in the last line after the short digs!'

'I am beginning to understand,' said I. 'But, Lucia, now you have the opportunity and no one is near, tell me all about a man, and what it is he does to one? What are short digs?'

'I'll sleep with you tonight, my pet,' she said, kissing me, 'but I shall have so much to tell that I won't spoil the fun by beginning now. Besides, once I get on that topic, I shall get so wild, I know, that nothing but my copious and repeated spending will relieve me or you,' said she, archly laughing and stroking my cunnie most delightfully. 'Now,' she added, 'come, dress, and put on my stays, and I'll put on yours, and we will go and exhibit ourselves to Mrs. Warmart.'

Having dried our mottes, Lucia put away her syringe and sponge, and then we returned to bed, but she asked me to let her have a good long look at my cunnie, which, she said, was such a perfect jewel she wished to examine it thoroughly. To be able to do this with ease, she asked me to lie down on my back, across the bed, so that my legs might hang down over the side. I did so. Then she fell to admiring my feet, ankles, calves, knees and thighs, kissing them all as her wanton eyes wandered to regions higher still. It was exquisite, all these warm and passionate kisses!

'Now, Susan, darling, put one leg over each of my shoulders. Ah, that is it! Now I have this sweet little cunt of yours in full view. Lie still, darling, whilst I examine it to my entire satisfaction in all its beautiful details!'

I lay quiet as a mouse. I felt her arms encircle my thing, and her hand approach my motte, of which she stroked the long curling bush, and then her fingers separating and parting the hairs that crossed the soft entrance to my cunnie. These delicate little touches gave me infinite pleasure. It seemed as though Lucia delighted in giving me fresh experiences and each experience brought me fresh pleasure. Presently, I felt her press her thumbs gently so as to open the top of my cunt.

'Oh, the sweet, sweet, little ruby clitoris!' she cried. 'Susan, you have such a pretty, pretty little tongue here! I really must kiss it!'

I cried out, 'Ah, Lucia, don't do that, darling! That is not nice!'

'Not nice?' she cried, raising her head. 'Do you mean, Susan dearest, that I hurt you? That my kisses there are unpleasant to you?'

'No, darling, but surely it is not a nice thing to put one's lips on such a part of the body as that.'

'Oh,' said she, 'is that all? Now darling, I like to do it to you, and I like it done to myself, and I strongly suspect when you have had a little more of it you will like it extremely. Just see if you won't!'

Down went her lascivious mouth to my cunt again. Really and truly, I had liked it there the moment I felt what the sensation was like. I had only cried out because I felt the small stock of modesty I had left repugnant to such an action. However, as Lucia said, she liked doing it, I did not mind, and I lay still.

But only for a moment, for Lucia, having seized my stiff little clitoris between her lips, began to mouth it, and to touch it smartly with her tongue in so ravishing a manner that I could not help crying out with the excessive pleasure she gave me. I did not resist, but I could not lie still! I moved under her devouring mouth driven half frantic with the powerful sensations of exquisite, almost painful delight she gave me. Lucia seemed prepared for this, for she followed all my movements with skill and patience. If I snatched her electrified prey from between her lips, she instantly seized it again whilst her fingers tickled my motte or gently plucked at my curling bush. Presently, she left my clitoris and ran down the line of my cunt with the tip of her tongue. I felt her face press my motte, and her hands smoothly pass on my belly until they reached my bubbies. She took possession of them. My nipples were sweetly

425

squeezed between her fingers while she felt my breasts and magnetized them with her caressing palms. Her cheeks felt so hot against my thighs they seemed to burn them. But, oh, how to express my astonished sensations when I distinctly felt her tongue, gathered as it were into a rod, penetrate deep within my cunnie's lips and touch the exquisitely sensitive Straits of Babel-mandeb?

'Lucia! Lucia! For God's sake, don't do it any more! You are killing me with pleasure. Dear girl, if you don't take care, I'm going to spend! I'm going... to spend, I tell you! Oh...oh... oh!' and I felt a flood leave me. It must have inundated Lucia's face, but she only continued her actions, until at last, having spent several times, I actually managed, by drawing my foot up and planting my toes on a delicious elastic breast, to push her away.

Like a tigress bereft of her prey, Lucia rose, fire flashing from her eyes, her cheeks red with passion, her bosom shining from the moist tribute I had offered. Seizing me by the thighs, she placed me full length on the bed, and then sprang on top of me. With her knees she opened mine and forcibly spread out my thighs, and then commenced a passionate amorous combat, for which in truth I was nothing loath. Our cunts seemed to fit, our clitorises clashed, and seemed to penetrate deeper than they had yet done. On I twisted, I wriggled, I fought valiantly and played my part to perfection, for I was maddened with the almost supernatural excess of voluptuous feelings this lovely burning Sappho inspired in me. At length, after a struggle prolonged until nature seemed to become exhausted, Lucia lay motionless, panting on my belly, until we had both somewhat recovered our lost breath. Then, still lying between my thighs, Lucia raised her head, and looking at me with inexpressible love she said, 'There, Susan! I have no more to teach you of the pleasure one girl can take with another. Some women even prefer such delights to those which man can give them. I don't share their opinions, but after you have learned what it is to be well fucked, you must tell me.'

'Oh, Lucia, I can't tell! I can't tell! Perhaps I may, after all, find a sweet cunt like yours better even than a fine prick!'

'Well. I don't think so!' said she, laughing. 'But it is getting late, my pet. Come, let us go to your room. Your bed is probably dry by now, and mine is swamped! Look at it!'

And so it was. We rose, washed our cunts, bushes and thighs once more, and went to my room. Our modest chemise once again disappeared from sight under our nightdresses, through which the hills of our bosoms made themselves very apparent. Then we got into my bed, and locking one another in our arms, we soon fell fast asleep.

I imagine my reader will say that it was wonderful how an innocent girl like myself could have been so quickly converted into a perfect lesbian. But, dear reader, if you are of the male sex, do you remember how quickly you learnt to love when the fair woman who first taught you what your prick was for took it, and pressed it in the velvet palms of her hands? After that first powerful appeal to your passions, how long did ignorance prevail over knowledge? Did you remain shy and coy or did you plunge at once into that delightful vortex of voluptuous passion? I know your reply; you need not answer. And you, sweet girl, when your eager lover first passed a passionate hand under your petticoats and, seizing the lovely prey of your ardent little cunt, glided a tempting finger into its hot depths, did not that sweet cunt beg you to listen to his prayers? Having once been ravished of your modest maidenhead, and felt the rapture of that stalwart prick, the soft pressure of those pleasant feeling balls, and the inexpressible poetry of the movements of the blissful fuck, tell me, did you hesitate to open your thighs a second, a third, nay a thousandth, time to your lusty lover? Ce nést que le premier pas qui coûte, after that, the progress is rapid! Once the spark has been set to the combustibles, the fire rages and so it was with me. Lucia had suddenly attacked me by my weakest side. Without knowing or thinking, I yielded, and my readers will see, I have never had reason to regret commencing a course of pleasure which has made my life up to now one continual feast; one endless song of happy delight!

The Prodigal Virgin

This lesson in caresses was about to continue. Marion's naked and wondrous legs had once again capitulated after various retreats, and mingled now with the stalwart limbs of the man. And this was only the second lesson which this expert and enthusiastic tutor had given her.

In a nervous silence, feeling as if she were going to a much graver assignation, the maiden had consented to accompany her brother-in-law for a second swim together. And she had not resisted or argued – after a brief start and hesitation – when he had led her toward the secluded nook which seemed designed for spooning.

She took some comfort in the fact that Mildred had smilingly consented to let her don a suit which she felt distinctly more proper than the one she had previously worn with Stanley. The garment – another one-piece affair, to be sure – was of cherry silk. It was much looser upon her body than the blue contrivance into which Mildred had managed almost to shove her on the day previous and hence it did not reveal so shamelessly each curve and protuberance of the perfect little body of Marion. Nor did it stretch into such gauziness as to make it a mere film, as had been the case with the garment which had led to such nerve-wracking familiarities.

But already had the maiden had reason, with beating heart, to realize that this very looseness might prove a source of danger, too. Not very serious danger, of course, since her reliable and loveable brother-in-law was pledged to 'mere kisses', although, as he had just carefully explained, the inevitable by-products of embraces and kisses could not be avoided.

She had been inclined to sit cross-legged upon the sand, looking solemnly at the man with grey eyes like a disturbed owl. She had resisted at first by instinct, perhaps the more because every nerve in her lovely body tingled for his arms and lips. When he had stretched upon the sand by her side, he began to draw her gently towards him.

'Stanley, dear, be considerate, won't you?' she had whispered a little huskily as, yielding, she was drawn to lie facing him.

'You're all wrapped up like a mummy,' he complained disingenuously, touching her lightly here and there on the loose little garment, which left her smooth sides and chest and back, as well as legs and arms, quite uncovered.

'Don't Stanley, I'm very nervous already,' sighed the girl, as his fingers strayed to the pit of her stomach. 'You can't, thank God, see my skin all through it, can you?' A wee, perturbed wrinkle showed on her white brow. 'It's horribly scanty at that. I'm very… uncovered, but Mildred said it was the most sedate one she had in all her seashore wardrobe. She showed me one and vowed I should have one by the end of the week just like it. It was of white silk. You've probably seen it. She got into it to show me. Hasn't she got a lovely body, Stanley? And when she saw how sort of confused I was to see how nearly nude she looked in it and to realize that she dared appear in public in it, she stepped under the shower and then showed me the effect of water on it. My dear, she looked positively bare in the clinging, drenched thing! I really think you ought to speak to her about that suit. Has she ever worn it on the beach and into the water?'

'Two or three times,' he replied. 'It's a popular favourite in the colony. They howl for her to go back and get into it when she appears in any of her other suits.'

'And you let her?' queried Marion wonderingly.

He shrugged. 'What could I do without making such a point of what, according to modern standards, is of slight importance, and then appear a spoil-sport and prude and a grumpy husband? To tell you the truth, I feel I have a right to be proud of having so lovely and so beautifully built a wife who, when her body is on view like a work of art, people gasp in admiration. To be sure, when she comes out of the water in that suit she is just the same as stark naked. She has to be – and sometimes she is – very careful how she sits. For a wee rose shows between her legs and I've seen men's fingers curl and their eyes gleam when they catch sight of it. And a cute beard and pink nipples are served to the eyes of all comers.'

'Oh, heavens, Stanley, how can you say such things!' wailed the shocked Marion softly, writhing, chest-to-chest with him and held in his arms. 'And how can you endure such things? She hasn't had a mother or father, except for Aunt Josephine and Uncle Frank, and I guess they have been the reverse of strict. Shouldn't you try to make her behave?'

'She behaves all right, the dear,' he remarked quietly. 'Don't you see that it's all a matter of social standards? This generation has decided that the prudish quibbles and fanatical reserves of a bygone time were just morbid – that they weren't really innocent or lovely at all. So life is flavoured with more of the honey of fun and frolic and of pretty things freely revealed and with less of the vinegar of prudish conventions. Oh, little sweetness, what a soft spot I've found to kiss!'

His warm lips were buried just beneath a pink ear. The girl sighed and stirred in his arms. And, for some fifteen minutes, the silence which reigned was broken only by such sighs and by the feverish breathing of two more and more agitated persons.

Marion quivered more and more with the surprising sensations awakened within her as her slender neck was decorated with heated yet gentle kisses. She had no desire to speak and perhaps thus break the spell, even if she could have spoken intelligibly. Under her round little chin the warm lips snuggled, softly kissing, even tenderly licking. Ah, she thought bewildered, then the tongue may help the lips – even elsewhere than upon the mouth! It is very pleasant – shameful, I'm afraid – but, oh, God, wonderfully pleasant! It's as if I were just a wee kitten being licked and cleaned. Oh… and my temple and cheeks and forehead… how he does kiss and lick my face! I could scream, scream! Heavens, he's licking my nose! I'm so afraid I shall cry out loud and maybe make him stop this marvellous, incredible shower of lovely caresses! Will he never take my mouth?

Such was the frame of mind of the excited and trembling Marion, so it is hardly surprising that, as the man's sensual lips were slowly laid upon the rosy, curving lips awaiting them, Marion gasped a trifle, tightened her bare and exquisite arms about the neck of her comrade and tutor, and performed the unmaidenly act of kissing him hotly even before his mouth had opened for that first mingling of their lips.

And the enraptured Stanley was to discover now to what an extent his pupil had profited by the first lesson in using more than just the portals of the mouth in demonstrating tender affection and luscious even if un-practiced passion. For hardly had their yoked lips exchanged two lingering and loving kisses before a small and impatient tongue was covertly at work upon his lips, striving to part them yet more, moving with lascivious abandon between them, resentful of the barrier of the still closed teeth which prevented the exploiting of Marion's new accomplishment.

He, too, was inflamed and sighing as he gave her moist, warm tongue the admittance which it mutely asked. He strove for self-mastery as he gave his tongue and the cavern of his mouth to the darting, coiling, licking caresses of the small demon which took possession thereof.

She was curved inward upon his half-circled body, nestling there in a protection and a retreat whose full measure of lascivious interchange she did not yet recognize. She was panting as their tongues writhed and played together, now in one mouth, now in the other. Her hard breasts heaved upon his wholly naked bosom – his bathing shirt was cut to the navel.

Their eyes were closed. Marion was pallid now with an agitation and a blissful palpitation of all her nerves almost too powerful for her endurance.

He compressed his lips upon the slippery tongue then slowly withdrew his mouth, allowing the girl's red tongue to glide between his lips. Marion moaned softly as she felt her prized possession removed. Writhing against his body, conscious now in shivering ecstasy of the rampant and hard engine of his masculinity upon which her warm, soft belly was almost rolling, the thoroughly aroused young woman collapsed in his arms. She lay with her cheek pillowed on his bare shoulder, panting and pale from excitement.

Gently he soothed and cradled her. He slipped a muscular thigh presently between her naked legs. Sighing, and half-unconscious of his manoeuvre, she squeezed the hard, bare leg between her own thighs.

His soft and resuscitating kisses were quite brotherly now, even if that clasped and intruding leg of his was far from brotherly in its intent and in its effect.

Slowly the colour revived in the oval smoothness of Marion's cheeks. She opened languorous, swimming eyes. Aware, suddenly, of a naked knee which had slipped upward to press upon her almost nude and throbbing crotch, she gave the brazen limb a shamed push, which it accepted as notice of eviction and moved some inches downward. 'Oh, Stanley,' she sighed, cheek-to-cheek with him now. 'Isn't that the most wonderful way to kiss? Don't you suppose we just gave each other the most entrancing kiss that was ever exchanged?'

'I would be willing to enter it in any oscillatory competition whatever, professionals not barred,' he said with his attractive smile.

'Do you and Mildred and other people kiss just like that?' she asked faintly.

'There is precedent,' he replied gravely. 'I didn't lay claim to the discovery, you know. And as for Mildred, she loves that kind of kiss.'

'Well, it must be all right then,' she murmured comfortably. 'For Mildred distinctly told me that we should kiss in any way that you wished and that I liked. She said it would give me aplomb and control. But I don't feel very well under control just now, Stanley, except by these great arms and legs of yours. Please, please, withdraw your thigh from between mine for it makes me feel... oh, I can't tell you just how!'

* * *

Well, get in between my legs then,' he suggested. 'Legs may hug as well as arms, Maro.'

For a moment she resisted, but presently she found herself, nevertheless, held by hard thighs which pressed her own. She snuggled against him now in an increased intimacy of contact which was very comfortable and very delightful, if only one could mentally ignore the great affair which made him male and which, she decided, he could not help having or even help its being so infinitely disconcerting and so agitating, so suggestive and thrilling.

She was pulling roguishly at the matted dark hair upon his great chest. 'You licked my whole face like a puppy,' she said. 'It made me feel so queer. But now I know why – all this fur shows that you are just a great St. Bernard or maybe a splendid mastiff.'

He grinned boyishly. 'Getting used to brother's big body, aren't you, Maro?' he commented. 'Not so frightened over seeing me in this rag of a two-ounce suit as you were?'

She shook her head, flushing. 'I guess I was silly about that,' she said. 'But you did – you do – look so very bare in it, and you're so big and white and hairy, only burned here and there. And I'd never seen any men this way, you know. But I do begin to like to see you this way, and you are splendid, you know. And I do begin to see, too, that it is rather foolish to be squeamish about being as unhampered and comfortable as can be for swimming or for any sports. But all this hair… it's just a trifle bothersome. Isn't it the least bit indecent to have it all on display?'

'Oh, all?' he exclaimed. 'Only samples, sweet sister. You'd be surprised!'

She flushed more deeply, but continued to twist the dark strands playfully and even to rub the exhibited nipples with soft hands in a new forwardness which she failed to recognize as such and which hugely pleased the man. 'It does make you like a great animal,' she murmured. 'I'd be scared if there were more of it!'

'My blessed Maro!' he exulted. 'You've found a sort of finger kiss that is extremely pleasant, and it's your own invention, as far as I am concerned. When you rub me there and twirl my nipples under your palms it gives me sensations!'

'Sensations?' she queried ashamedly. 'I'm not being disgustingly naughty, I hope. I – I sort of like to pet you here, and since my fingers seem to please you... well... could I just...' Her soft voice died away as, quivering, she found fortitude and courage to lay her warm lips on the pink circle and the rosier tip which imitated so absurdly the ornaments of her own swelling bust.

Stanley's surprise, as well as his pleasure, in this unexpected advance of his timid and modest sister-in-law was very genuine. For it was a novelty to him to learn that the ardent kisses of lovely feminine lips on such a sterile spot could have an effect so very pleasant. He yearned suddenly for more of those kisses.

As if reading his thoughts and content to thus assuage her own desires and his, since surely this was a kiss she had been taught was permissible between them, Marion let a rosy, shamed tongue mingle with the movements of her lips. For several minutes she kissed each nipple and licked each tiny tip, too, with growing gusto and pleasure. 'Oh!' she cried chokingly, showing him for an instant a rosy and intent face. 'You would be surprised, Stanley, dear, how very nice it is to pet you this way. And I'm going to do for you the same thing you did to my nose and my chin...' Her voice died away, muffled by the flesh and hair of his chest.

He shivered beneath the gentle, and then the feverish, suction which her dainty lips applied to each of his nipples. 'My little precious!' he sighed tenderly. 'That is absolutely delightful, and all your own, as I've told you. And since it feels so good, I'm beginning to envy the women who have babies and nurse them.'

'I'm afraid it must be really very naughty,' Marion sighed, raising a flushed face reluctantly, 'since it makes us both feel so... agitated. And Grandmother always said that we should be suspicious of things that we found very enjoyable, for the devil baits his traps with tempting sensations.'

'We've got a good many of the grandmotherly shackles still

to break, haven't we?' he smiled.

'Oh, I know she's old fashioned, but she is a dear,' his companion conceded. 'But until now I've had only her. Now I've got you and Mildred and I can't tell you how happy it makes me! Don't you think Mildred is a darling, in all ways, of course, but I mean for letting us, even coaxing us, to have such lovely spoonings together?'

'She's all of that!' he said fervently. 'She's a broadminded and clever old sweet, and she loves us both with all her heart.'

'But I just cannot understand,' observed Marion, as she pressed the narrow band of his bathing suit into a mere wisp and laid her flushed cheek on his white, hard stomach, 'how you can seem so indifferent or even amused when she lets everybody in sight kiss her whenever they meet – that Gerard Crandall and Charley Barlow and, oh, all the grown men and the boys, too.'

'She's very kissable,' said Stanley, unruffled. 'And it's a great treat for them to feel those lips of hers melt against theirs in that way she has of making a kiss a real event. It's the custom of the country also, my sweet.'

'Oh, I know,' murmured Marion with just a touch of what she failed to recognize as jealousy in her tone. 'I've seen how you lay your lips on those of Sylvia Crandall and Suzanne Barlow and all these other girls on a sudden impulse when something you have said or done has amused or pleased you. But, well, anyhow, you don't go out with any of them and kiss and kiss and kiss the way you do with me, do you?'

'Not even with Mildred,' he laughed. He took her head of dusky gold in his broad palms and, after rubbing his almost naked belly with her unresisting but reddening soft cheeks, he suddenly lowered the lovely head until one of the girl's cheeks lay right on his enlarged and stiffened sex.

For an instant, the maiden failed to recognize the nature of the contact. Then the warmth of velvet cheek and of swollen virility communicated through the thin black silk. He saw her lovely eyes widen and her face glow scarlet. Her white neck stiffened into revolt and he allowed her to raise her abashed head. 'Oh, my God, Stanley, how could you do a thing like that!' she gasped tremulously.

Her eyes started wildly into his and he saw that the maiden was shivering. It was clear that an episode which would have passed as a suggestive and welcome joke in the midst of the young colonists on the beach, and which would have aroused uproarious laughter and perhaps would have brought him a slap on the cheek and then a kiss from some young wife thus affronted, had torn this virgin's spirit tremendously. 'What?' he queried, with disingenuous innocence. 'Oh, you mean the laying of your cheek where little girls mustn't touch? It was nothing to get so stirred up about; just a momentary hard pillow for my small sister. Don't you recognize the fact that this puritan and chaste upbringing you've had has just succeeded in making you squeamish about bodies, including your own adorable body?'

Still wide-eyed, Marion pondered this for a minute. 'Perhaps,' she faltered, 'you may be right, Stanley, to some extent. I see what you mean, at least. Since we're all human beings together, why make ogres out of each other? Is it something like that? Yet certainly, for the sake of the race, we must maintain certain reserves, and you wouldn't want girls of your own household to be entirely blasé and hardened, would you?' She looked grieved. 'I don't think I've been as squeamish about bodies as you accuse me of being. I'm not conscious of having harboured bad thoughts about them or being unduly obsessed by them. Though, of course ...' She flushed again at her effort at a frank self-disclosure. 'Of course,' she continued, 'I've been affected by our petting. That couldn't be avoided, could it? But I think I was clear minded, at first anyway, in merely a keen admiration for your strong body.'

With a soft laugh, he caught her up for a quick hug and a kiss. 'You are the cutest thing, Maro!' he said. 'But you'll be the death of me yet! Listen, Mildred thinks you should pick yourself a nice, wealthy, attractive husband, and there will be plenty of aspirants. But consider this thought in case any man should strike your fancy strongly enough so that you accept his suit – you'll be condemning him to an unpleasant destiny because I'll certainly kick him all about the place and out the front door!'

'But good heavens!' gasped Marion, wide of eye once more. 'I don't want to get married! I haven't the slightest notion of it!'

'You'd better not!' he growled with a smile in his brown eyes. 'At least not until the real prince comes along, one whom I can wholly approve and think worthy of you.'

She paid no attention in her ardent desire to disclaim utterly her sister's benevolent plans. 'I'd far rather be just a sister to you and Mildred,' she said, 'and maybe a friend to your very best friends.'

'A worse fate – for you and for us – could readily be imagined,' he smiled.

'Yet,' suggested Marion, calming a little and continuing a gentle massage of his belly as she lay in his arms, 'yet, after all, it's sort of tyrannical for you to assume to forbid me, in case I wished. It's as if you were to announce possession of me, as if I were a conquered people or a newly discovered land.'

'Looked at like that,' he admitted, 'it sounds detestable of me.'

'Oh, not detestable!' cried Marion softly. With one bare arm she hugged his neck while her other hand trailed downward along the isthmus of dark hair which led from the grove on his chest. The hand nipped and pulled gently. It slipped beneath the fabric to follow that fascinating band of hair down over the navel. 'Not detestable!' she disclaimed again. 'Do you know, Stanley, I wasn't the least bit peeved, really. I rather liked you so bossy.'

He held his breath, maintaining an utter silence lest he should disturb her little reverie. For in that reverie the girl did not observe at all that the primitive construction of his suit made the present location of her caressing fingers on his abdomen rather perilous. In her interest in that trail of soft hair, she pursued it well below the indentation of his navel. And suddenly her fingers paused in brief bewilderment. Then she cried out chokingly in deepest shame. She snatched away her hand. She buried her rosy face in his neck. For the isthmus of hair had ended suddenly in a regular thicket. And, pressed downward into that thicket by the confinement of the strained fabric lay a bald, smooth, warm, hard something which her fingertips had momentarily touched – touched and then gropingly taken just the merest bit of its substance into a clasp which delighted him beyond words.

'Oh... oh, God, Stanley!' she gasped in a wee wail. 'I – I didn't mean... I didn't realize... can you ever forgive me?'

'Precious numbskull,' he soothed, the tan of his face suffused with red, 'it was just a joke on you. I let it happen – with delight, I assure you. You haven't committed the crime of the ages. No longer ago than last week, when we were having a beach picnic in the moonlight, a young schoolgirl of this colony performed the same exploration on my body. And Mildred, sitting on my other side, observed it and smiled at me. But this girl of whom I speak did it deliberately, out of purely sensual curiosity, all the while continuing to show me the naked bust which had escaped from her little suit and which had produced that swelling in my bathing costume in the first place. 'She was not sure of impunity at first, and her movements were very furtive and slow, but she soon saw she could act as she liked and she was too absorbed to notice Mildred's amused, sparkling eyes. She did not just touch and run, as you did, Maro. No, she grasped and toyed and fondled, but suddenly she withdrew her hand. She kissed me hotly and furtively on the thigh and she rolled over and buried her face in her arms. She was shaking like a leaf in the moonlight and Mildred vows she spent. And that same lady swears too that it was undoubtedly the first time this small but lascivious Betty had ever had the opportunity to touch such a nude affair, which may be correct.'

'Spent?' whispered Marion. 'Oh, yes… oh, don't tell me… I think I understand. But how could you and Mildred let that go on? I should have cried out if I had been there and I should have lunged at her!'

'It was by no means an unnatural thing for her to want to do, the sensual, curious creature,' observed Stanley. 'And so, when she found by slow experiment that it was permitted to her, she couldn't resist any more than I could. Yet I think this small Betty comes nearer to being in what we call a state of innocence than any other member of this group of young people.'

'Well, I don't like it!' announced Marion. 'You should all be ashamed – you and Mildred and the girl – and I'd have done something about it if I'd been there!'

'Who's being possessive now?' he laughed, far from ill-pleased by the manifest but unconscious jealously which moved his sister-in-law; a jealously of which he knew that even Mildred had not been entirely free at the time of the episode he had narrated, but which that charming wife of his had found provocative of sensuality rather than sadness. But this reflection stirred him to emulate the frankness of this beautiful maiden and to try to make clear to her the psychology of an earlier topic. 'You are speaking – and you've been pondering on the matter – of the way in which we kiss and fondle and take even greater liberties without regard for ties of marriage or kinship or anything else,' he said. 'That is pretty nearly universal nowadays wherever young people, married or unwedded, get together with a party of friends or even with a few strangers scattered among them. I'm not claiming it's pure joy for me to see Mildred's lovely lips crushed against the mouth of another man in a kiss from which each of them draws pleasure, but there's such a thing – it's a bit of rather abstruse psychology, Maro – as finding a queer enjoyment in what is theoretically an outrage and a grievance. It's certainly a brazen pilfering of my property by the man and a brazen delivery of it by Mildred with no account taken of me in the transaction whatever. And the woman may as well find that – often without her being able to explain or analyze it – she gets a thrill out of being robbed of her exclusive rights to the man's caresses and affection.'

'There are plenty of cases in which this tendency to gain a perverse delight out of being outraged may grow to an extent which a maiden like you would find incredible. I have known – I know now – a very highly placed man who was visited at his home by an old college mate in whose utter reticence he thought he could confide, and he carried his naked and squealing young wife to the bed of his guest and left her there. I know another who performed the unspeakable act of drugging his own unmarried sister, with whom I've always thought him to be unconsciously in love, and allowing his closest male friend to help him strip her to the skin. And they made of it a rite lasting more than an hour, not counting the subsequent two or three hours during which, at some risk of the girl recovering sufficiently to know what was going on, the two rascals did everything except take her virginity. 'This first man (he's a wealthy single man) whispered the tale to me himself at a club. I hardly knew whether to feel the more flattered that he should so highly rate my trustworthiness or to feel insulted that he should feel I would not violently resent what he had done.'

Marion was squeezing her soft lips with the fingers of one

hand as if to choke back agitated words. 'What... oh, my God, how foul! What else did they do to her?' she whispered shakily.

'I'd better not tell you,' he said. 'You're pretty overwrought already, sweet sister. But what I am driving at is that all the sensuality which really sways the world in shot with perversity. And these chaps were not rough-necks at all but very respectable and respected citizens impelled by lust to sudden rampage.'

'Tell me,' she said in a faint whisper.

'They removed their clothing,' he went on, 'and they coiled her fingers about their excited members. They lay beside her, pressing her between them. They lay upon her. They rubbed their excited tools—'

'Stanley!' expostulated the girl feebly.

'They rubbed their excited tools upon her naked body,' he continued. 'You've asked for this, Maro! They raised her loins and dragged her to the edge of her bed. Then they parted her legs to permit themselves to rub their stiff organs right in the groove of her sex. They laughed to see her face redden and her white body grow tense as what they were doing affected her nerves and gave her lecherous dreams even in her unbroken unconsciousness. The brother heard his maddened friend gasp out a plea that the girl should be violated, and an offer of a fortune for the privilege. He laughed, more than half-crazed himself, and he vowed that he himself would give much more than that if he dared possess her.'

'No, no, no!' gasped the trembling Marion, her voice rising into a little shriek. 'No more, don't tell me more! It's like a glimpse into the inferno of human – inhuman – foulness and brutality. Oh, Stanley, it hurts me somehow, wholly aside from shocking me unspeakably, for something of horror now seems to rest even upon the gentle, tender, lovely caresses since they lead to passion and passion leads to such excesses.'

'You're passionate, aren't you, sweetness?' said Stanley happily. 'I must confess that I didn't think you were until I saw your marvellous response to my kisses.'

'Mildred says...' whispered Marion shamefacedly. She paused, hesitating, and then laid her lips to his ear. 'She says I am very passionate by nature, like her and like our parents... like you. I don't know how she knows or even whether she's right. I didn't know it myself. If she is correct...' she breathed.

'Yes, Mildred told me you would be a darling volcano if aroused,' he said indiscreetly. 'She explained that she was sure you were passionate by nature.'

'How dare she tell you that and then go on to encourage us to be alone together and to pet!' cried Marion indignantly. 'Why, it's just as if she had said to you, "here's my hot-blooded young sister. Kiss and hug her and she'll get very excited and you'll see how very naughty she can be, though she poses as such a prim thing!" I don't think it was nice of her at all, really, I don't.'

'You know she just wanted to pry you out of your otherworldness, to counteract your upbringing, to make you one of the young set to which you were born,' he said mildly careful not to caress her in this guarded mood. 'And your fortunate brother-in-law is the chosen instrument of the process.'

'Are you just an instrument, Stanley?' she asked. 'Don't you really mean any of the sweet things you have done to me?'

'You know whether I mean them, sweetness, little beauty with the exquisite face and the dear dimples and the shining hair!' he whispered.

He was half-lying upon her now as they both turned suddenly, dangerously tender. And Marion, looking him full in the eyes, was trembling, disconcerted, happy, unresisting.

He buried his face, his moving lips, in her lovely neck. He kissed her upper arms, the shaven nooks beneath them. He let his lips return to her for a torrid kiss. And his mouth sank to a bare and comely shoulder, so very poorly protected, like its mate, by the loose, scant garment she wore. 'You would kiss and pet my body, would you, trying to outrage a poor, delicate creature when all I had done was to kiss and caress your sweet face!' He raised his head to observe with her loving mockery. 'Well, there is such a thing as revenge in this humdrum world, as dainty pirates like you may discover!'

* * *

Stanley, oh Stanley, Stanley!' sighed the maiden. Flat upon her back now, her bare thighs enduring between them the agitating invasion of the male leg which he had cast over her nearer one, her smooth and lovely shoulders warm from his exploring lips, Marion had hardly stirred and had not protested at all as the delicious kisses covered all the revealed skin of her upper chest as with an invisible garment. But since the wee slip of a suit was very deeply cut in a V-shaped front, and since the mouth of her brother-in-law rested now directly between the exquisite mounds which heaved on either side of his lips with the girl's agitated breathing, and since his lips contrived to push somewhat farther to the side the silk which so loosely and thinly covered her breasts and to rest caressingly against each inner slope for a moment, the dormant guardians of her fundamental chastity awakened, alarmed, as they had been when this same man had laid torrid, lascivious lips just beneath the promontories of the dimpled buttocks.

'Oh, Stanley!' Marion stammered, striving vainly to press aside the hands which bound her, shoulder and thigh, to keep her in position for this browsing which was to him a treat beyond compare. 'Stanley, dear, please, don't kiss me on my bust! And don't...

oh, don't uncover me and kiss me anymore!' she whispered. And she ended with a little whimpering wail for suddenly feverish, firm lips, which would not be frustrated by a loose, light fold of silk, had pressed the fabric even farther to one side. Lips that trembled, lips that shot heat through the weakly struggling Marion, fixed themselves in a long kiss upon the rosy bud which formed a glorious adornment at the very summit of the perfect, milky white breast.

'Oh, my God... my God!' burst from the quivering lips of the girl. 'Let me loose, don't kiss me there. Cover my bosom, Stanley! Oh, Stanley, you're driving me crazy! You don't w-want m-me, Stanley, you don't want me to insist upon going back home and never, never coming out alone with you again, do you?'

'I do not,' he replied. 'Nor do I expect to allow such an infantile action as that. Did anyone ever tell you, darling little Maro, that your breasts are beyond compare in sheer beauty?'

'Stanley, you're hurting me, making me lose my faith in you,' she cried plaintively, and yet moved, despite all her shame in this first revelation of her nude bosom to male eyes, by his earnest eulogy, as well as by the hot kiss which he now proceeded to lay upon her other nipple after his pushing lips had uncovered it.

Since he wished to utilize his hands otherwise than in holding her feebly struggling form as they had been doing, he eased his great body farther upon hers, pinning her down at hips and belly by a firm weight which he strove to keep from being oppressive but which added much to Marion's agitation.

'There – you're violating our compact!' she panted. 'You have pushed my suit almost down to my waist. And your lips, your lips! Do you want me to go quite mad!'

He raised a flushed brown head. 'Violating our compact?' he queried reproachfully. 'How can you accuse me of that, Maro? What am I doing?'

'You're half stripping me,' she quavered. 'And seeing me and kissing me in spots where not even my sister's husband has any right to. And you're humiliating me and making me feel that you don't respect me in the least, and treating me as if—'

'Ah, kissing you,' he sighed. 'And wasn't I to have that sweet privilege, dear, by our agreement?'

'Well, but I thought it meant only my face, and the stripping... that is certainly not kissing or spooning or petting, as we were to do within limits!'

'Would you wish me, then, to kiss your bathing suit?' he smiled. 'Kisses are for the skin, darling sister. Ask Mildred if you're in doubt of that.'

She was silent for a moment, palpitating, bewildered by his argument. With head still raised, he gloried in the rise and fall of the adorable, firm, bare breasts in the sunlight with the accelerated breathing of the maiden.

'Then you think I've committed myself to being kissed quite anywhere you wish?' she whispered faintly. 'But, my God, Stanley, at least have mercy and be contented with what you already have! For if you were to kiss me again on... where you did yesterday, I'm certain I should have hysterics. Your lips on my breasts drive me almost wild, and being half naked with you this way... I couldn't stand more, indeed I couldn't. So be a very sweet and dear brother and be kind to a girl who is trying to keep her word to you.'

'Then you concede to me this darling bosom, this torso of radiant, rosy white, this form which I have never seen equalled anywhere?' he whispered gloatingly.

Marion was silent, struggling in the throes of an internal conflict in which those monitors of her chastity found their voices almost drowned out by the thumping of the drums of her senses. For her brother-in-law had added to the force of his irresistible arguments and his even more irresistible personality by slipping his own almost nude torso upwards on her own. And now, as he laid his lips gently on her mouth, her naked breasts were pressed deliciously by the shaggy and muscular chest of the man. She squirmed gently beneath him but did not refuse him her warm and clinging lips. 'I – I suppose I must since you already appear to have me uncovered there for your kisses,' she whispered, 'and since I seem to have made a very foolish and un-foreseeing promise to you.'

'My young blessed!' he said fondly, making her gasp by the gentle friction of his chest upon her sensitive bust. 'And let me reassure you a little if I can by telling you that even this which we are doing is no more than 'petting', as petting is understood by the young lights of the up-and-coming generation. And I'll take the liberty of reminding you, too, Miss Stone, now that you have recovered a trifle of self-control, that your own sweet lips wandered, playfully, no doubt, at first, but later quite warmly and excitedly, upon my own body in these same regions.'

'I – I know I did that,' murmured the flushed Marion. 'I hardly realized. I know I was being held, but I did get so excited when I found how nice it was to do and how it agitated you too. And... oh, I don't know just why, but I seemed to go into a fever of indecent actions... your great body, hard and strong, but with skin so fine and soft... it just seemed to me that I must pet it a little and kiss your funny, cute little imitation nipples, too.'

'You did more than kiss them, my dear Miss Stone,' he observed with mock severity. 'And, if I am not mistaken, this very soft and delicate little hand had an audacity which shocked me to the very core. Vengeance in kind is my motto. And so how would you like it if I...?'

Instantly, the beleaguered and apprehensive Marion was in a shivering, writhing stew in which she tried, with futility, to slip from beneath the weight of his body. 'Don't... oh, I beg, I plead! It will be all over between us, I warn you, Stanley!' she wailed feverishly, for her brother-in-law had laid his flattened hand upon her body just beneath the denuded bosom and his extended finger tended downwards, touching the tiny pit of the navel in the middle of the belly of satin then still slipping farther as if determined to return the visit, the unintentional, indiscreet visit, so hastily paid to his own secrecies by a maidenly hand half an hour earlier. Under the fabric which still covered the abdomen it advanced very slowly. Almost at the verge of a silken thicket it paused.

'You threaten me, eh, lady, with the bane of your eternal displeasure?' he said thickly. This beautiful and nearly nude girlish body drove him more nearly mad than he could recall ever having been in these circumstances.

'No!' Marion almost shouted as his hand made another ominous move, this time touching soft curls. 'No, no!' cried the girl shakily. 'I don't threaten, I beg, I plead with you not to shame me to death by what it would almost kill me to endure!'

He smiled down into her reddened face and into her almost terrified eyes. Then he slowly withdrew his hand from within her very thin garment, and she released haltingly the breath which she had caught and held in her apprehension of that masculine touch upon her privacies.

'Oh, thank you!' she whispered tremulously. 'I knew you couldn't be so... so cruel as that.' It was perhaps in the outburst of her gratitude over being spared such an unendurably libidinous contact, that Marion now so sweetly succumbed to whatever else he had in mind for her in the way of somewhat less soul-shaking familiarities. With her glorious young breasts he did now as he pleased. And life for Marion became a succession of thrills which made her tremble and sigh and sometimes moan in the ardour which he awakened in the recesses of her tingling body.

Her lips and her bosom shared now the contact of his sensual mouth, and always she hugged and kissed him heatedly when his voracious lips drifted upward from their fair pastures below to grip and to hold hers. Their tongues writhed and licked in serpentine juncture and the shaking girl, moaning with the innocent lechery which this mutual caress always awakened in her, was too intent upon its joys to note clearly how one of his hands feasted here and there upon her body while their tongues were playing and their lips clinging and sucking. Every bit of her exquisite form he visited thus. And though her scant suit still clung in some places, he was unhampered by any fabric on her lovely legs and bust and belly.

It was with a panting regret that she released his neck from her clinging, warm arms when he manifested the desire to feast his maddening lips again upon her body. Her breasts almost ached with the straining delight of his kisses and lickings and of the soft suction which he applied every little while to the rigid coral treasures of her nipples. She was gurgling, panting, rolling at last from the immense passion and thwarted desires which arose from the caverns where they had slept. 'Oh... o-o-o-o-o-h, God in heaven!' she wailed softly at last. 'I think you are killing me with pleasure, Stanley, darling! I can't stand it, I can't! It makes me ache to be wicked, to pretend I'm your wife, to be your wife, your... your anything! You don't want me this way, Stanley. You want me to be still your decent sister. This is – oh, unspeakably lovely, but it makes me bad, bad, bad!'

* * *

The long silence which ensued upon Marion's quavering protests was broken only by the rasping sighs of the man and the softer and more plaintive sighs of the maiden. She now felt that her short lifetime of modesty and aloofness from carnal impulses had been transformed into burning, unformulated desires which wracked her. She realized that little by little her scant apparel was gradually slipping yet farther downward. Her arms had been entirely freed of the fabric now, the arm holes withdrawn over her hands. Upon a cream belly masculine fingers took a delicate pleasure.

Her eyes closed, the girl lay panting, too weak to give resistance to any of his tactile liberties. For Stanley had so ensconced himself now between the extended and naked legs that he lay directly upon her body, and Marion was victim of the atavistic and age-old fires which burn within the human female when made to serve as bed for the male.

For an instant, he knelt on the sand between the widely parted legs of the lass, and the instant sufficed for him to peel his bathing shirt over his head.

Marion, without opening her eyes, gasped as he lay once more upon her. For now she could feel clearly the mingling of their naked torsos, and the magical effect of the contact of their skins, of their bared bellies, led the girl, as well as the man, into ecstatic delight.

She shivered and clung to his neck as, relieving her of the weight she already adored to feel upon her body, he swept her breasts, her velvet belly, with his own nudity. With gently fumbling fingers he pressed still farther downward the crumpled band of silk which still clad Marion and also the short trunks which constituted all his own remaining attire. And it was upon the full, wee mound of her sex, upon the uncovered grove of silken ringlets which adorned that mound, that he pressed now not only the crisp forest of his own secrecies but the naked and rampant rod which had already fired the girl to frenzy and threatened the utter rout of her chastity.

Between her legs she felt the light swaying of a sack whose

nature she did not fully comprehend. And, even though a slip of silk still covered her wee cleft, it seemed to her that she felt the heat of that naked sack through the fabric.

Relying upon the trembling, weakened state of his young sister-in-law – conscious that she now shared his own fires to the full even in her ignorance and innocence – Stanley crouched over her somewhat higher and offered himself the sensual joy of rubbing his huge erection over the tender, heaving young belly.

But with this maddening contact savoured to the full, the appalled instincts of all her native purity collected their forces for one effort more in behalf of chastity. To Marion this would mean only one thing – she was to be used, nay, she was being used as a woman is used by a man.

'Spare me, spare me!' she half sobbed, and writhing beneath his covering body, she managed the supreme effort necessary to turn herself upon her face.

'Why, you silly, sweet, darling little wretch!' cried Stanley, and he fell upon the white satin of her bared back with gentler kisses as he sensed more fully her dismay. 'Did you actually think I was going to be false to my pledge when you have so loyally sustained yours? You're shivering, blessed baby. What did you think I was going to do to you?'

'I thought... oh, I thought you were going to... to take me!' quavered Marion, her golden head buried in her arms. 'When you had us both all bare that way.'

'Never!' he cried impulsively. And then he modified his pledge, 'That is, never unless both you and Mildred actually urge it, and unless your sister agrees that it will do no harm for you to have the pre-marital experience that so many of our unwed girls have had.'

She gave a little choked cry. 'Then it will be never,' she quavered. 'But, Stanley, how can you keep referring to all this as merely kissing when you know very well that you – that we – are acting most atrociously?'

'Kissing and spooning and a little petting,' he maintained, 'just a sweet, feverish enjoyment for both of us and with no evil effect whatever.' He was gloating over the silken expanse of her small and perfect back and shoulders, for the maiden was nude to the loins in the rear as she had been in front. He kissed the smooth skin in a dozen spots. His lips lay tenderly on the dimples which were revealed just above the crumpled fabric of the bathing suit. His palms smoothed the white, soft sides. And Marion, sighing and vibrating anew, had no word of expostulation.

Suddenly, he saw her tremble violently and heard her moan softly. And he noted that his swaying member was touching ever and again her exquisite flesh and that the effect of this recognizable contact was maddening to the girl. Raising the elastic cord of his trunks, he covered his virility. 'As I told you,' he whispered, 'kisses may be applied with more than the lips – with tender fingers, with skin touching skin. And you must not be too quick to blame yourself or both of us. For I tell you, precious sister, that such joys as we are sharing are indulged in with no qualms whatever by these cultured, highly bred young people of our set. Maidens and youths, young wives and husbands, have lain naked in each other's arms in this very hollow in the moonlight and in many another spot on this beach. And they permit themselves everything but that in the way of pleasures. And they take no thought whatever of whether it is their own mate or fiancé who is with them, since a new body always has its added charm of mystery and delight.'

'Stanley, dearest, it's inconceivable, what you tell me!' cried the maiden. 'But surely they must be very common wretches in spite of a veneer of refinement!'

'Not at all,' he declared. 'They are what we are accustomed to regard as the flower of our civilization, for you know that none but a chosen few can even get into this colony. But they simply decline to be bound any longer by rigid conventions which have deprived us of many, many hours of happy dalliance in the past.'

'Yet certainly,' she argued, turning her lovely flushed face sideways to allow him a quick kiss upon her lips as his snuggling mouth mutely quested it, 'certainly they cannot always restrain themselves – can they – from... from actual unfaithfulness to marriage vows or to betrothal pledges?'

He smiled, just a shade grimly. 'They cannot,' he admitted, 'and this moon which is looking down on us now has seen things which would make mere marital infidelity seem as innocent as rosebuds by comparison. Infidelity is frequent, to be sure, but since in the very next hollow in the sand hubby may be doing likewise with wifey's intimate friend, wifey fears no wracking reproach for giving herself entirely, but many of our friends (married and unmarried) pride themselves upon the fidelity and determination with which they have avoided normal penetrations of the body. Yet, in this avoidance, they succumb to perversities for the sake of the spasm, perversities which make the moon draw a cloud over its shining face and which would seem to you entirely incredible if I essayed to describe them.'

Marion shuddered, but her imagination was unable to apprise her in the least of his meanings. It did not, nevertheless, fail to inform her gentle pressures had so lowered the suit beneath her loins in the rear that some inches of the crevice between her buttocks must be very indecently revealed, for his lips were straying between pauses in his words and she could feel a moist and very perturbing tongue softly licking along that shameful crack. As she sent a small hand to repair the indelicate exposure in her rear, the slender wrist was gently grasped and the fingers rendered impotent, while, very slowly, the unveiling of the upper slopes of those snowy buttocks continued. 'I beg of you, Stanley, for the sake of heaven!' she cried softly. 'Can't you see that you are making me shudder with shame?'

'The shame, my darling, is an aphrodisiac, not that you are in need of one' he replied; nevertheless, he refrained from further revelations of her almost denuded person, and he pillowed his cheek luxuriously upon the nearly naked backside.

Struggling for self-control, Marion ended by tacitly acquiescing in being thus used as a pillow, while her soft thighs and her silken back were gently caressed by his wandering fingers. 'But surely you and Mildred, at least,' she murmured as remembered his previous amazing disclosures, 'do not yield to these shameful promiscuities.'

'Mildred is a young and adorable rogue,' he said. 'She loves to pester and excite these young chaps by showing this and that, usually as if by chance, and then smiling coolly upon them when they manifest agitation. Her marvellous breasts – worthy rivals even of yours, Maro – almost broke up a social gathering the other day when she showed them playfully, offering me non-existent sustenance from them.'

'My dear!' gasped Marion. 'I should think you would have expired of shame and indignation, and have beaten her or something.'

'That cave-mannish stuff is a bit outmoded,' smiled her brother-in-law. 'Though Mildred enjoys a simulacrum of it at times. And she is nothing loath to whack me sometimes in a little game she has invented in which I play the role of her child instead of her husband, until a certain moment in the proceedings. There are girls here, though, who like nothing so much as to be shamefully and painfully flogged under condition of the utmost possible indecency – and by persons with no right whatever over them.'

'Good heavens, I certainly can't comprehend that!' cried the maiden. 'Did you speak to Mildred about what we were talking of yesterday – letting that Gerry Crandall into her boudoir, I mean and letting him raise her bare foot to kiss it, exposing her terribly while doing so?'

'I did,' replied Stanley placidly. 'And we both laughed heartily about the way in which his eyes had bulged and his face reddened and… well, another symptom of his state which was quite manifest.'

* * *

Silence fell once again, but a silence speedily punctuated by husky girlish protests. 'Stanley, Stanley, you seem to have sworn to make me faint with sheer shame! What a place to kiss, right… right between there! Yes, I know I said you could kiss me, but I never thought you would be so low and vulgar as… oh!'

He murmured indistinct words which Marion barely caught.

'Yes – I do love your kisses! There, I've admitted it!' she panted. 'But to open me this way, in such a spot, and to lay your lips there and – and use your tongue, too! It makes me wild! I could faint with shame!'

Again with his voice muffled by the abundant flesh which masked it as he perversely explored with face and lips and tongue the rosy valley between the lovely buttocks which his fingers parted, Stanley murmured something.

'Well, yes,' she assented again. 'Perhaps it's more than just shame that moves me. I know I c-can h-hardly t-talk! Oh, God, Stanley, let me up! If you don't s-stop this m-minute, I'll g-get up and r-run away! Stanley, Stanley, oh, God, you've pulled off my suit entirely! I'm naked, naked!' With a gasping wail, Marion's voice trailed off into a series of panting sighs, but her backward-thrust hands battled to pry from her rear mounds the male face and the tongue which was just now engaged in an activity upon a rosy and crinkled nook between them.

'I vow, Maro,' he said thickly as he raised his head a mere inch, 'if you keep on struggling, I shall promptly roll you over and you know what I shall see then!'

'No, no, for the sake of heaven, no!' stammered the beleaguered girl. 'But, Stanley, I think you've gone crazy to kiss and lick me in such a place!'

'There's no restriction on my kisses, remember that, sweetness,' came his muffled reply. 'And, since the little lady needs an initiation into what kisses can really do to one, she shall have a very complete one.' With one final penetrating lick at the enticing and tiny aperture, he raised his head. 'Don't you venture to move or to squeal as I continue my lesson,' he said huskily. 'There may a dozen pairs of spooners all about us, although not near enough to spy upon us, but remember that I shall roll you right over if you scream!'

He bent forward over the quivering body of the sighing, thrilled Marion, who was shivering, he knew, from what had already happened. He slowly parted the lovely thighs which she had clapped together as soon as the opportunity was afforded her. His breath was hot upon the flesh of the snowy legs, which the moonlight gilded faintly. On the tender skin of the maiden's back, his swollen tool rested and moved as he leaned. She shuddered at the contact. All her exquisite body was trembling. He kissed the soft thighs. His glowing face glided between them. It pressed upward and inward.

Feeling the heated breath of the man upon the most secret of her charms, and realizing that it was exposed to his eyes and his fingers, too, if he chose, the girl clamped her thighs upon his. Even yet – even after undergoing that delicious if odious caress in the rear – she had no real conception of what awaited her from this lecherous, beloved brother-in-law of hers. She caught her breath suddenly, and then exhaled it in a tremulous sigh which was a groan of infinite delight and infinite shame, for his lips were feverish in a torrid and prolonged kiss directly upon the delicate rose of the tightly pressed lips, which his eyes had rapturously scanned before he had lowered his mouth. Kiss after kiss he gave her thus, and the girl writhed upon her naked belly amid the sand. And not even the fact that her involuntary movements made that monster which she had touched, but never seen, press silk-like upon her back and loins could make her refrain from continuing them.

He withdrew his mouth a little, but kept his head poised near the already gently pouting little crevice while his hands prevented the convulsive motion with which the nervous thighs would have drawn together. He inspected anew the delicious nook. His breath was hot upon it. His face slowly pressed lower. His tongue protruded. And Marion, shaking as if in an ague, groaned dully as she felt that moist, ineffable touch upon her sex.

From the instant that the licking tongue was drawn along the wee furrow, Marion's power even to desire immunity evaporated into nothing. She panted, moaned, gasped and trembled violently in the tornado of bliss which swept her whole being. She tried to raise her plump bottom to give him even greater access, and in this he allowed her to succeed. Now his eyes, gleaming with his own intimate pleasure, could detect, while his tongue feasted, the silken shrubbery of the genital mound beneath the somewhat raised body. Soft tendrils tickled his forehead, his lips, his nose. From the girl's lovely body arose the faint and delicate aroma of a healthy and excited young sex.

For minutes – minutes of maddening and increasing and tantalizing rapture for Marion, and of sheer delight in his ministry on the part of the man – he continued his licking of the pouting groove, a licking which became more and more fervent and bliss-dispensing. Now the panting maiden was frankly rubbing her raised loins against his turgid member, even seeking it out, if its pressure was lightened, in order that she might roll it against her flesh.

Marion cried out in ecstasy, and was stricken immobile for an instant as she felt the borders of her silt parted very gently and the tip of his tongue intrude between them. Almost sharply, she repeated the little cry as she sensed the dwelling of the tongue's tip after a moment's exploration upon a point which, throbbing, ecstatically made it welcome. And suddenly she was in violent motion beneath him, not trying in the least to escape this delicious fate, but too wild with frantic bliss to remain still. He compressed her into immobility, but the jangling, crying nerves continued to writhe in all her person.

It seemed to Marion that she had never before conceived of a heaven such as this into which she was so amazingly introduced. All her body swam in sheer ecstasy. Suddenly, she cried out sharply, trembling from head to toes, her buttocks heaving spasmodically, each heave accompanied by a groan that was almost a shriek as she deluged the working tongue of the man.

* * *

And was that a kiss too, Stanley?' queried a weak and shaky little voice two or three minutes later, minutes in which Marion remained mute and prostrate, slowly recovering from the shock of a rapture greater than any which her mind could have conceived.

'It was a kiss, with variations, Maro,' he said with grave elation. 'It was the kiss, in fact.'

The girl drew a long, tremulous breath. Her naked and shapely body wriggled in the soft sand which still gave back to the heat of her frame the accumulated and stored warmth of the day's sun. 'Then kisses must include pretty nearly everything a man and a woman can do together,' she concluded, 'for I had the feeling that I was absolutely giving myself to you, and was carried right into heaven! How wicked I've been, for a girl has no right to be happy like that with a man unless she's married to him, has she? Am I what they called ruined, disgraced?' She turned her head to where he sat on the sand by her side. Her great eyes were shining yet still suffused with languor. And she speedily averted them again, with colour returning to her passion-paled face, as she saw his great, well built body as naked as the dawn in the moonlight.

'You are still the immaculate virgin, Maro,' he assured her. He took her nearer hand as she continued to sprawl upon her face. 'Surely you have not been reared in such ignorance that you do not know how a girl ceases to be a virgin and becomes a wife, or a lover?' he said gently.

'No – I – my last governess explained certain things,' she murmured, flushing more deeply. 'I realize that you haven't really... taken me. Yet, what you did to me... oh, Stanley, it must be far more wonderful than such a horrid action as she outlined to me. And I don't see why husband and wife should bother about such a low way of mating as that when such a perfectly marvellous delight as you have shown me can be had instead. Especially,' she added naively and nervously, 'especially when that other thing hurts a girl awfully, doesn't it?'

He drew her soft hand to his person. He placed it upon his abdomen, where it remained, exhibiting grateful affection as well as admiration for this fine male body by sundry caresses of the fine skin and the hard flesh. He knew that not even in her brief glance at him an instant earlier had she caught sight of the instrument upon which her satin back had so lasciviously rubbed when she was in the throes of passion. And truly, its formidable stature and proportions were calculated to strike terror to the heart of any maiden, especially if she sought to compare its bulk with so delicate and small an orifice as that which had just undergone his inflaming caresses.

Patting the back of the soft hand which was now engaged in tenderly smoothing his belly and vainly trying to nip the hard flesh of its muscular substance, he slowly forced it downward toward his crotch. Hardly aware of the movement towards his secrecies, Marion suddenly found her fingers upon crisp, thick hair. She gasped and made a feeble effort to withdraw her imprisoned hand. 'No, dear,' he murmured. 'You mustn't be unduly startled or nervous. You are twenty, and few girls of your age remain in your ignorance of what the consummation of their future marriage really means. And in such ignorance, too, regarding the instrument of that consummation! Have no fear, sweetness; nothing is going to happen to you. Inform yourself – I wish it, and so would Mildred – concerning a reality which will be much in your life after I have given my shy sister-in-law away at the altar to some wealthy beggar who is totally unworthy of her.'

The girl's blood was drumming in her temples. Ever since she had first seen this pillar distending his scant garment, ever since she had felt it bearing upon her in their first embraces, ever since she had so unwarily touched for an instant its smooth tip beneath his trunks, and especially ever since she had borne its rampant nakedness upon her back and had been moved to caress it hotly with her skin, a longing akin to an obsession had smouldered within her being, a longing to touch this majestic affair again and more prolonged, a longing to acquaint herself with it.

She smothered a shamed, excited feeling as she surrendered her other arm and hand to such intimate exploration as he seemed to wish to enforce upon her fingers. The fingers which

he laid upon the base of the thicket from which sprouted the oak
of his virility were warm and trembling in his clasp. He coiled
them about the root of the shaft, which they could not encompass wholly. Her immense agitation, the rush of colour to the
one soft, oval cheek which he could see delighted him.

'No, no, Stanley, don't make me, please, I can't stand it!' she
panted softly.

'Nonsense, lassie, you have a right to know how a man is constructed,' he whispered. 'It's nothing to get so upset about.'
Patting her white behind with one hand, he took the tips of her
fingers with his other hand. He caused her thus to investigate his
dangling testicles, all the hairy realm of his sex. And then he led
her hand again to the sceptre which so dismayed and enticed her.

With unruffled, irregular breathing, with face still gagged
and masked by her arm, Marion now become excitedly enterprising on her own behalf. With soft fingertips she took cognizance of this marvellous plant upwards from its roots. 'Oh –
o-o-o-oh, it's impossible, one couldn't stand it!' she said in a
smothered whisper as she touched the swollen sex timidly just
beneath its great knob. 'And it's even bigger up here! Did you
really do that to Mildred? I should think it would have killed
her! Did she have to go to bed for weeks and weeks, and have
doctors after the first time?'

'She went to bed pretty frequently, not always in the night
either, but not because of damage done by this prick or because
of any aversion to its function.' he said with a smile.

'Pri-prick?' stammered Marion wonderingly. And then her
visible cheek turned scarlet. 'What a horrid, horrid word. I
remember now, I heard a wretched girl say it, and then, when
she saw I didn't understand, she insisted on explaining it to me.
But a nicer name is… well, manhood, isn't it?'

'As you like,' he conceded with a chuckle. 'But you'll be calling such an article "ducky darling" and "mother's pet" and even far less decorous words after you are wedded.'

'I certainly will not!' she maintained stoutly, and he took note that one eye was now half-visible through long lashes that fluttered, as the fair head turned ever so slightly and almost involuntarily toward him. 'Because,' she went on dreamily as she fingered with a sort of tender consternation the smooth knob, thereby causing him sensations which she was unaware of but which gave him much ado in the matter of restraining an outburst of lechery which would have dismayed her, 'Because I'm never going to marry, so there! If you think I'm going to submit myself to such torment as an object like this could inflict, you are very much mistaken, Stanley Cochrane! And I certainly cannot understand how Mildred... why, she must be abnormal or else I am... in construction, I mean.'

He laughed and called her 'baby' which, with the caresses of her body with both his hands now, she accepted without resentment, too absorbed as she was in her digital exploits to find more than increased pleasure in his endearments and his touches on her naked person.

'Mildred is built about like you, and I speak with some authority since I've seen you both quite intimately,' he went on. 'I tell you, Maro, that if you two lay side-by-side, with everything veiled except your rosy-lipped little cunts, it would be pretty hard to decide which was which, in spite of the warm hospitality which your lovely sister has so often afforded me.'

'Oh!' protested Marion in a strangled voice. 'How can you use such vulgar words, Stanley, and how can you remind me of the disgraceful way in which you have viewed my body?' But her eyes were bright as it flashed upon her suddenly what she held in her lithe, caressing fingers. The lashes drooped once more as she noted that he was observing her act, and the flush deepened on her cheek and brow and temple.

'If you are still incredulous,' he murmured, 'I have no doubt that Mildred would willingly let you see how commodiously and rapturously she houses this standard.'

'Oh, how perfectly unspeakable!' said the startled Marion. 'Why, I should never dare to look and I'm sure that she would be revolted to the soul to permit it!'

She had raised her lovely, flaming face as she spoke and, when she would have sunk it again into her arm, he caught her tenderly beneath the chin. 'For five minutes, Maro,' he murmured, 'you have been wanting and trying to look boldly upon my body. Let's have no more of that bashful fear of making your quite natural interest manifest.'

'I – I didn't want to be any more brazen than I was already being…' she faltered. Her lids drooped over startled eyes which had just caught full sight of the great column of flesh to which her fingers still clung. The white lids arose partway and the girl peered through her lashes. And suddenly the grey eyes were wide and entranced upon the masculinity of the man. 'Oh – oh, my heavens!' cried Marion wildly. 'How huge, and how white and rosy! Are they all this way, Stanley? If so, you can be quite certain I shall never marry! Not even my fingers made me realize how tremendous it is!' Writhing in eager convolutions, she revealed her round breasts, the nipples rosy because of being ground into the soft sand. The maiden strove to get her other hand upon the fascinating monster, yet she wailed in a new shame as he facilitated her purpose by overturning her. 'Stanley, Stanley, I'm quite naked! Oh, don't look at me. Let me lie on my face again!' she gasped.

'You lie quite still, until I can see fully what an adorable sister his Mildred has brought to me,' he commanded. 'If it comes to that, there is such a thing as reciprocity, and I'm peeled down to my real self, too. Lie quite flat, little darling, and stop shivering. Let me see this beard of dark-gold, this blessed little grove of silk. Part your legs, sweetness... yes, I know I've seen already, but not exactly like this, not all your glorious nakedness at once.'

In an infinity of shame, and in a gentle fever of growing pleasure, too, Marion made him the complete sacrifice of her modesty which he demanded. Hands cast to either side, and fingers curled into wee fists, she submitted to his ecstatic examination. Not even when, breathing excitedly, he allowed his hands as well as his eyes every liberty of access, and petted and kissed her from head to little bare toes, did she stage any revolt now. She screwed her eyes tightly shut at first, and her exquisite bust rose and fell with her agitated breathing. But, as he pursued his luxurious examination and made her nudity the pasture of his warm lips and his ardent fingers, her eyes opened. With a shy delight, she observed the admiration and pleasure to which her nakedness had given birth. With a wilder delight, she watched in fascination the increased turbulence of his swaying member, its almost purple and shining knob and its palpitation as he knelt to lean above her.

And now a small hand stole forth to resume a lascivious and, this time, uninvited possession of the strutting and superb virility. Kneeling upward, he allowed her to clutch with both hands once more his sexual regions. He noted the fitful breathing of the shaken girl, her gasping sighs and the light convulsions which ever and again shook her white body. He felt his own passions again reach the danger point. Quickly he rose to his feet and caught her up likewise. 'Well, sweet little Eve' he said, smiling at her and supporting her beneath the arms as she swayed.

'Oh, it's paradise, it's Eden!' she whispered huskily as she clung to him. 'But, Adam, it's forbidden fruit. I cannot deceive myself on that point no matter what sweet, consoling things you say. Imagine being naked, stark naked, with a naked man and doing all these wicked, marvellous things! And you the husband of my own sister, which makes it all the worse because it seems like a disloyalty on the part of both of us.'

'You're better informed, better prepared to cope with life and sex and what they bring than you were two hours ago, aren't you, dear?' he asked gently as he saw that those grey legions of conscience and purity were again active within her. 'And, as for disloyalty, I assure you that if your sweet sister were to come upon us now she would smile delightedly, and probably insist upon giving you at once the spectacle of those further pleasures which you know only by vague report.'

Norah

Reverend Nicholas came in, followed by his ravishing daughter. He did the honours. The young woman was very much intimidated, but very well brought up, and she bowed gracefully with a rapid genuflection in front of the two lords.

She was simply dressed in a small navy blue dress which just reached down to her knees. A small collar and two cuffs of white quilting were the only garnitures on her clothing. Her legs were half bare. She wore white cotton socks held tightly around her ankle by an elastic top.

The presentations completed, she looked around at the company. Mary, who looked rather exhausted, was an object of astonishment for the young girl. Here was a girl in a dressing gown at a cinema. Even if it were a private one, she did not understand very well. And why did she look so miserable, with her tired, red, and beaten eyes and her pale cheeks?

Not having noticed the screen hanging from the wall but not yet unrolled, she questioned her father: 'But, Daddy, you told me we were going to the cinema?'

'Exactly,' responded Lord Selwin. 'You're in a private cinema; a club. There is the screen we are going to unroll. The camera is behind us in the booth, over there near the fireplace. See the hole? We are about to witness a film that has a particularly interesting and exclusive character. I am certain that it will please you very much and greatly interest you.'

The assembled gentlemen devoured their young prey with the eyes of satyrs who were about to catch hold of a tender morsel.

Evangeline was really beautiful, and from what could be seen, she had an admirably formed body. Her breasts pushed out the front of her dress, and her behind nicely filled out the back of the cloth. Her legs were well curved and she had slender and delicate ankles. She had creamy skin, and her black hair hung down over her shoulders. It was held simply by a knot in back of her head. Her brown eyes were set off by the long, curved lashes that showed her candour and innocence. She had cherry lips, which were slightly full and well traced, showing precocious sensuality. She was a handsome girl.

'You can have the best place, in the front row, Evangeline. Here, kneel down on this praying stool.' said the Reverend.

Without hesitating, she obeyed like a good girl.

The screen was unrolled, everybody took their place, and the lights were extinguished.

The Reverend sat down on the couch and pulled Mary down beside him. The film began. The title flashed on: Saturday in the Convent of the Sisters of Christian Theosophy.

The spectators were first shown the pupils in the convent, marching two by two through the courtyard into a study hall, where the Mother Superior, Lady Cunigonde, met with them the last Saturday of each month at eleven a.m. to give them their grades, and, if necessary, to mete out any punishment. They were accompanied by Sister Mary Angel. Whereas Mother Cunigonde was a robust woman with a slight moustache, about fifty years of age, Sister Mary Angel was a ravishing young novice who had not had much experience in life before taking the vows.

There were three sections of pupils: the young from twelve to fourteen years of age, the next of fifteen and sixteen years of age and those seventeen and older. They entered as usual, with the youngest in front. All were dressed alike, in light grey frocks. The youngest had socks, the next oldest had half stockings and the oldest had light grey stockings.

They sat down at their places, and Sister Mary Angel went about through the class. The door opened, and they all got up and said in unison:

'Good morning, Mother.'

'Good morning, dear children,' was Mother Cunigonde's immediate reply. She went and seated herself in the largest black wooden chair. Then she began to announce the results of the history and geography composition, naming the best ones in each section and congratulating them. The farther she went down the list, the more severe became her tone of voice. She inflicted some slight punishments such as taking away desserts, forbidding going out on Sunday, and other similar sentences for the lower halves of each section.

'I have something particular to say to Daisy Cunningham. Daisy, come up here,' she said looking along the rows of girls.

A charming little blond girl, led by Sister Mary Angel, came forward. She was timid, pale, and trembling.

'Young lady, I have no compliments to make to you. Your

grades are extremely poor, two in history, one in geography, and zero in deportment. I also note that you spoke back to one of your teachers after you were reprimanded. This is not allowed. I also see in your notebook that you did not know the date when Charles VI became king. Nor do you know the date when our great queen Mary Stuart died. And when you were asked the name of the winning general at Waterloo, you answered Cambronne. That is an unpardonable idiocy. In geography, you located Singapore in India, the Cape of Good Hope in South America, and what is even more serious, you said that Glasgow was the capital of Ireland. Shame upon you, young lady. Sister Mary Angel, would you please note on the black board Daisy Cunningham – twenty-four blows of the rod on the backside, and, of course, no dessert tonight nor tomorrow, and no going out on Sunday.'

Upset and in tears, the pretty young girl resumed her place. 'Here, now, is the class average.'

And the ritual began again. First there were compliments, then reprimands followed by more or less severe punishments, continuing until the Mother Superior cried, 'Oh, what have we here? Adeline Montgomery! You, the daughter of a famous general with such a mark in French! There are nothing but mistakes. You do not make your past participles agree with anything. You write chemin de f-a-i-r-e and Chato-Bryan. You have twenty-seven mistakes on one page of dictation. You must learn your grammar, young lady. What a mediocre student you are, and at your age! No going out on Sunday will enable you to do some catching up. Oh, what is this drawing on the margin of your notebook… how horrible, a boy with very few clothes on! Oh, this is shocking! You draw much better than you write. Here… comportment. Ah, another zero, and there is a notation that you were caught coming out of the lavatory with a pernicious book. This is frightful, young lady. What was the title of this book? No? You won't tell? Very well, then, you will be severely punished. You are a bad one, young lady.' She appeared to be furious, but behind it all she was delighted. 'Sister Mary Angel, write two dozen with the rod and two dozen with the horsewhip.'

'Oh no, not that, I beg of you, Mother! I won't do it any more. I'll work hard... oh, that's too much. I don't deserve that!' the girl choked through her tears.

'Go back to your place, Miss Adeline,' she said authoritatively to the young brunette, who buried her face in her hands and went back to her seat. 'Now we come to the class of older girls. I hope to have some compliments to make. And, in effect, the grades of this class were very good, in particular those of Miss Norah Britchley were very brilliant, as she had the maximum possible in all subjects.'

However, a sealed envelope was pinned to Norah's notebook. Mother Cunigonde opened it and read what was inside. She seemed very much moved by its contents. First she paled, and then she blushed, but still said nothing. After thinking for a minute, she called, 'Norah, come here.'

The girl, who saw nothing amiss, went forward smiling, expecting some supplementary compliment for the excellence of her work.

Mother Cunigonde handed her the note, 'Read it,' she said.

The girl read it rapidly, blanched frightfully, lowered her eyes, and said between her teeth, 'The dirty beast, she told on me. I might have known.'

'Miss Norah, I cannot let this incident pass. But this is outside of my jurisdiction. The Convent Confessor alone can decide what is to follow. I shall warn him of this. I want all three of you, Misses Daisy, Adeline, and Norah, at three o'clock sharp in the parlour. I thank you all, young ladies. You may go now.' She got up. The pupils filed out of the study hall. For an instant, the Mother Superior was still. Her nostrils trembled, a wicked smile twisted her lips, her eyes sparkled, and her hands were shaking. The last Saturday in the month was the day she waited for. She shuddered with pleasure at the thought of the punishments she was going to inflict on the culprits.

The film dispensed with the hours between the end of the scene where the culprits were named and the time when punishments were meted out. The next scene took place in the parlour – a large and austere room with stained glass windows, and bars between the beams on the ceiling from which iron lamps hung. Simple chairs and benches covered with leather ran around the walls of the room and a large crucifix hung at one end. At the other end were two large Gothic doors, and between them was a bench on which sat the three young girls who were awaiting their punishment. The clock sounded three. The door on the right opened, and Mother Cunigonde came in followed by the Chaplain of the Convent, Reverend Conbite, a gabbros man with a strict air, greying hair, and a rosy face. He was corpulent and not very tall. He had comfortably prominent belly under his cassock.

'Daisy and Adeline, go into my office and wait for me,' said the Mother Superior, pointing to a door nearby. 'Norah, come this way.'

The Reverend, the Mother Superior, and Norah went out by the other door. The film followed them into the Chaplain's office. There were two successive doors; the inner one was covered with leather, and then there was a heavy curtain covering the entrance. It was an austere office, but showing a simplicity of taste. It was lighted by a stained glass window like the ones in the parlour. There was a large divan and two armchairs with ancient wooden backs, the arms of which ended in wooden balls. There were also four chairs covered with cloth to complete the furniture.

Near the fire place, a strange sort of seat – a small bench, wide and low, on legs – was pushed against the wall, its back made of nothing but a piece of curved iron about one inch in diameter in the shape of an inverted V. The back was much larger than the seat itself, and it arched downward to act as a support on the floor.

All around the room were shelves with rows and rows of handsomely bound volumes.

Father Conbite took up his habitual position behind the working table, and Mother Cunigonde seated herself on the other side of the table. Norah, her heart pounding with trepidation, was made to sit on a chair between the two adults.

'Father, I feel compelled to submit to your judgement the case of Miss Norah Britchley, one of our most brilliant students and quite a remarkable subject. I feel that the reduced means I have at my disposal and my general lack of competence in such matters do not allow me to try to broach this problem alone.'

'What does it consist of, dear Mother?'

'Read this, Father.' And she handed him the sheet of paper she had taken out of the envelope pinned to the girl's notebook.

The Chaplain read aloud, 'The night guardian feels herself under the obligation to single out Norah Britchley, whom she caught unawares, during her nightly inspection tour at about four o'clock in the morning in the older girl's dormitory, in the act of performing a reprehensible and solitary ritual. Miss Britchley had cast the covers down to the foot of her bed, not thinking that she would be seen at such an hour. Her actions leave no doubt as to the wicked and pernicious habits this girl has acquired, and it would be of utmost interest to drive home the gravity of her act, for the sake of both her health and her morality as well as those of her school mates.' The note was signed, Sister Stanislas.

The Chaplain set the paper down in front of him, and fixed a baleful eye on young Norah from across the top of his spectacles. She, in turn, had lowered her head and was blushing all over. The Chaplain asked her, 'My dear girl, I want you to answer my questions frankly.'

'Yes, Father,' she replied.

'Exactly what were you doing when you were surprised by Sister Stanislas? Her written information is not completely clear, and I must know.'

'Why... nothing... nothing reprehensible, Father.'

'Come now. Don't lie to me. You were in bed?'

'Yes, Father. I was lying on my bed, asleep.'

'And feeling too hot, you had thrown off the cover.'

'Undoubtedly.'

'Your legs, how were they? Curled up, or stretched out?'

'Stretched out, I think, but then I was half asleep. Just before that, I had woken up after a dream, a nightmare, which had left me all shaken. I don't remember very well.'

'Ah, you were all excited. And would it be possible to know the subject of your... reveries?'

'Oh... ah... yes, of course, Father.'

'Then tell us. We are listening.'

'Oh… it was a dream like one we all have. I was in a wonderful castle, somewhat of a prisoner, and my handsome Prince Charming came galloping up on his horse to deliver me from the old witch who was holding me there.'

'Fine, fine, go on.'

'Then my handsome knight fastened the reins of his horse to a tree next to the house. I waited for him, impatiently, with my heart beating, standing near the window. Silently he climbed up with the aid of the ivy vines. He came up to my balcony, came over the railing and into my room. I fell into his arms, overcome with happiness. I hugged him, he hugged me and he…'

'Come on, and then what? You are very romantic in your dreams, my dear girl. Go on. Don't be afraid. We are here to help you.'

She hesitated for a few minutes, but he insisted, as also did Mother Cunigonde.

The girl was somewhat fearful, but she said, 'And he… kissed me… on the lips. I felt myself melting in his arms. After that, I don't remember any more, and I woke up all excited. I was sweating and my body was damp.'

'And,' cut in Mother Cunigonde, 'what she won't tell you, Father – I found out by lengthily questioning Sister Stanislas – is that she was ardently entwined with her pillow, with one hand pressing hard and rubbing between her tightly closed thighs, while the other hand was stroking her bare breast. She had pulled her night shirt up over her stomach, and she had slid off the shoulder straps. She was naked or almost so, pressing the pillow against her body between her legs and deriving considerable pleasure from this. The sighs and grunts that were heard left no doubt as to her state of sensual exhilaration. This shameless girl, Father, was wallowing in intense and solitary pleasure, and it was most certainly not the first time. Her dream, let me tell you, is nothing but a lie.'

Mother Cunigonde appeared to be furious. She had spoken rapidly, almost all in one breath, half rising from her chair, one fist pushing against the table and the other arm gesticulating; she was using her finger or her open hand to punctuate her accusation. She continued excitedly, 'She deserves exemplary treatment. She has to be cured of this vice, that's for certain, but first she must be punished as she never has been punished before. Oh, she should be made to remember what it costs to become too licentious and vicious a creature. Soon she will begin dragging others down after her. That would be the limit; my school becoming an offshoot of Gomorrah. The cult of Aphrodite would reign and destroy all the good education which we take such pains to instil in them.'

Norah was terrified. She had never seen the Mother Superior in such a state. She trembled with fear. These vague menaces seemed more fearful to her than did the price which she was going to have to pay.

'You are right, my good Mother. We must do something about this. First, Norah, do you admit the truth of these events?'

She nodded her head, and lowered her gaze toward the floor.

'And was it the first time?'

She made no answer, but instead heaved a heavy sigh.

'I asked you, was it the first time?'

'Of course not, Father. Her silence is worse than an avowal,' burst in Mother Cunigonde.

'Have you been… fingering it for some time now?'

No answer.

'How long, one month? Three? Six? More?'

She nodded affirmatively.

'Heavens!' the Chaplain could not keep himself from exclaiming. He too began to get in an aroused state, as could be seen from the large hump that began to rise between his legs, even though he was sitting down.

These scenes were very well photographed. They were shot from every possible angle and from all distances, and the protagonists were shown under all aspects.

'It is time to do something, if it is not already too late. At any rate, don't be scandalized, but we must examine you. I was a doctor before becoming… what I am. Consequently, don't take offence at what we are going to do. Come over here, near the sofa. Cunigonde, undress her.'

Norah leapt to her feet in protest. 'Undress me! Why? What for? I'm not… I don't want… Mother! Mother! Leave me alone! You have no right!'

'No arguments, little one. The Chaplain gave an order, and I intend to carry it out. We are going to examine you, medically speaking, that is. We must watch over the state of your health.'

During this scene, the Chaplain had risen to his feet, gone over to a small stand, and come back with a glass in his hand. He unlocked his desk and took out a bottle of brandy and a small flask of colourless liquid. He put about ten drops of this into the glass.

Norah was still struggling.

Mother Cunigonde struck her on the arm and on the head,

and pulled her by the hand. She cried out in anger, 'It's useless to try to run away or to struggle. You're shut in here, and you won't get out of this room until we let you out. And also, the walls are thick and the door is doubled, so you can scream your fool head off and no one will hear you. So you can cut out the shouting and get undressed. Naked, do you understand? Take off all your clothes, even the medallions from around your neck... that's it, completely naked. Then we'll examine you and look you over as we please. Hold still there!'

The Chaplain, his short-sighted eyes shining out from behind his thick glasses, came toward her. He held the glass in his hand. 'Here, drink this, it will make you feel better. Calm you down, it's good for you. I put a few drops of sedative in the glass,' he said with his unctuous voice.

The sedative was, in reality, the concentrated extract of Spanish fly. Norah stopped struggling for an instant. With a trembling hand, she took the glass from the priest and drank its contents jerkily, in little mouthfuls. Naturally, she was not used to drinking any alcohol. When she had finished, she set the glass on the bureau.

'There you go. Now show some signs of life. Undress yourself, Norah, or we'll have to do it for you, and we don't want to tear your clothing if we can help it,' said Mother Cunigonde.

'Oh, please, Mother, have pity on me. Don't ask me to do that. Oh, Father, you can't make me do that. It's awful. What do you want to do with me? Can't you examine me... like I am?'

'Take off your dress and then we'll see. Perhaps we can arrange something,' said the old trickster.

She fell into the trap. Helped by Mother Cunigonde, she

unbuttoned her dress down the back, slid her arms out of the sleeves, and stopped there, looking wonderfully charming in her light underclothing. The strict convent rules only applied to the exterior uniform, the stockings, shoes and hat. The rest was up to the parents of the girls, and Norah's mother, who was rich and elegant, had spoiled her daughter. Her underclothing was of fine silk trimmed with lace. She of course wore no corset, but just a little belt which pressed against her thighs and held up her stockings. She was absolutely ravishing in her scanty lace and silk.

Somewhat agitated by the slowness of the operation, Mother Cunigonde made a surprise movement and caused her dress to slide down to the floor. Norah uttered a little cry, and tried to pull up her dress, but the Chaplain seized hold of her quickly with his hands, preventing her from bending over to reach the dress. He held her with his hands behind her back. The Mother Superior hesitated no longer; she unfastened the garters, and despite the contortions of the girl, slid the belt down to the floor. Before the unwary girl had time to react, the Mother Superior had also drawn the string holding up the panties, and they too fell down to her ankles. Then with one quick motion, she took the girl's slip at the bottom and whipped it up and off over the girl's head.

Norah howled with shame feeling herself completely naked in front of these two villains, but she was not given the time to think for a second nor to protest to any extent. They brutally pushed her against the sofa where she fell over on her back. The Chaplain held her wrists together above her head and he attached then with two leather straps fixed into the wall. At the same time, Mother Cunigonde had ripped off the girl's slippers, and then the stockings, which were the only article of clothing remaining on the girl.

The poor thing twisted her body in all directions, trying everything she could to shake loose from their clutches, but they were much too strong for her, and she was completely at their mercy. She screamed and cried, supplicated, implored, and promised to do anything if only they would let her alone.

In the twinkling of an eye, they had tied her ankles to the other end of the sofa, and she lay there, stretched out and winded, powerless and naked. She had a crying fit, and she moaned ceaselessly. The only thing that had not been removed from her body was the slender chain of medallions that she wore around her neck.

'You're a tough one, little idiot,' cried Mother Cunigonde, who was perspiring freely. She wiped her forehead with the back of her hand and brushed off the drops of perspirations resulting from the efforts she had made. 'And there you are, all tied up now.'

The Chaplain got down on his knees, and with his concupiscent eyes he carefully examined the milky body stretched out before him.

Norah was panting, and her lovely breasts, which were high-cupped and firm, heaved up and down rapidly.

He began to touch the peaches-and-cream flesh of the young maiden. His eyes sparkled and his nostrils flared perceptibly as he inhaled the moist odour of this faultless body. His nose made the journey from one armpit to the other, which gave off a chaste smell from the small tufts of hair growing there, and then he stopped in between, fingering the nipples of her breasts. He noted that they had come out of their shells; that they were pointed and hard. Norah shuddered under his touch.

Suddenly, a strange languor seemed to overcome her, and the gentle titillation of his exploring fingers had the curious effect of opening up and making blossom the secret parts of the young victim. The drug had taken effect and was acting strongly on the solid and healthy temperament of the girl who had already felt the distant call of sexual orgasm.

Sensing a slight and involuntary spreading of her thighs, he ceased his caresses. He leaned over, screwed his cupped ear over the snowy hill of her left breast like a lemon squeezed, and listened to the heart, which, overcome by fear and artificial excitement was pitter-pattering in anticipation. Gently, he pinched her cheek, as doctors do, but for him it was a rare and sensual sensation to touch her skin, which was as smooth as the petal of a flower. His gaze crept down over her thorax, to her stomach, and it rested on her tender navel. He extended a finger, tickled the outside rim, and then pushed on into the depths of the sensitive hollow.

Surprised, Norah cried out, and without realizing it, she spread apart her legs as far as the cords would allow. He looked on down and perceived the slope and the undergrowth that covered Mount Venus. He decreased the pressure of his finger and drew it slowly up the length of her stomach, and her legs stayed open. He continued to delicately stroke the smooth skin, and soon he had moved his hand to the critical area, and his fingers crept in among the short, thick-set, and silky hairs.

Mother Cunigonde was still standing at the end of the sofa. She plunged her gaze down toward this unveiled virginity. She was without reserve in her admiration of the perfect outline of the untouched and palpitating slot. Norah had ceased to react. She appeared to have collapsed, and she let them do what they wanted. Ardent tremors began to run through her veins, and her limbs were shaken by intense spasms, which also shook her nipples and her lower stomach. Her cunt began to be animated by spasmodic contractions, and it became moist to the touch. Desire, unknown desire, the orgasmic flame, began burning inside of her body, penetrating into the depths of her very soul.

His hand descended slightly farther. One finger reached out toward the moist vulva and penetrated into the opening crevasse. It pressed on into this newly turned furrow and separated the virgin walls until it came up against the stretched and hard membrane of the excited clitoris.

From the depths of her throat, Norah heaved out a long, heavy groan. Mother Cunigonde freed her ankles, knelt down at the foot of the sofa, and raised the girl's knees slightly, spreading them apart so that the enraptured cunt would be more accessible to the man's touch and gaze. The drug had taken effect. Norah was fully in heat, and the only thing left to do was to gratify her thirst for satisfaction.

The Mother Superior thrust her face forward, hesitated for an instant, and then suddenly placed a glutton's kiss on the virginal vagina, and then she immediately began to peck away with her tongue at the exposed cunt lips. So as to better get at her prey, she pushed the girl's legs farther back and exposed, in a monstrously indecent manner, the writhing twat. She lapped at the pink protuberance below, and with little pecking motions of her lips she brought her tongue into the middle of the contracted opening.

Norah panted and shook all over in heat. She arched her stomach and brought her kidneys into play, thus better offering herself to the immoral caresses.

Father Conbite again plunged his finger into the umbilical aperture, which tore a moan of suffering or pleasure from the unfortunate girl. Then he slid his hand downward rapidly and grabbed the whole twat with his fist. The palm of his hand came away soaked with the abundance of fluids exuded by the virginal cunt. He seized the clitoris and began to shake it with one hand, while the other was squeezing and rubbing one of her tits. At the same time, he chewed and licked at the other tit.

Under the affect of the quadruple excitement, Norah burst. She was completely beside herself with frenzy, belching up incoherent cries, arching her back and contracting her muscles. She blew an odorous fart right into the mouth of the horrible woman, which did nothing to daunt the activity of the latter. The unleashed girl howled her pleasure, and finally completely beside herself, she had such a violent spasm that if she had not been firmly attached, she most surely would have rolled onto the floor. Her breasts were swollen and their turgid nipples were almost double their normal size. Her vulva was in a frenzy of activity, opening and closing in rapid sequence. Her stomach billowed out with demonic contractions. Never had either of the two members of the cloth seen such an unleashing of sensuality. The girl continued to moan like a woman at the final extremities of sexual orgasm. As soon as one spasm died down, another rose to take its place. Mother Cunigonde, in an absolute fury of excitement underneath her skirts, continued to work away at the frenetic cunt with her skilled tongue. She lapped and licked the fluid which continuously oozed out from the crazed cunt.

'I can't hold it any longer!' Father Conbite cried suddenly. 'Let her calm down for an instant. Don't fan this impure fire for a bit. Prepare the praying stool, here, beside the sofa. Now let's flagellate her for a while. After the joy and the pleasure comes the pain, and then the pleasure by way of pain, and so the cycle will be complete.' He undid the thongs holding her wrists.

Norah lay stretched out, breathing hard, but inert, her eyes closed, her head inclined to the side and her lovely auburn hair spread in disarray over the pillow. Every now and then slight shudders continued to shake her and to make her contract all her muscles. Her breasts remained hard, and the nipples were still pointed.

He brought over the praying stool, and they raised up the half-unconscious Norah. 'Kneel down,' he commanded her.

As if inebriated, without realizing what she was doing, her head pounding with fire, she obeyed them. Immediately they fastened her wrists to either end of the cross bar.

The Chaplain bent down and began to turn a small crank in the front of the seat. This seat separated into two parts, with the gearing mechanism hidden under the leather of the stool. The smooth surface of the seat frustrated all the efforts Norah made to keep her legs together. When this operation was completed, she was fixed spread-eagle there, with her knees about two feet apart. It was then an easy matter for the two fiends to lead a leather thong around her shins and fasten it to hooks on either side of this rather extraordinary praying stool. Then the Chaplain cranked back the inclined planes of the stool's seat.

In this way, Norah exposed her whole body defencelessly. Her inner thighs were spread out and she was entirely at their disposition. Her body was in an almost vertical position, but if necessary the metallic support could be adjusted to lean her forward or backward as her executioners so desired. It seems that this instrument of torture had once been used during the Spanish Inquisition, and since then it had been perfected with modern methods. Her stomach, the upper part of her thighs, her breasts, and her arms were all prominently displayed. Norah cried out with fear. She had no idea why she had been tied up this way. However, she very quickly began to find out the goals of her tormentors.

'You acted like a slut!' cried the Mother Superior. 'Like a shameless and licentious creature, like a girl who cannot control her sensuality! Why, just a few minutes ago you showed us your temperament of unbridled eroticism, Norah. But when left to your own devices you go at it all by yourself, and with your pillow at that, like the vicious girl you are. Even yesterday, and the day before, and the day before that; for these many years you have gotten into the habit of practicing your solitary vice. So then, this vice, we are going to try to cure.'

She continued in the same vein, 'Father Conbite and I are first going to administer sixty blows with the rod, thirty apiece, and afterward, when you are all softened up, well heated up all over your body... after this, to cure you... he's going to make a woman out of you, Norah. He's going to fuck you! He will be your Prince Charming, the one in your dreams. When you once again collapse beneath our caresses, he is going to use his stiff tool to penetrate by force into the virginal flesh of your cunt. You'll be well serviced, and I can assure you it will cure you of your libidinous desires to satisfy yourself all alone, against the rules of nature.'

The Mother Superior got more and more worked up and excited as her own words continued to tumble out. 'Yes, you, a young virgin, we're going to make a woman out of you, a real woman, by breaking open your cherry and forcing apart the virginal flesh, by ploughing into your vagina, by forcing the way into your matrix, by fertilizing it in a natural way. This is your fate, the penalty you must pay for your sins. Now you know!' Then, turning to the Chaplain, she said, 'A little patience, Father, to work now, and be sure to impale her pitilessly. I'll leave you the back. I'll start by stroking her belly, her thighs, and breasts... ah, if that doesn't warm her up again, and if she doesn't come ten times in a row after we have warmed up her circulation like that, then I'd let myself be raped by a whole regiment of Horse Guards!'

'Calm yourself! Don't overdo things, Mother!' cried Father Conbite, somewhat outraged by her show of indecency.

Mother Cunigonde undid the long cord that she wore around her waist and that hung down the length of her left leg. It was not a particularly closely woven cotton cord and no thicker than a finger. She folded it in four lengths and used it as an instrument of flagellation.

For his part, Father Conbite had selected, from the dozen he kept in one of the drawers of his desk, a handsome rod, long and slender and made out of a supple branch. It was a light weapon, one that would not wound any more than would a nun's cord.

They took up their positions on either side of the prisoner, he behind and she in front, and they began to strike the girl. The Mother Superior began with the outstretched arms, going from the wrist to the shoulder. At each blow, the four strands curled themselves around the delicate flesh leaving four red marks on the outraged skin.

On his side, the Chaplain began with the calves and the thighs. Carefully and forcefully, he placed one blow beside the other as he mounted toward the centre of the body. He began with the right side, and then went back and did the left one.

There was something extravagant in Norah's cries and contortions. She was tied by the shins and the wrists, which left the rest of her body free to twist and turn in all directions.

Before they had completed ten lashes, Mother Cunigonde cried out, 'She makes too much noise with her howling. Let's gag her!'

Once this operation had been performed, the unfortunate girl could do nothing but moan through the folded towel covering her mouth. The two tormentors were excessively excited by her crazed contortions, her exaggerated hip movements, her plunging forward and her brutal backward motions, depending on which one of the two struck her. It was a lewdly satanic picture to see the girl's lovely body jiggle, arch, and twist itself in such a lascivious manner under the blows.

The pretty breasts flung themselves about in all directions as they were lashed several times by the quadruple cord. Their nipples turned an angry red. Her back was covered with marks from her shoulders all the way down to the point where her coquettish ass jutted out, and her legs and thighs had taken on a deep pink colour. Up to this time the two experts had left untouched the ass and the stomach, which were still creamy white. This was the dessert, the most succulent dish saved for last.

'Let's blindfold her!' the Chaplain cried suddenly.

She had a minute of repose, during which she begged them with her eyes, as she emitted muffled and unintelligible sounds through the gag. Her eyes rolled around in their orbits, and she defended herself so well by jerking her head around in all directions that they had to try three times before they finally succeeded in blindfolding her.

Then began the final act of the drama – at the same time, in rhythm, on the stomach in front, and on the jellied flesh of her ass behind, the last ten lashes fell, violently and well-spaced.

The flames of hell devoured the tender flesh of the poor girl. Her skin was red all over, striated with violent marks, but there was not a single open wound, not a drop of blood. Her flesh was still entirely intact.

'Set up the rest and swing her forward.'

What she called the 'rest' was a rod holding up a horizontal bar in the shape of a half-moon. This rod was set into a hole in the middle of the front of the praying stool. The curved part of the rest was to uphold the abdomen of the girl, at about the height of the navel.

The rest was set in place. Then they unblocked the mechanism and swung forward what could be called the back of the praying stool, to which were tied the two wrists of the patient. She was tilted forward so that her stomach came in contact with the rest, and it was fastened there by a strap.

Norah lay half suspended in mid-air, with her hands held against the cross-bar of the stool's back, and her stomach held against the rest, her back more inclined than horizontal and the cheeks of her ass outrageously opened. It could have been that her cunt was bubbling intensely; in between her legs the flesh around the desired slit, which had remained white, was now convulsing and becoming red with excitement. The little hole was moved by constant contraction. All the details of this effervescent sexuality were shown to advantage by means of a frightening close-up.

'It appears to me, Father, that there is one part neglected by your rod,' cried the Mother Superior, pointing her finger toward the exposed area. 'The skin is all white in the slot from her cunt hairs all the way up to her coccyx. I think that it would do her good to finish the job we started. You take care of that angle, and I'll finish off her tits. We can't leave undone what we started... patience, Father, only a couple of minutes more.'

She placed herself beside the suspended girl, took up her cords, and began to flagellate the well exposed nipples. During this time, the Chaplain skilfully lashed the sexual parts, producing frightful bounds and muscular contractions.

All her muscles contracted in an ultimate effort to defend herself. From the right, from the left, from above and from below, the vicious lashes left their traitorous kisses on the most tender parts of her flesh.

The Chaplain could restrain himself no longer. He quickly unbuttoned his cassock from the hem to the waist, and raised it up and tucked it under his belt. His legs were bare, and his horrible cock could be seen.

Ah, the Mother Superior had been quite right when she had said that Norah would be copiously serviced. What a prick! What a gland! What a joyous weapon! It jutted out of his groin like the mast of a ship. The prick was not overly long, but it was thick and husky, and at the end it was ornamented with a Machiavellian mushroom. It was evident that this tool required hot and juicy women for satisfactory fornication.

He drew near and sank to his knees between the legs of the unfortunate girl. He brought his hungry dick in contact with her inflamed slot.

'Not so quickly, my friend. You won't get in that way.

Think, she's still a virgin; her cunt has not yet been reamed out like mine, and, God knows, even I have difficulty taking you on.' After saying this, the Mother Superior took from the desk a small jar of fine, liquid lubricant. She copiously dosed the monstrous rod, and to finish things off, she dipped her well-anointed fingers into the vestibule of the vulva. She pushed her middle finger against the hymen, sought the little opening, pushed, and forced her finger in, enlarging the narrow passage by forcing the walls apart. Her finger came out all bloody. Norah had uttered a horrible groan from the sharp pain of this intimate violation. 'It's your turn now, and good luck,' she said laughing.

The Chaplain coupled up with Norah. He grabbed her around the waist with his hands covering the cheeks of her ass, and he pushed desperately with his hard-on against the little opening. But he could not get it in. The difference in size between the two organs, the weird, flattened form of his tool and the smallness of her cunt prevented him from succeeding.

Fortunately, Mother Cunigonde came to his rescue. With the thumb and fingers of one hand, she spread to the maximum the still unaccustomed cunt lips, and seizing hold of the cock, she guided it to the proper spot. The end of the foreskin went in between the lips. 'Now... go ahead... push... push hard,' she told him.

He pushed, braced himself, and pulled with his arms. Suddenly, everything slid over to the side.

'Clumsy!' cried Mother Cunigonde. 'What would you do without me? You'd be in a fine pickle with this tiny-cunted virgin and your enormous crowbar that can't find its way in.' She began again, spreading apart the entrance as far as she could, and again placed his prick into the slot, and then she exclaimed, 'Don't budge! Me, I'm going to make you enter this resistant cunt.' She seized a horsewhip from one of the desk drawers and, bracing herself, she delivered a whopping blow on the ass of the Chaplain. A triple cry sounded forth, the Chaplain from surprise, Norah from the atrocious anguish of the piercing pain, and Mother Cunigonde from joy and triumph at seeing her strategy succeed.

Under the violent blow, the Chaplain had lunged forward, and he had overcome all the proffered resistance with his formidable thrust. The narrow sheath was dilated to its extremity, the cherry had burst wide apart, and, with the aid of the lubricating fluid, the battering ram had furrowed a passage.

With grandiose alternation, the piston churned in the narrow cylinder, and in a short time it violently ejaculated its flood of boiling sperm. The virgin female was for the first time fertilized by the male.

* * *

Norah was quickly untied and carried over to the chaise lounge, over which Mother Cunigonde had spread a bathrobe. She was unconscious, pale, and defeated. Mother Cunigonde rapidly sponged her bloody cunt, which was all sticky with mucus and sperm. These were only the natural damages, and with a fine sponge and soapy water she carefully washed the external parts. Then, sliding a basin under the girl's ass, she administered internal washings with a special rubber syringe filled with warm milk mixed with several drops of a disinfectant.

The Chaplain was enjoying his recent pleasure. He was seated in his arm chair with a fully satisfied air at the thought of his glorious exploit. From time to time he rubbed his itching ass, which helped him to meditate on the treatment he so much enjoyed administering to his little protectorates.

The Mother Superior rang, and Sister Mary Angel came in by a door at the end of the room.

'She has had her fill for today, Mary Angel. Take her to the infirmary for a couple of days. Then put her in a private room. She won't sleep in the dormitory any more. That will make things easier for us if we want to… visit her. I leave her in your care.'

Before leaving the room, the Mother Superior spoke to the Chaplain. 'Are you satisfied, my friend?'

'Very. It was a very interesting experiment, but the Spanish fly will continue to have an effect on her for another day or so, and I believe that I…'

'No, no, my friend, she needs to rest. The shock was considerable, and the Spanish fly will continue to tickle her for a while. Don't get impatient. Mary Angel will derive great pleasure in caring for her.'

'Yes, I suppose you're right, but for my own self, my Dear Mother, all this has just made my mouth water and I am far from having my account settled, as you would say.'

'Don't worry about that. I still have two more victims to be punished, Daisy Cunningham, who is due twenty-four blows of the rod, and Adeline Montgomery, a charming brunette who will take double that number. While I am taking care of Daisy, you can do what you want with Adeline. Why don't you call in Sister Mary Angel, if you want, and you can entertain yourself at will with this girl, who was caught reading Aphrodite, that delightful book by Mr. Louys. I have been informed that she lost her virginity some time ago, although she has never, I think, been fucked by any man. Get her to tell you her story. It should be quite amusing. You can relate it all to me at supper.'

Thus it was decided. The Mother Superior left the room and went into her office which was adjacent to that of the Chaplain's and furnished in exactly the same way. She rearranged her dress somewhat, retied her belt, washed her face and hands with water, opened the door to the parlour, and called out, 'Daisy. Come into my office. This way,' she said, indicating the open door behind her. 'As for you, Adeline, our Chaplain, Father Conbite, would like to have a word with you. Go in that door, but don't forget to knock first.'

The younger girl was quite upset, but Adeline was even more frightened when she learned that she was to be punished by the Chaplain, because he had the reputation of being very severe. Nevertheless, she obeyed, knocked at the door, waited an answer like a good girl, and then went in. Heavily, with a muffled sound, the large door closed behind her. Mother Cunigonde had an enigmatic smile on her face, and taking Daisy by the hand, she drew her into the office.

The Gilded Lily

Naughty, naughty!' She giggled, and screamed again when the old man reached down and pinched her behind. The next minute he was whispering in her ear and she had stopped laughing and was wriggling against him like an eel. Another champagne cork popped at the table and the producer and the girl dissolved in the jostling crowd.

'I guess we might as well elbow our way in,' said Larry.

'If you folks want to eat first there's a dining room upstairs.' Matt Greer pointed to stairs near the checking booth. 'There's a show to amuse you while you eat,' he winked, and then glanced at his watch. 'Should be able to catch it if you hurry.'

'What do you say, Lily?'

'I'm ready,' she smiled.

Matt Greer whistled between his teeth. 'That's what I like to hear. I'll see you both later.'

They took the stairs to the second floor.

An impeccably dressed hostess met them in the hall. 'How many in your party?'

'Just the two of us.'

'Would you like a table for two or would you prefer to be with a larger group?'

'Let's join a larger party, Larry. They're all having so much fun.'

Larry nodded. 'It's okay with me.'

'Would you follow me, please,' said the hostess, turning to lead the way down the corridor. Lily tightened her grip on Larry's hand. There was no back to the woman's dress! She was entirely naked from her bare shoulders to the rounded pert cheeks of her bottom. Larry felt his penis quiver as he watched her buttocks swinging along in front of them.

As they approached a door at the end of the hall, she turned and handed him a small silver key attached to a numbered piece of bamboo. 'In case you want to be alone, this is the key to your room,' she said smiling. 'Should you wish special service, you'll find a buzzer beside the bed.' With a knowing glance at the front of Larry's pants, she went back the way they had come.

The door in front of them opened into a low-ceilinged room illuminated only by candles on a dozen tables all facing a small stage at the other end. Long emerald drapes hung along the walls. As their eyes grew accustomed to the dim light, they saw most of the tables were occupied by groups of people talking in restrained voices. Everyone was seated on low, zebra-skinned hassocks.

Out of nowhere, another young girl appeared as smartly dressed as the hostess in the hall. She motioned for them to follow, and led the way to a table. This time the fact that the girl was also nude down her backside didn't surprise Lily, but she saw Larry appraising her full rump as if he was tempted to reach out and pat it.

They joined a party of six near the stage. One of the men got to his feet and Lily recognized him at once. He was Rex Rayn, the star of Too Late the Dawn, one of the films in which she had had a bit part not three weeks before. Naturally, he didn't remember her, and Lily didn't intend to mention the fact that she was in the film.

One after another, Rex Rayn introduced the party, and then motioned for the hostess to bring more bottles of champagne. Beside Rayn was a pixie-faced blonde with pouting red lips and wide, innocent blue eyes; definitely not his wife. On her left was a dark-haired man with a weak face who looked more like an accountant than Rayn's business manager and agent. His name was Sark. His date was a tall, busty redhead. The other couple was a Mr. and Mrs. Fox. He was white-haired and looked senile, she was perhaps twenty years younger, but not young enough to carry off the black leotards, sequined yellow blouse, and red sash outfit she was squeezed into.

Somewhere in the background there was music – soft, heady music that wafted through the room and set the atmosphere.

The girls in half evening gowns were serving long silver trays of food to the tables.

Larry leaned close to her. 'Go easy on this,' he whispered.

'What do you mean?'

'Matt calls them "party stimulators". They're hors d'oeuvres mildly spiked with some kind of aphrodisiac, not enough to do any harm, really, but you can get awfully high on them.' He nodded toward the big-breasted redhead who was popping them into her mouth like peanuts. 'Rayn's manager is going to have his hands full,' he said, grinning.

Lily sampled several of the appetizers and found them slightly sweet with the flavour of some unusual liqueur. Following these came more trays, and silver flagons of bitter-tasting beverage that seemed to tease every taste bud in her mouth, sharpening it for more of the same. There were dishes of food she had never seen or tasted before, seafood combinations defying description, Oriental sauces that you poured over thirty-six small, individual dishes containing choice titbits of fish, fowl and meat, all highly seasoned and unique to the palate.

Long before they were finished, Lily felt a soft glow invading her entire body, as if she were being turned on a spit over a fire. She thought she detected the fragrance of jasmine in the room, and realized it was incense.

The effect on the people around her was clearly evident. They were more relaxed, more informal. Rayn's arm was around his blue-eyed blonde and he was caressing her breast. The weak-faced manager was ogling the redhead's bosom hungrily and, at the far end of the table, Mr. and Mrs. Fox seemed quite fascinated by the voluptuous behind of one of the hostesses bending over a nearby table. Everyone in the room was gradually loosening up; they leaned back, drinking slowly, talking in subdued voices, savouring the same delightful dream-like sensations that were flowing through Lily.

What a relief, she thought. Not a worry in the world.

And she knew that no matter what had happened to her from that moment on that it would seem like the most natural thing in the world. Everything was perfectly wonderful.

Suddenly a blue spotlight illuminated the stage in front of them. Several of the zebra-skin hassocks had been placed in a semi-circle on the raised dais. In the centre was a gleaming white one almost six feet across and decorated with a Moorish design in gold. The emerald drapes on both sides of the stage parted and a group of dwarfs made their way quietly into the audience. Lily almost laughed out loud. They reminded her of The Wizard of Oz, and the thought of Dorothy suddenly appearing on the stage to say 'there's no place like home' was almost too much for Lily to bear. She couldn't resist leaning over and asking Larry where Matt had hidden the magic slippers.

Larry grinned back at her. 'They must be looking for them now,' he quipped under his breath.

Three little people who couldn't have been more than three feet tall approached their table, smiling. Without a word, they scurried underneath as if intent on a game of hide-and-go-seek. If Lily hadn't seen them, she'd never have known they were there. They made no movement, no sound. But something in the room had changed. There was a feeling of almost restless expectation. The music had stopped. The blue light remained focused on the white leather hassock in the centre of the stage.

They didn't have long to wait. From the folds of the curtain emerged a statuesque bronze-skinned brunette in a filmy negligee that enveloped her nude body like a misty pink cloud. She slithered into the spotlight, stretched languidly and seated herself on the white hassock. Through the sheer silk the dark round orbs of her breasts rose and fell as she simulated a yawn. As if it were a signal, two other girls materialized beside her wearing nothing more than black silk stockings, tiny maid's aprons and small white-winged caps perched jauntily on their heads.

With slow, delicate movements they gently slipped the negligee from the brunette's sculptured curves. This done, the girl lay full length on the hassock, arching her body and flexing her long legs. Her hands – the white palms pressed against her dark skin – moved caressingly up her thighs to her stomach. The provocative mount between her legs was devoid of pubic hair, and, as her long fingers touched and stroked each of her bare curves, everyone could see the brown nipples of her high-pointed breasts growing erect.

Kneeling beside her, one of the maids produced a silver flagon of oil. Each dipped their hands into it and applied them to the girl's body as if they were polishing mahogany. In the blue light she glistened with a rich silver sheen as the maids aroused each sensitive nerve of her exquisite form with pressures and manipulations of their own invention.

Hardly had they finished when a man entered the spotlight. Instinctively, Lily remembered pictures she had seen of Greek Gods. Here was a living Greek God as handsome as she was beautiful. His body was lithe and muscular with curly black hair and facial features that could have modelled the intaglio of an ancient coin. As he moved toward the girl, Lily was certain she had never before seen such a sensual expression on a man's face. With a deft movement, he whipped away his loincloth and she sucked in her breath. His penis was in full erection – a throbbing, rigid rod that looked to be ten inches long.

Suddenly Lily felt small warm hands touch her legs. She jumped and looked down in surprise. Then she saw one of the male dwarfs who had crawled under the table. He was trying to push her legs apart.

Embarrassed, Lily glanced toward the other people at the table. The expression on Larry's face puzzled her at first. He was staring through half-closed eyes at the stage, his breath whistling between clenched teeth. Then she saw why. Just below the edge of the table cloth there was a movement. Larry's fly was open and his stiff penis was being rubbed up and down by another small hand. Beyond Larry it was difficult to tell what was happening; however, she noticed that Rex Rayn had pulled the tablecloth well over his and the blonde's lap. From the hypnotic way they were watching the stage Lily had no doubt as to what was going on. Of course, that was why they were there: the dwarfs were quietly masturbating the guests.

Half smiling, Lily spread her legs and the fervent little hand moved under her skirt.

On the stage, one of the maids was applying oil to the youth's body as he half reclined on one of the zebra hassocks. His tool had never slackened in its immensity; rather it had grown with the incessant massaging the girl was giving him. It stood out like a flagstaff, its base concealed in a bush of black hair. In the centre of the spotlight the brunette was receiving her final anointment for love: her maid was lavishing her ripe body with kisses and tongue lickings until, finally, only one place lacked her attention. And this she promptly remedied, sliding between the brunette's legs and lowering her face below the shaved mount. The girl flinched. Her whole body responded to the sensations moving through her. Her slender arms relaxed and dropped to the sides of the white leather where her fingernails raked whiter welts along the smooth soft skin. Only her lips seemed alive and they moved up and down to the purposeful lapping of the girl's tongue in her crotch.

Lily was unconsciously enjoying the same pleasures. Beneath the table a finger was stroking her swollen clitoris. She pushed her hips forward, exposing more of herself wishing it was a little mouth instead of a finger exciting her.

Beside her, Larry sucked in his breath, made a hasty grab for his napkin, and pushed himself back from the table with it clutched between his legs.

'Damn, I lost some!' He withdrew the napkin and Lily saw the thick gobs of come on it.

She pressed his arm and glanced appreciatively at his semi-stiff penis. 'If I weren't such a lady, I could be very jealous of the little vixen who caused that.'

'For her size, she's mighty damn good at it,' Larry said. 'Christ, look at that!'

Lily turned back to the stage. The youth was standing over the girl who had been massaging him, his hands buried in her hair. With a sudden movement, he jerked her head forward and impaled it on his fleshy shaft. The corners of his mouth turned up in a wicked grin as he shoved her head roughly back and forth, flexing the muscles of his buttocks and thrusting his tool deeper into her mouth. Her white cap had fallen to the floor and the tiny apron was twisted around her waist, revealing the thatch of hair between her legs. At first she appeared frightened by the viciousness of the act, and then her arms came up and twined around his legs. She was enjoying it almost as much as he.

And watching the girl forced to suck the man off was highly exciting for Lily. The unseen finger was working her clitoris into spasms of pleasure, making her frantic to go off. She drew her skirt up to her waist and spread her legs wide apart so nothing could hamper him. Glancing down, she could see his finger slipping wetly in and out. Her silk briefs were pulled aside and the juice was trickling through the fabric and saturating her seat. On an impulse, she lifted the tablecloth and looked underneath. The tense-faced little man made an effort to conceal what he was doing with his other hand between his own legs. Lily reached down and caught hold of his excited little peter and began rubbing it as he had been doing. With both hands unencumbered, the dwarf pushed them eagerly into her crotch, his tiny fingers strumming her sex juices into a lather while his undersized-root thrilled and stiffened to the touch of Lily's experienced hands.

On the stage, the brunette's body was heaving up and down. Whimpering sounds came from her throat, and her long legs stiffened with the unbearable pleasure. The youth, too, was straining; every muscle in his body stood in rippling relief as he built toward climax. The girl between his legs was beside herself. Her bottom wriggled excitedly each time the shaft buried itself in her mouth. She wanted to swallow every inch of it, to strangle herself on it. Her head moved back and forth faster and faster; one of her hands reached up and squeezed the youth's scrotum, pumping it as if she thought she could force the sperm out of the rigid spout by the pressure of her hand on his swollen bag.

Suddenly the boy rolled his eyes upward until only the whites were visible. He made a mighty effort to tense himself, then jerked his cock out of the girl's mouth and lunged for the brunette on the hassock. In one motion he swept aside the other maid and rammed his quivering penis fulllength into the brunette's pussy. She screamed as their bodies locked together, jerking in spasms... once... twice... three times....

The blue light slowly dimmed and the stage was once again in darkness.

'God, damn!' Larry exclaimed.

Lily withdrew her hand from under the table and closed her legs. The little people were quietly leaving the room the way they had come in. She felt it first, then held her fingers close to the candle and examined them. They were covered with a colourless sticky mucous. Only in this town could such a show be staged for a private party. Everything about the evening had excited her, yet left her unsatisfied. Her sex burned and itched, but she could wait; sometimes the agony of waiting was the best part. After all, they had the whole night ahead of them.

* * *

Janet Hall came home earlier than she had planned, but not too early. Lily had telephoned her at the school shortly after she had talked with Larry so there wouldn't be any slip-up with her arriving on the scene at the same moment Larry was meeting Lily. In a way, she almost regretted the arrangement. The more she thought about it, the less she was interested in the novel she had borrowed from the school library that afternoon. She yawned and lay the book aside. It was a warm evening and the sea was calm. Too nice a night to stay inside, she decided. A walk along the beach was just what she needed to get rid of her uneasiness. Maybe if she had made Larry take her to Matt Greer's party instead of Lily... but even as she toyed with the thought, the old familiar bitterness welled up inside of her.

Snatching up her sweater, she strolled out of the house and walked down to the beach. A gentle breeze played across the water and her flats made soft purring sounds on the loose sand. The sound and the sea reminded her of how she had loved coming to the beach as a little girl. Her parents had rented a cottage, the same one every year, and they went there almost every weekend. During the summers, they always stayed there for at least two weeks. Janet had been just a baby when the young girl came to work for the family. She didn't remember much about that; but she would always remember the good times she and Sheila used to have racing barefooted over the sand until they both dropped laughing and crying from sheer exhaustion. Janet was about sixteen then and Sheila was very old – at least in her thirties; a petite full-bodied girl with honey-coloured hair and beautiful white teeth that gleamed like pearls when she threw back her head and laughed.

Janet was more than fond of Sheila; she loved her. And in her strange way, Sheila had returned that love. How well Janet remembered the first time. It was three days before her seventeenth birthday on Saturday night right after her bath. Sheila had come in with a huge Turkish towel to dry her and Janet grabbed one end of the towel and was teasing her. Before she knew what happened, Sheila had caught her in her arms and was kissing her on the mouth. At first Janet was frightened, and then she liked it because it tickled; so different from the way her mother or father kissed her. And she had begged Sheila to do it again and again until the girl was blushing. But she did do it again – and she did something else Janet never forgot: she put her hand between Janet's legs and every time she kissed her she rubbed her with her finger until the tickling felt so good she almost cried out.

From that moment on, Janet made her do it whenever she could and, other times when she was in bed thinking about it and wanting it, she discovered how to make the pleasurable sensation herself. Then there was the horrible experience the following summer.

As usual, they had come to the cottage for a two-week vacation that summer. She had looked forward to it all year because it meant that Sheila and she could be together more than ever. But for some reason the woman had changed. She was different. Instead of making excuses to be with Janet as she had in the past, she seemed to try to avoid her. Then one day, by accident, Janet discovered why. Sheila was meeting a man. He was much older than she was and lived in one of the cottages year round. Once she knew, Janet spent every minute of the day planning ways to spy on them, plotting how she would get rid of him and have Sheila all to herself again.

She watched them go into the dunes together, arm in arm, the way she and Sheila had always done, laughing, whispering, happy beyond words – and Janet burned with jealousy. She hated him for putting his arm around her waist as if he owned her; she hated him for daring to kiss her, for holding her, for having secrets. She was tormented by hate. That and pity for Sheila who had been taken in by it all.

Then one afternoon she followed them to the man's cottage, a small white house that sat back from the road and was surrounded by tall bushes with pink snowball flowers. She had crept under the cottage listening, straining her ears to hear what they were saying. But all she heard was an occasional whisper and, once, Sheila calling out in a pleading voice that frightened her. She needed help.

Perspiring from fear, Janet crawled out and fought her way between the bushes and the house to a window. Using the corner of the cement foundation blocks, she climbed up and looked in a window.

Sheila was on the floor naked, rolling and moaning with her hands holding her stomach. What was wrong with her? Was she sick? Why didn't the man do something for her? She was begging for the man to come help her... then she saw him, hunched over in the far corner of the room, and he was grinning at her!

Janet was on the verge of running for help when the man stepped forward and she saw the front of his pants were open. He was holding his thing! It looked like a long stiff hose and he was rubbing it with his hand as he staggered toward Sheila. Just before he got to her he sort of sagged at his knees, and his thing began spitting white stuff out onto the floor in front of her... just jerking and squirting while he laughed horribly over poor Sheila's body...

She had run then, crying as if her heart would break, biting her lip so badly it bled all over the front of her frock.

She wanted to bleed, wanted to die.

It wasn't until years later that Janet understood what she had seen. She had never forgotten it; it marked the beginning of her hatred.

Funny how walking along the beach had made her think of it; the experience had been one of those nightmares of growing up, an explainable thing, something you could analyze and understand now. Nonetheless, it had left its scars.

Remembering it brought a strange feeling to her, a reckless, vengeful sense of unrest. She shivered under her light sweater. Oh, to torment a man as Sheila had been tormented, to drive him to his knees begging and whining for her favours... how stimulating it would be.

She quickened her step and turned toward the highway and the way home. The moon had risen higher, casting a light on the pale ribbon of concrete. She hurried along, wrapped in her thoughts.

Suddenly she was aware of an automobile behind her. She stepped off to let it pass. But instead of going by, the car slowed and drew up alongside her. Inside, the shadowy figure of a man leaned over and looked at her.

'Excuse me,' he said. 'I wonder if you could tell me where I catch the cut-off into West Hollywood?'

'Five miles further,' replied Janet briskly.

'Thanks. I've been driving all day and I'm getting kind of beat. Could I give you a lift in that direction? I need someone to talk me awake.'

Janet shook her head. 'No thank you. I just live a short way. I can do just fine by myself.'

'Hey, now, wait a minute,' the man laughed. 'This isn't a

pick-up, I'm a cop.'

Surprised, Janet took another look at the man. He was a policeman, and in uniform. She felt rather awkward. 'I – I am sorry,' she apologized. 'I thought–'

'Of course,' the officer said, amused. 'You're perfectly right to be careful, but I am going your way and if you'd care to ride, I'd certainly appreciate it.' Then he added, 'It is rather late to be walking, you know.'

'Well, thank you,' said Janet, laughing at herself. She opened the door and got in. As they started off, she glanced out of the corner of her eye and caught him with a wide grin on his face.

'I'm Dick Salburg,' he said by way of introduction.

'Do you make a habit of running down women on the highway, Mr. Salburg?'

'Only the pretty ones,' he smiled. He was a big man, square-shouldered and thick-chested, like Janet imagined all policemen were. In the light from the dashboard she could see he was towheaded with wide-spaced eyes. There was something about him... perhaps the way he held his head or maybe it was his mouth, but he reminded her of someone. While they made small talk she kept trying to remember.

'I stay with my brother up in Burbank. He has a small gas station, nothing much, just big enough to make him a few bucks during the winter so he can take off and go fishing the rest of the year. He's nuts for fishing, built himself a boat, the kind you can sleep on. He lives on it too. What a life... here, care for a cigarette?' He offered her the pack.

And then Janet knew what it was about him. It was his hands. They were tremendous, with thick blond hair along the backs of the fingers. He had the same hands, the same mouth and face, as the man who had been with Sheila!

Quietly, she accepted the cigarette and watched with fascination as he pulled the lighter from the dash and held the glowing tip toward her. As she drew the smoke into her lungs, her heart was beating hard. 'You... ah... you haven't ever lived around here before, have you?'

'Me? Are you kidding? I'm strictly a north Californian. I couldn't begin to stomach the Hollywood crowd down here.'

'Then you're not here on vacation?'

'Heck no, it's all in the line of duty,' he grinned, 'and only temporary at that.'

Janet felt light-headed all of a sudden. The man wasn't a stranger; she had carried his image with her for too many years. It was foolish of her to think he might be the same one, but he was the same type – the big, hairy, masculine kind that a woman like Sheila would have loved. And before she had taken three drags on her cigarette, a wildly exciting plan was already fitting itself into the confused pattern of her mind. 'The red bungalow on the left is where I get out,' she said.

'Gosh, so soon?'

'I told you it was hardly worth the trouble.'

The car came to a stop and he reached over and opened the door for her.

'Are you going the rest of the way into town tonight?' she asked.

'If I don't fall asleep and pile up somewhere along the way.'

'Do you... ah... do you think think a cup of coffee would help?'

'Would I? Lady, just try me.'

'All right, come on.'

At the door, she accidentally dropped her purse and made sure he brushed against her as he stooped to pick it up.

Inside, she flipped on the light and turned to him with flashing eyes. Before he knew what had happened, she'd wound her arms around his neck and was kissing him. 'I want you awfully bad,' she hissed between clenched teeth.

'God, damn, baby!'

'Don't talk... just kiss me... just a little.' She leaned against him, pressing her thigh into his groin.

He responded as she'd expected. His arms circled her like bands of steel, his hands pawing at her sweater.

'No, wait...' She pushed him from her.

'What?'

She held him at arm's length, studying the growing protrusion in the front of his pants. Then in a voice that wasn't her own she whispered, 'I like men that are big...'

He made a grab for her and she let his hands rush clumsily over her body, let him enjoy it for five seconds before she broke away.

'Let's get undressed first... hurry, in the bedroom...' She ran through the living-room, dropping her sweater, kicking off her shoes.

He lunged for her, and she pushed him down on the bed. 'Your clothes... I want to take off your clothes.' She tore at the buttons of his shirt, pushed his arms behind his back and was dragging it off. Then she saw what she knew he would have with him – a pair of handcuffs. Deftly she lifted them, pushed his arms further back and closed the metal jaws with a click. He was handcuffed to the bed post.

'What the goddamn hell is this?' He jerked his arms roughly.

Without a word, Janet methodically undressed him. When she'd finished, she stood up and examined her handiwork. 'Why Mr. Salburg,' she said mockingly. 'What's wrong? Don't you want to make love to me?' She burst out laughing at the sight of his limp penis dangling between his hairy thighs.

His face was the colour of a squashed tomato. 'You bitch... you damn crazy bitch. Turn me loose!'

'Not yet, sweetheart, I've got something very special for you. I wouldn't want you to run off and miss it.' Very deliberately, she bent down and grasped her ankles, then, very slowly, she straightened up, running her hands the full length of her legs to the top of her nylons.

Dick Salburg stopped his struggling and stared.

Janet was glassy-eyed, her breathing laboured. Her fingers flew over her buttons, touched the zipper, then, trembling slightly, she slithered out of her dress.

She stood in front of him like a statue, watching intently. His eyes grew wide as they moved over her body. She pivoted very slowly so he could see all of her, and then her fingers began fluttering like the wings of a bird caught in a snare as they wove a design of caresses over her shoulders, across her breasts and down to her hips, where she toyed with the black lace edging of her garter belt. She arched her whole body towards him, offering him her charms, and while standing there, she gently massaged the silky mount that swelled between her thighs.

Salburg twisted on the bed. His eyes were bloodshot. 'God almighty!' he gasped hoarsely.

Janet trembled with excitement. The smile on her face

was set like a mask. She couldn't force her eyes from his penis. It had hardened into an upright phallus, the foreskin drawn back nakedly from the heart-shaped head. And it was throbbing...

She arched herself even more, bringing her body inches from his face. With painful deliberation, she unhooked her garter belt and let it drop to the floor. Seconds later, her brassiere lay beside it. She was weaving now, her head thrown back, her slender hands manipulating ever so lightly the firm flesh of her breasts. Her fingers made ovals around the rosy, erect nipples, and then glided down her flanks to massage the warm rotund cheeks of her buttocks.

Salburg groaned, clenched his fists, and fought against the encircling bands of steel until scorching pain shot up his forearms.

Janet made a V of her hands and pressed them to her crotch, drawing the silk tight over her mount. A sigh of repressed pleasure rushed from her throat; her pink tongue darted out to moisten her lips. Extending the middle finger of her left hand, she eased it gently between her legs, pushing it all the way, the silk tightening with it. When she withdrew it, the finger was glistening wet. The musky odour of her spunk swirled around her like perfume. She held her hand out to him. 'Lick it,' she commanded. He did, and a long slender drop of translucent fluid dripped from the cone of his penis into the curly blond hairs of his crotch.

Hooking her thumbs into the thin silk of her panties, Janet slowly peeled them down her thighs until her pubic mount thrust out in a tangled jungle of moist hair. She left them there, spread her legs even further and gently caressed the curve of her flawless belly.

Salburg was writing on the bed, mouthing words incoherently. He begged her to release him, swearing he would do anything she wanted if only he could have his hands free.

But Janet shook her head. 'I know what you would do,' she panted. 'You'd take it in your hand and masturbate... like that...' She formed a cylinder with her fingers and made the lewd motions in the air.

'Damn it all, you're driving me crazy! I'd like to break your neck!'

'But you love it, don't you?' She smiled, turning sideways so he saw the profile of her lush round behind protruding over the tight silk panties, the swath of blond fur jutting out in front. With one hand on her behind, her legs bent, she pushed her index finger between her lips of her cunt and moved it around and around.

He tried to shut his eyes but the spectacle was too much for him; he sat hypnotized by the girl's every movement.

Her body took on a rich pink glow. It grew shiny with oils released from her pores. The curve of her arm flexed rhythmically; the muscles of her thighs and buttocks joined in the tempo set by the urging, demanding caresses she lavished on her greedy sex. Yet not once did she take her eyes from his quivering penis. She watched it for each new sign of excitement, thrilling to the stimulation as much as he was. And the wonderful difference was that she could satisfy hers while he suffered with his.

Cascades of pleasure swept her each time she saw him try to twist on his side so he could rub his turgid member against something, anything, for relief. But she had gotten him in such a position he could only turn part of the way, not enough to do him any good. There was nothing with which to sate the burning necessities of his penis. Nothing.

Janet squealed in ecstasy. Her finger moved so rapidly it was a blur, her buttocks rotated faster... faster... she could feel herself coming... working up to it... climbing toward the peak with wave after wave of increasing pleasure.

At the last minute, she shoved her hips toward him, gave a final stroke, then pulled apart the lips of her vagina. The abnormally developed clitoris stiffened and jerked before his eyes and Janet rocked with the intensity of the orgasm.

Hardly had the first spasms subsided when she saw Salburg convulse, and a jet of white sperm shot out of his trembling penis. He gagged in agonizing pleasure as it squirted thick and fast, lathering his stomach and thighs.

She collapsed on the bed beside him and stared numbly at his drooling staff.

'God!' he gasped. 'That never happened before in my life!'

Janet was too content to care. He had gone off and she had wanted to torture him up to that point, without his final enjoyment. But what difference did it make? She had made him suffer, so she had succeeded. She squeezed her thighs together deliciously. The little rosebud head of her clitoris still protruded from between the coral red lips. She reached down and touched it with the tip of her finger, pushing the gland firmly against her pelvic bone. It was slippery and hot. Almost reluctantly, she released it and pushed her panties the rest of the way down her legs. They were sopping wet. She took them off and without a word, pressed them against his warm scrotum. His flaccid penis began to stiffen.

'That's much better,' she said.

'Better, like hell! You've had your kicks, now how about turning me loose?'

'Funny man. So you can rape me?'

'No. Honest. You can't just leave me here.'

Janet returned her hand to her clitoris, casually rubbing it as she spoke. 'Why can't I?' she asked. 'I could feed you and fan you, and then we could do this every day. Now wouldn't that be nice?'

'Jesus, woman, what you need is a good fuck, then you wouldn't be interested in playing games.'

The corners of Janet's eyes crinkled. 'Didn't you enjoy yourself?'

'Enjoy myself! I didn't get a thing out of it, at least not as much as you did.'

'I hardly expected you would,' she said. 'Too bad you couldn't control yourself.'

'For crying out loud, what do you expect?'

Janet looked away disdainfully. 'I guess that's about all I could expect from a man. It's all they think about, you know.'

'Well, I'd like to know what the hell you're thinking about,' he said, watching her push aside the hairs of her vagina and fully expose her clitoris.

'Do you think I'm beautiful?' she asked him simply.

He wanted to say he thought she was about as beautiful as a rattlesnake in heat, but instead he concentrated his gaze on the pulsating organ she was displaying for him and said, 'I've never seen anything to beat that, baby.' And he meant it. 'Come on, now. Turn me loose. I'll make you feel things you never dreamed of.'

Janet raised an eyebrow and studied him closely. She had to admit he wasn't really bad looking. Still, she hated him for his masculinity – the possessive male, only one step above an animal. 'I've never been touched by a man,' she said defiantly, 'and I don't intend to be.'

'But what's wrong with that?' he frowned. 'A guy can give a girl a hell of a lot of happiness. Come on, let me show you.'

She would have to let him go sometime, the problem was how to do it without getting hurt. 'If I turned you loose, what would you do?'

'Make love to you like you really want,' he said truthfully.

She looked at him sharply. 'But I don't!' she insisted. 'If you ever tried that, I'd scream rape from here to high heaven!'

'Okay, okay, don't get excited.'

In a calmer voice she said, 'If you were to promise me, I might reconsider...' She glanced at his penis. It was only semi-hard. She didn't want him thinking about it now.

'All right,' he muttered, shifting his body on the bed. 'You got me cornered. I won't try to rape you.'

'Is that a promise?'

'It's a promise. The key's in my left pants pocket.'

She found it, stepped around behind him and unlocked the handcuffs.

With a cry, he bounded off the bed and grabbed her. She tried to scream, but he smothered it with his mouth. She felt his sticky cock rising hotly against her stomach.

She wrenched her head free. 'Damn you! Damn you!'

He bit her shoulder, and his hand flew over her body, touching and caressing the sensitive places he now knew so well because she had showed him. He cupped one of her breasts and lowered his head to the nipple; tickling it with the tip of his tongue and feeling it grow erect.

Janet struggled in his arms, trying vainly to force him away. But he was too powerful for her. Beating on him was like beating on a wall. His whole body imprisoned her. He was slipping lower, trying to force her to the floor. No! If she could stay on her feet... down he went, until his powerful hands closed over the lobes of her buttocks, holding her in a vice. She wriggled frantically. He tightened his hold so she couldn't move. He was on his knees. Her rigid clitoris stuck out in front of his face. Without hesitating, he sucked it into his mouth.

She pounded against his shoulders with clenched fists... pounded until she was weak, then suddenly she realized she was cradling his head tenderly and that her fingers were stroking the nape of his neck. All her strength was gone and in its place came the acute pangs of pleasure.

Salburg tongued her clitoris furiously. He licked underneath and around the twitching gland, tightened his lips, and let just the shaft slide in and out, forcing the rapid motion by jerking her hips back and forth faster and faster until she couldn't stand it any longer. Pushing his head hard against her creaming vagina, she came.

The instant he felt the spontaneous suction against his mouth, the violent shudder that coursed through her limbs, he dropped his hand to his inflamed cock. One pump was all he had to give it, and his seed squirted hotly against the calf of her leg.

Afterwards, when they had rested, he tried to apologize, but she was too spent to care. She put on her lounging robe and took him to the door.

'Listen,' he said, just before leaving, 'I want to help you. I like you a hell of a lot. Between the two of us we could get your trouble straightened out.'

She looked at him with a mixture of longing and uncertainty in her eyes. If only she could believe him, trust him. The experience hadn't been near as horrible as she had thought. She had to admit, there had been a difference – a man had made the difference. Perhaps, after all, there was hope...

'Don't think about it now,' he said, smiling at her. 'You and I'll be seeing each other again, and that's a promise I intend to keep,' he added, leaning down and kissing her lightly on the forehead as he went out the door.

* * *

The show was over. People got up and left in pairs or groups. 'Let's see how things are going downstairs,' Lily suggested.

'Yeah, they should be going full blast by now. Sure you don't want to stop at the room first?'

She hugged his arm. 'Later, Larry.'

There was a new kind of excitement in the corridor. People were fumbling with their room keys, opening doors and slamming them. A skinny man in pink drawers burst out of one room and ran squealing into another. Tight on his heels was a fat man wearing glasses. The front of his enormous purple silk bathrobe flapped open, and Lily saw his pudgy hand clutching his stubby penis as he waddled past.

'Hermann, doll, open the door, you foolish boy!' He beat on it with his free hand. 'Naughty, naughty... Hermann? Doll?'

Larry shook his head sadly. 'Matt sure knows some queer people,' he said.

If there was confusion upstairs, what was happening downstairs was pure bedlam. People weren't sitting at tables any longer; they had been removed and gigantic coloured pillows were substituted. Everyone was rolling around the thick carpeted floors, a tangle of humanity that had finally managed to dissolve all existing inhibitions. The only ones still standing were a few of the girls serving champagne in the nude. They stumbled and staggered through the sea of writhing bodies, holding the bottles aloft until hands reached up, hauled them – bottles and all – into the melee.

Surprisingly enough, most people still had their clothes on, a problem quickly being remedied. One couple was wrapped in each other's arms deep in a bright red pillow. The man's hand was buried between the woman's thighs and she was twisting like a snake while he kissed her. Around them sat a circle of middle-aged couples watching with bright-eyed curiosity. In another group a young girl was crying and clutching part of a shredded dress to her nude shoulders while three women pulled on the material until it gave with a resounding rip, leaving her with nothing but the shreds. With a cry, all three fell on her like wolves, pinching, kissing, caressing, burying her under them.

Matt Greer crawled out of the thickest part of the crowd that had been surrounding a half-nude redhead. He was laughing uproariously. His coat was gone, his shirt was ripped and the front of his pants were soaking wet. 'Here, you two! Catch!' He hurled a bottle of champagne across the room. Larry caught it just as the dark-haired hat-check girl, minus her tights, wrapped her arms around Matt's neck and hauled him to the floor like a sack of oats.

From somewhere at the far end of the room, a microphone

sputtered and squawked, a loudspeaker droned, 'Movies, everyone, movies!'

Larry tucked the bottle under his arm. 'Come on,' he said, taking a firm grip on Lily and wading through the crowded bodies.

The chaos quieted for a moment, and the occupants shuffled to the pillows to arrange themselves as the room darkened and a giant screen illuminated on the ceiling.

They found an empty pillow and slumped down while Larry worked the cork out of the bottle with a bang.

'Chug-lug, chug-a-lug,' someone chanted in the darkness.

Lily tilted the champagne bottle to her lips and quaffed a good portion of the cool, bubbly liquid before passing it to Larry.

The screen darkened and the title appeared: A FARMER GIRL'S DELIGHT, Starring Tom and Annette.

Sporadic applause rippled through the audience. Someone dropped a bottle and it smashed.

Overhead, a handsome man in overalls was shown looking toward a ramshackle farmhouse. The camera pulled back to reveal him urinating in the bushes. There was a quick close-up of his penis before the scene changed and he was walking toward the farm.

Lolling on the front porch on an old sofa was a tousle-haired girl with a large, pouting mouth. Her ragged skirts were casually drawn up to her thighs.

As the man paused at the gate, their conversation appeared on the screen:

'Hello, pretty, your pa home?'

'Nope, they took the wagon to town. Why stranger?'

Tom's hand was doing something in his pant's pocket while his lecherous eyes roamed over the girl's body.

'Just wondered,' he said. 'You're a cute one to be left home all alone.'

Annette smiled and inched her skirt higher.

Tom walked onto the porch, his hand still busy in his pocket.

'How about you givin' me a little kiss, honey?'

She wrinkled her nose. 'I ain't never been kissed, don't reckon I'd like it anyway.'

(Muffled laughter from the audience.)

'Wouldn't do no harm to see,' said Tom. He made a grab for her and when she ducked, he managed to rip open the top of her dress.

'Now see what you done,' she said, taking her time covering her breasts.

'Here, let me fix that,' Tom said, reaching for her. In the next scene, they were kissing and his hand was feeling under her dress between her thrashing legs. The camera moved in close enough to let everyone know she was naked underneath.

'Did you like it?' he asked.

'Couldn't rightly tell, stranger. Maybe if you were to try it again...'

He kissed her again, and this time she spread her legs.

'What say you and me do a little fucking?' said Tom.

Annette's skirt was around her hips and his finger was moving in and out of her pussy. The camera panned to the front of Tom's overalls where his thick penis was protruding from his open fly.

In the darkness, Larry reached over and touched Lily, trailing his fingers over her tight skirt, feeling for the crisp mound with the slippery silk stretching over its hump. She covered his hand with hers and pressed it against her.

Tom grinned as he shucked off Annette's ragged dress and lay down on the sofa beside her.

'You'd better be careful, stranger. I'm a virgin.'

(An outburst of laughter from the audience.)

He fondled her for a moment, and then slipped his penis between her legs. She expertly wrapped them around his back and they pumped away while the camera moved around to catch it from all angles. They made love furiously, thrashing on the old sofa until it threatened to collapse from their violence.

The camera moved to a side view, capturing glimpses of Tom's hairy tool sliding in and out of Annette's dark muff. In a moment, he withdrew, and those watching close caught a fleeting view of one or two feeble spurts from his pecker as the scene jerked and blacked out.

'Hell of a time to run out of film!' someone shouted, followed by general laughter.

In the next sequence, Annette and Tom were changing positions. She climbed on top of him and lowered herself onto his rigid prong. From behind, the camera pulled in so close the whole screen was filled by an enlarged view of her full buttocks and hairy cunt gaping and sliding juicily up and down Tom's fleshy shaft...

Lily tightened her legs on Larry's hands as his fingers caressed her hot sex. She had pushed up her skirt and slipped off her panties. Doing that in a crowded room with so many people around gave her a delicious sense of naughtiness. But she was too aroused to care if anyone saw her or not. The possibility that someone might, however, excited her all the more. She turned her head and looked into the darkness.

On a nearby pillow, she could make out the shadowy figure

of a man on his hands and knees, and then realized he was on top of a woman.

There were sounds she had not been aware of before of people breathing, sighing, gasping; the rustle of clothes; the rhythmic contact of bodies; a girl saying, 'Fuck me, fuck me,' over and over like a broken record; a man's triumphant cry, 'I'm coming! I'm coming!'

Lily felt for Larry's penis. The bulge was iron-hard. She unzipped his pants and shoved her hand through the opening, fumbling to push aside his shirttails while he anxiously shoved his hips toward her.

It was out of his shorts and the inside of his trousers were clammy from the juices he had already secreted. Her fingers closed around the hot column, forcing him to moan as she dragged it out of his fly.

'Wait,' he whispered, and with his free hand he unbuckled his belt and pushed his pants down.

His cock seemed to expand in her hand and she cuddled the warm, throbbing member as if she was afraid it would escape her. Her fingers crawled down the length until the head was cupped and poking against the inside of her palm. Exerting any pressure on the sensitive knob made him groan and swivel his loins in rapture. She explored it minutely, searching for new ways to give him pleasure.

On the screen, Tom pulled his limp penis out of Annette and the camera focused on the last trickle of sperm as it oozed from the shrinking gland and dripped to his overalls like a remorseful tear.

A man sighed, 'Jesus, I came right with him!'

'I know,' a woman's voice replied. 'Be sweet, honey,' she paused, 'finish me with your...' The last word was whispered so low it was inaudible.

Then from across the room, the man who had shouted before tried to get another rise out of the audience. 'How'd he get that hard-on so quick?'

There had been no pause in the film, but now Tom and Annette were dragging the old sofa into the front yard and his prick was again in a state of miraculous erection. He stripped off his overalls, lay down on the couch and began jacking-off. Eagerly, Annette slipped between his legs until her face was directly over his penis, then the camera shot low and recorded her avid expression of pleasure as she watched.

While lying on their sides, Larry drew Lily's leg across him and put his between, fitting his penis into her vagina. She had never made love that way before, but as the new sensations assailed her, she pushed her hips forward to meet each thrust, digging her heel into the small of his back to urge him on. The lips of her pussy stretched like a rubber band around his organ, compressing her clitoris until the entire length was rubbing against his moist barrel with intense feeling. They had welded their bodies into such a perfect fit that the slightest movement sent excruciating pangs of pleasure through each of them. Their hands roamed freely over the other's body while following each erotic scene on the screen overhead.

Annette was clutching Tom as he quivered with a paroxysm of delight. Unable to stand it any longer, she lowered her head to take the gland in her mouth, but he pushed her away. The instant he came, the camera faithfully drew close to catch the quick flashes of his semen from his convulsing organ. And before he could stop her, Annette was greedily licking it off his stomach.

Lily groaned as her orgasm opened inside of her like an umbrella, radiating pleasure upward through her loins, downward through her legs. The suction-tight clasp of her vagina alternately squeezed and released Larry's organ as it spewed its load into the hot furnace of her sex.

He slipped out of her with a prolonged sigh of satisfaction. Through half-lidded eyes he tried to concentrate on the screen's figures, but their movements registered slowly. Annette was taking a douche while the camera played on her cunt. Tom's hand entered the frame, grasped the slim rubber nozzle and began fucking her with it.

She was smiling when she said, 'I guess this is better than nothing,' and the last thing Larry remembered was a picture of Tom's shrunken prick dangling limp but happy between his legs.

The screen flashed THE END, blacked out momentarily, and then glared white. A series of upside down numbers followed, and a new title appeared: A GIRL'S BEST FRIEND.

The spectators greeted it with a round of applause. There were hurried calls for more champagne, and a few people made quick exits to relieve their kidneys.

Lily sat up and glanced at Larry. His eyes were shut and he was snoring soundly. Without disturbing him she got up and made her way between the people and pillows until she reached the door. She was dizzy from the champagne and the thing she wanted most right then was fresh air.

She walked through the empty lobby and out the front door to the patio. Looking over the Pacific she took a deep breath and immediately felt better.

'Lovely night, isn't it?'

Startled, Lily turned. She hadn't noticed the man leaning

against the railing at the end of the patio. He was wearing evening clothes and straightened up as she looked at him.

'It is lovely,' she said.

He walked toward her. 'Would you care for a cigarette?' he asked, drawing a silver case out of his pocket and offering it to her.

'Yes, thank you.'

'I didn't see you inside. Have you been here long?'

'Since before the movies.'

'What did you think of them?'

She shrugged and smiled. 'Interesting. I imagine that type of thing will always have a big box-office appeal.'

He chuckled and lit her cigarette. 'Anything the public bans has box-office appeal. Are you in films, Miss…?'

'Caldron. I've done small parts.'

He paused for a moment, and then said, 'I guess most people at Matt's parties are.'

'And you?'

'My name's Kurt Rothman.'

'Oh!' Lily exclaimed. 'I'm sorry, I didn't recognize you, Mr. Rothman… it's so dark out here…'

'Directors don't always have the opportunity to meet people as people, if you know what I mean.'

'I believe I do.'

'And what kind of girl are you?'

'Just people,' she smiled.

'That's what I like to hear.' He looked at her more closely. 'Would you care to take a stroll around the grounds with me? I could use a little exercise.'

'Just around the grounds?'

'That's all,' he said.

'I don't know. After all, I am with someone.'

'Are you afraid something will happen?'

'What could happen?' she asked.

'Nothing that already hasn't,' he said.

'Are you certain of that?'

'Of course not,' he said. 'It doesn't pay to be certain of anything.'

'Are you married, Mr. Rothman?'

'At the present, no.' He grinned. 'Would it make a difference?'

'Yes, I think so.'

'Then you have nothing to fear. Shall we go?'

She nodded. They started along the gravel path that led away from the club and through a terraced garden. The fragrance of the flowers hung on the night air like heavy perfume.

'Have you been to Mr. Greer's parties before?' she asked.

'Once or twice,' he said. 'They're always the same.'

'You sound as if they bore you.'

'Not necessarily. They amuse me, despite being a bit mild.'

'Mild?'

'Perhaps the word is childish. I mean the films and everything. Most of the people here need that stimulant before they can enjoy sex. It's really a shame.'

'Why do you say that?'

'Well, isn't it? Think about it a bit. When people get so jaded that they have to watch other people make love or see films on the subject before they're aroused enough to indulge themselves, isn't it too bad? My first wife was like that. It got so bad she started wanting me to bring home girls from the studio and make love to them while she watched.'

'And did you?'

'Once or twice, but I tired of it. Since she had to have it that way there was nothing to do but to get a divorce. Things are better now.'

'If you don't need those things, Mr. Rothman, why do you come to these affairs?'

He thought over her question carefully before answering. 'Perhaps,' he said, 'I come to these horrid parties just hoping to run into someone like you, someone who may feel much as I do about things. You know I had a hard-on for you the minute I saw you on the patio.'

'You shouldn't talk like that,' she said.

'Why not? It's the truth. I think you know I had a hard-on.'

'My, you are easily aroused, aren't you?'

'Only when I meet someone like you,' he said.

She laughed. 'Now that's very original.'

'I'm afraid it's not, but frankly, it's the only way I could think of putting it.'

For a few moments neither spoke as they walked.

'What are you thinking about?' he asked.

'Oh, nothing, really.'

'Anything to do with what I said?'

'Partly.'

'Does it excite you? I mean just thinking about it?'

'Yes, I guess it does.'

'It does me too,' he said. 'I bet you're the type of girl who likes it hot and fast.'

'I'm afraid you're wrong, Mr. Rothman.'

'Am I?' he said. 'You somehow strike me as a girl who would like a man to do everything, everything under the sun. Then later I believe you'd like it fast.'

She didn't answer him, only smiled to herself. 'I was thinking of a girlfriend of mine. She's a virgin and she'll never see twenty again.'

Kurt Rothman stopped in his tracks. 'Is that the truth? She's that old and still a virgin?'

'Cross my heart,' laughed Lily.

'That's unbelievable. It really is. She must be sick or something.'

'She's attractive, healthy, everything a man would want. She simply dislikes sex, that's all.'

He shook his head. 'One of the rarities of the twentieth century,' he said.

On the grounds behind the club, the garden opened onto a large oval swimming pool. As they passed under some low palm fronds, he turned and gently put his hands on her shoulders.

'No, please,' she said. 'I'm terribly tired.'

He drew her close to him. 'You're not helping my hard-on, you know. I've already creamed a little in my pants just talking with you.'

She struggled in his arms, making a half-hearted attempt to free herself. 'I wish you wouldn't say such things. I've only just met you.'

'You'll never know what it's like.' He was breathing hard against her cheek. 'You don't realize what a man feels when he's tempted by a beautiful woman; when he gets a powerful erection and it starts to get juicy. It's a terribly unsatisfied feeling.'

'But there are girls in the club...'

'Not them,' he said, sharply. 'They're all bitches. All I have to do is mention my name and they flop on the ground with their skirts over their heads. It's bad enough fighting that sort of thing at the studio; even those that work for me. They all want something more from me, more money, a better part, marriage, more alimony. You name it, they want it. And the way they think they can get it is with their cunt. That's why I never have anything to do with them. I'm sick of them.'

'How can you be certain I'm not after the same things?' she said.

'I'm not,' he said, 'but the fact that you haven't made a play of any kind makes me hope that you're different. You talk different, you appeal to me differently. I need what you can give me, and I need it badly.' He pushed his hips up against her and she felt his tremendous organ pressing against her hips.

'I am beat,' she said, making her voice sound as sincere as possible. 'You'd be terribly disappointed with me tonight.'

'I'm only human,' he said. 'I guess that's my whole trouble. The only way I get complete satisfaction is…' He stopped talking.

'Yes?'

'Oh, don't pay attention to me. Sometimes I talk too much.'

'I'm always a good listener,' she said.

For a moment he said nothing. His erection moved and she felt herself tending to push toward him.

'Well… it's just that I need sex. More of it I believe than the average man. Since I've never got anything from doing it with the women I'm forced to associate with, I've had to find another way out. It's an organization. One that's extremely secret. The members are people like me; we enjoy sex for sex's sake. Since no one ever knows the identity of a fellow member, you can understand how perfect an arrangement it is. Until I met you this evening, I've never had any other temptations, but in the few minutes I've known you, I can't shake the feeling that you and I have much in common.'

'Perhaps we have,' Lily said. 'This organization, is it something like what happens during Matt's parties?'

'This is mild compared to that. Say, you aren't interested are you?'

'No, I–'

'Have you ever heard of a Black Mass?'

She thought for a moment. 'Wasn't there something in the newspapers about a year ago?'

'That's right,' he said. 'A group was arrested in New York. Caused quite a lot of publicity for us.'

'Then that's the organization?'

'Yes,' he said. His voice was eager when he asked her the next question. 'Could you possibly see yourself attending a meeting with me a Black Mass where anything and everything is done, where sex is the God and you its disciple, could you?'

'I… I don't know.'

'Is it because you're afraid of doing those things? If it is, forget your fears. You have no idea how wonderful it is! Imagine, anything, anything your heart desires, you can do. It's a debauch, an orgy that goes back to the Dark Ages when the Church was ridiculed. Only the form is religious now. It's simply become a worship of sex. Everyone wears hoods; your presence would only be known to me. God, just the thought of it…' He began rubbing himself against her again.

'Please,' she said, 'we really must get back…'

'Tell me you'll go and I won't ask another thing of you tonight.'

'I don't know,' she said. 'This has all been so sudden. I'd like to think it over.'

'Let me call you next week.'

'Well... all right.'

'But please think about it between now and then,' he said. 'Let your imagination run wild. Even then, you won't be scratching the surface.'

She promised she would think about it and give him her answer when he telephoned.

'One other thing,' he said as they started back toward the patio. 'In each Mass, there is always a virgin deflowered, a girl who in one night learns more about sex than most people in a lifetime...'

Oh, my gosh, Lily thought, Janet!

Darling

He drove the car rapidly down the street, looking occasionally at the girl's figure, huddled against the door. Mostly he watched the empty road and felt the car glide over the pavement. He turned down Seventh Avenue, and she still hadn't spoken. At 10th Street, he stopped the car and turned toward her. She leaned her elbow against the door handle and was already half on the sidewalk, calling, 'Thank you' over her shoulder when he reached over and pulled her back into her seat.

'What's the hurry? What's your hurry?'

'I'm tired, Paul,' she explained.

'My God,' he answered. 'You're fine all night. I really think you're relaxing and having a good time, but you always make the goodnight the briefest, coldest moment of the day.'

'I'm sorry,' she said again humbly. 'You know me.'

'I don't know you, Gloria. Does anyone know you? Do you ever sit still long enough to be known?'

She was getting impatient, and she said, 'For crying out loud, how often can you go over the same theme? No, I don't sit still. No, I don't like dragged-out good nights. No, I don't care if I never see you again. Yes, I'm tired.'

'Look, honey,' he interrupted her, 'I'm not going to rape you.'

She smiled cruelly at the suggestion. 'No one's going to rape me. It takes a very cooperative woman to get raped. A man might get me to the floor, but he wouldn't get further.'

Paul said, 'Why speculate? Why don't you let me love you the way I want to? I swear to you Gloria, the way I feel about you, it would be wonderful for both of us. I'd really make you want it. I'd make you want it till you cried for it.' And he put his open mouth on her ear. 'It's not fair for a woman as beautiful and sensuous as you to put men off. You were obviously put on earth to satisfy, not torment us.'

Feeling his tongue nuzzling wet inside her ear, she shuddered with excitement and horror. 'Get away from me,' she said with anger, and he couldn't hear the terror in her voice. 'When I'm willing and ready to give myself to a man, I will. I don't need you licking my face like a stupid dog to convince me.' His fury relieved the bitterness inside her.

The man was livid at her gross refusal. 'You whore,' he whispered to her. 'You whore with a virgin's cunt. What are you waiting for? When are you going to give your rare gift away?'

'It's not that,' she told him tiredly. Her voice was calm. 'You know it's not that. It's just that I'm not interested.'

'Not interested?' he shouted. 'What the hell are you talking about? You sound as if you're returning a library book.'

'I don't want it!' she screamed. 'I hate the whole phoney slobbering business.'

'You're a teasing bitch,' he spat at her. 'And you'll never

know what it means to feel like a woman.'

'What does it mean,' she mocked, 'to feel like a woman? What's so different and special about being a woman?'

'You fool!' Paul roared. 'You'll never know what it means to spread your knees and say to a man, "fill me with your prick because I'm dying from emptiness".'

'Don't,' she begged. 'Don't talk to me like that. Don't dare.'

'You'll never know it from me,' he continued as if he hadn't heard. 'And no man is going to wait as long as I did. Give it up, baby. Put on pants and wipe the mascara off your eyes and make it with the girls. Mona's Bar is full of dikes just waiting for you. They've seen the dead look in your eyes, and they know it'll take a woman's hand to make you feel like a woman. You disgust me. You're worse than a whore.'

She listened with rapt pain, thinking, he's going to hit me when he's finished, and she waited with an ecstasy she did not understand. Her heart felt as though a strong hand were clutching and numbing it. 'Why don't you hit me?' she breathlessly demanded.

Paul looked down at her with a contempt that was as cold as his wanting of her had been hot. 'I wouldn't touch you baby,' he said. 'I'll just let you rot untouched. The ladies like to get a virgin. When they see the blood on their hands, they know they've got them forever.' He practically pushed her out of the car without so much as a glance back.

She stood motionless until she heard the drone of the engine fade away around the corner of 6th Avenue. The street lay dark ahead of her.

Oh, God, oh God, she thought, I hate men. I hate their hungry faces and their moving hands. I hate them when they press against me and I feel their pants bulging. I'll never let one love me. Imagine being naked on a bed, and having them crawl all over you and pull your legs apart. When you lay flat and broken like a defeated enemy, and they stick their stiff prick in you, that's the only part of them that's got feeling left. They're like crazy animals till they spurt their vicious fluid in you. And then you're supposed to kiss their feet and pretend that you enjoyed it. They'll never have me. Nor will a woman. I don't want some woman's tongue and long-nailed fingers to stroke me into an excitement that interferes with my thinking and breathing. Yes, I'll do it myself. And I'll go to my grave never having been a fool for some sexual machine.

Numbly, Gloria pushed her shoulders against her door. It opened for her, and she closed out the silent street behind her and placed her hand on the dimly lit banister.

At first she didn't feel the hand that covered hers. Her heart was beating so loud in her chest from the distasteful scene with Paul, and her thoughts were cutting out the world around her. But as she moved up the first step, she felt the iron-like hold, paralyzing her. She looked down from her height into cruel eyes. The blue of the man's eyes was so light that his face looked like a portrait painted by a madman who had left the eyes where the soul should be the dead white of the canvas. A shock of black hair covered his head. His mouth smiled grimly at her mute terror.

'Come down off the step, lady,' he whispered. 'We're going to have a little party.'

She opened her mouth to scream, realizing that no sound could come out of her. And then she felt his knife edging into the small of her back pressing against her with the frigid indifference of steel.

'I gotta fuck some bitch, and you're the lucky cunt.' He

laughed soundlessly. 'It's an honour baby, 'cause I got a cock as big as the Eiffel Tower.'

Listening to him, she regained her senses. I'll talk him out of it, she thought. 'Look, mister,' she implored, 'I'll give you all the money I have. I'm a virgin… I'm a virgin and I'm getting married next week and you'll ruin my life if you… if you… take me. Because then my fiancé will never marry me. You see, he wants a… a pure girl.'

The man looked at her with his vacant eyes. 'I like virgins,' he whispered. 'C'mon virgin, we'll bleed all over this fancy hall.' Effortlessly, he pushed her down to the floor in the little black alcove behind the stairway. She found her voice to scream, and he slapped her face until her ears were deafened with a ringing inside her head that cut off the whole world. 'Unbutton my pants, you whore,' he commanded.

'No,' she gasped, 'no, I can't touch you.'

He grabbed her hand and placed it solidly across the mound in his pants.

'Unbutton them, you bitch. My prick wants to be free to dig inside of you.'

She felt his knife against her ribs. With trembling hands she unbuckled his belt.

'That's it! That's it! Do a good job, virgin.'

She moved her fingers to the first button, and he shoved her hand deep inside his pants so she could feel his hot, pulsating flesh.

'Faster, faster, you cunt,' he commanded.

Slowly and miserably, she undid the last button. He wore no underpants.

'Pull my fly open… pull it open!'

She did as she was told. His prick was folded primly

between his thighs, covering his balls.

'Now pull it out. Gently, gently... with all the love in your fucking whore's heart,' and again he laughed madly and excitedly. His cock leapt out straight beneath her fingers. It was veined and white, almost purple at the tip. It was huge and massive, bigger than anything she thought a man could fold between his legs. 'Kiss it,' he said. His voice trembled. 'Open your virgin's mouth and suck it.'

She thought she would vomit with disgust and horror.

'Suck it! Suck it, you pure cunt!'

She put the tip of his prick in her mouth, feeling it jump with life against her teeth.

'Spread your teeth... spread your teeth!' he screamed under his breath. He grabbed her head, pressing it against him so that his prick went cruelly between her teeth, gagging her at the back of her throat. 'Lick it. Lick it like it's candy. Better than the best at Fanny Farmer, huh?' He laughed again and pulled her head back, sticking his hand crudely in her mouth and pulling her tongue out. 'Here, here,' he directed, 'where the vein bulges. Suck it up and down. Play with my balls. Play with my balls and suck the shaft up and down... ah...' He seemed hypnotized by the motion of her unwilling head. 'Enough, you bitch. I'm going to come inside you like a Fourth of July celebration. I'm going to explode inside your pure cunt.' He threw her head down, twisting himself quickly on top of her body. Then he got on his knees and pulled her legs around his kneeling body. His prick bobbed stiff and angry before him. He took his knife out and bent his head near hers.

Good, he's going to kill me. I'd rather die. I'd rather die...

But delicately and surely, he slit the crotch of her panties, exposing the soft black hair of her cunt. He did not touch it, but kneeled, sucking his breath in and out and staring at the cleft in her as she grew faint with naked terror. Not touching her cunt, he took his heavy penis in both hands, and lowering his body, with one thrust he rammed inside her. She screamed with pain, but his hand was ready on her mouth, not letting any of the pain out; keeping it locked in her cunt. She felt him scraping the bleeding wound in her.

'You're dry baby, bone dry. Ain't you having fun? I'm having fun. You got the tightest cunt I ever been in… tight cunt, sucking me in… tight-cunted bitch…'

Her body from the waist down was writhing with pain. He put his hands beneath her hips, and she felt his fingers digging into her ass. They found the hidden hole, and two fingers crushed mercilessly into it. He reamed her with them, stretching her anus until she thought the tender membranes would split. Her body was trapped and full with him. No out; no freedom for her body. Stuffed and imprisoned with his intrusive prick and fingers.

Then, miraculously, a great heat and throbbing started under her heart, and moved to meet his raging penis. She burnt with humiliation. Was this desire, this crazy itch and burning in her cunt? His penis rubbed against her taut clitoris, and when every nerve in her body was stretched like wire, and her thighs felt aflame, all the restraints in her body let go and she felt the pendulum throb in her cunt. It was like a ballooning of her inner flesh, like a fish's mouth. Open… close… open… close… she felt herself losing consciousness. Her pussy oozed its pent-up juices, smoothing the passage of the piston between her thighs. She felt it grow even bigger as if it were a balloon inflated to the bursting point. Then that humongous cock began to jerk and spasm as it erupted a flood of burning sperm.

She lay still, not wanting ever to move again. But he was up on his feet, more cruel than when he had thrown her to the floor. 'Get up you bitch,' he ordered. 'Button my pants.'

She got to her knees, her head level with his softening prick.

'Put it in and button me up.'

She fought a desire to stroke the velvety head.

'Put it in, bitch.'

She pressed his prick between his thighs, and numbly kneeling before him, began to button his pants. They were both silent. She lifted her head to his white eyes. 'Come upstairs to my apartment,' she begged.

He laughed into her face. 'I got what I wanted, virgin. Ask your uptown friends to carry on.'

But she knew that only this man with the white eyes could bring all the fluids of her body pulsing hot to her cunt. 'Don't leave me,' she implored. 'Don't leave me to die.'

He pushed her head away from his covered prick. 'I got what I wanted, cunt. Now try fucking the Eiffel Tower.' And he kicked her away from him and sauntered out of the hall.

She put her face against the tile floor and started to sob as relentless need gnawed at her body. 'Come back,' she cried against the tiles.

She lay there for almost an hour, hoping she would hear him turn the knob of the door. Then, knowing he was gone for the night, maybe forever, she dragged her body up the stairs.

Gloria turned the lamp on over the bed. She fell across the mattress, dazed. Her feet, their shoes still on, touched the floor. She lay still, knowing that the last half an hour had made her a slave to a pair of white eyes. As the image of his eyes floated into her blackened mind, she felt the urgency throb in her cunt. She moved her hand to the slit pants, and pressed cold fingers against the inside of her cunt. It was wet there. She pulled the fingers before her face and saw that they were covered with blood. Like a child, she thrust her fingers in her mouth, sucking them, hoping to get a taste of him mixed with the blood. The mustiness of his sperm made her dizzy with excitement. Her fingers slid back to her cunt. Up and down they moved against the small, hard pit of her clitoris, up and down, deadening her insides with her hungry desire. Up and down and harder and harder, till she was hurting herself as he had. At last she felt the flow of sensation that he had given her, but weaker, much weaker than the dawning she had known with him. She gasped with frustration and the tension of near-orgasm, and fell into a restless sleep.

The next morning, a persistent ringing in the room brought her swimming out of a dream in which she had been float-ing in a pool, flat on her back, her belly facing the sky and swelling, swelling like a carnival balloon until she thought she would burst. Her eyes wandered to the diving board. There, poised as though he would fly rather than dive, was her father. He laughed with his white eyes, and started to float toward her distended belly. She shrieked, and woke up, her screams competing with the blasting of the telephone.

'Yes, yes, yes!' she cried as though it were the telephone and not a person soundlessly far from her room, urging her to respond. 'Yes,' she muttered, and pulled her bruised hips around. She reached out and picked up the receiver. Almost before she could speak, a husky voice said, 'Gloria, is that you baby?'

'Yes,' she said blindly, still not fully conscious.

'Look, baby, this is me, Paul. Darling, I didn't sleep all night. I'm so sorry about yesterday. Look, I just had a bit too much to drink. I'm sorry. Are you there?'

'Yes,' she answered wearily. Paul and the things he had said, she thought disconnectedly. What was it he said yesterday? What happened with him yesterday? She couldn't remember. Only something had happened after Paul. What was it? And then the white eyes floated out of her dreams, gripping her stomach, and she was completely, shockingly awake.

'It's okay, Paul. Really. I guess I deserved what you said.'

'No, Gloria. Look, I'm just a conceited ass. If a girl doesn't sleep with me, I make a whole case study out of it.'

She pictured Paul's dark, gentle eyes, and his fine soft hands. 'A girl should want to sleep with you,' she said. 'If she doesn't, then she probably does have a screw missing someplace.' And she thought, My God, I really got my screws bolted in place last night. No more loose screws. Except now I'm one big loosened screw. All of me, so no one can hear the rattling.

'Gloria, baby, are you there? Can we just forget about last night? I promise, I won't say another word about us... I mean that way. It's a beautiful day, the sun is shining and the winter chill is gone. Let's drive up to Westchester and have some lobster in the Rye Inn.'

'That would be great,' she said. 'Get me out of the city today.'

'Gloria, you're an angel. I don't think there's another girl who'd forgive me for last night. I don't know what got into my head.'

Sense, she thought. Last night was the first time you ever sounded like a man... the first time you ever made me feel like a woman. She shook her head. Christ, do I have to be beaten and bullied into being a woman? Well then, beat me, bully me, I have to live. For the first time I want to live.

'I'll pick you up in an hour. Is that okay?'

'What time is it now Paul? Ten o'clock? Good. Come over for coffee and eggs at eleven, and by twelve we'll be on our way.'

'Great,' he said, his voice relaxed and relieved. The husky whisper of the first few seconds of conversation had evaporated. 'I'll pick up some cheese Danish and we'll have a picnic. I love you, Gloria. I love you even if I am a stupid ass.'

Too bad for me. Too bad the stupid asses go for me. And they admit it, too. The stupid asses are always very honest. I wonder if we can make a deal. I turn him into a man and he pays back by turning me into a woman. No, the only thing he could turn me into is a cow – a big, fat, contented, cud-chewing-in-the-green-fields cow.

'In an hour then, baby,' Paul sang.

'I'll be waiting for you,' she answered.

When she hung up the phone, she was dreadfully alone again, and she realized that she was afraid. She pulled herself off the bed and kicked off the shoes she had worn all night. Her toes felt stiff and cold. She walked to the window and rolled the bamboo blind up. The windows were dirty on the outside, the way New York windows always were. Because you weren't allowed to sit out on the sill and wash them, the way you could in Kansas City. In Kansas City, you lived in a house that had two floors; two floors of a wooden house, and the windows always glistening and clean. Her eyes filled with hopeless tears. Here she lived on the fourth floor. A wonderful studio with all the light she needed to paint. Of course, artists didn't really need light anymore, doing their crazy patterns of colour. The artists didn't go out into the sun the way Cézanne had. It didn't matter how a tree looked with the sun coming through the leaves. Artists were city dwellers now, painting sunless images in sunless rooms.

She opened the window and looked up and down the quiet brownstone-lined street. Down below, a car was parked badly. Two girls with short hair and tight jeans passed, touching in their walk and dress and faces told the world that they were in love; that at night they gripped each other's short-cropped heads, and dug into each other's hidden sex. They had looks of frozen, corrupted purity.

Small fenced-in trees lined the street. A skinny man with corduroy pants passed carrying a canvas under his arm; another sunless artist. Yhen a young man wearing horn-rimmed glasses, scurrying like the rabbit in Alice in Wonderland, rushed by balancing thick books against his tweed coat. Gloria laughed. Boy oh boy, you'd better read fast. You've got lots to learn, my bright young man. Hurry, or you'll die before you finish St. John's list of classics. We're all insane, reading and painting and blowing tunes. And all the time we want a thick-tongued maniac to grab us in a dark hallway and jam sex into us. All the money I wasted on paint and canvas and school. All the time I was just a cunt, an unused cunt. Those are the biggest cunts of all, cunts as big as our heads.

She closed the window, suddenly afraid again to be alone in the room. I wonder if he knows my name? I wonder if he'll look me up in the book and come back? But I must forget about him. I must forget and go on living.

She walked into the bathroom, the pale eyes invisibly following her. She leaned over the bathtub, the gesture bringing a throb of pain to her temples. She turned the hot water tap; soon smoke and splashing water filled the tub.

She walked out into the small kitchen and filled a kettle with water. She set the kettle on the stove, and turned the automatic gas jet. A flame shot up and she jumped back, suddenly realizing that she was standing in her kitchen, staring transfixed at the white eyes in the pattern of spots and cracks on the wall. Oh God, I'm trapped. I'm trapped.

Gloria wandered into her studio, the main room of her top floor apartment. The walls were covered with her paintings. An unfinished canvas hung on the wall between the two windows. Her canvasses were too large for her to use an easel. She painted by dipping into brilliantly-hued buckets of paint, and splashing her frustration and confusion across the white canvas. All the colours of her life leaped at her from the walls, and she felt surrounded by mute enemies. She fell across the sofa in the middle of the room. It was covered with an Indian throw. Tiny flowers and men on camels marched along the border of the couch. She reached over to the coffee table that she had made out of wrought iron legs and an old mahogany kitchen table. The first cigarette of the day tasted like blood in her mouth, and she smashed it out in her Mexican pottery ashtray, and went back into the kitchen. She poured the boiling water through a drip coffee-pot, and poured a full cup of black steaming coffee. She brought the cup into the bathroom, putting it down on the closed toilet seat and unzipping her black dress. The rapist, the white-eyed devil, hadn't bothered to take her dress off, just pulled it above her knees. He didn't care that she had full, nipple-tipped breasts. He didn't care that her white back exposed the long slim line of her spine. He didn't care that the musk of her body lay hidden in her armpits, that her hips curved out from a small sculpted waist; he only wanted to get to her cunt. No other part of her existed for him, not her head or her heart or her round, throbbing, blue-veined breasts. Only one place his prick wanted to go; only one thing it cared about. His prick and her cunt could fly to the moon.

She lowered herself into the tub, and the water turned pink with her clotted blood. She grew faint. The water rushed into her cunt, settling hot in her moss-covered cavity. It brought the memory of him back to her with painful immediacy. I must find him. He's got to come back to me. Does every vagina feel the same to him? Didn't he feel, inside me, that he'd come home? Will he want another woman tomorrow? Is he with another woman now, shoving his magnificent prick into her pink, hot flesh? The thought brought tears of rage and jealousy to her eyes.

She took a soft sponge and soaped her body – her thighs, and the blood coating them, her slightly-muscled calves, her arms and breasts, and her tear-stained face. Her body felt the prickly sensation he had left in it, a blind glutting desire. She remembered the Greek fable about Io. Io had wandered between heaven and earth, a gnat biting at her, leaving her no peace, torturing her with its persistency.

I'm just as damned. He's left a scar in my cunt. An itching, burning scar. And only his prick can heal it. He's got to come back to me. He can't leave me to wander the earth like Io. She started to cry. But I'm an artist. I've won a drawer full of prizes. I've been shown in the Whitney exhibition. He can't have ruined me. He can't have left me with nothing to live for but his enormous cock. Just thinking of the rigid boned flesh that had jutted from beneath his hard stomach made her tremble with excitement. I'm lost… lost.

She pulled herself out of the tub and dried her body with the big Cannon towel. She wiped herself gently, with rhythmic concern. When she put the towel between her legs, her thighs pulled tightly together, as if her secret need had its own secret will. Her fingers wandered to her hot vagina. She separated the taut lips with her fingertips, exploring the smooth inner membranes that were the colour of conch. She felt the throbbing clitoris. It jumped at her heated prodding. 'I can't,' she murmured. She knew that if she flung herself across the bed and induced her own pulsating orgasm, she would be left with a hotter desire. Only the white eyes could save her. She walked into her bedroom, feeling the cruel urge between her legs. Her eyes reflected torture. I'm going crazy. I am crazy.

The green tweed suit, the fawn cashmere sweater, the thick hand-crafted belt, the mascara, powder and lipstick, the stockings, garters and thin-heeled shoes were all draped and painted expertly on her when the doorbell buzzed. Only the urgent itch inside of her didn't change with her cool, fresh-looking exterior. Her secret, hot, hidden desire laughed at her allegiance to civilization. She could put on fourteen sweaters and twenty-two strings of beads, and she'd still be naked and hungry inside.

She opened the door gaily for Paul. 'All is forgiven,' she announced before he could speak, fearing a drawn-out apology. 'Let's just forget it and not even mention it again, especially today.'

He put a bouquet of tulips and lilacs into her hands, and dared to kiss her timorously. 'You look beautiful,' he said, his eyes admiring her fine shoulder-length black hair, cut in straight bangs across her forehead. Her mouth was painted a fashionable orange. 'You are the coolest lady in New York.'

Very cool, she thought, even as the furnace raged in her groin.

'Well, let's scramble the eggs. I'm starving. Something about not sleeping all night must give you more time to be hungry.'

She was afraid he'd apologize again. 'You should have taken a pill. It's too much of a bore to toss all night.'

He followed her lead. 'Next time I don't sleep, I will. But,' he slipped in an oblique apology, 'if it's for the same reason, I'll just blow my brains out.'

Brains, she thought with contempt. Who gives a fuck about his brains?

Gloria pulled eggs, butter, bacon and cream out of the small refrigerator next to the stove and oven. She took a bowl from the cupboard and cracked four eggs into it. Beating them, she felt almost normal. Paul powdered salt and pepper into the bowl.

'You always forget the spice, honey.'

She laughed. 'I don't believe in spice.'

He put his arm around her. 'Is it really hopeless for me?'

'Is what hopeless?'

'Am I going to love you all my life as if you're a distant statue, a marble goddess?'

'Why not? I am a goddess, you know. I'm Io. Ever met her?'

'No,' he said, sensing the desperation behind the humour.

'Io is the only goddess who had an itch, a real terrific itch.'

He didn't answer her.

'This itch,' she continued, 'drove Io all over the whole damn earth, across the Caucasus to the shores of Exxine, across the Macotic Strait into the arms of the Amazons, out of Europe to the continent of Asia...' Her voice droned on incoherently.

Paul took her by both shoulders and shook her gently. 'Baby, what's got you? You sound miserable. Really beat.'

'It's nothing, Paul, nothing. I've just got a long trip in front of me, that's all.' Then suddenly, and inexplicably for him, she said, 'Have you ever seen a man with white eyes?'

He answered her tone instead of her words, 'Maybe you'd better lie down for a few minutes, Gloria. I'll bring the breakfast in when it's finished. You've got deep shadows under your eyes. Honey, if you don't feel well, if I hurt you more last night than you'll admit, we don't have to go anywhere. There's a Mozart concert on WQXR. We can just sit here and listen to it. Then we can have an early dinner and make a short day of it.'

'Yes,' she said, feeling dizzy with the need inside her. 'I'll lie down, but don't try to get out of that drive to Westchester. It's just what I need for my artistic nerves.' She kicked off her shoes and stretched lengthwise across the bed.

In fifteen minutes, Paul was beside her with a full breakfast tray – coffee, toast, bacon, soft scrambled eggs, and a gorgeous cheese Danish. He put the tray on her night table and sat on the bed beside her. 'Can you tell me what's wrong?'

'Nothing is wrong. I just didn't sleep too well. I'm a bit tired, maybe a little manic or depressed. Darling, do you think I'm a manic-depressive?'

Paul placed his hand on her back. She wanted to grab it and shove it between her legs. 'What I said last night really upset you Gloria. I'm a pig to speak to a sensitive girl like that.'

'It was true yesterday, Paul,' she said, looking into his gentle eyes with a mixture of loathing and insatiable desire. 'But it's not true today.'

'What do you mean?' he said, his voice hopeful.

'I mean last night I was a frigid bitch and rotten to you.'

His disappointment showed in his voice. 'Oh.'

'But today I'm not frigid.'

'Gloria, what are you saying?'

'Make love to me. Make love to me now.'

'Baby,' he implored, almost killing her desire with his comically-serious face, 'I didn't mean what I said yesterday. I want you. Oh, God, how I want you, but only when you're ready.'

'I'm ready, Paul. I'm ready. Do I have to get down on my knees and... and unzip your pants?'

There was a shocked silence. Paul winced. He was used to the ceremony, the eager asking and the grudging permission before he made love. He was not prepared for this dry, toneless command. Sex was a game for him, played in a very prescribed way. 'Have something to eat first,' he hesitated to regain his composure. Sure he'd fuck her, but she had to play the game.

In frustrated rage, Gloria picked up the parsley-sprinkled eggs and flung them across the room. They fell in a disgustingly mushy yellow heap. 'Fuck me!' she screamed. 'Fuck me for Christ's sake! You do know how? You have a prick, don't you?'

His face grew black with rage and fear. His anger aroused him until Gloria saw a bulge swell in his pants. Eagerly, she laboured with his belt buckle and unzipped his sober pin-striped trousers; found his prick decorously pressed against his left leg. He wore Brooks Brothers pink underpants. She reached into the slit in his shorts and freed the stiff, hot flesh. It stood wondrously firm before her eyes. The head was wide and hot and throbbing. She caressed the entire veined shaft, not seeing Paul's eager frightened face above her. She saw nothing but his taut rod, and felt nothing but the draining emptiness inside of her. She put her mouth eagerly against the cap of his prick, and sucked it with long intakes of breath. She swirled her tongue around the velvet helmet, and then ran it down the length of his lance. She licked around the base, sucking his balls into her mouth one at a time. She worked back up to the head, pausing only a second before swallowing the entire cock, burying it in her throat until her nose brushed the thick hair at his root. She felt his legs tremble and released him. 'Put it in me Paul, put it in me quick.'

He was silent with tension. 'Take off your clothes,' he commanded.

'No, no,' she screamed, 'no time! Just ram it in me.'

He ripped at her cashmere sweater, pulling it up around her neck, and pushing her methodical head away from his prick at the same time. He tugged at the pink brassiere beneath the sweater, but his nervous fingers couldn't find the hooks. Instead he pulled it up, so that it cut her under the arms. At last, his mouth found her taut nipples. She felt a shiver of hot lust as his tongue wandered over them.

'They're stiff like your prick. I have two pricks.' Then she pulled his head away from her, because the need to have him inside of her was becoming unbearable. 'Fuck me Paul,' she pleaded looking at his gentle, dark eyes. They brought him humanly close to her, and she felt her body grow chill. 'Close your eyes. Don't look at me, just fuck.'

'Gloria,' he implored. 'Gloria…'

She knew his humanizing of it had killed it for her. Her nipples grew soft. She lowered her hand to touch his prick. It was still stiff, and he was breathing hard, but it was not the thick, cruel prick of last night's lover. This one felt hard and thin, hopelessly thin to her touch. Disgusted, she turned on her side. And at that moment, from behind her, Paul's prick found its way between her legs and into the hot cavity of her desire. She thought it was too late, but his firm cock, moving in and out of her with a crazy, excited rhythm, was suddenly filling her with fire. Maybe? She pressed hard against him. She grew dizzy with the intensity of her need. 'Harder, Paul, harder, give it to me! Give me a prick of hate, not of love! Give me a prick of hate!'

Her throaty, insane demand freed Paul's orgasm. It rushed trembling all the way from his shoulders, throbbing down his breast and stomach and groin and emptied into her cunt.

'Not yet!' she spat in fury. 'I need more! Fuck me! Fuck me!' She continued to thrust her hips against him, fighting to regain the sensation, but Paul had grown soft inside her. She pulled away from him, her cunt wet with his sperm and the soothing liquids that had started to flow in her. She picked up his lax cock and balanced it in her palm. 'I could crush it, you weak bastard. I hate you.' She burst into tears of frustration, her fingers pinching her hungry clitoris.

'You're crazy,' Paul hissed, but he lowered his head to her cunt and pushed her hand away. 'Let me,' he said gently. He covered her emptiness with his mouth.

She leaned her head against the pillow and thought, as long as he doesn't take his mouth away, I can live. His tongue was inside her, gently licking her enraged clit. She felt a trembling, exhausted calm. She touched his dark head. 'Thank you, darling,' she said weakly. 'Thank you.' But even while sobbing her thanks, even as his tongue and teeth in her cunt calmed her insatiable need, she knew it would not bring the blasting, blinding release she had known under the stairs. It took a cock of contempt to do that. She felt as though a slave was salving her hot, tired insides. She arched her body sensuously against him, but it would take a master to cut the chords of her nerves. At the urgings of his mouth she felt the liquids flow gently down her body. The slow, tenuous pulsations of the orgasm began. Cheated and relaxed, fulfilled, and yet hungrier from the entranced, controlled throbbing of her cunt, she lay back amongst the pillows and tasted her tears.

Paul put his head on the pillow next to hers. His face had a look of mortification mixed with pain. After months of gentle cultivation, he was shocked to discover this aggressive madwoman. Was she always repressing this abandoned sexuality or had his patient courting driven her to frenzied carnality? Maybe there was another man. His face contorted with jealousy.

They lay next to each other, not touching, in heavy silence. He thought she was sleeping, but when he looked over at her, he found her lying flat on her back, her eyes opened wide to the ceiling. She had an expression of entranced agony. 'Gloria,' he said. 'Gloria, what is it?'

Her face showed she had not heard him. He leaned over and took her shoulders, feeling her shudder.

'Gloria, are you sick?'

She turned on him, repeating his question mockingly, 'Am I sick?'

'I can't tell,' he said hopelessly, 'if you love or hate me.'

'Neither,' she sighed. 'You don't even exist for me, really.' She turned heavy, feverish eyes on him.

'I do know I would never want to make love again like we just did. I guess I'm rather old-fashioned, but I like to lead the woman. I don't like to feel drawn up into her emotion.'

'I guess you are old-fashioned,' she agreed with distant disinterest.

'I think,' he countered, 'that you'll find most men are like me.'

She laughed hollowly. 'Then maybe I will take your suggestion of yesterday. Maybe I will try women.'

His face grew grim with the insult. A woman had never rejected him with such scrupulous and utter detachment. 'What you want is some kind of animal fury. Not love.'

'No, I just want you to kill the bug in me.'

He got up on his elbows and looked down at her breasts. The sweater and brassiere still pulled below her armpits. Her breasts were forced into taunt points by the pressure above, the nipples erect and pebble-hard. He felt the blood rushing to his penis, pressing it authoritatively through the slit in his drawers. He was horrified that his body desired this crude woman. He pressed his penis up against his leg, zipping his pants with nervous speed.

Gloria watched with a smile on her face. 'Don't worry, Paul,' she giggled contemptuously. 'You won't get in me again. You don't even get near my bug. You don't even flutter its wings.'

'What are you talking about?' he said, embarrassed that she had seen his fear. 'You talk like there's a mosquito eating at your–'

'Cunt? Pussy? Snatch?' She laughed again.

'Gloria!'

'That's all it is,' she screamed. 'Stop reading your fancy psychology books. Stop turning women into goddamn monuments or the Virgin Mary. There's only one Virgin Mary, and she had a mighty rough time. I don't want God in my cunt. I just want a man. Are there any? Do you know any?' The white eyes floated before her, and laughed into her flushed face.

'I think,' said Paul, 'that you should see an analyst.'

'Great,' she answered. 'Do you know of one with white eyes?'

'What are you talking about?'

'I want an analyst with white eyes. I want him to fuck me back to sanity.'

He leaned to look closely at her, and his chest brushed the protruding breasts. Again his penis urgently pressed against his pants. Then his tongue was searching her closed, cool lips. 'Let me!' he cried. 'What difference can it make to you?'

Gloria pulled her head back and said, 'Try, just try to be a man for me.'

'Yes, yes,' he said, not hearing the accusation in her voice. 'Let me try.' He pulled the sweater over her head. His fumbling fingers caught the snap on her brassiere and pulled the restraining cloth away from her mounds. He ran his hands eagerly over her soft, warm tits, pinching the nipples between his thumb and forefinger. He didn't dare look at her face. With a grunt, he pressed his mouth against the stiff pink knobs at the tip of her tits. He sucked at the pinpoint hole in her nipples, trying to drain milk from the breasts that had never suckled. 'You darling, you darling,' he murmured against her softness, each sound and breath giving the warm breasts new sensations. Then he levered himself up and stuck his cock eagerly between the valley of her tits. The channel was dry and he crushed the mounds of flesh tight against his shaft, feeling the pulsation, the separate heartbeat. His penis expanded, fatter and stiffer, pressed against her woman's body. And still she didn't move.

Blind with the heavy, throbbing need of his prick, he reached his hand under her skirt, pulling at the garters and fragile stockings. He lifted her body half into the air, and clumsily hauled the panties and stockings off in one long silky piece. He slid her skirt off last. Gloria lay flat on the bed, completely, ravishingly naked. He got on his knees beside her, and ran his fingers up her delicate ankles, her thighs, her hips, her fragile waist. His tongue followed his fingers, tasting her cunt, her breasts, her belly, the fleshy inside of her thighs. He crushed himself against her smooth stomach to relieve the tormented steel rod growing out of him. He rubbed helplessly against her cool skin. Up and down, up and down, until he heard her even breathing grow rapid and gasping. Only then did he look into her eyes, seeing them glitter at him from a terrible depth. Her mouth was closed, and she looked nearly unconscious with her beautiful head crushed into the pillow.

'I love you. I love you. I love you,' he groaned, tenderness mixing ecstatically with his fierce love-hungry prick. Her eyes looked back at him with pure hate, turning his stomach cold. With rage and frustration, he pulled her passive legs apart, and rushed his blood-heavy prick into her pink and sensitive flesh. Her pussy was almost dry, and its unconscious resistance to his penis made him grow harder and more enraged. He tore into her, forgetting the woman or thing beneath him. He knew only that he was dying in his tortured cock, and that the hot elastic channel of inner flesh was giving him back his life. He ground up and down, in and out of this hot path, hypnotized by the rhythm of his desire. He clutched at her shoulder and whispered into her ear to the cascading of her body, 'I love you. I am helpless in you. Love me!' Then he felt the passion imprisoned in his prick rush forward for freedom. From his muscled thighs, his knotted stomach, his prick grew rigid and leaden, and when it had to break from its own weight, it shot sperm deep inside her in convulsive spurts. He fell exhausted against the pillow, his face mixing with her perfumed black hair. 'Darling, my darling,' he gasped, catching his breath, his body buzzing into normalcy, but when he looked down at her face he saw her eyes were cold.

'Leave now,' she whispered, her voice dead.

'Gloria, my darling,' he almost wept.

'Leave now, or I will kill you,' she repeated.

Her white face wanted him dead. He got up from the bed, zipping his trousers. He bent to speak to her… to plead for communication, for time.

She said in a trancelike voice, 'Leave quickly, Paul, or I promise I'll kill you.'

The Story Of Monique

Monique stretched cat-like on the couch and ran her fingers lightly over her erect nipples. Closing her eyes she tried to resume her nap. But the images behind her eyelids persisted. She could still see the convent, the voluptuous girl, the huge breasts with the golden needles stuck in the nipples. Her hand wandered down to her moist pussy...

She must have fallen asleep, for when she next opened her eyes the shadows were longer in the room and her aunt Sonia was lying naked next to her. Monique was barely awake and already the woman was sitting up and rubbing her excited and juicy pussy against the hard peaks of Monique's tits. Monique came fully awake as that voluminous cavern absorbed the end of her breast.

Monique reached under and caressed Sonia's buttocks. Her aunt was rocking up and down, fucking herself shallowly with Monique's erect nipple. They hardly talked as this continued for some time. Sonia eventually tired and resumed her position at Monique's side, only this time she inverted her body so that her head lay between Monique's thighs and her pussy was offered to her niece's willing lips.

Monique felt Sonia separate the folds of her cunt with her tongue, and she reciprocated. The activity was pleasing, but hardly satisfying after all she had experienced the past several days. So she lay back and daydreamed while she absently licked Sonia's crevice and darted her tongue into her secret grottos. So absorbed was she in her reverie that her aunt's attentions did little more than cause a mild stirring in her loins.

Sensing her distraction, Sonia sighed and rose from the bed. 'If I had known this would be the result of your meetings with Selma, I would never have participated in the introduction,' she said ruefully. Her true disappointment wasn't very great, however, and she was smiling as she left Monique to her introspection.

As usual, Monique found herself in the woods near the shore late in the afternoon. Monique thought it a strange and wonderful coincidence that as she walked along the path through the trees who should materialize but her best friend Janine approaching from the other direction. Surprise and pleasure was clearly visible on Janine's face as they hurried toward each other and embraced.

'Monique, I'm so glad to see you,' her friend gushed. 'I have to admit, I thought I might, knowing as I did that you were coming here for the summer. I couldn't resist taking one of the cottages near the jetty when one of them became available.'

Monique smiled and held her hand as they walked. 'I'm glad you decided to come. I thought we wouldn't be seeing each other until after I returned to Paris.'

'Well,' the girl continued, 'at graduation we did promise to get together as soon as possible. And what could be sooner than this.' She laughed good-naturedly and plopped down next to a moss-covered tree trunk. 'I saw Max before I left to come here. He's in Cannes this week, you know. And he expressed some interest in seeing you.'

'Oh, really?' Monique's interest was piqued now. Max was nice to be around. It seemed as though he always had been. His parents had been old friends of Monique's, and the two children had often played together. He'd grown into a fine handsome man, and she'd thought more than once what it would be like to make love with him. Janine's voice interrupted her reverie.

'Of course, my uncle is up to his old tricks again. Ever since Mother and Father died in the accident...'

Monique turned to face her. 'So how is he behaving toward you now?' she asked.

Janine shrugged. 'The same, I guess. He comes to me every night always crowing his displeasure at something or other. He usually ends up baring my bottom and spanking me violently.'

'The lecherous bastard. Does it really hurt you?'

'Sometimes,' admitted the girl ashamedly, 'but now I can usually take it, except when he goes at me between the legs.'

'What? He whips you between the legs?' Monique said with disgust.

Janine nodded. 'Generally he uses a flat ruler. He likes to tear my shift from me until I'm naked on the bed, then he either has me stand, legs apart, bent over the bed, or lie flat on my back. He hits either from top to bottom, or sideways, almost always on my bottom though.'

'And then...' Monique prodded, suspecting what was coming.

'Well...' she hedged, 'he usually ends up by sucking me twice between the legs till I come, while his finger is rammed up my ass.'

'And what else?'

'Okay! Okay! He likes sticking his big cock up my asshole.'
She blushed as she said it and looked down at the ground.

'Does it still hurt you?'

'Not really. Actually, it's even quite good.'

'And what about the maid, doesn't she see anything while this
is going on?'

'Oh, Solange, he takes her into his bed sometimes. Usually he
drives his rod into her slit and she cries a lot, but out of happiness I suppose. She doesn't sound like she's in pain.'

Monique nodded, certain the girl wasn't really asking her for
advice, and not really willing to give any. She didn't feel qualified to pass judgment on anyone, especially after some of the
adventures she'd recently experienced. So with an expression of
sympathy – just for the sake of propriety in Janine's eyes – she
helped her friend to her feet and they continued their evening
walk, talking as old friends do and immersing themselves in the
wonderful moments of their common past.

The next morning Max called her and invited her to come to
the city. She accepted. When she left, Sonia was smiling cryptically – probably, Monique thought, because her aunt had
hoped she'd won a convert to her lesbian beliefs and pleasures.
This visit could show otherwise.

When she met Max at the restaurant he'd chosen, she proved
to be quite a hit. The eyes of the men in the place gravitated to
her breasts the moment she passed the door. The way they
looked at her made her impatient to leave. Max, as tall, fair and
handsome as she remembered him, told her he had something
special planned for the evening. When he explained that he was

taking her to the movies, however, she began to have doubts.

The film was already running when they arrived. Max had made arrangements for them to use one of the private viewing booths that occupied the balcony floor. He politely refused the offer of an usher to accompany them to the proper room, and led Monique up the stairs to a door at the end of a richly carpeted corridor. When he handed her a velvet mask before they entered, she knew the adventure she'd anticipated was about to materialize.

Max knocked four times, waited a moment, and then opened the door. In the cubicle were three men, two women, and a girl of indeterminate age. It was a very old movie house decorated in the classic style. The cubicles were a part of the balcony, and were separated by high partitions. To see into the next cubicle it was necessary to climb onto a high chair and balance precariously while peering over the top. There were no introductions.

Without preamble, Max went right up to one of the women – an attractive redhead of about thirty – tore open her blouse, and pulled into view two very firm and very pretty breasts. He leaned over and began to suck the pink nipples until they stood erect. The other woman, who was already surrounded by the three men, freed herself from their attentions for a moment and drew close to Monique. She lifted the thin sweater Monique had worn and exposed her luscious tits to the sight of the excited men. Then the woman bent and emulated Max's actions, sucking and pulling at the boobs with her teeth. The men were suddenly swarming around Monique, running their impatient hands over her thighs and buttocks as they lifted her skirt.

An insane, uncontrollable excitement was taking hold of her. She closed her eyes and let the woman knead and suck her breasts. She opened them again at the sound of a long, drawn-out sigh and saw that one of the men had lifted the skirt of the woman and was blindly kissing her ass. His teeth left little marks on the taut skin as he nibbled and licked. The other two men continued to do the same to Monique, laving the soft skin of her backside with their tongues and dragging their teeth across her luscious curves. She leaned over the back of one of the seats, offering her rump to the concupiscence of the eager strangers. Their mouths resumed covering her flesh with tingling kisses. In the dim, flickering light she could see Max, propped against the wall, offering his dick to the lips of the young girl. His tool was long and hard; the cap was a thick mushroom on the slender stalk. The girl was sucking it slowly, the bulk of the shaft disappearing down her throat with each swallow.

Suddenly a nose began to infiltrate her buttocks. She spread her legs to grant it easier access and bent still lower to offer the sight of her salivating cunt to the eyes of the panting men. A tongue insinuated itself between her pleated lips and caressed the enlarged love bud. Monique felt her legs go weak as the wet stroke washed across her sex, lingering on the slit and darting inside once again. The tongue scoured her, searching out her innermost secrets. She kept her eyes open as she was tongue-fucked, absorbing the sight of the girl sucking at Max's hard pole. It sent a ripple of heated lust through her. The cock went in and out of her mouth the way a dick would a pussy...

One of the women sauntered over to Monique and placed herself in a similar position, bent over the couch with her back to one of the men. The lips of her cunt gleamed wetly in the dim light. The man standing behind her pulled her to him by the hips and rammed his cock up into her offered pussy. His stiff shaft easily penetrated the yawning slit and slid in to the balls. He began pumping violently, drawing back as far as he could without withdrawing from her sheath, then driving into her again and again until she seemed a puppet manipulated by invisible strings so exaggerated were her spasms. The sighs of the rest of the participants were covered by the soundtrack of the movie, but Monique could hear the man next to her murmuring to the woman.

'You're mine, mine to fuck as I please. This is all that is real,' he grunted as he pounded his meat in deep. 'Do you like the way it feels? Do you like feeling my big, hard cock all the way inside you? Can you feel it stretching your pussy?' He reached around and started grabbing at her swaying tits. 'I love fucking you,' he continued. 'Now fuck me the way I'm doing it to you.'

He stopped pushing against her and took a short step back. The woman almost immediately took up his rhythm. She continued to lean forward, but she thrust back and forward with her ass, drawing his cock into and out of her. He was now the victim of her whim, and she wriggled her hips and banged against him in a motion calculated to maximize her pleasure.

The other woman in the room, half lying on a chair, was offering her spread cunt to the suction of anyone who wished to partake of it. When all of the mouths, cocks and fingers were busy elsewhere, she busied herself by burying her own digits in her desperate canal and masturbating until the sign of her passion began to ooze from her love box.

Monique released herself to her climax as the tongue-lashing she was receiving neared its inevitable conclusion. She hardly heard the young girl on the other side of the room gurgling as she received in her mouth the load of sperm that shot geyserlike from Max's dick. The thick cream filled her cheeks and choked her as she struggled to swallow it, finally letting much of it fall from her lips back onto his thighs. He nonetheless continued to ram his cock into her throat, forcing her to accept his strokes by holding her head in place at his belly.

Monique was biting at her own arm to smother the cry of intense joy she was experiencing as she came. Her legs were trembling so violently she nearly fell in a faint upon the couch. Even this failed to gain her a moment's respite. One of the men took her crossed arms away from her breasts and began passionately sucking the sensitive mounds. While this was going on, the woman next to her was still being fucked, and making dramatic efforts not to scream her satisfaction. The other girl who was waiting to be serviced finally rose and came to Monique, joining the man in sucking her tits and rekindling the flame that had just died down. Fingers rubbed the flesh of her torso and found the entrance to her already lubricated cunt. Finally she was made to rise and then was bent over again. She felt a hard prick knocking at her buttocks. It was strong but thin and penetrated easily in her so-often-distended anal sheath. Soon her breasts were heaving under her, slopping at each thrust of the flesh pole in her welcoming asshole. The belly of the man responsible slapped persistently against her cheeks.

Max still was not done with the girl. Monique saw him talking to one of the women, and then he placed a bank note between the cheeks of her ass. She walked away gesturing to the girl to offer herself to Max. The girl positioned herself with her back to one of the chairs. She spread her thin legs, thereby exposing her barely-fleeced pussy to Max's hungry gaze. It was all he needed. His erect cock bobbed from side to side as he approached the girl and pressed his belly to hers. Monique saw him rear back and place his cock head at the entrance of her cunt. Then he pushed into her. He went in without obstruction, the youthful body obviously having already been deflowered.

Monique continued to watch him fuck her wildly for several minutes – grabbing at her developing breasts with hands and teeth, lifting one leg and draping it around his hip so as to deepen the penetration – before she became too involved in her own roiling sensations to pay any further attention. She gave herself passionately and without shame, hoping that the sounds of the film would cover the noises she was making.

The man remained in her for quite a long time. His motion was expert and heightened their mutual pleasure. First he would plunge in and out as though he planned to wring the juices from his body in the space of mere seconds. Then, when it seemed as though his rock-hard member must unburden itself, his rhythm would slow and he'd guide their passions to a more manageable level. When this was accomplished he pumped her faster and faster once again, the cycle repeating itself until she was sure she must scream from the incredible feelings cascading through her.

Max continued to bang the young girl while she lay back in calm acceptance of his treatment of her. She rocked her hips in time to his penetration, milking him and taking her pleasure, though Monique was sure Max was aware only of his own actions and his own impending orgasm. When it happened he pulled his cock from her grasping slit and shot his load against her belly and thighs. Before another moment had passed, one of the women rushed over and licked it all away, popping her fingers into her mouth and relishing each collected glob.

The film was nearing its end and the rest of the theatre patrons began to file out. The sound of their passage in the hall outside was loud and distracting. But once Max and the rest of the men were sure that the theatregoers couldn't see into the cubicle, they surrounded Monique and lowered her onto the floor. They spread her arms and legs so as to contemplate the opened flower of her pussy and the crinkled starfish from which flowed a thin rivulet of sperm. Monique protested, even though she knew it would fall on deaf ears. The sight of her seemed to enflame them.

'Fuck her, Max,' they urged. 'Fuck her good and hard.'

His cock was thick and hard and eager to comply. Monique spread her legs wider still and watched as he rammed his massive member in her. It was painful for a moment. But then the pleasure took over. Monique squirmed and moaned and started to meet each of his thrusts with her dripping love box.

'Fuck me! Fuck me harder!' she ordered. 'I want to feel your balls against my ass!'

He pumped wildly and did as she asked, drilling so deeply that his belly smacked against hers and his balls flopped against her delicious buttocks. Then he pulled out of her without warning.

'Turn over, bitch… stick your ass up in the air and spread those legs so I can see that hot box.'

She did as she was told, and turned as Max pulled her toward his glistening tool. He was kneeling, facing her butt. His cock was still so hard the head seemed swollen to twice its normal girth. His jabbing at her pussy lips was just getting her more and more hot. He was so large. He was thrusting blindly now, hitting her clit, sending shivers all through her muff. Monique couldn't stand it any longer. Her hands reached down to guide his prick into her waiting cunt while the others watched with naked lust in their eyes.

He began to thrust harder as she settled his cock head on her slit. It entered easily as Monique backed up right against him. 'Do you like the way it feels?' asked Monique huskily. 'Tell me how much you like your prick in my cunt. Tell me how much you enjoy fucking my pussy.'

'Instead of telling you, I'll show you,' Max gasped. He quickened his pace, darting the full length of his shaft into her, pulling out, then plunging in again.

Monique could feel the tightness building in her stomach. She knew they were both going to come. Max moved faster and harder. She was trying to meet his every move. She thought he would erupt in her first, but she couldn't wait for him. The sensations, the spasms were too demanding to wait any longer. They went from her head to her toes, cantering on her cunt. As Max pumped her she grabbed for his shaft, squeezing it when it was mostly out of her, feeling the torrent rise in him. He exploded in a shower of white cream that coated her pussy channel and leaked from its entrance in a thick stream.

When they'd finished, Max helped Monique to dress and led her out of the cinema. She experienced a slight feeling of shame, but at the same time there was a glow of satisfaction and desire not yet fulfilled.

She fell asleep immediately upon her return to Sonia's villa. Her restless mind conjured images of pleasures not yet experienced and needs she couldn't allow to go unfulfilled.

* * *

One week later, Monique was on a train bound for Paris. She couldn't forget the wounded look in Selma's eyes when she'd told the woman that Claudie Merval had called and told her that some sudden employment opportunities had become available…if she returned immediately. Monique had hesitated not at all, though she felt her 'education' had been prematurely terminated. She was sure, however, that she would see Selma again. She realized there was no chance that the Nordic mistress of pain would permit her to escape permanently.

She put the book she'd been reading back on her knees and watched the passing landscape through the large picture window. The train was panting through a dry country of olive trees and thorny bushes. The sky was grey, promising storms and winds. In the compartment, despite the open windows, the heat was almost unbearable.

Monique examined her travelling companions. One was a priest, if his black suit and constricting collar were any indication. He was reading his prayer book, but his eyes were more often reading the curves of Monique's legs than the lines of the psalms. By his side slouched a red-faced merchant whose complexion deepened each time he caught sight of the white flesh above Monique's stockings. In another corner, two lovers were kissing passionately without paying any attention to the other travellers with whom they shared the cramped quarters. Monique closed her eyes and imagined the welcome she would receive at the hands of Claudie Merval. Claudie... there were so many remembrances attached to that name; she owed the woman so much for taking a personal interest in her welfare and education. Sadly, some of those educational episodes were already fading in her memory.

The two lovers were still embracing when the train came to a sudden stop. The girl's skirt had ridden up, exposing a generous expanse of thigh that had attracted the eyes of the men in the car. Monique smiled to herself and felt a naughty twinge. She made a pretence of resuming her reading, but through her lowered eyelids she could see the men trying to get a closer look up the girl's skirt. She guessed they saw the buttocks that no panties covered. They didn't dare to lean over for fear of being too obvious and ruining the show. Instead they twisted and turned and sought every advantageous angle from which they could obtain a better view. When the dark shadow of the girl's pussy hovered into view for just a moment, they both put their hands in their pockets. Monique could see the movements of their fingers under the suddenly swollen material. A moment later the couple rose from their clinch, realizing they'd reached their destination, and left the train.

Determined to continue the fun, Monique slowly parted her knees. Under the material of her short skirt, the compass of her legs opened. The passion-entranced girl wasn't the only one not wearing panties. The lustfully inquisitive eyes across the coach could now see the joint of Monique's thighs and the enticing slit of her cunt. It seemed to her that their eyes were like a caress on her unveiled secrets. The two men looked at each other with knowing confidence, smiled, and this time leaned down for an unobstructed view.

Monique had to admit to herself that she was enjoying the exhibition in front of perfect strangers. She was hot under the heavy cardigan that moulded her imposing breasts. The nipples were thrusting against the material as if they would burst free; the bra she'd put on was much too small. She was consumed with a sudden desire to show them her tits. Her temperature seemed to rise in direct response to her fantasy. She sponged her temples and mechanically unbuttoned the first button of her blouse.

'Are you hot, my dear?' asked the merchant. 'Your face seems terribly flushed.'

Monique hesitated a moment in front of the red and sweaty face of her companion, but some inner demon was pushing her to answer to his ill-concealed desires. 'Yes, I'm very hot,' she breathed throatily. 'I was wrong to put on a blouse so thick in this heat…'

'Well, change it,' suggested the man, hopefully.

Monique smiled, and did her best to appear ignorant of the true meaning behind his request. 'I wouldn't mind… but here…?' She looked around the compartment, at the corridor window with the shade drawn, at the priest.

'Don't worry about me,' he assured her, 'my prayers absorb all my energy.' But Monique could see that his palms were sweating.

'The same goes for me,' piped up the merchant too quickly. 'We wouldn't think of making this trip unpleasant for you.'

Monique hesitated, then turning around she pulled her suit-case to her from the rack. In the mirror on one side of the carriage she could see that the two men were avidly staring at her. She opened her blouse unconcernedly, removed her bra – holding it out absently so that they could see – and then removed the blouse entirely. Her bare back was offered to their greedy eyes.

Monique knew her magnificent breasts were fully exposed to them in the mirror. Her nipples were dark and hard from the excitement of the moment. She felt an urgent desire to turn around and offer them the full view of her tits. The blood was beating at her temples and her throat was dry and parched. She made a show of picking up the filmy blouse that she'd chosen to put on, but she hesitated, accentuating each movement. She put the blouse back in the suitcase and lifted her arms as if she was about to riffle through her belongings and look for a different item. The motion made her breasts jiggle wondrously, and she could hear the sharp intake of breath across the compartment. Just then the train lurched and started to roll forward once again, giving Monique the excuse she needed to fall backwards between the two red-faced men.

She began panting and moaning immediately as she felt the voracious mouths on her tits, pulling at the nipples, aspiring the red strawberries for an ardent sucking. She protested, weakly, for the sake of propriety, and then allowed them to do whatever they wished.

Their hands became more demanding, fumbling under her skirt. They massaged her thighs and slid between the lips of her twat, stopping to caress the engorged love bud that was already damp with the juices of expectation. The heads were suddenly lowered, abandoning the nipples. Monique smiled voluptuously; that perpetual curiosity, the 'Peeping Tom' complex that waited to be awakened in every man. They all wanted to see that obscure object of their desire, and before penetrating it, they wanted to study the delicious aperture and its moss-covered borders, the thick and slightly palpitating lips.

Monique made a final weak effort to free herself. Her spread-eagled body was pushed onto the cushioned bench. They tore the skirt from her, revealing the mysterious mouth between her thighs. Both heads immediately leaned over the offered secrets. The ardent tongues probed and prodded at the exacerbated flesh of the exposed clitoris. Monique panted quietly, arching her back to offer her belly to a more intimate penetration by the men's lashing tongues. She could feel her orgasm approaching. They licked her insanely, arousing in her that blind, unseeing passion that demands nothing other than its fulfilment. They alternated penetrating her crevice with their tongues, sometimes inserting a finger or two to stretch the willing folds and allow easier entrance. The fine-spun gold on her mount was sopping with their saliva as they left little of her unwashed between her belly and her thighs.

It seemed unlikely that she would be brought to completion,

though, when the brakes of the antiquated train began to squeak and the transport perceptibly slowed. The two upstanding men panicked. A station was approaching and each participant suddenly, hopelessly, tried to regain some semblance of composure.

Monique got up and dressed quickly. The adventure came to an end as suddenly as it had begun when the train stopped and a matronly woman entered the compartment, seating herself solid as the Rock of Gibraltar opposite the two men. Monique frowned and decided she wasn't yet finished with them. She avenged herself by making them mad with desire, opening her thighs from time to time and affording them a full view of her yawning cunt, still oozing its juices.

Monique was the first to leave the train. To her disappointment, she learned that the connecting train to Paris was going to be delayed until the following morning. In response to her inquiry, a man on the platform advised her that she could find lodging at a small hotel by the edge of the woods near the station. From there she could, if she wished, take a bus to Paris instead should the train fail to arrive.

The building was a modest but pleasant one, with whitewashed walls and bright shutters at each window. It contrasted sharply with the dark tonalities of the pine woods surrounding it. It was furnished in common country style, but dust on the floor and on some of the tables indicated that customers must have been scarce. By the counter in the small dining room a man in shirt-sleeves was just finishing his lunch. He dispassionately evaluated Monique when she entered the room, but she noticed that his eyes lingered on her bobbing tits and the jutting nipples.

'I'm Cesar Jouve, the boss,' he said, a string of meat hanging from his mouth. The way he stressed the word 'boss' indicated his satisfaction with the self-appointed title.

Monique explained what had happened and asked for a room, which he provided with a listless shrug and a demand for the appropriate number of francs. When he called out, a young girl of perhaps sixteen appeared to assist Monique to her room. Her name was Sweet, she said, and Monique could readily believe that. She was tall and lithe and curvaceous, though she'd not yet fully outgrown the coltishness of youth. Her hair was dark with red highlights and her eyes were an intriguing shade of green.

To Jouve, the girl must have been sweet indeed, Monique came to realize later in the evening, for as she snuggled between the warm covers that swathed the bed in her room, she heard the familiar sound of the whip emanating from the bedroom across the hall. She knew it must be Jouve and Sweet, acting out that voluptuous song, for there were no other guests. She nodded.

So even in the most remote backwaters the whip was king. What part of Sweet's body was being attended to now? Her swelling breasts?

Monique's hands were busy on her own body as she thought of this. She left her right mound, lathered with her own saliva, and started on the left. Her other hand was busy at her cunt, dipping into the secret grotto and becoming saturated with its juices. She removed the fingers and rubbed the right nipple with the musky oil. The engorged cap rapidly became pebble hard. She lifted the breast to her mouth and lapped at it with her darting tongue. It circled the darkening peak. Then she sucked her finger and returned to rubbing her clit. Her masturbation, stimulated by and combined with the moans and smacks coming from the other room, were the most exciting things she'd experienced alone in her life. She accelerated the pace of her activities as the cries became more violent.

The crack of the whip had ceased not long before, and Monique knew the man was fucking the girl. Her orgasm rose in a tidal wave of pleasure as she imagined the delicate body of Sweet used in bestial manner by the 'boss' of the hotel. She could almost picture his dark, thick cock shuttling in her mouth, or filling the tautness of her young pussy. Better still, she could picture herself lying with her, massaging the alluring limbs, kneading those pert breasts, and licking the lightly furred mount to a state of excitation. The image remained with her as she drifted into oblivion...

Diary Of An Angel

Wednesday, the 11th

In spite of my state of fatigue, Kenneth came into my room last night and did with me what he pleased, paying no more attention to Ursula than if she had not been in the room. My terror was such – now that I know of the possible consequences of pleasure – that I could not lie still, even though Kenneth swore under his breath and pinched me brutally. Stammering and crying, I explained that it wasn't because of him; it wasn't for any reason but that I didn't want to be pregnant. When he heard that, he laughed, saying that I was still too young to find myself in Ursula's situation, and that he advised me to forget any lies Angela might have told me to the contrary. But this did not reassure me, for I know his own capacity for telling untruths. Had I not, but a few hours before, had more than adequate proof of it? But I dared not say anything, especially with Ursula there. For all his coaxing, though, Kenneth could do nothing, even though he said he was determined not to spoil me and that I had but to leave matters to him. Every time he would put his member to my opening, it would shut of its own accord, and finally even against my own will, for he was losing his temper again and I was beginning to be more afraid of it than of the possible outcome of his pleasure.

The same thing repeated itself several times. Putting his tool in my mouth, he said he was going to punish me, and he pushed his penis to the very depths of my throat, nearly choking me. And as he did so, his temper worsened. He said then that if I played the little fool and held back for so much as an instant, I would suffer for it. Placing me once more upon my back, he pulled at me, prying me apart with his fingers until the end of his staff was placed at the opening. But the moment he let go with his fingers, it snapped shut again, constricted by the same force that was making my entire being shrink with icy fear. Cursing now, and calling to Angela, he turned me over, and passing his wetted finger over the dent in my buttocks, and he inserted it into the other hole, then took out his finger and, bending down, titillated that hole with the tip of his tongue until, to my horror and shame, I felt it open. Suddenly realizing what he was about to do, I fought wildly to free myself, scratching his body with my fingernails, hoping that if I caused him pain he would let go. I then heard Angela's cool voice.

She ordered Ursula to get up and hold me down. Ursula, of course, obeyed immediately. She pulled my arms away and stretched them out in front of me, causing my head and chest to fall forward on the bed. Held thus, I couldn't move. My back was arched and my buttocks were exposed to Kenneth's enquiring tongue.

I don't know just when he substituted the smooth end of his

pole for his tongue. But I suddenly felt it penetrate me gradually, my hole closing around its hard length in a tight grasp as little by little he eased his way further in until at last his balls were resting upon my opened cunt.

Circling my waist with his spread hands, he began to move. The pain I felt made me cry out to him to stop. He did stop, and remained thus, his prick throbbing inside me. And then I felt a soft moist mouth cover my slit and a strong tongue drive into my cunt, until now it opened wide too, seeking its wanton pleasure from Angela's wicked dexterity. I knew it must be her, for Ursula, beads of perspiration pouring down her face, was still pinning me down with all her force, made stronger by the hatred that animated her. The grip of her hand had become like iron. I could hear her convulsive breathing as she watched us, tightening her fingers from time to time until I thought my bones would be crushed.

In spite of the pain, I felt that the moment was near when, for all the horror of my situation, I would be unable to prevent myself from yielding to the now well-known feeling of rapture. Gradually, it was enveloping me and making me stir my buttocks as Kenneth explored them. I could hear myself panting, sighing, I could hear myself sobbing and imploring him all at the same time, I could hear myself telling him I was willing to undergo anything they wished if only they would allow me to satisfy my lust. And when Angela's lips left me, I begged her to come back and continue. I was beyond myself with excitement, my dripping, craving hole was searching her mouth, but instead, I felt another tail penetrate me. Colder and stiffer than Kenneth's, it slid into me and began to move, synchronizing its action to his. Finally, enraged and not caring what happened, I let them hammer into me at their will;

then, swooning with pain and delight, I sank into a delicious oblivion.

When I came to myself again, I saw Kenneth's tall figure standing between Angela's wide-flung legs. They had piled pillows so that her orifice was level with his loins. His hands on his hips, his arms akimbo, he furrowed her slowly, idly, hardly moving his body, his flesh so deeply inserted that all I could see were the superimposed triangles of fair and dark fur grinding against each other. With every jolt, Angela emitted a guttural cry, biting her arm with such force that traces of blood appeared on her fair skin. Her face was something terrifying to behold. Although her eyes were wide open, nothing could be seen of them but the whites.

Kenneth was studying her face and body, seemingly taking great care to time his movements so as to delay as long as possible the moment of her release. After a while she pleaded with him to move more quickly, saying she could not contain herself any longer. But, instead of doing as she had asked, Kenneth began to withdraw himself. I watched, fascinated, as his long rod emerged unhastily, like a thick rope. And as he backed away, Angela repeated her injunctions that he should not leave her now. But Kenneth retreated until his prick was altogether in sight. I let out a gasp of choked surprise, for, fitted around its rim was a stiff circular brush of coarse black horsehair, which stood out around the tip as stout as wire.

Hardly knowing what I was doing, I reached out my hand and touched it. Each bristle seemed as sharp as a tiny steel needle. Kenneth, his eyes never once leaving Angela's face, pushed my hand away and, placing his collared end against the mouth of Angela's orifice, he went back into her, each black bristle turning out as he did so and making an incongruous black ridge around the pink slot before vanishing completely, followed by the thick stem that supported them. After a second of immobility, Kenneth started moving in and out of her in long sweeping strokes. I could almost feel the spikes lacerating her soft inner tunnel as, with increasing speed, they rubbed up and down its length.

Instead of feeling pain, Angela only begged Kenneth to go at it with greater ferocity. She placed her legs on his shoulders so that he could probe her to the last inch of his possibilities, so that the instrument of torture could reach the last depth of her hole. She now seemed to be suspended from his shoulders, only her neck and head touching the bed. She clawed wildly at the shawl beneath her, and as she was approaching the moment of ultimate fulfillment, I saw that her transport had reached such a pitch, that indifferent to the consequences, she was readying to scream. I clapped my hand to her mouth in order to stop her cries, allowing her to bite me cruelly while she wriggled like a snake, her body racked and contorted with ceaseless spasms of mingled agony and delectation, avoiding and then seeking Kenneth's terrible thrusts until all of a sudden she became rigid and, as though stricken to death, fell back upon the bed. And just when it seemed life would return to her body, Kenneth once again withdrew, wanting it seemed, to prolong her agony even longer still. With my hand still clamped over her mouth I watched Kenneth's grotesquely ornamented staff as it slid out of her, dripping with a creamy white substance and felt the sharp cut of her teeth as she bit into me still harder yet. At this point, blind with desire, and still feeling the pain Kenneth had inflicted on me, I lifted my hand from Angela's mouth, placed my knees to either side of her head, and lowered my cunt over her open mouth. Her tongue immediately sought my wet hole and roughly she began to suck at me. I then bent down so that my face brushed against Kenneth's staff and placed my own mouth to her soaked loins. Kenneth rose above us and he removed his strange ornamentation. I moved my tongue up and down the length of her opening and, as she began to shudder with a violent containment, I placed my tongue flat against her cunt and pressed down hard, sucking with my lips so that she moaned and from her I swallowed long draughts of the tepid grass-flavored milk that gushed from her hole down my throat. It was then as if Angela were simulating with her mouth my own actions, for as she was still in the throes of ecstasy, she clamped her mouth full over my cunt and sucked, causing me to grind down on her face, seeking the motion her tongue no longer gave. After her pleasure subsided, I raised my dripping mouth to Kenneth's still throbbing staff and took it between my glistening lips and onto my tongue. Almost immediately he spurted forth his own milky juice and I do not know if it was Angela's regained awareness of her tongue in my hole or if it was the impact of Kenneth's release against the back of my throat, but I too then stilled so that I could feel wholly the explosion of pleasure in my loins as I rested hard on Angela's pliant mouth.

During all this time I had not devoted a thought to Ursula. It seems so hard to believe that, in this short time, I have become so depraved that I could not care about her being there. I only remembered her after Kenneth had left me. Even then I didn't care that she had been witness to these disgraceful scenes in which, finally, I had taken a willing part.

I still held Kenneth's shriveled end in my mouth, my lips locked around its base, when, pushing me away from him, he darted towards Ursula's bed, calling out to Angela to come to her senses.

I was so placed that for quite some time I had had my back turned towards her and had not been able to see what she was doing. Now turning around, I saw her sprawled out on the bed, her thick cotton nightgown tucked up in a bunch under her chin, her legs wide apart and between their long, pendant thick lips, she held what could be seen of one of Angela's little whips, the sturdier end of which she was using as if it were a man, prodding herself violently in what seemed a sterile attempt to obtain relief from the furious desire burning inside her. Her cheeks were a flaming red. Although she was pronouncing his name, she hardly seemed to notice Kenneth watching her with an air of bemused curiosity. Meanwhile, the thin plaited leather stick moved rhythmically in and out, its smallness contrasting strangely with the breadth of the gap that hungered for it and which it was searching in vain. Angela stretched herself and yawned. She got up in a leisurely fashion and went over to look at Ursula. Seeing what all the excitement was about, she started to laugh. Without further ado, she caught the slender lash-end of the whip, gave a tug, and pulled the instrument from its sheath. Holding its slimy length away from her, and a look of disgust on her face, she left the room, announcing that she was going to bed.

This painful scene seemed to arouse Kenneth, for his prick was rising again. Holding it in his hand, just out of Ursula's straining reach, he waved it in front of her in the most offensive manner while the wretched girl, her hand rummaging in her slit, her eyes riveted to the object of her desire, sought by her own means to obtain a semblance of relief. But her efforts were wasted. She lay there panting, her lips parched. Her cunt yawned, angry and wet, a yearning chasm; and Kenneth held himself just out of range. There was a look of madness in her eyes when Kenneth, tiring of this game, decided to leave us. I begged him not to leave me alone with her, for I was indeed almost out of my mind with fright. Looking down at himself significantly, he said that I would suit his purposes, and in spite of my great fatigue, I followed him, letting him do with me what he wished, learning by my docility to feel no pain even if I felt no pleasure.

I fell asleep before he was through with me.

Thursday

I had quite forgotten about the picnic Mama planned for today. The vicar had been invited and he joined us early in the morning and we went out at half-past ten. The sun was already very hot. We drove to Stanton Forest in the barouche.

We found an agreeable shady spot not too far from the road and we settled ourselves under the trees. Miss Perkins and I unpacked the hampers of sandwiches and other things, and set out the food on a large white tablecloth on the ground, decorating it with moss until it really looked very festive and charming and earned me the compliments of both Mr. Gareth and Mama.

After our meal was over, and the vicar had said grace, Mama suggested that we children go for a walk, reminding me that if I kept a sharp lookout I would surely find some interesting plants or flowers to press in my diary. I blushed and thanked God for the half-light of the tall trees which permitted my confusion to pass unnoticed. Ursula, who had scarcely touched her food, asked to be allowed to stay behind, saying that she felt rather weak, what for the heat of the day. Her permission was granted; she remained with the three grownups, while the three of us went off obediently.

Angela announced gaily that she would help me find some attractive shrubs for my journal, and talking about this until our voices were out of the range of their hearing, Angela started to imitate dear Mama, parodying her voice in the most shocking disrespect.

Kenneth bared his organ and placed it in my keeping, and thus we walked along. He seemed quite unconcerned by the indecency of our attitude, and talked in the most natural way with Angela until, at the edge of the path, we came upon a nest of grass snakes, curling and twisting in a tangled, loathsome knot. I let go of Kenneth with a shriek of alarm, staggering several steps backward in an attempt to flee. But Kenneth took hold of my wrist and told me not to be babyish. Dragging me back to where the hideous heap of snakes was, he crouched down beside his sister who, with fascinated interest, was scrutinizing the writhing, slimy mass at her feet. To my utter horror, Angela advanced a white finger and probed and fondled those reptiles. Then she even picked one of them up, twisted it about her arm, not one bit troubled by the contact of its cold, viscous skin.

I felt gooseflesh prickling all over me and fought against a mounting sensation of nausea. Kenneth, his limb still dangling through the gap in his trousers, trimmed a small stick with his penknife and began to play with the snakes, lifting up several at a time and letting them slide back into the seething nest. They amused themselves thus for quite some time, silent and absorbed, while I watched nearly overcome by disgust.

Then Angela put an affectionate hand on Kenneth's arm. 'Dear Kenneth!' she exclaimed, her eyes full of merriment and dancing. 'Dear Kenneth, just imagine!' In her voice was a strange note of exultation that made me look down at her. She was smiling; her eyes were glittering as she drew out her handkerchief and, selecting one of the snakes, put it on the square of white linen, tying the ends together so that the creature could not escape. Then, lifting her skirt, she put it in her pocket and carefully smoothed down the folds in her dress, she got up and said that she felt that the time had come for us to rejoin the party.

Kenneth had watched her all this time without saying a word. His brow was puckered as though her intentions were not at all clear to him. But then he must have reached some sort of conclusion, for he started to laugh softly. Getting to his feet, he went towards Angela and crushing her against him, he kissed her passionately on the mouth until she thrust him away, breathless, saying that we ought to get home as soon as we could induce those fools to move. She took the lead, seemingly thoughtless of the nasty thing she had under her skirts. Kenneth made me hold his staff again, and did not let me release it until we were well within earshot of the party. I stumbled along behind them, dizzy with apprehension of I knew not what, picking nervously and at random any small plant that grew along the way.

When we rejoined the others we found Mama and the vicar and Miss Perkins engaged in a lively conversation; they never seem to tire of talking about problems and principles and forthcoming Church bazaars. Ursula, making no visible attempt to participate in the conversation, stiffened when she saw us approach and kept a keen eye on us, doubtless wondering what we had been up to.

She looked quite ill and I was astonished that no one had noticed this. From time to time, as though following her own inner thoughts, she unconsciously wrung her hands as though pleading with someone, in some mute and hopeless dialogue. I began again to fear that at any moment she might break down and no doubt Angela had noticed the same danger, for, putting her arm affectionately around Ursula's waist, she helped her up and the two walked away under the trees, where I saw them talking together for a while. When they returned Ursula had changed completely, now appearing quite gay, smiling at Angela and looking at her with an expression of positive adoration on her pale face. I could understand none of this, but instead of feeling comforted, I shuddered as I wondered what new piece of devilish mischief Kenneth's darling sister had been dreaming up.

Rising, dear Mama said it was time to return if we were to get home in time for tea. After packing everything up, and burying the leftovers, it was a very gay party that rolled up to the house.

We played games that evening and went upstairs at a rather late hour. Dear Miss Perkins seemed reluctant to let the vicar go, although it is frankly beyond me what she can find of interest in him. He is so dreadfully dull and so severe that he puts the damper on any fun one could have, and I shouldn't be surprised if he – who is so upright and stern and so godly – found our dear Miss P. a trifle 'fast' as they say.

While wishing Mama good night, Ursula, to my surprise, asked Mama if we could have the horses to go riding tomorrow morning.

'Why, of course, my dear Ursula,' Mama replied.

And Ursula thanked her with such exaggerated profusion that I grew concerned again.

'I am so delighted to hear that you are well again. I shall have word sent to Joseph at the stables to have the mounts saddled and ready for half-past seven.'

I was so tired I could hardly find the energy to undress. When Kenneth came into my room, a feeble, useless 'No!' escaped from my lips. I think he realized that truly I was too worn out to be of any use to him and I dare say he found his pleasure only in the fact that Ursula, her body trembling like a leaf, was obliged to sit and watch us. As for myself, indifferent to the scandal, I waged a losing battle against sleep and only woke up when he slapped me. Soon after, I returned into an exhausted slumber.

Friday

It was with the greatest difficulty I woke up this morning. Every bone in my poor body was aching. I could hardly remember what happened with Kenneth late last night or how I had ever managed to wake up and conclude the day's happenings by writing them down. I have learned, I do think, to write in my sleep. Some evil spirit guides my pen and aids my hand across the page.

The very thought of going forth for the morning ride made me hurt. Miss Perkins helped us get dressed. In this way I was spared a tête-à-tête with Ursula. Pale and drawn though she was, she kept up the conversation, probably so as to divert dear Miss Perkins' attention from my listlessness. For, to tell the truth, I don't know how I am going to go on much longer. I have no strength left in my body. And my mind is so depressed, I am so despondent...

Kenneth had used and abused me; I felt I had no more resistance left. The strain has been too much. It is not my fault... and yet, of course, it is, and my fault alone. Whilst hating Kenneth, the very notion of his (I cannot write the word) makes my heart beat more quickly, and my blood tingle there in the very place where my shame is seated. I know that I should loathe both of them. Yet even so, the memory of Angela's lips, blush though I do at the thought, sends a delicious thrill down my spine, obliterating all sincere sentiments of guilt.

It is only when I am temporarily out of their clutches that I realize I am in their clutches. It is only when I am, for the time being, away from them that I realize what they are turning me into a monster like themselves.

When we came down, Angela and Kenneth were already astride their horses and waiting for us. They both seemed in excellent high spirits and talked a great deal as we rode off, Angela turning now and again to give Ursula a smile of secret understanding. I had no idea what was between them. And although Ursula smiled back fawningly and preened herself under Angela's advances, I could not help noticing that look of fleeting dread that raced across her face when she thought she was not being observed.

My mind full of questions and foreboding, I hardly noticed the moment when, having reached the woods, we were nearing the fatal place I knew so well. And I was seized by an irresistible impulse to wheel my horse about and gallop back to the house. Bringing up the rear as I was, the plan was feasible. I was already gathering in the reins in preparation for spinning Sunbeam about, when Angela, her fiendish mind having, apparently, divined my thoughts, ordered me to ride out in front of her. Her voice was harsh. Meekly, I did as I was told.

Having dismounted, I fumbled with my horse, pretending to be unable to attach him properly, and when Kenneth came back to give me a hand, I asked him in an agonized whisper what was in store for me. He laughed, patted my cheek, and said I had nothing to fear. Angela, he said, was going to rid Ursula of the fruit of her sin, for this purpose using an old method she had learned from her nanny in India. I almost cried out, saying that I knew they were lying about the poor girl's condition, abusing her naiveté to torture her for their own evil pleasure. But a selfish fear for my own safety stilled the words rising in my breast, and I said nothing.

By the time I had recovered my wits, Angela had undressed her victim and was taking out from beneath her skirt a ball of flat, ribbon-like cord. She directed Ursula to lie down between two small saplings. Still chattering in a gay and soothing manner, Angela tied her outstretched arms to one tree and her legs to the other, explaining that it was of the highest importance that she remain immobile. Trembling and as pale as death, Ursula complied without a word of protest.

Kenneth's eyes followed his sister's every movement. Almost absentmindedly, he was holding his flesh in his hand until, as though seized by a sudden frenzy, he tore off his clothes and, begging Angela to do the same, got her to leave Ursula. The two rolled over on the moss in a savage embrace. It seemed for a while as though nothing were going to appease their hunger for each other. Breathlessly and with unbelievable brutality, they sought pleasure in each other's body, shifting from one position to another, exploring every shameful crevice, and this with such rapidity and such fury that one could have thought that they were people condemned to death and had but this moment left to them in this world, a moment they wished to exploit in order to satisfy their every mortal yearning. Their bodies, like two flounders, made a slapping noise as they collided wildly, both of them soaked with perspiration and saliva. The strange sound of this battle echoed through the forest stillness, from time to time punctuated by a sudden rustling of the breeze or the faint strangled gasps that came from Ursula's mouth as she, shaking in every limb, tried in vain to rid herself of her bonds.

And then, as suddenly as they had gone for each other, like a pair of mad dogs, they parted as if by common consent, and they drew off a distance, smiling and panting. I saw to my surprise that, fierce though the battle had been, Kenneth at least had lost none of his potency during it.

Coming back to where I stood (for I do not think I had stirred a muscle throughout that time) Kenneth looked meaningfully at his still charged weapon and I obediently took it in my hand. He bent over me and undressed me, making me change his shaft from hand to hand while he slipped off my sleeves. Using my chemise, he wiped his brow and his armpits, then rubbed his lean supple body until his skin glowed and with a sigh of satisfaction he threw away the crumpled rag and pressed himself against me. My face was buried in the fur of his chest, and I stayed thus, with my eyes closed tight, until I heard Angela call out that everything was ready.

At the same moment, I heard a scream come from Ursula. It rent the air and went through every nerve in my taut body, causing me to jump away from Kenneth and in spite of myself to rush towards Ursula. Then my brain registered what I was looking at.

I stopped dead in my tracks, like a hunted animal that knows there is no way to escape. My flesh crawling with horror, I stood still and watched.

Angela, still quite naked, her body stained with streaks of brown and muddy green, stood before Ursula holding the snake in her hand. Ursula's legs were widely opened, held in place by the tapes. (I realize now that she had thought it all out in advance. To carry out her scheme, a considerable length of tape was necessary, and she had plainly left nothing to chance.)

Ursula, thus quartered, her eyes starting out of her head with fear and revulsion, struggled to free herself, and, of course, couldn't. Angela, the greenish reptile wriggling between her fingers, was asking Ursula if she were ready, saying that, after all, these screams were unnecessary, that all this was for Ursula's own benefit, and that good breeding required her to at least put up a show of gratitude.

Ursula was speaking, but no sound came from her lips. Bending down beside her, Angela, with a smile playing over her face, pulled Ursula open; widening the opening with her fingers. She stared into Ursula's eyes while she did so, all the while waving the small snake over Ursula's body. Ursula tried to scream; she tried to plead with Angela for mercy, but still no sound escaped her lips. Slowly, Angela lowered the snake, holding the lips of Ursula's vagina open.

I shut my eyes, grasping the air for support. I thought the earth was giving way underneath me.

I heard Ursula say, 'Gag me, gag me quickly or I'll scream!' and then I heard no more until, after what seemed an interminable silence, Kenneth began to speak.

'Bless my soul,' he said, 'I believe the dear girl has fainted, damn me if she hasn't.'

I heard him walk forward over the springy moss, calling out to me to come along. When I opened my eyes I was standing over Ursula, looking down with curiosity at her white body and ashen face. The snake was still clutched in Angela's hand and there was a cruel look on her face.

'Jolly good, don't you think, eh?' Kenneth chortled. 'She'll think you actually did it. I might as well jam her now myself. She'll not even know the difference.' He knelt down and pushed his way into her inert body. 'Quite a joke, I'd say. And this time she's going to have a pretty little bastard right enough, I'll see to that!'

Angela, greatly amused by this new game, diverted herself with the tapes, which she pulled and released, jerking Ursula's legs into the air and letting them fall back down again. This pleased Kenneth enormously. The impact on his prick, he said, was delightful and 'by George, I'm too worked up to bugger her.' Lifting her buttocks into the air, he breathed deeply, gasping each time he filled his lungs, and while his body was shaken by long spasms of ignoble satisfaction, he released himself in Ursula's very depths....

Not knowing what else to do, I went up to my room. That's how I got here. I am still here writing all this down in my diary. I can't explain why I'm doing it or why I do anything. Perhaps I find some strange kind of solace in being able to put everything down in black and white so that, at least, it exists on paper. For I'm not sure it exists in my mind. And, too, my diary already contains so many horrors, that it cannot hurt to add a few more that I am writing of my own free will instead of being constrained.

Anyway, I don't care anymore. I haven't any friends. My diary is something at least...